P9-DHG-930

loving time

also by leslie glass

HANGING TIME

BURNING TIME

TO DO NO HARM

MODERN LOVE

GETTING AWAY WITH IT

loving time

LESLIE GLASS

BANTAM BOOKS

NEW YORK TORONTO LONDON SYDNEY AUCKLAND

LOVING TIME

A Bantam Book / November 1996

Book design by Maura Fadden Rosenthal

Library of Congress Cataloging-in-Publication Data

Glass, Leslie.
Loving time / by Leslie Glass.
p. cm.
ISBN 0-553-09692-3
1. Policewomen—New York (N.Y.)—Fiction.
2. New York (N.Y.)—Fiction. I. Title.
PS3557.L34L68 1996
813'.54—dc20 96-12544
CIP

Published simultaneously in the United States and Canada

Bantam Books are published by Bantam Books, a division of Bantam Doubleday Dell Publishing Group, Inc. Its trademark, consisting of the words "Bantam Books" and the portrayal of a rooster, is Registered in U.S. Patent and Trademark Office and in other countries. Marca Registrada. Bantam Books, 1540 Broadway, New York, New York 10036.

PRINTED IN THE UNITED STATES OF AMERICA

BVG 0 9 8 7 6 5 4 3 2 1

for edmund and the graduates

jhu

and

rcs

class of 1996

acknowledgments

Readers are often surprised to learn that it takes almost a year for a manuscript to travel from an author's desk through its many stages of production until it finally becomes the book they've been waiting to buy. The process begins with editorial Close Encounters of the Third Kind, moves right along through many scheduling, marketing, promotion, and sales conferences. The pages themselves go through a complicated copyediting, production, book design, and printing process. Meanwhile, the difficult packaging decisions are made and realized, the cover design, cover art, and copy are completed.

A beautifully produced book is the author's dearest wish. For fulfillment, it requires the work of dozens of gifted people. Bantam has an editorial, production, packaging, marketing, and promotion dream team. Thank you especially, the truly daring and visionary Publisher, Irwyn Applebaum, and world's most challenging and supportive Associate Publisher—my brilliant editor—Kate Miciak. Thank you Managing Editor Susie West for production orchestration; Jamie Warren Youll for gorgeous cover designs, Betsy Hulsebosch for marketing, Barbara Burg for publicity, and my publicist, Susan Corcoran. Thank you Linda Biagi for foreign sales.

But, wait a minute! Before a single book can appear in a store, another powerful group of Bantam people have to go to work: The Mighty Bantam Sales Force, which comprises the true, and not-often-enough-sung, heroes of publishing. This is the Force to which we authors pray every night: "May the Force be with me." Thank you especially, Sally Johnson, Central District Manager, who said the magic words at the right moment, as well as Bantam Salesperson Cinda Van Deursen in the Eastern District; David Glenn and A. Scott LePine in the Western

District. Thank you Telemarketers and those in Special Markets and National Accounts, and everybody else who gets those books out there and tells them not to come home again.

For help with the fictional Psychiatric Centre in LOVING TIME, and the field of psychiatry, thanks to Richard C. Friedman, M.D., gender expert, psychology professor, and consultant extraordinaire.

Does the Eagle know what is in the pit?
Or wilt thou go ask the Mole?
Can wisdom be put in a silver rod?
Or Love in a golden bowl?

thel's motto
William Blake

loving time

raymond

one

Raymond Cowles died of love on the evening of his thirty-eighth birthday. It happened on Sunday, October 31, after a long battle for his soul. As with many bitter conflicts, the end was abrupt and unexpected. In the same way as love had come on him unexpectedly and caught him by surprise after a lifetime of loneliness and despair, death crept up on Ray from behind without his even knowing that his release from ecstasy and anguish was at hand.

Since his twenties, Ray had flipped past the passages about love in the books he read. The movie versions of passion and lust seemed stupid and unbelievable to him. Love was supposed to happen to men like him when scantily dressed, big-breasted women flashed the look that said "I'll do anything. Anything at all."

Lorna had looked at him with those eyes; other women had, too. Many other women. Sometimes Raymond had even thought he'd seen it in the eyes of Dr. Treadwell. He never got it. Love to him was like a foreign language for which he had all the clues but couldn't figure out the meaning. And he had learned to live without it as his own personal cross to bear, like a dyslexic who could never really read, or a patient with a terminal illness that wouldn't go all the way and end his misery for a long, long time.

Until six months ago, Raymond Cowles thought he had all his problems solved. He had made work the focus of his life, tried to find the same satisfactions in his personal life other people experienced in theirs. He wanted to feel what other people felt, and when he couldn't, he acted as if he did.

Then, six months ago, Ray Cowles finally understood what life was all about. He fell in love. The paradox was that real love, the kind that smacked into one so hard it turned a person all the way around, didn't always happen as it should. The great passion of Raymond Cowles's life came too late and was spiritually messy. Even though he was a man experienced at battling demons, Ray's new demon was the worst he'd encountered.

With Dr. Treadwell's help he'd conquered all the others. First the demons that told him he was a bad child. Then the ones that told him he was stupid, not up to his studies. The big ones that said he was incompetent at his jobs. And always in the background there were those demons that told him he could never attract a girl, never satisfy a woman. These particular demons continued to torture him even after he met Lorna, the endlessly sweet and understanding girl he married.

The killer demon told him he was a failure at everything, even the years of psychoanalysis to which he had resorted half a lifetime ago for a cure. This was the demon that whispered to him in his sleep that his sudden and overwhelming passion at age thirty-seven was beyond disgusting and immoral. Love, for Raymond Cowles, was a fall from grace into the deepest pit of depravity from which abyss he was bound to fall even further into the very fires of Hell.

In the months prior to his death, as Raymond fell deeper from grace into lust and corruption, he wanted nothing more than to surrender at last to the first real feeling of contentment and joy he had ever experienced. But he wanted to fall and be saved with his love absolved. Surely everyone had the right to surrender to passion and be released from the excruciating anguish of sin. He had that right, didn't he?

But absolution didn't come, and once again Raymond Cowles's dreams were full of far-off women—high on cliffs when he was on the ground, or on shore when he was way out at sea. In dream after dream, these women waved their arms at him and told him, "Watch out, watch out." And each time he awoke in a panic because he didn't know what to watch out for.

Then on October 31, at the very start of his new life, Raymond's world collapsed. He felt he had no warning. He was cornered. For a few moments he was alone. And then he wasn't alone. He was trapped with a person who wanted to kill him.

"Save me, save me." He tried to scream into the phone, into the hall, into the lobby of the building, out on the noisy street. *Save me!*

He longed to reach for a life preserver, but there wasn't one. Where was one? Where was a lifeboat? Where was safety?

Help!

At the end he was mute. He couldn't cry out for help or make the move to save himself. In his last moments of panic, when Raymond Cowles was too frantic and distraught to make a sound, the very thing he had never been able to watch out for slipped out of the noisy Halloween night of dress-up and reveling on Columbus Avenue and took his breath away.

two

At midnight on Halloween, two hours after Raymond Cowles died, Bobbie Boudreau slouched into the French Quarter. His mood matched the atmosphere of the seedy bar perfectly. To a Cajun from Louisiana, this was as far from the real French Quarter as a place could get. The old jukebox was a poor stand-in for even the worst live band and there was no compensation for the lack of a weary stripper migrating slowly back and forth across the bar. Charlie McGeoghan liked to tell Bobbie he'd named his dump the French Quarter because he'd heard New Orleans was a wild place, and even the word *French* sounded pretty wild to Charlie.

The old Mick got only two things right. It was too dark to see the menu and newcomers' drinks were always watered. Bottom line was, Charlie hated anything wild, and his hole was nothing more than an advertisement for missed chances. Which was pretty much how Bobbie himself felt tonight. He didn't like basic principles like justice, wisdom, and truth getting all fucked up.

Bobbie had been told a long, long time ago that the Lord always evened things out in the end. But sometimes it just didn't seem that way. The Lord's mysterious ways were awful slow, too slow for Bobbie Boudreau. Bobbie liked to hum a little tune to the words "The Lord's too slow for Bobbie Boudreau." When he got tired of the wait, Bobbie had to step in as the Lord's agent and speed things up. He was working such a case now. In just a few days the coin would drop in the slot, the wicked would slide down the tubes, and the meek would inherit the earth. He was looking forward to it, banged the door of the bar going in.

"Hey, Bobbie." Charlie's skinny wuss of a nephew glanced up from mopping the counter. "How's the war going?"

Bobbie grabbed a stool. "We lost, *frère.* Lost on all counts."

"Well, as they say, time heals all wounds. What can I get you?"

Bobbie shook his head. "No, Mick. It don't. Fact is, time makes it worse and worse."

"Oh, come on, Bobbie, don't start that Mick stuff. You know how my uncle feels about that."

"Fuck your uncle."

Brian McGeoghan's nervous eyes raked the murky, nearly empty room. "Good thing Charlie ain't here, Bobbie. He told me to throw you out when you get like this. He can't afford any more insurance."

Bobbie jerked his head at the vacant bar stools around him, his sullen mouth softening at the happy reminder of those occasional, teensy-weensy scuffles that occurred when he was forced to avenge some asshole provocation. "Throw me out with not one soul here to bother me? That's a good one. Give me a beer. Just one, I'm working tonight."

"Okay. . . . One's fine as long as you don't make trouble." Brian McGeoghan smiled suddenly. "Wouldn't want you drunk in the operating room either, would we?" He pushed a frothy draft across the battered surface.

"Hey, *frère,* I'd never do anything to hurt a patient," Bobbie intoned solemnly. Bobbie hadn't been a surgical nurse since his MASH days in 'Nam a long, long time ago, but Brian didn't need to know that. "Never."

The beer tasted like shit. Bobbie drank it down quickly, then had another. The second tasted better. He considered a third. Then two assholes came in, sat a few stools down from him at the bar, and began talking softly. One was bigger than Bobbie was, a mean-looking white with fleshy pockmarked cheeks and a drunk's red-veined nose. The other looked like an Irish mole. Bobbie didn't feel like breaking any bones tonight, so he paid up and went outside.

At one A.M. the streets were finally quieter. No more parents hustling along clumps of kids in costumes. Not so many dressed-up faggots. A few here and there. Faggots never bothered him. Anyway, Bobbie had things on his mind. He was working a case, wasn't looking for trouble. He wandered over to Riverside across the stretch of dead grass to the Henry Hudson Parkway. He liked watching the cars speed along next to the Hudson River, the mile-wide slash of black water that separated New York from the rest of the country. In Riverside Park he would sit on the grass or a bench and tell himself the stories of his life exactly the same way, over and over—all the horrors right up to the day the bastard Harold Dickey and the bitch Clara Treadwell unjustly cut off his balls and destroyed his life after a thirty-year career in nursing. Because of them Bobbie Boudreau was no longer a nurse, not a nurse of any kind. For almost a year he'd been a cleaner, floor polisher, garbage collector, lightbulb changer—not even a plumber, electrical engineer, or handyman. His asshole boss said he had to work his way up for even that kind of work.

When he wandered along the labyrinth of underground passages that connected the six buildings in the huge hospital complex dressed as a janitor—a fat clip of official keys banging against his hip—Bobbie looked as if that seniority was already his. He was both big and broad, still hard enough in his spreading midsection to look disciplined. There was an air of authority in his movements. His face was solid with concentration and purpose. He had the belligerence of someone in charge. Seldom did anyone stop him. When they did, it was usually for directions. Doctors, nurses, administrators, maintenance, even security intent on their own troubles rushed past him every day. Those who took the briefest second to glance his way felt immediately reassured that he was just your average good-guy hospital worker, like they were—honest, trustworthy, caring. A person who would not waste a second before fixing something gone wrong. And he did fix things gone wrong.

He was about to cross the viaduct that formed a bridge over the Ninety-sixth Street entrance to the Henry Hudson Parkway when a powerful stench of excrement startled him. He was filled with disgust even before the bum shambled from behind a bush. The bum was muttering to himself; his sorry-looking penis still hung out of pants not yet buttoned and zipped.

Bobbie swerved to avoid him, but the bundle of rags figured he'd found a mark and didn't want to let him go. "Hey, pal," he called, forgetting to zip his fly as he hurried after Bobbie.

"Fuck off."

"Hey, pal, that's no way to talk. You got a dollar? I'm hungry."

The bum followed Bobbie onto the bridge, whining. "I'm hungry, man. You know what it feels like to be hungry? All I need is a dollar. One dollar. What's a dollar to a rich man like you?"

The piece of shit was disgusting, had no control. He stank; he defecated in the bushes like a dog. And now the filthy mongrel was following him across the bridge, mocking him. It was a mortal insult.

"I said fuck off."

The bum grabbed at his arm, whining some more. Bobbie didn't like to be crowded. A thin stream of traffic, heading north, whipped by behind them on the parkway. The light changed and a car crossed the intersection below.

"Hey, pal, think of Jesus. Would Jesus walk away from a friend in need?"

Bobbie stopped short and drew himself up to his full height. He was six two or six three and weighed two hundred and thirty pounds. The piece of shit was talking to him about Jesus. Bobbie stared.

The guy figured he'd scored. "Yeah, gimme a dollar. But for the grace of God I could be you, pal."

He was wrong. Bobbie could never be him. Bobbie was good. Bobbie was clean. He was efficient. He was in control. Bobbie didn't stop to think any further. He picked up the offense that thought it could be him and tossed it over the railing. His move took two seconds, maybe three. Some deeply soothing sounds followed: a grunt as the asshole was picked up, a scream as he fell, then the thud as he hit the ground. If the bum survived the fall, he didn't live long. Almost instantly there was a series of crashes as an oncoming car, speeding up to enter the parkway below, struck him, braked abruptly, and was in turn bulldozed by the car behind. Bobbie kept walking. It all felt exactly like the Lord reaching down with His grace and punishing the wicked.

At three A.M., feeling on top of the world—like the right hand of God itself—Bobbie slipped into the Stone Pavilion of the hospital through a service door on an empty loading dock at level B2. After the incident with the bum, he had gone home to change into the gray uniform of a maintenance crew he didn't work on and to pick up a toolbox that was not part of his job. He hadn't yet acquired the correct jacket, so he wasn't wearing one, even though the temperature had dropped way down again. The stolen plastic ID clipped to the stolen shirt identified his own slightly freckled, flat-featured, unsmiling face below slicked-back, gray-flecked curly hair as that of a senior maintenance worker in the Psychiatric Centre where he was no longer allowed to go.

Bobbie liked thinking that if the two bastards who ruined his life knew he was still around, they'd finish him for good. They thought they could kill people and get away with it. Bobbie snorted at the fact that he was too smart for them. They didn't know he was still around. He hummed his little God ditty. "The Lord's too slow for Bobbie Boudreau."

He turned down a branch in the tunnel that began its descent to level B3. He heard the clicking of the relays in the machine room that provided electricity to the nearest bank of elevators. He passed on to the long, long pump room that drove hot water through the pipes and radiators of all twenty floors of the Stone Pavilion and heard the fierce hiss of steam, jetting harmlessly into the air from dozens of safety valves. Then he passed the deep-cold quiet of the morgue at the center of the *H* in the building's courtyard, a ridiculously long way from everything.

Abruptly the ground started to rise up to level B2 again. The color of the stripe on the floor changed from yellow to blue, signaling passage into another building, the Psychiatric Centre, the funny farm. Whatever you want to call it, Bobbie Boudreau was coming home to finish the work he'd started.

three

At seven-thirty A.M., Dr. Clara Treadwell felt some satisfaction at the miserable weather as she walked the half-block from her impressive penthouse overlooking the Hudson River to her impressive executive suite with the same view on the twentieth floor of the Psychiatric Centre. The sky was battleship-gray, hanging low over the choppy water. Although it was only the first of November, already it was a winter day, a harbinger of the many dismal days ahead.

She flipped up the collar of her navy cashmere coat and congratulated herself for insisting on returning to New York yesterday straight from Sarasota, instead of spending the night in Washington with the Senator as he had wanted. He was getting very demanding lately, almost like a husband who couldn't stand sleeping alone a single night. She decided it was time to start setting limits for him. Getting home by five-thirty, she'd had the evening to pick up her messages, return calls, go over the dozens of memos and reports she had to deal with as Director of the Psychiatric Centre, Chief Psychiatrist, Chairman of the Department of Psychiatry at the medical school, and Mathew McPherson Appleton Professor.

When she'd been a medical student at the university and later a psychiatric resident at the Centre, Clara Treadwell never thought she'd have a single one of those titles, much less all of them. Nor did she ever dream that she'd be appointed to a President's Commission on Mental Health and meet the Senator who'd made that cause his life's work. When she'd been a resident, she never would have believed that a woman past forty-five could not only attain such status but could also attract a man of similar accomplishments (and far greater wealth) and that they could fall in love with all the passion and excitement of teenagers.

Every day when Clara Treadwell awoke in her stunning apartment, decorated with fine antique furniture and painted in shades of beige and peach to soften the light and flatter her complexion, she felt the thrill of her accomplishments all over again. The apartment, a perk of her job, cost her only a dollar a year. That was gratifying in itself. But even more thrilling was the fact that she was the first woman ever to have it.

She was the first woman Chairman and Director of the Psychiatric Centre, the first to be head of the department and the first to have the name professorship. Her freshly washed hair whipped around her face in the wind off the river despite the generous dose of hairspray she'd given it. She ducked quickly into the cavernous building, patting her hair back into place.

"Morning. Morning," she murmured as she waited for the elevator, conscious of her position and how important it was to acknowledge the people around her.

She unbuttoned her coat, could not resist showing off the sleek new suit and trim body under it. She had to admit her figure wasn't perfect anymore, but she dressed well, moved gracefully, and knew she still looked—if not great—at least good enough to attract attention wherever she went. It was with the warm feeling of being able to assess herself critically and come to an objective conclusion that Clara Treadwell entered the elevator of the Psychiatric Centre. For nearly six minutes, as the crowded box made its tedious progress upstairs, she concentrated on her strategy for the various meetings at which she would preside that day, feeling a sense of mastery in all things.

Then, as the elevator doors opened on the twentieth floor, her body tensed at the unwelcome sight of Harold Dickey hurrying out of the executive suite. The tension started with the familiar tingle at the base of her neck that felt as if, once again, she'd been bitten by a tiny insect pest she'd repeatedly neglected to squash into oblivion.

"Ah, there you are!" Harold's face creased into a delighted smile. "I was hoping to catch you."

"I'll bet you were," she muttered coldly, brushing past him. Harold reached out and took her arm, halting Clara's retreat. The tic in her cheek, which twitched only when she was absolutely exhausted or impatient beyond enduring, made its first tentative throb. She sighed. "What do you want, Hal?"

He smiled his old smile. "Just you," his smile said.

She shook her head. Not a chance. Not a ghost of a chance.

"Did you have a good weekend with the Senator?" he asked.

"Harold, you were coming from my office." Clara said the words slowly, giving herself a moment to calm down. She was deeply angry at his pushing, pushing, pushing her so that very soon, if he didn't get a grip, he was going to force her to squash him.

"Yes, yes. I wanted to chat with you before the meeting about your proposed changes in the guidelines of the Quality Assurance Committee. I thought it might be useful."

"Oh?" she said. Another management problem for her to finesse.

This was how Hal blackmailed her to be with him. When she didn't make time for him, he became difficult. He played the devil's advocate in her meetings, raised questions that engaged the others on the committee in hours of wasteful debates about trivial points. Often he changed people's minds about the issues.

Harold Dickey had quickly withdrawn his hold on her arm, but his face was still softened by that obnoxious expression of adoration no woman can bear seeing on a man she doesn't admire. They were stopped right outside the entrance to the executive suite, where Clara's assistant, the vice chairman, the chief resident, and various other functionaries could observe them perfectly well.

Harold's expression was particularly offensive to Clara because he was way over sixty now and past his prime. His hair was white and had receded far enough to reveal the dome of his bright shiny skull. His stomach had grown, and so had the fleshy pouches under his eyes. The gray Brooks Brothers suit he wore was shapeless. He still ran, and still played tennis, but his fire was gone. The only thing about Harold that was the same as when Clara had been a resident under his supervision eighteen years ago was the mustache. The white mustache had been very distinguished then, made him look dapper and a little dangerous. It still made him look a little dangerous. But now he *was* dangerous.

She'd been lenient for a long time—understanding, gracious, thoughtful, sensitive. She'd given him projects and even referrals. Just last night she'd referred a patient to him, Ray Cowles. She remembered with annoyance the conversation she and Ray had had about it. Ray and Hal were difficult children who irritated her almost beyond endurance. Let them bother each other; they deserved it.

Clara's day was not starting well. Every man in her life required boundaries and discipline, not diplomacy. She had to spend precious moments dealing with each one. Having to take the time to reason with them annoyed her. Her tic made its second throb. She shook her head impatiently to make it stop. "Harold, I'm late for a meeting."

"Oh, my. I wouldn't want to keep you," he said with that asinine adoring smile. "What time would be good for you?"

"No time. I have the day from hell today."

"Do you want to have dinner later? I could hold my thoughts until then."

"No, I have an association meeting."

"Great, so do I. We can go together." He looked hopeful.

Clara's lips compressed with disgust. She shook her head at how he just wouldn't let it die. She had married and divorced twice, had had many lovers, and had made her way through the complicated politics of two other psychiatric institutions since Harold had been her mentor, her supervisor, her lover. Now, after all these years, even though she was his superior in every way, he still had the supreme arrogance to think that he could get her back. Harold Dickey had not figured at all in her deliberations about returning to New York after a thirteen-year absence. The return of his desire, his continued and growing interest after much discouragement, had surprised her at first. Then she was amused; she thought he could be useful. Now, however, she felt different.

"Hal, I said I'm busy."

"I like that outfit," he murmured. "You look very pretty, Clara. Is it new?"

The navy suit was new. His commenting on it was inappropriate. She was the Director of the Centre. She could force him out, eviscerate him. She'd done it to many better men than Dickey would ever be. She was terminating him, no question, just as she had terminated Ray. And Hal was absolutely certain she wouldn't. The tic in her cheek throbbed, confirming her decision.

He smiled. "Have a good day."

four

Almost before dawn on November 1, Maria Sanchez heard her son, Detective-Sergeant Mike Sanchez, rise from his solitary bed and cross the hall to the bathroom, yawning loudly. The bathroom door closed. Five or ten seconds later his water splashed loudly in the toilet. The toilet flushed. Then came the sound of heavy rain as the shower pounded the bathroom tiles. Each day it was the same. It took Mike exactly twenty minutes to urinate, shower, shave, and dress.

Each day Maria spent those twenty minutes waiting for her bitter coffee to brew and watching the joggers stretch at the entrance to Van Cortlandt Park, then disappear, their legs pumping easily up and down. The joggers ran in the summer heat, in the chilling rain. In the winter months they appeared before the sky began to lighten, some not even wearing sweatpants or jackets, their breath making steam. Maria knew who some of them were, what buildings they lived in, at what hour they took the Broadway elevated train that ran within view of her window into Manhattan.

Mike told her she was the kind of witness they liked to have on the stand in court, a person who knew what was going on around her, noticed when something was different and remembered it later. It made her feel good when he said that. Her *hijo* was an important man. He didn't have to patrol the streets or wear a uniform anymore. He'd had his picture in the newspaper. Maria still showed the clipping of her son to her friends. She was proud that everybody in the neighborhood knew him, came to him asking for things. They thought her *hijo* could personally fix all their parking tickets, speeding tickets, all their problems with any government agency, including the IRS. She never told anyone otherwise.

She also knew her son could have any woman he wanted. Even without the uniform, he was a good-looking man, still excited them. The single women in the neighborhood kept their eyes on him, flirting all the time. And some of the married women, too. Maria didn't blame them. No one had trouble when Mike was around.

The walls in the old building were thin. Behind the bathroom door she heard him burp, then adjust the water in the shower. The faucet whined as he turned up the hot and the pipes began to clank. She hesitated, unsure of what to do. She had a box of wooden matches in one hand and her favorite rosary with the pink cut-glass beads in the other. She was a superstitious woman, knew timing and ritual mattered. Yesterday was Halloween. She wouldn't have lit a candle yesterday for anything. This year God had finally intervened for Mike. Mike's wife, Maria, who had left him five years ago, was finally dead of her leukemia. Halloween was over and November 2 was tomorrow. Could she start the ceremony a day early, light just one candle now, or should she wait?

Maria Sanchez had celebrated November 2, Mexico's Day of the Dead, faithfully for all of the thirty years she had lived in this Bronx apartment overlooking Broadway, the elevated train, and Van Cortlandt Park. This year, however, she'd begun her shrine to the dead two months earlier than usual. She took out the old, old photos of her mother and father, uncles and aunts long gone; mementos of other half-forgotten relatives; the relics of her two babies, dead in infancy many, many years ago in Mexico, and those of her husband, Marco, when he was young. She studied them one by one, then arranged them on the heavy, carved wooden table, along with offerings of food, candles, and the prayer cards she got from her church.

The shower droned on in the bathroom. As she weighed the odds of her desire against the possibility of doing wrong, the coffee perked, and the sky lightened to day. Because her daughter-in-law had been too religious to divorce, Maria was glad she was dead. Then, ashamed of the sinful thought, she quickly extracted a match from the box, struck it, and inhaled the pungent sulfur odor.

Instantly, a thousand memories jumped out of the smoke, crowding the match tip as it flared. Then, as she reached out and lit one of the dozens of candles she had placed around the table and sideboard, her memories began to separate and go to their places. Some traveled to the silver pocket watch that had not worked since the day her grandfather died, some to the baskets of fresh and dried fruits, some to the chilies and herbs tied in bunches with thin bakery string, some to the stacks of letters with ink so faded on the brittle paper that the words could hardly be deciphered anymore. Still others flooded into the bright, artificial lilies and roses that reeked of plastic no matter how many times they were washed.

As the candle smoked and guttered, Maria lowered herself to her knees and began to pray. This year she did not pray for the dead, who were either in Heaven or not as God saw fit, but for the soul of her son, whose heart had refused to heal for so many years in spite of the many eager women who took him to their beds. Mike had been a husband with no wife for a long time. But now the wife-who-was-not was dead. It was only right that her son should have his soul back, so life could begin again.

"Just take a look at him, *Todopoderoso,* a man of thirty-four, almost old enough to be an *abuelo* and not yet a *padre,*" Maria complained softly to the Almighty in her own mix of Spanglish.

"*Esta un crimen en contra la naturaleza,* no? I ask you not for myself, even though I wouldn't mind taking care of *dos bebes,* or even *tres.* I ask for *m'ijo.* My only child. You took the first step. Now take the second. Whisper in his ear, *Todopoderoso,* tell him it's time to love, to marry again. *Dios,* are you listening . . . ?"

Maria never prayed to the Son of God. At the center of her shrine she had placed one lone crucifix, a very small and painless one that showed no signs of suffering on the serene face of *Jesucristo.* There were no nails sticking through His hands or blood dripping down His chest, and His crown of thorns was all but obscured by His healthy head of long, curly hair. The crucifix was surrounded by small prayer cards colorfully adorned with rosy angels and many poses of the *Virgen y Jesu.* Maria preferred the Mexican Church with its emphasis on the love of mother and child to the endless Italian celebration of tortured saints—skinned and beaten and burned—and otherwise martyred Christians in the church she attended. She always prayed to *Dios Todopoderoso* and to the *Virgen.* No one else.

Her fingers moved to the next bead. "Ave Maria . . ."

Her son, Mike Sanchez, stood in the hot shower for a full five minutes, savoring the only privacy he had. He dreamed in the hot rain, scrubbing at his skin absently with a rough loofah, wondering, as he always did these days, if April Woo was showering in Queens at this very moment. Wondering if indeed she showered. He didn't know if she showered. Maybe she bathed instead, in green- or blue- or pink-scented bubbles.

So which was it—shower or bath? Every day he thought about it, and every day not knowing made him anxious. He could not imagine her asleep at night either, since he didn't know what she wore to bed. This was the kind of thing that irritated him. He was a detective. He could find out anything about a dead person he hadn't even known, but there were a lot of very simple facts about April Woo he just couldn't find out. The living could be tricky. Every time he asked April a question she didn't like, she flashed him the kind of look that proved her claim that Chinese torture was the best.

It also annoyed him that he couldn't get a grip on his feelings about her, a female cop who didn't need a gun to waste a guy. Tough. And he never liked the tough ones for more than a few hot New York minutes. Still, she was the one he thought about.

Okay, so say it was a shower. He visualized April Woo taking a shower. That wasn't hard. He'd driven her home a few times and knew she lived on the second floor of the neat red-brick house she shared with her parents in Astoria, Queens. There were white curtains in the windows. He had no trouble imagining her soaping her slender body behind the white bathroom curtains. For a few seconds he allowed the vision to turn him on.

Then suddenly, without any warning, April's sharp, beady-eyed mother intruded on the scene. She leaned out the window and screamed at him in Chinese. Mike could hear the harsh guttural sounds, the meaning as clear as any deep-throated growl of a well-trained guard dog. April's mother was as thin and mean as his own mother was plump and sweet.

As Mike washed the soap away and then turned off the water, he realized he had heard something after all, but it wasn't in Chinese. It was a passionate whisper in Spanish. He stepped out of the shower, straining to hear. He felt a chill enter the steamy bathroom and was puzzled. He could almost see the cold air drift in under the door and freeze the moisture. He knew what it was. His mother's prayers had summoned the ghosts of her family all the way from Mexico. And now they were beginning to arrive.

Mike didn't know any of those long-gone relatives. He didn't want anything to do with them. Of all those lost to his mother, only his father had died here. Three years ago Marco Sanchez had collapsed in the kitchen of the Mexican restaurant where he had been chef for twenty-three years, and no one had thought of calling 911. They had called *him.* He was the cop who had a handle on the system. But it had taken him over an hour to reach the restaurant. By then his father was dead.

"What are you doing, *Mamita*?"

Maria looked up, snapping her mouth shut so hurriedly her soft chin quivered. She hadn't heard her son move back across the hall to his room to dress for the day. Now he was wearing a gray shirt and shiny silver tie, gray tweed jacket, cowboy boots. She didn't see the bulge of his gun under his jacket, but she knew it was there. Mike stood at the far end of the living room jammed with bright heavy furniture studying her as if she were a suspect in a crime.

She frowned. It didn't take a famous policeman to see she was on her knees praying. Her fingers moved to the next bead. "Do you know what tomorrow is?" she asked softly.

"Yes, tomorrow is the Day of the Dead." *In Mexico, not here.*

She nodded. *Correcto.* "I am praying for the dead."

He didn't say he thought it was too late to pray for the dead. She already knew he thought that. She knew his job was to collect the dead and study their lives to find out how they died. She knew he didn't want those dead, or any others, to follow him home. But as long as he was unmarried and fatherless, the dead were all she had.

"I'll pray for you, too." She leveled her gaze at him defiantly, willing her prayers to enter his heart.

"Thank you, *Mami,* my prayers are for you, too." In a weak moment after his father died, Mike had moved back to his childhood home to keep his mother company for a few months. That had been three years ago. He wondered if she planned to dismantle the shrine any time soon.

Then, as he did every morning, he told her he had to get an early start on his day and took off after coffee without having breakfast. As he left at seven-thirty A.M., November 1, it occurred to Sergeant Mike Sanchez that it was time to move out and get a place of his own.

five

The detective squad room of the Twentieth Precinct was a long room on the second floor with windows facing the north side of West Eighty-second Street. Nine desks stuck out from the windows, like boat slips. Seven had a telephone and a typewriter, an ancient tilting, rolling chair, and a metal visitor's chair. So far only two desks had computers. But not everybody knew how to use them anyway, and there weren't enough printers. Opposite the marina was a holding cell.

The place didn't look much different from the set of *Barney Miller,* the TV comedy series about detectives that had made Detective April Woo think it would be fun to be a cop when she was a kid. The difference between then and now was that a lot more people died and you couldn't ever count on a happy ending.

Tilted back in her old swivel chair, the phone tucked under her ear, April was thinking about *Barney Miller* because Monday had hardly begun and already she was having a *Barney Miller* conversation. She looked up at the ceiling, her small nose wrinkled with exasperation.

"Yes, ma'am, the police *do* care that your toilet is clogged, but we can't come over right now and fix it."

"Why not?" The demand was nearly a shriek. "You're right across the street. You can send someone *across the street,* can't you?"

"No, ma'am. We can't send anybody anywhere for a flooding toilet. We're not plumbers." April had already explained this several times.

The shrill voice rose. "You mean there isn't a *single* person in that *whole* fucking precinct who knows how to fix a toilet?"

April smelled Sanchez long before he stood over her desk, guffawing and trying to get her attention. The powerful, spicy-fruity sweetness of his unnameable aftershave traveled way ahead of him wherever he went. She had known the moment he entered the little ell at the entrance to the room, where there was a bench for people to sit on while they waited for a detective. It had taken her almost a year to get used to his smell, but a lot of people never did. Occasionally Mike had to punch out some fellow officer who didn't know him and thought he could get away with calling Mike a spic or a faggot.

"So? Are you sending someone?" the woman screamed in April's ear.

April had the feeling this call might be a leftover trick-or-treat from

Halloween. Cops were always pranking each other. She had a powerful urge to sneeze. But maybe it was Mike's aftershave. The need to sneeze came from way back behind her nose. It was unpleasant, worse than a tickle. It felt as if the explosive seed of a chili pepper had lodged up there in her sinuses.

Sai Woo, April's mother, liked to tell the story of April's birth to explain her daughter's occupation, which was unlike those of any of her friends' children. From the start of her life, Sai said, April had been difficult. She said April had resisted coming into the world, so her poor mother had to push her, push her out by force. When she finally emerged from the womb, April's head was elongated like a squash, and her nose was badly twisted out of shape. She looked as if she smelled a really bad smell. That's how April became suspicious, the reason she was a cop, Sai explained.

To offset the bad omen of her resistance to life, April had been given the Chinese name Happy Thinking, just in case her head remained the shape of a squash. But even though she had grown up beautiful and smart, she was still disobedient in many ways. Insisted on always seeing things from the worst side, never the best. And refused to get married, have children, be happy.

April held the receiver away from her ear. "No, ma'am, I already told you we can't assign a police officer to a clogged toilet."

Unless the toilet happened to be stuffed with body parts that wouldn't go down the drain. Briefly, April considered asking if that was the case here, then decided against it. Even in New York it didn't happen that often.

"You have to." The woman wouldn't give up. "The man downstairs is a maniac. If the water goes through the ceiling, he'll come up here and kill me."

"Sounds like you should call a plumber right away." The chili seed exploded and she sneezed, shaking her head just like the dog did when it was annoyed.

The sneeze made April think of the dog. She had given it to her mother to divert Sai from her preoccupation with April's unmarried state. The orphaned poodle puppy came from a case April had had several months before. A famous dog, it had been the only witness in two homicides. April had worried that her mother might not accept any creature that wasn't Chinese, but after the case was closed, she went through all sorts of paperwork to get it anyway.

Turned out to be worth the trouble. Even though the puppy wasn't a Shih Tzu or Pekingese, the Chinese dogs of emperors, Sai had liked the poodle and solved her problem by making it Chinese. She gave it the name Dim Sum, which meant Touch the Heart Lightly. And immediately the strong-willed animal and its many needs took over all the attention in the house.

The puppy had to be trained, had to have lots of toys and learn not to teethe on the furniture. Had to have special cooking. When Dim Sum arrived, she had weighed hardly three pounds and didn't even know how to play. Now she was nearly six pounds of confident apricot-colored poodle that behaved like a tiger. Whenever Dim Sum was annoyed or impatient or angry, she shook her tiny head and sneezed hugely. Sai Woo, who had never had a moment of true enchantment in her life, was enchanted. And forgot about her daughter's wasted childbearing potential.

April sneezed again.

"God bless," Mike said.

The woman on the other end of the phone line continued to scream. "Oh, my God, you should *see* it. I'm not kidding, Niagara Falls."

April giggled.

"Are you telling me you'll come only if I'm *dead*? Is *that* what you're telling me?"

"No, ma'am. I'm just telling you we can't fix your toilet."

"Bitch!" The woman slammed down the receiver with a crash.

Finally, April glanced over at Mike, now innocently sitting at his desk with his back to her, a file open in front of him. Only a slight tightening of her lips betrayed her suspicion.

She was a classic beauty with a delicate, oval face, expressive almond eyes, rosebud lips, swan neck, and willowy figure. She didn't look like a cop.

"Buenos días, querida," Mike said without turning around. *"¿Cómo estas?"*

Her lips tightened some more. She didn't answer.

He swiveled around. "What did *I* do?" he demanded, palms up.

"That woman just called me a bitch because I wouldn't come over and fix her broken toilet."

Mike shook his head. "That's what's wrong with this city. Can't ever get a fucking cop when you need one."

"Nice." She gave him a hard look. "Anyone you know pranking me?"

"*Querida,* please. Who would do such a thing?" He smiled his big, friendly, engaging, seductive smile that was so sexy and so un-Chinese.

"Yeah, yeah. Who would do such a thing?"

Sanchez grinned.

April did not at all feel like grinning back. It really annoyed her how Mike Sanchez projected himself as the sincere, stand-up kind of guy the public could rely on, and everybody bought it. Women went for the Zapata mustache and the powerful aftershave. Juries believed his testimony. In spite of his being a bit on the laid-back and relaxed side, rumor had it he was a comer in the Department.

"Busy night last night?" Mike slapped some files around on his desk and changed the subject.

"You mean because of Halloween?"

April checked her watch. Eight-thirty-three. All crimes and misdemeanors that had occurred the night before were on color- and number-coded forms, waiting for the Detective Squad Supervisor, Sergeant Margret Mary Joyce, to assign them for investigation.

Major cases brought a million people swarming in. April had heard about the accident involving a homeless male who either jumped or fell off the bridge at the Ninety-sixth Street entrance to the parkway. One car hit the victim, the other rear-ended. It had been a mess to clean up. A twelve-year-old, who hadn't been wearing a seat belt in the front seat of the second car, slammed into the windshield and was in a coma. Two other people had been hospitalized. The John Doe was in the morgue. April shrugged again. "Guess nobody important died," she murmured.

The call about Raymond Cowles came in at ten-thirty. Some wife who didn't appear to have access to her own apartment wanted them to check out her husband. He hadn't turned up at the insurance company where he worked and was expected at some important meeting. Sergeant Joyce said it sounded like a case for the two of them.

six

On the way out Mike stopped to pick up the keys to the unmarked puke-green Chevy he'd been using for the last week. Outside the precinct door he offered them to April. "You might as well enjoy it while you can, *querida.*"

He nodded at two uniforms on their way in, then paused for a second to raise his arms as if in a great embrace of West Eighty-second Street, Columbus Avenue, the whole plum of the Upper West Side where the two detectives from Queens and the Bronx were lucky to have been assigned and which April might soon leave.

April's eyes were on the solid block of three-story, mud-colored town houses across the street from the precinct. Somewhere in one of them was a flooding toilet she'd refused to deal with. It was far from the worst thing she'd ever done as a cop, but she felt kind of bad about it. Maybe the woman was old and didn't know what to do.

For a few seconds, she stood on the sidewalk jingling the car keys. It was only the first of November, but already the air was cold and damp, just slightly on the pungent side. Maybe they'd have another bad winter.

Walking the Chinatown beat for four years, April used to gauge the changing seasons by the intensity of the garbage smell as it sat on the sidewalks waiting for pickup. Last winter there had been no less than eighteen snowstorms in New York. The city had been paralyzed again and again as mountains of snow and garbage cut off access from the sidewalks to the frozen streets. Yet the air had smelled sweet and fresh.

Most of the year that April had been in the Two-O, she had traveled around in an unmarked car working cases with Sergeant Sanchez even though there was no such thing as partners in detective squads. He called their relationship "close supervision."

Close supervision of one cop over another could have several meanings, April knew. It could mean her work wasn't up to standard and needed watching. Which it didn't. It could mean Mike was her rabbi, showing her the ropes. Which he thought he was. Or it could mean he was just constantly hitting on her. Which he also was.

April hadn't liked the arrangement. She didn't like being second-guessed or watched, didn't like being close to anyone or involved. Cops who were too involved made mistakes in the field. They got hurt. Mike had jumped in front of her gun once to save her life. She could have accidentally shot him. It still upset her to think about it. He knew as well as she did that involvement could mess up judgment, could be lethal. And still he worked pretty hard at involving her.

"I'm nostalgic already," she muttered, buttoning her jacket.

Mike shot her a glance. "You mean that?"

"Well, it's not so bad here. Bad would be Brooklyn. Staten Island. Lots of things worse than being here."

They found the car in the police lot in a tight spot, squeezed inside carefully, and banged the doors shut at the same time.

"Why didn't you just get the pay, then?" he demanded.

"You know why." April slammed the car into reverse and made a number of tight maneuvers that almost resulted in disaster for two blue-and-whites and the Commander's navy Ford Taurus.

"Hey, chill out. It's not the end of the world."

"I'm fine."

"Yeah, then why wreck the Captain's car?"

"I don't know. Maybe I made a mistake." It was the first time April had said it, maybe even the first time she had thought it. But now that the truth was out, it hit her hard. "I liked being a detective. I mean I *really* liked it."

She pulled out into the street and jerked to a halt, narrowly missing a speeding bicycle messenger. "Sorry," she muttered as Mike's lowered head hit the dashboard.

"Get out. I'm driving," he snapped.

"I'm sorry." April leaned over solicitously. "Are you all right?"

"No, you nearly killed that kid. Get out." Mike's Zapata mustache quivered with outrage as he smoothed back his fine head of hair with both hands, checking his profile in the mirror.

"I didn't even get close to him," April protested. "Get off my case."

She'd said it a thousand times. *Back off. Leave me alone.* What did she want with a vain, sweet-smelling, overheated, hairy, smiling non-Chinese person who would not stop calling her "darling" in Spanish no matter who was around to hear him? She wasn't his darling.

"Fine." Now he probed a nonexistent bruise on his forehead. "Fine. You fucked up, and you want me to stay off the case. Fine, I'll stay off the case."

"*I* fucked up? I made the list, didn't I? You know how many good people didn't make the list?"

April pulled out into the street carefully and stopped on Columbus at the red light.

"Fine," Mike said a fourth time. "You wanted the rank more than the pay. You wanted a command of your own some day. Huh? Was that it? Maybe you like me so much you wanted to get away before you did something your *mother* wouldn't approve of. How about that?"

"Okay, you win. You can drive." April unfastened her seat belt and flung open the door.

"Get back in here. I don't want to drive. It's only two fucking blocks."

"Damn," April muttered, slapping her seat belt back on. Yes, yes, and yes. She'd wanted the rank. A lot of cops didn't give a damn. They got promoted to detective and made it to first grade. They got a lieutenant's pay and were happy without the rank. But she wanted the rank. The catch-22 was this: To get the rank you had to take the test. If you were a detective and scored high enough to make sergeant, you lost your job as detective because each advancement in rank meant going back into uniform and out on the streets again as a supervisor.

So, by forcing herself to study for and finally take the sergeant's test, she'd put herself in the position of possibly losing her status as a detective, her accrued days off, and a lot of other things. There was no telling where she'd end up and how long it would take her to get back into the detective bureau. If ever.

So why had she done it, when she already had sergeant's pay? She did it because only after you got to the rank of captain could you be promoted further without taking any more tests. Since the sergeant and lieutenant and captain tests were given only when the ranks got thin, you could hit them right or not. Five years ago, when the last sergeant's test had been given, she had been too green to score well. Mike had taken his sergeant's test when he was twenty-nine. He was already a sergeant when he went into the detective squad. Last time he had the chance, Mike passed on taking the lieutenant's test because he already had the pay and liked his job. If he had another opportunity now, he'd probably take it. They were silent for two blocks. April double-parked on Columbus. She tossed the car keys at Mike before getting out.

Raymond Cowles occupied an apartment on the fifth floor of the building located on the corner of Seventy-ninth Street and Columbus Avenue. On the ground floor was Mirella's, one of the many popular, pricey restaurants in the neighborhood that the officers from the Two-O never patronized.

The first thing April did was look up toward the fifth floor. The building faced the park at the back of the Museum of Natural History. The park looked gloomy now in the gray autumn light, with the few remaining leaves on the trees shriveled and brown.

The doorman was a small, skinny man with a uniform that bagged out all around him. He held a handkerchief up to his runny nose and began protesting as soon as Mike and April were in the lobby.

"Well, I couldn't go up and open the door just because she asked me to. I don't have the key, now, do I? What did she want me to do, break down the door?"

April produced her badge.

"Yeah, yeah. I know who you are. You were in that other case. A couple of months ago. The salesgirl, right . . . ?"

April made a vague movement with her head.

"I thought I remembered your face. You came around asking—"

"Does the super have a key to the Cowles apartment?" Mike interrupted impatiently.

The doorman turned to him with a frown. "No, not everybody wants to give you their keys. Can't make 'em if they don't want to, can you?" He pushed the button to summon the elevator. The door slid open. "Five E, end of the hall on the right. Probably just sleeping off a drunk."

"Let's hope so," April murmured.

seven

All morning Bobbie Boudreau had trouble concentrating on the heavy polishing machine that could so easily spin out of control and hurt someone bad. Something about what Brian had said in the French Quarter last night pissed him off. Brian had said the old Mick had told him to kick Bobbie out before he made any more trouble. Where did the old shit get the idea that he made trouble? *He* didn't make trouble.

All he wanted, all he'd ever wanted in his whole life was to be treated with simple justice. Where was that justice? It pissed Bobbie off thinking about it. So he punched someone's lights out in a bar a few times. So he went to the bitch's office and took a few things out of her desk. So fucking what? That wasn't trouble.

Trouble was his asshole of a father beating the shit out of him when he was too little to fight back, then shooting every single one of Bobbie's precious chickens—the business that was going to bring electricity and a telephone and a TV to the house and make them rich. Trouble was that crazed drunk running inside for his fucking hunting rifle, the only thing in the house worth owning. Bobbie could still see his raging bull of a father, still big even with the sickness, still powerful as God, as he stumbled out into the yard shooting at the fifty screeching hens that charged in all directions trying to get away, only to collapse in bloody heaps of feathers. The fit didn't let up all the times the old man had to keep reloading to get them all. He could hardly stand up, but that didn't stop him from shooting at everything in sight, shrieking at Bobbie all the time. Something like "You little shit, you shit-eating dreamer! I'll kill you, too."

The cancer and a few other things finally took the bastard out soon after Bobbie decided to join the Army. Bobbie could pinpoint the day his father started spitting blood to the day Bobbie made up his mind to believe the recruiter who came to his school. That soft-voiced black Major told him personally the Army was the only place in the country a black man could get a fair shake.

"Only in the service is everybody—and I mean *everybody*—treated the same."

The Major personally offered Bobbie Boudreau, who had never in his life owned a new pair of pants, pay every month no matter what, a place to live, a uniform that would give him respect and make him look good.

"You want to look good, boy, don't you? You want to develop your abilities? Get an education and have a career?"

You gonna believe this bull? Boy?

The man had to be kidding him. A new pair of pants. A jacket, boots that laced up above the ankles. A career for him? The blood in Bobbie's family had been so mixed up for so many generations that by the time he was born, the seventh of ten calico children, no one even knew anymore what aunt, what uncle, what granpappy, or granmammy came from which racial and ethnic background. He had black, Indian, French blood. You name it. He wasn't anything *specific,* and that was the problem that bothered him most growing up. Who did he get to be? Wasn't nobody like him either inside or out.

He was a strange mixture of colors, his skin freckled, his hair a reddish frizz, his eyes the only ones in the family that were a mild-seeming washed-out blue. Big, gawky, shy to the point of paralysis, Bobbie Boudreau was called *nigger* by the white kids he knew, *white* by the black kids, and *trash* by the Creoles. There wasn't a single place he fit in.

Sure he wanted to look good, be treated like a man. He wanted to look every bit as good as that black Major. A light-skinned black, but not as light as he. He wanted to sound like him, too. Be him, in fact. If that guy could get ahead, why not Bobbie?

Every time he saw that tape recorder in the bitch's drawer, Bobbie was reminded of the hard road he'd traveled, how desperately he'd tried to get past it all, and the nowhere he'd gotten. He'd started at the top and one asshole after another had shot him down just like those chickens. He'd had perfect fitness ratings in his military training. Perfect. He knew he wanted to be a medic. He had good hands, followed orders well. He got the highest ratings in his MASH training unit.

Then before 'Nam *one* tiny mistake. During a surgical procedure when he was assistant to the surgical nurse, Colonel Stasch asked for a hemostat. Bobbie took one from the green tray, handed it to the nurse, who handed it to the surgeon. Colonel Stasch was from the Midwest somewhere. He was known as the Hitler of surgeons, made all the nurses cry.

"It's the wrong size." Colonel Stasch threw the hemostat across the operating room and glared at Bobbie—not the nurse who'd handed him the wrong thing.

He snarled at *Bobbie,* "What's the matter with you? Yes, *you,* fuzzball. Are you a moron? Can't you speak English? Answer the question. Can't——you——speak——English?"

Bobbie almost choked trying to get the words out. "Yezzuh, ah trah," he'd murmured, head down so the bastard couldn't see the hot blood burning behind his pale blue eyes.

"*Trah,* what the fuck is that? You come from some kind of swamp, boy?"

The patient lay on the operating table, all covered up with green sheets except for the slit in his gut nearly six inches long, with a drain stuck in it and the nurse swabbing away at the oozing blood with sponge after sponge while the procedure was delayed. Bobbie raised his eyes as far as the instrument tray. A small streak of blood was visible on the scalpel Colonel Stasch had used to make the incision. It lay on the green cloth alongside several others. "You're not worth shit, boy. We should send you back to where you came from."

Bobbie's own blood suddenly blurred his vision. He was bigger than the skinny doctor, and he had quicker hands. He could grab the scalpel and slit the bastard's throat before anyone knew what happened. He ached to do it, could see it all. But even as he saw himself kill the bastard, he made a decision. He would not slit the asshole's throat. He would find other ways to cope. He'd let Justice wait awhile.

Ever since school Bobbie Boudreau had been ashamed of the way he talked. In the Army, he was teased about the way he talked. He'd already begun listening very carefully to the way the doctors he admired talked. It was after the incident with Colonel Stasch that he bought a tape recorder and started practicing simple words. Hello. Good-bye. How are you? Yes, sir. Right away, *sir.*

Last night he'd ached to pick up the tape recorder in the bitch's desk and say something into it.

"Hello, bitch. I'm here."

No, better would be, "Hello, bitch, count the days." He could say in the tape recorder, "You're dead."

In the end, though, he said nothing. The bitch might recognize his voice.

eight

It was a routine call, but April's heart beat faster as the elevator door slid open on the fifth floor. It was always that way. Her mouth parched up dry as a desert, and a strange metallic taste materialized as if she'd been chewing on a bullet. Her hands became clammy. Her heart raced. Her heart was always racing. Somewhere up there in her neck, or even higher, at the back of her throat. Or else her heart beat in her mouth, and her head throbbed as if with a migraine.

Every time it was exactly the same. The brain charged up the electrical circuits with a power surge that jolted the whole system into a state of alert. A thousand signals transmitted at the same time. Warning signals. Memory bank activation. Pictures of a dead child hidden under a pile of garbage in a backyard, shooting flames, explosions, flying debris, choking smoke, guns going off, a suspect hit, a cop shot, a huge mirror crashing to the ground crushing the woman under it. Burning clothes, skin. Blood. Suspects' voices, and those of the dead.

As each new case began, ghosts from the old ones kept whispering in April's brain, telling their cautionary tales over and over. Never take anything for granted. Never! Never accept only what you see in front of you. Never automatically believe the things people tell you. Never just open a door. Never! Behind it could be something. Could also be nothing, too. But you never knew . . .

It was a well-known fact cops keeled over and dropped dead sometimes on nice quiet days when nothing at all was coming down. Their hearts just stopped after too many power-surges to the system. Some had post-traumatic stress symptoms, too, like soldiers after a war. And a lot of cops had problems with normalcy. They took charge on the job but couldn't stand gearing down to daily life. Breakfast and lunch, and families who didn't understand what being hit by jolts of adrenaline—two, three times a day—was like.

April had a weird feeling about this one. She glanced at Mike and swallowed. It was very quiet in the hall. Mike's mustache bristled with the tension. He must be feeling the same thing she was. The thing was, you never knew whose nightmare behind the door was about to be yours.

It was a small building, six apartments to a floor. Here, on the fifth floor, the *New York Times* still lay on the faded blue carpet by two apartment doors. One was at the end of the hall on the right. The ancient wallpaper was stylized, spiky bamboo, in metallic blue and silver. It was supposed to be exotic and Oriental, but evoked no Orient April knew. The paper was scarred and peeling in places, and so was the matching carpet. The aroma of toast lingered in the stale air.

Leaning against the wall and staring down at the newspaper in front of 5E was a thirty-something, wispy blond woman in a shapeless beige coat. Her fine, even features should have manifested a pretty woman, but they didn't. Anxiety was so deeply etched on her thin pale face, attractiveness had been all but erased.

As April and Mike headed down the hall toward her, the woman looked up and uneasily watched them approach. Finally, when they were only a few feet away, she opened her mouth tentatively. "Are you with the police?"

"Yes, ma'am. Sergeant Sanchez, Detective Woo." Mike flipped open his badge.

The woman waved it away without looking at it. "That's all right, I believe you." Her hands fluttered around the drawstring of a well-worn shoulder bag. "I'm sorry," she added immediately. "About the trouble, I mean. I didn't know what else to do. They wouldn't let me in. They said to call the police." She pointed toward the elevator, meaning them in the building, then looked down again at the newspaper. "Strange."

April nodded. It usually was. "You're . . . ?"

"Lorna Cowles. His office called when he didn't come to work. I guess Ray didn't tell them we're separated."

"I see." April could smell the woman's fear. It filled the space around her like an aura. She looked bleak and far more frightened than anyone in such a situation should be.

"They said he was working on something that was due today. A report for some meeting. It's not like Ray to be late." Lorna Cowles glanced nervously at the door, then away.

"Do you have the keys?" Mike asked her.

"Me?" The question seemed to amaze her. "No. I already told you—he moved out. He didn't even want me to see it. I—I've never been here." She dragged a hand through her fine shoulder-length hair. It was very pale all the way to the roots. A natural blond without makeup. She seemed bloodless, bleached and hopeless all the way to the bone.

Mike rang the bell a few times. There was no sound from within, none at all. "Police," he said. "Open the door."

"I told you, I did that already. Ray's *responsible.* He wouldn't be in there and not answer—"

Mike produced the thin strip of plastic that worked only when doors weren't double-locked. April touched the woman's arm to get her to step back and give him some room.

At the unexpected contact, Lorna Cowles shivered, then reached down to pick up the newspaper before moving away. "This is so intrusive. . . . Ray really won't like this. . . ."

Mike's hands moved quickly with the plastic strip, angling it around the tongue of the lock just right. There were lock picks in his pocket, but he didn't need them this time. The Medeco wasn't locked. After only two tries, the door popped open.

Mike turned to April, cocking an eyebrow. *Ready?* She nodded. He pushed the door open and went in.

"He's probably away." Lorna Cowles hung back. "I'm sure that's what it is."

"Do you want to wait here?" April asked her gently.

"I—I don't . . . Well, what's . . . I mean what do people—"

"It's your call." April left her to her choice and followed Mike into the apartment.

The living room and dining area made a quick, precise statement. They were spare, unfinished. In the living room were a sofa, a glass coffee table with two empty wineglasses on it. A stereo component system and compact disks were laid out on the floor at the edge of a colorful area rug. A standing halogen lamp still burned brightly in the corner by the uncurtained windows. Under the lamp were two unopened cardboard mover's boxes. In the dining area were a round café-style table and two wicker café chairs. The only thing on the table was a bowl of wrapped Halloween candy, the kind you passed out to trick-or-treaters. The bowl was about a quarter full.

It looked as if Cowles had only recently moved in, and he and a friend had just finished dinner. April took it in instantly and would not forget her first impression. Out the windows she could see the back of the museum and the leafless trees in the park. Mike had stopped at the bedroom door. The total stillness of his attitude, the stiffness of his back told her the man they were looking for was in there.

"Looks like a suicide," he said softly, going in.

April followed him to the door, then stopped as Mike had so that she, too, could form an impression. They worked the same way. Later, they would ask each other the same questions, shake the answers around like a dog with a sock, follow the same thoughts to their conclusions. But for now they just looked.

Raymond Cowles lay on one side of his queen-size bed, the side with the bedside table next to it. He was lying on the rumpled beige sheets, wearing suede loafers without socks, faded jeans, and a blue shirt buttoned only halfway. He was on his back, his arms at his sides. He was beautifully dressed and looked like an actor in a movie.

The way the room appeared only half–lived in, with no reading light by the bed, no clothes on the floor, no paraphernalia of a life scattered about, it almost seemed as if someone could shout "Action" and Raymond Cowles the actor would get up to finish the scene.

Raymond Cowles the man wasn't getting up, though. He'd finished his last action when he put the plastic bag over his head and taped it with masking tape around his neck. His life had gone with the air in the bag. He was the color of putty.

"Oh, God. *No!*" Lorna Cowles had finally made it into the apartment. Her fist flew to her mouth, and she screamed, "Oh, God. Oh, God. Take it off! Quick, take it off."

April took her arm. "Come on, let's—"

"Take it off," she screamed. "Don't let him—"

"It's too late. There's nothing we can do." April guided her out of the room.

"Is he—?" Suddenly Lorna wanted to go back.

"He died hours ago. Long time ago." April led her into the kitchen. Here Raymond had taken an interest. Pots hung from a pot rack. Rows of glass jars filled with beans and dried pasta, a shelf of spices. A bowl of fruit, ripe. Two used cloth napkins and matching placemats lay on the counter along with some crumbs and an empty bottle of wine. White wine, a California chardonnay.

"Oh, my *God.*" Lorna Cowles was horrified, stunned. The fist went to her mouth again. "He cooked for someone."

Apparently he had. April found a clean glass in the cupboard, filled it with water, and handed it to Lorna.

Lorna took a sip, then turned and vomited in the sink.

April swallowed. This was the way it happened. Mike hit the redial on the phone to find out if the deceased had called anyone before he died.

Then he went into the victim's bathroom looking for the sedatives Cowles would have needed to take to get drowsy enough not to fight asphyxiation, and she was in the kitchen with the vomiting wife.

When the vomiting wife was finished, April handed her paper towels and some ice water.

"Oh, God . . . Who would do something like that to him?" Lorna slumped against the counter. "Who would do that?"

"What makes you think someone else did it?" April murmured.

"Well, *he* wouldn't. Ray wouldn't do such a thing. He believed in God. He believed in eternal Heaven and Hell. He would *not* have done this to himself." Lorna fixed her light blue eyes on April. "Don't even consider suicide. I'm sure it wasn't. Please, don't cover it up like that. Find out who did it."

"Sure," April said. Of course they would investigate. It was their job to investigate. But it looked like suicide to her. In the other room April could hear Mike calling for Crime Scene and an ambulance. Maybe he'd found something that made him suspect Cowles's death wasn't a suicide. That changed things.

Lorna Cowles reached out, as if somehow to connect with the last bottle of wine her husband had drunk. "Poor Ray," she murmured.

"Don't touch," April said quickly. "Don't touch anything else."

The woman's hand jerked back. "Don't touch," Lorna Cowles told herself. "Don't touch."

nine

Ten minutes later Lorna Cowles was out in the hall of her estranged husband's new apartment, weeping noisily. "Ray would never kill himself. He'd been *analyzed.* He was saving for his retirement."

April handed her a tissue.

"We were so close, liked all the same things. Neither of us cooked. Restaurants were our thing. We went out a lot. . . ."

April waited for her to blow her nose.

"I don't understand. He said he needed to be alone for a while. That's all I know. Maybe his psychiatrist knows."

April could hear Mike's voice on the phone. Then everything was quiet. She knew Sergeant Joyce was on her way over.

"He *couldn't* have killed himself." Lorna started again, shaking her head so hard, her fine pale hair flew back and forth.

April let some silence build up for a few seconds. More silence. Finally she asked, "What makes you think so?"

Lorna frowned. "He didn't know how to make pleats." She held her hands up and pleated the air with her fingers to show April what she meant. "The bag was pleated around his neck. Didn't you see that? How could he have done that?"

He probably did it before he put the bag over his head. Suicides often planned everything. April cleared her throat.

"Ray wasn't manually dexterous," Lorna insisted. "He couldn't cook, couldn't hammer a nail. You see?"

What April saw was a pale, slender woman who no longer appeared helpless and tragic. The tension and fear that had been engraved so deeply on Lorna's face when they'd first met her was gone. Now she was angry, indignant. April wondered what kind of life insurance the deceased had. She fell silent, waiting for the widow to tell her more.

Just then, down the hall, the elevator door slid open. Sergeant Margret Mary Joyce, her hair awry and her face set in a scowl, slouched out. As April's favorite color was blue for the Department, Sergeant Joyce's favorite color was green for her heritage. Today she wore a forest-green jacket over an unmatching green blouse and dark-brown trousers.

On Sergeant Joyce's bad days April thought she looked like a badly dressed fire hydrant with a badly dyed blond wig. On good days April acknowledged that her supervisor's small Irish nose—which tilted up at the tip instead of becoming flat and spreading out as April's did—was quite appealing. Her skin was nice and white, even in summer, because she never went outside except on a call. She was plump, but hardly fat. And her hair was not really *so terrible* in and of itself. It was just hacked off without a plan, dyed the wrong color, and not often enough. Sometimes the front of her hair stuck straight up, and April itched to do something about it.

Sergeant Joyce's eyes were dark blue, too close together, and she squinted when concentrating, which was most of the time. But she was very serious, wanted to prove to the world that women were just as good in law enforcement as men. Maybe better. She, too, was a comer. That's why she was there, didn't want anything in her squad to get by her, just in case the squeal turned out to be an important one.

She walked past April without acknowledging her. "Are you Mrs. Cowles?" she asked with no attempt at sensitivity.

As Lorna looked the newcomer over, her uncertainty returned. "Are you with the police?" she asked anxiously.

"Yes, I'm Sergeant Joyce." Commander of the Detective Squad, she didn't say.

Right away April could see that Lorna didn't like her. "I already told the officer everything I know." She cocked her head toward April, who was suddenly busy with her notebook.

"You mean Detective Woo?"

Lorna glanced at April. "Uh, yes."

Sergeant Joyce looked doubtful. Looking doubtful or scathing was her thing. "Well, you'll probably think of some more things over time."

"I may think of a lot of things," Lorna replied sharply, "but I know my husband, and I know he didn't kill himself, so you better start looking for the monster who did."

Nothing like antagonizing the cops. The way Sergeant Joyce hammered her flat feet on the worn hall carpet as she walked away gave every indication that it was not up to the newly widowed Lorna Cowles to tell the police what their job was. Without another word, she went inside. Eager to get into the apartment to view the deceased.

ten

Sergeant Joyce's lips were gone when she returned. They had disappeared into her mouth, where she chewed on them thoughtfully as she considered the situation. Inside the apartment the Crime Scene team had already begun its work. Joyce made a slight motion with her head at April as she stared steadily at Lorna. April knew that scrutiny. It meant *We're going to strip all the covers off this woman and see what's underneath.* It was a common police tactic that April and Sanchez used only on alternate Tuesdays with clearly guilty suspects. Today was Monday. The woman was the victim's widow, and clearly not at her best. With her, they wouldn't have used it.

April's left eyebrow arched at her supervisor. *You want me to go or stay?*

Joyce raised her shoulder a half an inch in reply.

Stick around.

Inside the apartment, muffled conversation as the two men from Crime Scene went about their job of dusting for prints and photographing and sketching and measuring and bagging anything that could conceivably be used as physical evidence in whatever case might be made in court many months from now. If it ever came to that. Sanchez was searching for an address book, for leads on the girlfriend, Cowles's dinner companion. April wanted to be in there with him.

Out in the hall, silence. Now the Sergeant was guarding the door like a brick chimney, her hair on end and her mouth shut tight on her lips. She studied the widow this way for what seemed like a few eternities. Lorna's beige coat had fallen open. Underneath, a tan sweater was unevenly tucked into a straight plaid skirt of the palest blues and browns. It appeared the woman had dressed in a hurry and rushed over. Still, her tights matched and so did the paisley scrap of silk tied around her neck. Sergeant Joyce's eyes finished the tour of Lorna's person by scanning her polished tasseled loafers, which were similar to those of her dead husband except hers were not suede, and the shoulder bag that had seen better days. A most conservative-looking person. A drink of water. Pale and exhausted, Lorna did not give the impression of a killer. But April had seen her change colors three times in an hour, now, and had a picture of her as a chameleon.

Sergeant Joyce released her lips from behind her teeth. Her pink lipstick was now outside the lines. She was ready to speak. "Mrs. Cowles, are you all right? Would you like a cup of coffee?"

Confused by this sudden concern for her well-being, Lorna glanced quickly at April, the cop who had seen her vomit in the sink without gagging herself.

"I touched. I'm sorry," she said, so softly the brick chimney was taken aback.

"What?" Sergeant Joyce turned to April for an answer.

April reached into her own shoulder bag, pulled out her diminishing pack of tissues, and offered it to the Sergeant, pointing to the bow in her own lips.

"What . . . ? Oh." Sergeant Joyce accepted a tissue and dabbed at her mouth distractedly. "What do you mean, you touched?"

"I know you're not supposed to touch anything. I threw up," Lorna said flatly. The Chinese cop wouldn't let her clean the sink. Her eyes flickered at the clicking sound inside the apartment. "What's that?"

"They're taking pictures."

Down the hall a door opened. A gaunt elderly woman in a pink flannel bathrobe cautiously emerged from her apartment with a garbage bag. "What's going on?" she demanded querulously. "I'm a sick woman. I'm not supposed to be disturbed."

Sergeant Joyce motioned with her head toward the woman. Without a word, April crossed the hall to talk to her.

"Who are you? What is this, a convention?" The woman peered at April through watery eyes.

"We're with the police. There's been an accident," April told her.

"Don't tell me. I don't want to know. Just get out of here as soon as you can." She thrust the garbage bag into April's hand and closed her door with a bang.

In the six years April had worked the Fifth Precinct in Chinatown, first walking the beat, then as a detective, no one had dared call her a bitch or hand her their garbage for disposal. In Chinatown, people believed the law existed for one purpose only: to cause trouble for perfectly innocent citizens. The police were there to imprison or deport them, steal their money, and maybe beat them up in the process. In Chinatown, police were treated with fear and respect.

But here, on the affluent Upper West Side, no one was afraid of the police. No one respected them, and no one was grateful when they did their job. Here, the police were held in contempt by the rich, and cursed and shot at by the poor. Considering the fact that the police department was the city's only hedge against chaos, April sometimes thought being a cop was worse than a thankless job; it was a cruel joke. Maybe that was the reason so few Chinese wanted it.

She marched to the door marked EXIT with the old woman's garbage. Near the door something touched her. She brushed her face with her free hand. Nothing was there. Still, for a wild moment, her armor was pierced and she felt elation. What was it? No one was anywhere near her. At the end of the hall, Sergeant Joyce stood talking to Lorna Cowles.

Must be her mother who traveled around with April sneaking her ideas in whenever she could. Many years ago Sai Woo had told April that the air was in constant motion, not with wind and rain and snow and sleet but with the activity of powerful gods and ancient spirits that could do whatever they wanted to human life. She had warned April to watch out for them and try to decipher the hidden meaning in everything in order to make the gods work for, not against, her. For spirits could blow hot or cold in a person's face and alter his feelings and his life in an instant. Turn a man away from his wife, toward evil and ruin. Turn a woman toward the golden light. You never knew what they were going to do.

This was another way in which April was disobedient. She refused to believe in golden lights and shabby gods that had been lost even to China for more than half a century. She was American, lived in a rational world where things could be explained. Where things *had* to be explained. Every day of her life, every case she worked had an official beginning, had to be written up on numerous forms. Every case had to be officially opened, investigated, and officially closed. The blanks on the forms were small. There was no room for subtlety.

Yet the system turned out to be more tricky and complicated than any capricious spirit her mother could invent. Even when the laws were crystal-clear, lawyers and judges shrouded the path to punishment in an impenetrable fog, putting a dozen different spins on every count against every criminal. People killed one another in riots, on the streets, murdered them brutally in their own homes, and their lawyers got them off. They stole cars and sold drugs and assaulted children and were out on the street again without blinking. Who knew why this was happening?

Every day April tried to make sense out of events that made no sense whatsoever. And still, every once in a while, she had a golden moment of absolute happiness that challenged reason. Now, standing in the hallway of Raymond Cowles's apartment building with an old woman's bulging plastic bag in one hand, she wondered if perhaps the flooding toilet and the old woman's garbage were spirits telling her she was wasted and unappreciated here in this uptown Caucasian world.

It occurred to her that this part of her life was a test that was over, like the sergeant's test she had taken. Except her sergeant's test had been a retest. Months ago, she had missed her scheduled appointment for the exam because a suspect had been trying to kill her at the time. So they had given her another chance at it. Only this time no board of real people was there to ask her questions and evaluate her answers. Instead of a board of three, one sour-faced uniformed Sergeant had given her the written exam, then set up a video camera as if she were a suspect in a particularly nasty homicide.

"Please direct your answers to the camera," he'd told her.

Who knew if anyone ever actually looked at the tape. Maybe they—whoever *they* were—just decided it was time for a change for April Woo, as they had when she was transferred out of the Fifth Precinct. Perhaps it was her destiny to return there now because she was an Asian and that's where she belonged. Only this time maybe she would go in triumph, as a Sergeant, a Supervisor.

Maybe wearing a uniform and eating delicious Chinese food every day was her future. The correct future. Recently she had met a doctor who had his office in Chinatown. George Dong seemed to be interested in her despite her age, which was nearly thirty, and her job, which was demanding at best. Maybe something would come of it. The thought shot a shiver down her spine, sending the golden moment on its way. She opened the exit door.

The building was too small for a back elevator. Only a landing with a recycling bin, a shelf for newspapers, a garbage chute, and the back stairs were behind the door. The recycling bin and the shelf were empty. Whatever had been in Raymond's garbage had already been removed. April remembered that his Monday paper was on the carpet in front of his door, but there was no sign of a Sunday paper. Most people kept at least a few sections for a day or two. Funny. She dumped the old woman's garbage down the chute.

The hall was empty when she came out. Sergeant Joyce must have taken Lorna Cowles to the precinct to answer some questions of her own. April headed back into the apartment.

No one from the M.E.'s office had arrived to pronounce the corpse dead yet, so Raymond Cowles was still in his bedroom lying on his back on the bed with the plastic bag neatly taped around his neck. The photographing was finished, but someone April didn't know was sketching the room, measuring everything and labeling distances and angles. He was shorter than she and weighed twice as much; he was working intently and ignored her.

She moved closer to the bed to get a better look. The beige covers of the bed were pulled back in an untidy mound. The body lay on a rumpled sheet that had some stains on it. Whatever body hairs had been there earlier were gone now. If Raymond Cowles had struggled at the end, there was no sign of it. His arms were by his sides. Under the plastic, his unseeing eyes were just slightly open. April reached out to touch his hand. It was cool, rigid. She crouched down to look at the long, slender fingers with their short nails buffed to a low luster. His left ring finger had the indentation of a ring, but there was no ring on it now. The only visible bruise was on his neck—a hickey, round and red and put there before his death. There was no guessing what kind of marks might be hidden under the shirt and trousers.

"April," Mike called from the living room.

April straightened up. The sketcher continued to ignore her. She opened the drawer of the bedside table with the crook of her finger, even though she knew Mike would already have looked there. Inside was a large jar of K-Y jelly and about a year's supply of latex condoms in packets of three.

The man had been interested in eating and sex. She closed the drawer and left the room. Mike had arranged some items on the dining-room table, which was still gritty with gray fingerprint powder. The items were in clear plastic bags, already neatly labeled. Among them was a pill container with twenty-five Kaminex remaining from a prescription of seventy-five, a notepad with the name Harold Dickey and a phone number written in blue ink on it, and a copy of *Final Exit.*

eleven

"Halloween." Sergeant Joyce spat out the word with disgust. "Worst night of the year as far as I'm concerned." She threw herself into a chair in the detective squad's interview room, where the TV was on, set to a surgical procedure. The removal of what appeared to be an eyeball was in progress.

April leaned against the wall behind the monitor so that she wouldn't have to watch it. Mike sat in the chair opposite her and stroked his mustache.

"One of my kids ate two pounds of candy and threw up half the night. The other one dressed like a washing machine—covered his head with a box from the supermarket and had his sister staple up the bottom. She forgot to put any holes for his arms, so the poor kid couldn't collect anything." Sergeant Joyce shook her head fondly. "Can you beat that?"

April and Mike exchanged glances.

Joyce sighed gustily. "Well, what do you think?" She directed the question at Mike.

He winked. "Kids are great," he said. "I wouldn't mind having a few myself."

"No kidding." Joyce shot him a mean look. "Why don't I believe that?"

"I have no idea."

"Well, I wasn't talking about kids. I was talking about the case—Raymond what's-his-name."

"Okay." *Whatever you say.*

The words "ovarian cancer" jumped out of the TV speaker.

Sergeant Joyce's head jerked around as if she hadn't realized the show was on. "What the fuck is that?"

April's stomach rumbled. She jiggled her foot impatiently. It was lunchtime. The minutes were ticking away, and there was a lot to do.

"Looks like the TV. You want it off?"

"Yes, I want it off. I want it always off. Who turns that thing on, anyway?"

Mike leaned over and hit the power button. He shrugged again. If the squad supervisor didn't know that Healy turned on the surgery channel every chance he got, it wasn't his problem.

"I hope it's suicide," she said suddenly, pulling at her hair. "Our record is really getting to stink."

April smiled. Yeah, here they were in what was called a quality-of-life precinct: the West Side north of Fifty-ninth Street, Central Park West to the Hudson River. The area included a number of high-profile churches and synagogues, the New York Historical Society, the Museum of Natural History, Columbus Avenue, where the TV networks were, Lincoln Center, several colleges and a university, a huge hospital complex. The list went on and on. This was where robberies, muggings, panhandling, car thefts, drugs, and rapes of the homeless were the major contenders for their time. Homicide was not exactly a daily occurrence around there. People didn't like it. It made them nervous.

"It's Healy. I know it's Healy. He must have been rejected from medical school or something." The Sergeant smirked at them, wanting them to know that even when she said she didn't know things, she really did.

"High school," Mike shot out.

"All right, all right. What about the stuff in this guy Raymond's apartment?"

"You mean the book and the Kaminex?"

"Yeah."

"There's a precise description of the plastic-bag suicide in the book, complete with some discussion about alcohol and tranquilizers. If you drink too much and take too many, you fall asleep before the bag's attached. He had that section highlighted," Mike said.

Or someone had. April thought of the neat job and wondered how a man might have a lover in for dinner, have sex, get dressed, comb his hair. Then what? Did they have a fight and break up? Was he so despondent he headed for the bathroom, popped a few pills, wandered back into the bedroom to call his shrink?

Then what?

He took the pills, put a plastic bag over his head, lay down on the soiled sheets with his shoes on, and went to sleep? Wouldn't he want to write a note telling the shrink what had happened? Desperate people usually wanted to tell, to explain themselves.

"The book could be a plant," April said. Could be there were no tranqs in his body.

"Halloween," Joyce muttered. She was back on Halloween. "What's the significance of that, huh?"

"Maybe it was just a coincidence," April suggested.

"Lots of movement, lots of noise in the area last night," the Sergeant was lamenting. "You know in these buildings, not all the kids trick-or-treating live there. Sometimes they bring their friends over and do it together. People open their doors without looking."

April shifted her weight and started jiggling her other foot. Why was Sergeant Joyce fixated with Halloween? Halloween probably had nothing to do with it. The guy was unhappy. He offed himself. After a bottle of wine and dinner and sex all over the sheets? Love bite on his neck.

"Maybe it's not a coincidence," Mike said. "If you kill somebody on Halloween it could be a trick. The joke's on the victim. If you kill yourself, the trick's on the people left behind. You think Cowles had a sense of humor?"

April shook her head. Sometimes killers did, but suicides usually didn't. Raymond's wife had said he was seeing a psychiatrist. The same Dr. Treadwell had prescribed a tranquilizer. Maybe Ray had had trouble sleeping, but maybe he had had a mental problem. April had already dialed the number on the pad found on the table beside Ray's body. Harold Dickey was also a shrink. According to Ray's appointment book he'd seen Treadwell, the other psychiatrist, on Friday.

The two psychiatrists seemed to be the key. April checked her watch. It was after one. The person who had answered Dickey's phone said the doctor was usually in his office between one-thirty and two. If they hurried they might be able to catch him.

"Let's go talk to the shrink," April said.

Sergeant Joyce pushed her chair away from the table, scraping new scuff marks on the dingy green linoleum floor. She scowled at Mike. "Be nice," she warned.

twelve

The old fire room on level B3 where Bobbie Boudreau spent his breaks had been too small to rehabilitate during the many improvements and additions to the Stone Pavilion since its original construction in 1910–13. The room, a space of about eight feet by ten feet down a rarely traveled jog off a main passage, had been passed over again and again. Its door was green like all the others, but without a label to designate its purpose. Without a label, the room was ignored. It hadn't been of use to anyone for many years until the day six months ago Bobby found it in one of his janitorial ramblings.

When he found it, the dust in the little room was so old it was no longer furry. It had hardened into a gritty crust that refused to come off even with soap and water. Stacks of red fire buckets with clumps of ancient sand still clinging to their sides and bottoms lined one wall. A large axe and a smaller one, both badly rusted, hung on the wall above three folding stretchers made of wood and canvas piled one on top of the other. Rolls of rotting fire hoses almost prevented Bobbie from opening the door. That first day when he pushed inside and breathed the hot stale air of the forgotten room from the hospital's distant past, he'd felt as if he had discovered another country for himself—almost like the cardboard box he'd jerry-built into his own space in a corner of the ramshackle structure the Boudreau family called home when he was a kid.

He'd stumbled on the place only a few days after his mother died in a room not so very different from this in a brownstone a dozen blocks downtown. And it was there, camped on the only cot still strong enough to support his weight, that he brooded on the bitter humiliations and injustices he had suffered in his life, culminating in the final ultimate castration by the bitch Clara Treadwell, who ruined his life and killed his mother.

It made Bobbie's jaws hurt—set his throat afire, his whole head and brain, in fact—to think how evil that bitch Clara Treadwell was, how much he wanted her dead. After all his years of faithful service at the hospital, caring for the craziest of the crazy, people so vicious and dangerous the other nurses were scared to handle them. He'd cleaned up their shit, their vomit, dressed their wounds when they stabbed or burned themselves, stopped them when they pulled out their hair. He'd sedated them, calmed them with his touch. They'd loved and depended on him, and she'd swatted him down like a fly for a death he had had nothing to do with. *Nothing* to do with. He'd been scapegoated, humiliated, drummed out of his whole life when all he'd done was his job as he was told to do it, nothing more, not a thing more.

And it wasn't the first time in his life this had happened, not by any means the first. How could life be so unfair? The answer was that people like Clara Treadwell always abused their power. They always hurt little people. They hurt anybody they felt like hurting. And good people had no way to protect themselves.

It was actually a photograph of Clara Treadwell in the Medical Center's newspaper that gave Bobbie the idea of cutting out letters, pasting them into messages, and delivering them to the bitch herself. Her picture appeared with some regularity. He'd seen it in the *Post* when she was appointed to the President's commission. The same picture appeared in the Medical Center newspaper. A month later there was an article about her condom lectures and her proposal to put condom machines in the adolescent clinic and inpatient departments of the Psychiatric Centre to prevent AIDS. The article talked about the furor her proposal caused.

That photo had also featured Dr. Harold Dickey, Chairman of the Quality Assurance Committee—the other fuck who deserved to die. Years ago Bobbie had walked into an empty patient room on a locked geriatric-depressive ward and found Dickey and the young Clara Treadwell groping each other behind the door. Lots of things just didn't change. In the recent newspaper photo they stood beside a condom presentation on a blackboard. Dickey's hand cupped Treadwell's shoulder. Both were smiling.

For a few weeks after that photo appeared in the newspaper Bobbie put condoms in Treadwell's files, left them on her chair in the boardroom, in her desk, in the toes of the running shoes in her closet. The locks were changed in the executive suite, but that never kept him out.

He sat on the cot, staring at his collection of bitch photos taped to the wall. The one that galled him the most was the one with the smiling arrogant foolish hypocritical Dr. Dickey. Those two thought they could get away with anything, thought no one knew what their relationship really was, what they were up to. Bobbie felt powerful, knowing about them and knowing they didn't know he knew.

Like the colonel years ago who never knew how close he'd come that day to dying, Clara Treadwell didn't believe she was in mortal danger. She didn't believe in Bobbie's power. He could see it in the way she walked, in the smile in her publicity photos. Foolish woman was going to lose her old lover. He stuck the photo back on the wall. Since the bum had had his accident and fallen off the bridge, Bobbie had felt very calm. The pieces of his shattered life were coming together again. He didn't like messes, knew exactly how to kill so no one suspected a thing. Accidents were his speciality. He'd gotten a bonus he hadn't expected with the bum, and the next two were scheduled. He checked his watch. One-twenty-five. Time to go to work.

thirteen

At one-thirty P.M., in gray sweatpants and a gray sweatshirt with no slogan on it, Jason Frank jogged down the five flights of open stairways from his office and apartment to the main floor. The stairs, like those in an old first-class European hotel, had been a major attraction for him when he moved there eight years ago. The twenties-era building was unique. It had two ways of getting up and down: the large, old-fashioned, see-into cage elevator and the open stairs. Wide landings went all the way around the building, forming an elegant square from the marbled lobby to the fifteenth floor. The wrought-iron railings were painted black, decorated with insets of brass leaves and elaborate vines.

Once grand, it was all getting pretty shabby now. The diamond designs on the bottom half of the walls, formed from black and white half-inch tiles, were no longer perfect. Many of the tiles were chipped or broken. A few were missing altogether. The well-worn marble stairs were cracked and hadn't been polished to a high shine in decades. The ceilings, decorated with moldings and golden rosettes, were in need of a paint job and some new gilding.

The building was a co-op. Recently the board had taken a poll to see how many owners wanted to spend the hundred-thousand-plus dollars it would take to make the necessary repairs, but the outcome hadn't been revealed yet. As Jason hit the main floor, the doorman glanced at his watch.

Emilio was twenty-five and watched everybody's comings and goings with an avidity that was unusual even for the chummy Upper West Side. He had seen the doctor's last patient come down and was pretty sure the man was gay. It made Emilio worry about the doc. If the doc had gay patients, did that mean he was gay himself? It was the kind of thing you just had to ask yourself. And now, ten minutes later, Dr. Frank was in a sweatsuit heading for the door.

"Going for a run, Doc?" Emilio asked.

Jason smiled. No, he was going to rob a bank. "Morning, Emilio."

"Not for over an hour and a half. It's afternoon now." Emilio opened the heavy glass-and-wrought-iron door.

Dr. Frank walked out. He didn't look gay. He was about six feet tall, taller than Emilio's five ten. He was also a lot thinner than Emilio. The doc had a lean runner's body, medium-brown hair, cut pretty short. He looked kind of like a Kennedy, one of those privileged kind of people. Well-built, good-looking, with a good background and all his shit together. Except he had a beard now. More than three weeks' worth of beard, and he was still scratching at it. Emilio studied the doc as he went out the door. Was he gay or not?

"Watch out for those raindrops now. It's going to rain."

Jason didn't answer. He was very careful not to say much to Emilio. The young doorman had some problems with his identity. For a while the young man had been telling all the people coming to see Jason that he and Jason were colleagues because Emilio was studying psychology at the community college he attended at night. He said he could tell things about them just by the way they walked.

That kind of thing amused colleagues but made Jason's patients extremely uneasy. Jason had to tell Emilio to keep his speculations to himself and not do a single thing more than open the door. That was his job and his limit, to open the door. He had considered knocking the young man's teeth out but decided that was an overly aggressive and unproductive approach to the problem.

Outside, he sniffed the moist chilly air and shivered. He hated the cold, considered it a personal enemy he had to conquer every year. It was November already. Pretty soon he'd have to stop running outside and start traveling across town to work out at the 92nd Street Y. Jason hated that. It took up too much time. Six months of the year, when it was warm, he ran in Riverside Park. He ran in the morning before he saw his first patient or sometime between twelve and two. He had a rationale for everything he did, and in the eight years since he had qualified as a psychoanalyst, he had worked out his days and hours exactly to fit the requirements of his profession, which was unlike any other.

He taught medical students and psychiatric residents. For each hour-and-a-half lecture, it took about forty hours of preparation. He taught at three different levels. Every level had to know certain things by the end of one of his talks. Medical students got the basics. The same subject for residents was much denser and deeper. For colleagues in associations he had to write the papers in advance. Jason got paid nothing for teaching and nothing for supervising residents. The personal cost of becoming an important analyst, a mover and shaker in a rigid and unyielding field, was something no analyst talked about.

No one got paid for the thousands of hours spent writing articles for psychoanalytic journals. Nor for the hundreds of dollars it cost to reprint the articles and send them all over the world to people who wanted them. Jason was paid an honorarium for about half of his speaking engagements, but even those did not begin to cover the cost of the hours and hours it took to prepare. And the days to give them, because a speaker didn't just fly somewhere and speak, then get on a plane and go home. A speaker had to meet students, had to have lunch with the head of the department, colleagues who wanted to interact. Sometimes it was too far to go home. He had to stay, have dinner and spend the night.

For conferences, topics had to be approved in advance by the program committees. Then presenters had to hand in papers in advance so the discussants could read them and prepare their rebuttals. Of course, one had to stay and listen to other people's papers. Often Jason was asked to be both a discussant and a presenter. When he got back home, exhausted and drained, he was immediately plunged into a grueling round of twelve-hour days packed with teaching and patients and had stacks of unopened mail waiting for him. That was the career track for someone who wanted to make a difference in the field. Jason was on that career track, an independent attached to an institution that considered teaching an honor that shouldn't be polluted by any recompense.

He crossed Riverside Drive at Eightieth Street and broke into a comfortable jog. Up at Eighty-fifth Street was the huge hospital complex, one building of which was the Psychiatric Centre where he had trained and where he now supervised and taught.

He passed the Centre without looking at it, didn't feel like going in, which was the reason he didn't have a full-time job there. Jason had never acquired the taste for politics and committees and endless meetings. The only way for an independent like him to earn a living was in patient hours. And he knew exactly how many patient hours he had to book to support his writing and teaching. He was never really idle, never without a thousand demands on his time. He had married twice. He'd left his first wife. Emma, his second wife, had left him. Whenever he wasn't working, he was thinking about that.

He barely noticed the majestic Hudson River or the cliffs of New Jersey on the other side of it. He was worrying about his wife acting in movies, living in California, who spoke to him on the phone at a scheduled time every week and told him there wasn't a thing about him she'd ever loved. It was at this point that he broke into a sweat.

When he reached Ninety-fifth Street, he was thinking that he didn't have a car, a country house, a child. The question was, could he cut back his activities and spend some real time with Emma? That was the issue. It seemed that only a major sacrifice would impress her. That was how far women had come in their evolution from passive helpmate to separate working partner. It was clear that two careers meant no time for anybody. Emma had given him five years of hers and ended up desperate enough to act in an erotic film to get his attention. Now that she was successful in her own right, she thought it was perfectly fair for him to sacrifice his work to hers for the next five years.

Up at 110th Street, sweating freely, Jason turned around and started back at a faster pace. By now he was no longer thinking of any of the things that oppressed him. The endorphins had kicked in. His energy was renewed. He felt he could run for an hour and not feel any pain later. Which wasn't true. He felt optimistic about women in general and Emma in particular, felt somehow it would all work out. Which probably wasn't true either.

As he passed the Psychiatric Centre for the second time, he glanced at the entrance. He almost fell over his feet at the sight of the only two cops he knew heading into his turf again.

fourteen

Shrinks were a strange species, April thought. The hospital complex was called the Medical Center, but the psychiatric building was named the Psychiatric *Centre.* The Centre's towering marble entrance and vast lobby also insisted people take it seriously. A quick check before April and Mike left the precinct confirmed that both of Raymond Cowles's shrinks had offices in this intimidating building. It was the kind of place that made cops feel like they came from the reeking lower levels of society's dung heap.

As soon as Mike was on the other side of the revolving door, he stuck a finger in the collar of his gray shirt and pulled at his shiny silver tie, stretching his neck. He didn't exactly fit in with the M.D.s of the world. The bulge of his holster was just visible around his left armpit. His sharp clothes and sharp watchfulness, his gleaming black hair, and the bravado in the smile under his abundant mustache didn't help either.

April shifted her bag from one shoulder to the other, hoping the security guard having an animated conversation with a maintenance man across the wide stone floor would not suddenly realize he'd just let in two people with guns and call the cops. They headed for reception.

"Can you tell me where I could find Dr. Dickey?" Mike asked the pretty woman at the desk.

She gave him a big smile and tossed her mop of curly red hair so that it bounced around. "Dr. Harold Dickey?"

Mike gave her a big smile back. "That would be the one."

"Do you have an appointment?"

Mike showed her his gold shield. "Of course," he said.

"Nineteenth." She handed them visitor passes.

"Thanks." Mike Sanchez turned away, then swung back. "What about Dr. Treadwell?"

"The Director of the Centre? You have an appointment with her, too?"

Her? Mike's eyes opened wide as he turned toward the elevators. "Yeah," he murmured, "her, too."

Surprised, April touched his sleeve. *The woman director of the Centre was the shrink of the dead man?*

Mike jerked his head at the guard by the door, who continued his discussion without looking their way. Some security. Also the woman at the desk forgot to tell them they had to check in with the Nursing Supervisor on the third floor to turn in the bullets to their guns. Nobody was allowed to walk around a mental hospital with a loaded gun.

April was troubled by a number of things, not least of which was that Dr. Treadwell was a woman. She had no idea why it bothered her. It occurred to her she might have felt the same distress if the doc were Chinese. One didn't want trouble for one's own. April pressed the up button a few times. Then Mike punched it. They looked at each other. With six elevators it seemed to be taking a long time. The crowd grew as they waited. A number of the people waiting were wearing white coats. Others had interesting patterns shaved into their heads, multiple pierces, weird-colored hair, and strange clothing. Mike looked increasingly unhappy.

It took an eternity to get to the third floor, to find the head nurse, give up their bullets, watch them being labeled, bagged, and locked in a filing cabinet. Standing at the elevator a second time, April saw Mike drop two replacement bullets into his pocket, just in case.

It was one-forty by the time they got to the nineteenth floor, and the matronly woman at the desk rang Dr. Dickey's office to see if he was free.

"Dr. Dickey, two police officers are here to talk to you." She turned her shoulder to shield the receiver. "No, they didn't. . . . Yes, Doctor."

The receptionist hung up the phone. "Fifth door on the left," she told them crisply.

Fifth door on the left. April's lips tightened as she thought of Raymond Cowles with the neatly pleated plastic bag over his head. Ray had had two shrinks. One turned out to be the Director of the most prestigious psychiatric hospital in the city—maybe the whole country—a woman, no less. And the other was who knew what. No one was going to be happy with this case.

The fifth door on the left opened before they got to it. A plump man in a gray suit stood in the doorway, warily watching their approach. His bushy eyebrows and expressive mustache, along with dark eyes that kept moving as if they didn't intend to miss a thing, dominated his pink-cheeked face. The man was past the midpoint of his life but still radiated a feeling of power and energy as he sprang back into his room and motioned for the two detectives to enter.

"Dr. Dickey," he said mildly, introducing himself. "How may I help you?" As shrinks often did, Dickey gave the impression of already knowing how he could help them.

"I'm Sergeant Sanchez and this is Detective Woo," Mike said.

"Is there a problem?" Dickey cocked his head.

"Do you know a man by the name of Raymond Cowles?"

Dickey moved his head over to the other shoulder. *Yes, no, maybe so.* "Should I?" he asked.

Mike shrugged.

Dickey regarded him coolly. "Why don't you fill me in on the facts, and we'll see what I can do to help."

"Fine. Raymond Cowles was found dead in his apartment this morning."

Dickey's bushy eyebrows moved together into a deep frown while his eyes darted back and forth, as if searching for some clarification. "This is not a person I know," he murmured finally. "I'm puzzled . . ." He opened his hands questioningly.

The three of them still stood in the small space in front of Dickey's unimpressive wooden desk. Dickey didn't ask them to sit down. His hands were open, palms up. "What does this have to do with me?"

"Raymond Cowles wasn't a patient of yours?" Mike asked.

Dickey shook his head. "No," he said emphatically.

"You didn't know him?"

"No."

"Your name and number were on a notepad beside the body."

Dickey winced, then shook his head again. "A lot of people know of me. That doesn't mean I know anything about this. I never met the man."

"He had your number. Did you speak to him?"

"I never spoke to him."

"Do you know Dr. Clara Treadwell?"

Dickey's dark eyes darted from one to the other. "Of course, she's the Director of the Centre. Is she . . . ?" He flushed.

April kept silent, watching the doctor's face. She noted that he was cool and reserved, was not concerned enough even to ask how Raymond had died. Then Dr. Treadwell's name came up and he blushed like a girl.

"What about Dr. Treadwell?" Dickey asked suddenly. "Does she have some involvement with this? What happened? I'd like to know what happened."

"You didn't know the deceased?"

"No, but anything that involves the Centre . . . I'm the chairman of the Quality Assurance Committee." Dickey drew himself up to the position. "I would have to know . . ." He smiled engagingly, imploring them to tell.

Mike glanced at April. "Thanks, we'll get back to you."

When they left, Dickey followed them out into the hallway. For a second, it almost seemed as if he intended to go upstairs with them to visit the Director. Then abruptly he turned back into his office and softly closed the door.

April made a face. "Why bother to lie? We'll only find out anyway." She punched the up button for the elevator. They waited for it.

"Oh, *querida,* everybody lies. Don't you know that yet?"

At two P.M. the two cops stepped out of the elevator on the twentieth floor. They studied the empty hall. In only minutes, they'd traveled a long way from the unadorned academic offices on the nineteenth floor. Here, an expensive patterned carpet covered the floor, a warm beige paint job and horsey prints decorated the walls. Straight ahead, oversized mahogany doors marked the entrance to the executive suite.

Uneasily, Mike and April walked through the doors. Inside, the reception desk was vacant. So were the upholstered chairs and sofa. The reception area looked like a living room. Around it a number of smaller mahogany doors were open or closed on more living room–like offices.

Before Mike and April had time to consider making a move, a thin dapper man in an expensive-looking gray suit and a red-and-white polka-dot bow tie appeared in one of the doorways and sauntered toward them. A small inquisitive smile was painted on his sculpted, upper-class face.

"Is there some way I may be of assistance?" He spoke with the assurance of a man who was sure he could.

Mike took out his ID. "We're here to see Dr. Treadwell."

The man's small smile did not waver as he examined the ID. "I'm Dr. Goodrich, Vice Chairman of the hospital. You may tell me what your business is here. I'm sure I can help you." A look of concern replaced the smile.

"This is something that concerns Dr. Treadwell personally."

"Anything relating to the hospital also concerns me." After a few seconds of awkward silence, Goodrich smiled again.

"We have no reason to believe at this time that the matter we've come about is related to the hospital." Mike smiled, too.

April hated standing there with her mouth shut while two men acted like jerks. She cleared her throat. "Would you tell Dr. Treadwell we need to inform her of a death? I think she would agree that it would be better for her to discuss it with us now than read about it in the newspaper tomorrow."

Dr. Goodrich's pale face reddened. "Can you tell me who it is, so I can warn Dr. Treadwell?"

"No. I'm sorry."

"Wait here. I'll see if I can interrupt Dr. Treadwell."

Goodrich turned and rushed headlong to the central closed door. In a moment he was back, closing the door silently behind him. "She'll be with you very shortly. Come this way." He led them to the closed door on the right, opened it, and ushered them into a large corner office with striking views of the Hudson River and the New Jersey Palisades.

He indicated two chairs in front of a huge desk with drawers on the wrong side. "You may sit down."

"Thank you."

Mike and April remained standing. April noted that Dr. Treadwell's office was about double the size of the detective squad room in the Two-O, which contained nine desks and a holding cell.

Almost instantly, the connecting door to the next room opened. No one would mistake the dark-haired woman who entered for a secretary. She wore a close-fitting navy suit that was striking in its simplicity. The skirt was cut just above the knee. A printed chiffon scarf of subtle earth and winey tones was tucked into the space where two buttons were open at the neck. Her stockings and high-heeled shoes were a subtle match to one of the burgundies in the scarf.

But the suit told only half the story. The other half was projected in the authority of her walk on nice slender legs, her flawless makeup, the comma of her dark hair. April was impressed. This woman looked very young to have such a high position.

"I'm Dr. Treadwell," she told them in a soft voice.

"Sergeant Sanchez and Detective Woo," Mike murmured.

The doctor glanced from one to the other and sat down at her desk. Her second-in-command with the fading blond hair and exemplary cheekbones didn't have to be told what to do. He had retreated to the door and left without saying good-bye.

"You have some information?" Dr. Treadwell said.

"We found the body of Raymond Cowles in his apartment this morning," Mike told her.

The sharp intake of Dr. Treadwell's breath drew some saliva down the wrong tube. She began coughing.

"Would you like some water?" April asked, thinking this was the second woman today to gag over the death of Raymond Cowles.

Dr. Treadwell raised her hand, shaking her head. "I'm sorry. This is a shock. . . ."

"Take your time. I can imagine it must be very difficult to lose a patient like this," Mike said.

Dr. Treadwell frowned. "What are you talking about?"

"The wife of the deceased told us you were his psychiatrist."

Clara Treadwell shivered. Her tufted leather chair swung around toward the window. When the chair swung back, her face was composed. She reached into a drawer of her desk, brought out a pocket-size tape recorder, placed it in the middle of her desk.

"Please sit down and tell me what happened." She indicated the two chairs opposite her.

April glanced at Mike. He smiled at her, inclining his head toward the tape recorder. They sat.

"November first. I'm with Sergeant Sanchez and Detective Woo," Dr. Treadwell said, her eyes on Mike. "I'd like to establish a record, if you don't mind, Sergeant."

The thing was voice-activated. Dr. Treadwell did not touch it. Mike lifted his shoulders in a small shrug. He scratched the ear that had been burned the worst in the explosion last spring. This sure was a switch. Usually they put the tape recorder on the desk and did the interviewing.

"Sergeant, you may begin now."

Mike said, "At ten-thirty this morning we received a call from Mrs. Cowles."

Mike told Dr. Treadwell as much as he felt she needed to know, which wasn't much. He held a lot of information back for a later date. The doctor stopped him from time to time for clarification, as her colleague, Dr. Dickey, had done. But Mike wasn't telling any more than he absolutely had to. They didn't have the autopsy yet, didn't know the cause of death.

As he spoke, Dr. Treadwell's hand flew up to her eyes, stretching her fingers to cover them both. To April, a person's eyes were the doors of knowledge. Between the eyes was the pathway to the soul. Dr. Treadwell's stretched fingers between knowledge and soul could not shield her deep distress from April's view. The Centre's director's face could be blank, but never so deeply blank as those of Asians, who had a much longer history of *save the face or lose the neck.* What April saw behind Dr. Treadwell's fingers was fear, just as, earlier, April had seen fear in the widow. What was it about the deceased that scared these women so much?

When Mike stopped talking, Dr. Treadwell dropped her hand to the table. Now the eyes were open and sincere in the front, and closed only from behind.

"I want to cooperate with the police in every way," she told them.

"Thank you. That will make things easier." Mike smiled.

Dr. Treadwell went on. "But I'm a little uncertain what I'm at liberty to reveal in a matter like this . . . the ethics of confidentiality . . . I'll have to consult a lawyer."

That was it. Interview over. April glanced at Mike.

"The deceased was your patient," he said.

Dr. Treadwell shook her head. "Not at the time of his death. As Director of the Centre, I can't take private patients. Ray Cowles was a patient of mine, years ago. Over a decade ago—more like eighteen years to be exact—"

Abruptly, the doctor stopped talking. She picked up the tape recorder and turned it around in her hand. "I'm very saddened by Ray's death, Sergeant. Thank you for telling me."

Dr. Treadwell gave the two detectives a small, saddened smile and pushed the button to stop the recording. April was right. At the mention of the lawyer, the interview was over. They were dismissed.

fifteen

Mike and April exited the Psychiatric Centre and crossed to the no-parking area where they'd left their unit. The sky had thickened into a dense rain cloud that was just beginning to unburden itself in a very fine drizzle. It was colder, too.

At the car, Mike smoothed back his hair and held out the keys. "You want to drive?"

April shook her head. She opened the passenger door and slid in, slamming it harder than she meant to.

Mike jogged around to the driver's side. Just as he reached for the door handle, the sky opened up. Sheets of fat raindrops plummeted down. He dove into the car, banging the door and sprinkling water all over the front seats, shaking his hands in April's face.

"Hey, watch that." Cold on April's cheeks, the rain felt fresh after the hot dance in the executive offices upstairs. She laughed, relieved to be out of there.

Mike settled in his seat, adding to the musty old car a mix of aromas that included fruity Caribbean aftershave, Old Spice deodorant, and wet wool. He didn't make a move to start the engine. He was busy with the rain on his face, with his sleek wet hair. The torrent streamed down the windshield, completely blocking the world outside.

This was how he liked it, stuck with April in a very tight space. This was when he was tempted to tell her the stories of his life and ask to hear hers. This was when he most wanted to take her in his arms and kiss her. All the windows were fogged up. From outside in or inside out no one could see a thing. He glanced at her, but she was studying the rain pummeling the windshield, didn't say a thing. He knew if he tried to kiss her, she might take her gun out and kill him. April seemed to think love was some kind of curse. He didn't know why any woman would be as hard and unyielding as that.

"I've decided to move," he said suddenly.

"When did you decide that?"

He laughed. "This morning. In the shower. I was thinking of you, and I decided it was time to get a place."

Sitting in the car with the rain hammering at them, April could almost imagine it. The downpour sounded like a shower. She didn't want to think of Mike without his clothes. "Let's go. I've got a lot to do. I'm hungry. It's almost two-thirty."

"What do you think of it?"

She shook her head. "It's hard to get a shrink to tell a straight story. Even in homicide cases, they always claim patient confidentiality." She sighed. "Maybe we'll never know what happened to Cowles."

"Not that."

April laughed. "Well, I'm glad you shower, if that's what you mean. But thinking of me? I don't know, Mike. . . . You got a hundred and one girls crazy about you. Why think of me?" She turned to him, her face appropriately blank.

"You're the detective. You tell me."

"Nope. I'm not in your head."

"Yes," he said. "You are in my head."

She shifted uneasily. Uh-uh, she wasn't going for monkey business in a unit. Why didn't he give it a rest?

"Okay, then, what about you?" he said.

"What about me?"

"You shower or bathe? This is important."

She made a *tsk*ing noise with her tongue. She knew of officers who had gotten up to things in their units. Knew the cooping places along the Henry Hudson Parkway. Precinct life was practically living together. There would have to be some monkey business among the uniforms. Some of it consensual, some of it not so consensual. Nobody liked to talk about it, but sexual harassment happened. A lot.

As for the detectives, they were so together there were bunk beds down the hall from the squad room for people who didn't want to go home on night shift–day shift turnarounds. With the exception of Sergeant Joyce, April was the only woman in the detective squad. Sergeant Joyce went home to her kids. April went home to her parents even if it turned out to be for only two or three hours. She went home, thought about Mike, then came back, saw him, and wanted to get away again. It was weird.

"I'll tell you what," April said. "If I'm so much in your head, I'll think it and you tell me."

"Fine."

Although April showered every morning, she thought of all the bath beads and bubble baths lined up on the shelf above her bathtub. She bathed at night and on weekends.

"You do both," he told her. "Bath and shower. How's that?"

"Adding the third option gave you only a thirty-three percent chance of being right."

"Well?"

Well, she could lie and say he was wrong, but she wasn't much of a liar. "You're right," she admitted.

"Good. You should trust me more." The rain had slowed to a trickle. With a grin, Mike wiped the fog off the inside of the windshield, then started the car. "So what do you think about my moving out on my own?"

That wasn't a good question to ask April, who had moved out only as far as the second floor herself. "I don't know. You ever live alone?"

"Entirely all by myself alone? No."

"Me neither."

He swung around in a wide U-turn. "You ever live with that guy—what was his name?—Jimmy?"

"No."

"Thank you."

"What for?"

"You were honest. I asked you a question, you didn't slide around on it, saying it wasn't my business. You answered the question."

"Well, I *didn't* live with him," April said, indignant now. "Why would I want you to think I did?"

"Doesn't mean you weren't sleeping with him."

"I'm not a nun."

"*Querida!* I'm relieved." Mike laughed, then hit the hammer and ran a red light.

sixteen

"I didn't do it, you fucker. I didn't do nothing. God gonna come down and she gonna rip your heart out. She gonna give your babies boils and plagues. That's what she gonna do." The invective from the woman in the holding cell came out in a long, bitter tirade. When it was over she began again. The woman was wearing three or four layers of clothes, all torn and reeking. She wouldn't sit down on the bench against the wall. Occasionally she kicked at it.

"There's roaches in here," she screamed.

No one denied it.

"Hey, get me out of here. I didn't do nothing. You put me in jail for *nothing*." She hung on the bars of the holding cell, trying to get her fat head through. Her face was puffy and blotched. Her stringy hair was tied in a few loose knots that hung down on either side of her face.

The four people in the squad room were on the phone, ignoring her.

"Hey! You. Fucker. God's gonna rip your heart out."

Detective Aspirante, at the desk closest to Ginesha, the civilian secretary who answered the phones and took messages, crossed his legs. "Pipe down, can't you see we're working here?"

"I can see it. I can see you fuckers working." The woman started her own private spitting contest. How far out from the bars could she land one?

For a few seconds it was almost peaceful—Ginesha, Aspirante, Mike, April, all talking on the phone, looking out the windows at the rain pounding Eighty-second Street.

"Aw, shit, don't do that. Come *on*." Aspirante was on his feet. "That's disgusting. Jesus." He looked around for help. "She's spitting on the fucking floor."

Sergeant Joyce came out of her office with a file in her hand. "What's the matter, Aspirante?"

The woman in the holding cell screamed at Joyce. "He hit me. That fucker hit me."

Joyce made a disgusted face at Aspirante. He shook his head.

"Oh, no. I didn't even bring her in. Healy brought her in."

"He knocked me down and raped me, too. That's the one." The woman pointed at Aspirante. "He's a cop. I knew he was a cop. God's gonna rip his head off. She is."

"What's her story?" Joyce demanded.

"Some old guy crossing Broadway stumbled into her grocery cart. She was napping on a bench. Heard the cans rattle in the cart, got up, and knocked him flat with a broom handle. Broke his arm with it."

"Get her out of here." Joyce turned back to her office. "We got a raper coming in." She went into her office, kicking the door closed behind her.

"Hey, Woo . . ." Aspirante began.

April listened to the voice on the phone, ignoring Aspirante's approach. "Well, when is he coming in? Uh-uh, I see."

"Hey, Woo. The Sergeant wants you to get the Broom Lady out of here."

April swung her chair all the way around to face the wall and the window, ignoring him.

Mike hung up. "What's your problem, Johnnie?"

"She spit on the floor." Aspirante directed his attention to three fat gray lugies on the floor.

"I got to pee. I got to pee. Get me outta here. I got to pee. I mean it. I really got to."

"Hey, Woo. The lady's got to pee. Take care of it, will you?"

"Yes, you have my number. Give me a call if you think of anything else." April rang off. She turned to Aspirante and spoke in a quiet, hard voice.

"Don't do that again." She enunciated clearly. "Didn't you see I was on the phone?" She looked up at him. It was a long way to the sneer. Aspirante was about six feet two, weighed about two hundred and thirty, maybe forty, pounds. Of that maybe an ounce or two was intelligence.

"You were on the phone?"

April stood up. Now it was five five to six two. "I'm off the phone now," she said evenly.

Aspirante thrust one hip out as if to stop her from getting away if that was her intention and looked way down at her, truculent. "Well, while you were on the phone we got ourselves a crisis. The lady here has to ur-in-ate. Then the Sergeant wants her out of here."

"It's not my call."

"When a lady has to pee, Woo, you're the only one here to take the call."

April didn't say any of the things that came to mind. She had a fleeting thought that Aspirante would not be a friend if they met one night in a dark alley. But that was nothing new. In dark places, she didn't think anybody would be a friend. Behind Aspirante, Mike got to his feet. Shit. Now the cavalry was on the way.

"Mike, I want to talk to you," April said. "I'll take care of it, John. You can go back to your cage now."

Aspirante's eyes narrowed. "What's that supposed to mean?"

"It means we've all got work to do." Mike came around the side of the desk. "She said she'd take care of it. Now you go 'Thanks.'"

But Aspirante couldn't say thanks. It was a lot to ask for him to get himself centered in his big body and figure out where he was. He took a moment to do that, tried to figure out if he'd won or lost the battle, couldn't tell. He stood there watching April call downstairs for a uniform to deal with the Broom Lady, get her to the bathroom and the papers sorted for the next step in the process. Healy was in the interview room talking to the injured man's son. If the son wanted to file an assault complaint, it would be hours before the woman was back in her spot on the street. By then the rain might have slacked off. Aspirante went back to his desk. Goldie, a uniform with a long history of dealing with the homeless and crazy, came to take the Broom Lady away.

"You get yourself in trouble again, Mamie?" she asked the Broom Lady. "What are we going to do with you?"

Mike leaned against April's desk. "What's up?"

"The doorman on duty last night in Cowles's building was a temp. It was the first time he'd worked there. He didn't know anybody, so he had no idea who came to see whom last night, what time they came, or what time they left. No idea at all. He said he wasn't feeling well, anyway. Had a bug and almost didn't go to work."

"So we'll have to check with the other doormen. Maybe they know who Cowles was seeing. Or the shrink. She probably knows."

"Mike, both shrinks said he wasn't their patient."

Mike nodded. "True, but Cowles's appointment book showed he had an appointment with Treadwell two days before he died. She's an attractive woman. Maybe they didn't meet as doctor-patient."

April chewed her lip, thinking about it. Could be they were lovers. "Maybe. Mike, did anything bother you about all those condoms?"

He lifted an eyebrow. "Like what? The guy was into sex."

"The semen stains on the sheet," she muttered.

"How do you know they're semen?" He kept his face straight.

"*Supposing* they turn out to be semen stains. Then what?"

"Okay. I get it. Why was it on the sheet? Why wasn't it in the condom, if he was such a believer? Or in the partner, if he was just too hot to bother with one?" Mike scratched his scarred ear. "Maybe he didn't get anywhere with the dinner date and jacked off into the air after she left."

"Yeah, could be," April agreed. Could be either of those things. People were coming in. She checked her watch. It was after four, time to go home. Tomorrow they were on the four P.M. to one A.M. shift. The day after that was their turnaround. Start at eight A.M. again. By then they might have an autopsy report.

Mike stood there, nodding. "It's something to think about."

She could tell he was trying to make up his mind whether to ask her to dinner or something. All that talk of semen and ejaculation must have turned him on. It was too early for dinner, though. They'd just had lunch. Finally he said, "Wanna go out for a beer? We could talk about the case."

Now April kept her face straight. "Sure, Sergeant. We could do that."

seventeen

All Monday afternoon Harold Dickey was flooded with memories of his affair with Clara Treadwell, begun nearly eighteen years ago when she was just a green resident. Then his job had been to follow her through her first cases and teach her the process she needed to learn to be a first-rate analyst. Each session she had with a patient had to be discussed, interpreted by him. He corrected her mistakes, watched her every step. It took hours every week. The Ray Cowles case had brought them together. Ray's treatment had been their common interest, the beginning of their passion and her development as a gifted psychiatrist. With Ray between them as their beating heart, their love had blossomed. Then, only four years later, Ray was cured and successfully terminated. Clara presented a paper on his case. It was published. Her star began to ascend in the psychiatric firmament. And she left Harold far, far behind.

By six P.M., hours after his visit from the police, Harold Dickey could hardly contain himself. Anxiously, all afternoon he'd been checking his watch again and again, wondering what Clara was up to. How was she taking the terrible news? What was she doing about it? As the hours crawled by, he became more and more upset at her delay in calling him to set up a plan of action. They had a lot to do. She should have gotten in touch with him by now. She had a patient death on her hands. He'd had a visit from the police. She needed him now. Right now.

Harold's watch told him it was way past six. In the old days he never had to wait for Clara Treadwell. In fact, it used to amuse him that he couldn't get away from Clara. She was always there, flying to him in every free moment she had, teasing him, tempting him with her bright, eager smile. Sexy, sexy girl. Undoubtedly she'd been the brightest student he'd ever had. What a combination of brains and drive and high-voltage sexuality. Clara Treadwell had been like a shot of adrenaline for him every day. She'd pursued him relentlessly, and he had not been able to resist her.

Harold stroked his mustache, remembering. Before Clara, in all the years of his tenure at the Centre, he'd never been interested in a colleague. Of course he had dabbled with secretaries, psychiatric nurses, and occasionally a social worker, someone sweet and pliant like Sally Ann, the nurse he'd met in his first year of medical school back in Texas and married soon after. They were still married. They had stopped loving each other a long time ago but had never bothered to divorce.

Theirs was the typical story. Sally Ann had been important as the breadwinner for a number of years, then quit to have children. By then he was a doctor and she was no longer on the same social level as he, was no longer interesting or important. For thirty years now, they had been living in Hastings, sharing the same house. But there had been very little conviction on either side for a long, long time. He didn't know or care what she did. He'd always had someone else on the side.

Harold never looked at any of his colleagues, though, never thought of becoming involved with a resident. He'd never even considered it. Those serious, homely women of the fifties and sixties who went into the field never appealed to him. Even in the early seventies when Harold's star had risen and he was at the top, the very top, and the women began their invasion into the profession—first just a trickle of them, then a few more bright young things with longer hair every year until the number of girls was past the halfway mark—he didn't think of them. And now there was a real crisis in the field. More women wanted to be psychiatrists than men.

And Harold had never looked at any of them. Only one had ever gotten his attention. Carmen—Clara. Clara who was Carmen the temptress and destroyer of men, though he didn't think of her that way then. Clara Treadwell, who had been Carmen, had hung around and seduced him. Without meaning to get too deeply involved, he had helped her out. By the time she left, he was so deeply in love with her, he couldn't imagine life without her. But Carmen/Clara had moved on to other men, another life, without giving him a second thought. And he'd had to endure living without her. Now she was back, the risen star while he was the falling one.

He sighed. Of course Clara had been very bright. She'd been destined to succeed. But Harold knew she could never have succeeded to this extent without his interference years ago. He had intervened on her behalf with Lawrence, the last chairman of the department, who died soon after retiring three years ago.

He tapped his watch with an impatient finger. Three years. It was hard to imagine that three years had passed since his old friend, his own mentor and supporter, was gone. It was *impossible* to believe that in Lawrence's place, running his hospital, was Harold's own protégée. Somewhere a beat had been missed. He, Harold, had been the meat in the sandwich between Lawrence and Clara, nestled between them in a wonderful harmony. And now one was dead and the other . . . Well, the other was keeping him waiting.

Harold looked around at the office he'd occupied for over three decades. Here he had done his great work in genetics, when Lawrence developed the genetics department and made him chairman. He'd kept this office all through the sixties and much of the seventies when the funds were rolling in and genetics was the wave of the future. By the eighties it was over. The explosion of molecular biology had eroded the genetics division of the psychiatry department, which was finally absorbed into the division of neural sciences and directed by an M.D.-Ph.D., a clinical psychiatrist and molecular biologist.

Harold wondered how he could make his point to Clara. He was angry now. He really should have immediate access to her at all times. There were vitally important things he needed to discuss with her. He glanced at the phone, willing it to ring. His life was a steady stream of students and patients and teaching. Why didn't the phone ring? Okay, there had been changes in his field, big changes. But he'd always had his teaching and his residents and his patients and his role in keeping the hospital on track. He'd always had that. It was Clara no longer treating him with respect—no longer loving him the way he should be loved—that made him feel diminished, hurt. Since her coronation as Queen of the Centre, he'd wanted to stop the hurt, but he couldn't find a way.

Every day he'd promised himself he wouldn't think about it, wouldn't feel lonely and betrayed by her. And every day when he saw her confident, glowing face, the pain hit him anew like a deep and anguished grieving that had no end. Her gifts were there in his office, in his closet at home, on his wrist. Before, they'd held the honored place in his life, trophies proving her great love for him, her gratitude for all he had given her. But now that she'd taken Lawrence's place upstairs and was squeezing the love from his heart like water from a sponge, her gifts to him had become painful symbols of her ownership of him. Now when he saw the awards given him for his work so many years ago and the gifts from Clara now identified as his only true and enduring love, all Harold Dickey felt was the unbearable loss.

Brilliant clinician that he was, he could not find a way out of his own case.

He checked his watch again: 6:16. He couldn't wait any longer. He reached for the phone and tried the Director's office. No answer at reception. Harold tried her private line. No answer there either. He was stunned. He couldn't believe that Clara had left without him. It wasn't possible. Once again anger flooded the calm stream where he tried so hard to live in peace. Clara knew he hated to be ruffled. She *knew* he didn't like to be challenged. Why did she deliberately humiliate him? No, surely it was an accident, a misunderstanding. It had to be.

He twisted on the hook, searching for an excuse. Maybe it wasn't Clara's fault. Maybe she was in a meeting with the lawyers about Ray's death. He remembered that Max Goodrich had stopped him in the hall earlier and told him the police had been to see Clara.

"We have to protect Clara," Max had told him, as if Harold might not be on the team of those deeply committed to protecting Clara.

"I'm sure there's nothing to worry about," Harold had replied. But the truth was, an investigation into the ancient history of the Ray Cowles case would be very worrying indeed.

For the last three years, Harold had been convinced that Clara would come back to him if her troubles with the Centre ever got big enough. Now the trouble was big enough, but where was she? All afternoon he had tried not to think of her living up there in the ether, way, way above him, where the power was. At 6:20 he decided it was time to go looking for her.

eighteen

Clara Treadwell did not instantly engage the Psychiatric Centre's legal machinery. She detested the hospital's general counsel, Ben Hartley, and decided she would not worry, or take any steps about the Cowles situation until there was an autopsy report determining his cause of death. By her last meeting of the day, however, she was too impatient to endure any more aimless debate about trivial matters. She walked out.

Recently, her span of attention had begun to vary quite a bit. In Washington, where the issues were big ones and the players big-league players, she was alert and fully engaged every second. But in the smaller arena of hospital and university life, the endless round of meetings about hospital departmental problems made her New York life seem routine, almost small-time. The petty politics of the individuals involved, each clinging so desperately to his own little sliver of the power pie, took up a lot of time. The system was an old one, unreformed and clogged with personal agendas. Instead of looking forward to the massive challenges of the new century, psychiatry seemed to be scuttling sideways like a crab, scared and on the defensive. One in ten psychiatrists was involved in a malpractice suit. Insurance companies had cut their payments so far back, they were subsidizing only fifteen days of managed care whether the patient had a food disorder, was a substance abuser, paranoid schizophrenic, or sociopath. Chronic illnesses couldn't be cured by fifteen days in the hospital, but no one was listening. No one cared.

As for therapy, insurance companies were demanding the psyche be treated the same way allergies and heart disease were. They expected pathology to be managed chemically, or surgically removed with a few intensive sessions of dynamic psychotherapy. Psychiatrists scrambled for faster and faster ways to do their work. It was like walking back in time to when only the rich could afford mental illness. It was small wonder that Clara Treadwell felt better in the intoxicating air of Washington, where power was an alcoholic kick that had no hangover.

Today, at 5:45, she slipped out into the soggy dusk and headed the one block home. Gratefully, she found her apartment as she had left it—large, beautifully decorated in an understated way, everything in its place. Only now it smelled of furniture polish and the flower arrangement that came from the florist every Monday. This week it was an unusual combination of blue irises, orange lilies, and some white and pale green blossoms in lilaclike bunches that Clara had never seen before. The arrangement had been unwrapped by the cleaning lady and placed on the butler's tray in the living room. Clara detoured into the living room to smell them. The lilies had a strong aroma, but the white blossoms were not lilacs. They had no perfume.

The rain had stopped hours ago. Now, high above Riverside Drive, it was quiet and serene. Clara moved quickly into the bedroom and played back the messages on her answering machine. Her lover, Arch Candel, the Senator from Florida, had called her three times in her office that day and twice at her home since five P.M. The two messages on the machine told her the same thing: Arch had a free moment and wanted to connect before the evening began. The machine played on, running back through the messages from the week before and the weekend that had not been erased or taped over. She waited for messages from Raymond Cowles, found one from a week before, and erased it. Then she shut the machine off and retraced her steps to the living room, where she poured herself some vodka and opened a can of tomato juice from the drink cart.

Finally she headed for the bath, her cordless phone in one hand and the lifeless bloody Mary in the other. She put the drink down on the side of the tub, dumped some bath salts into the tub, then dialed the phone and turned on the water at the same time.

"Senator Candel's office."

"Oh, it's Dr. Treadwell, returning his call." Clara wandered back into her bedroom and began stripping off her clothes.

"Oh, Dr. Treadwell. The Senator's in the car. Are you at home? I'll have him call you on the car phone."

"Yes, I'm at home for"—she glanced at the gold watch that had been a gift from her second husband—"forty-five minutes."

"Fine. I'll let him know."

"Thanks." Clara hopped to get out of her skirt and panty hose, tossed her pink silk bra on the expensive heap she'd made of her clothes on her bed. Naked, she took the phone with her and padded into the bathroom, where the bathtub was almost full. When she sank into the hot, fragrant water, she groaned with pleasure.

Not five minutes into her watery retreat, Clara thought she heard the doorbell ring. She was up to her neck in bubbles, talking on her portable phone to Arch in his limo in Washington. She sat up, shivering at the sudden change of temperature. Then she sank back again, telling herself no one could get past the doorman. She tried to relax and listen to what Arch was telling her, to respond appropriately to his account of his day. He liked to stay in constant touch, liked to talk.

The bell rang again.

"Listen, darling. Someone's at the door. I have to go."

"Who?"

"I have no idea. I'll go check."

"Well, come right back, darlin'. I'm worried about you."

"There's nothing to worry about. I'm fine."

"Call me anyway. I'm worried about you."

Arch's voice had the camouflaging southern softness that always impressed Clara. She liked southern men. They had that studied gentleness, taught from the cradle, that was relentlessly soothing on the surface without in any way concealing the rifle on the rack in the back of the truck, the pistol in the cupboard, in the drawer of the night table. It never failed to turn her on.

"Maybe you need some help."

She smiled in her scented bath. Every time she told Arch about a problem, he wanted to send someone in from Washington—the CIA, the FBI, the Justice Department—somebody big, to help her out.

"Thanks, baby," she murmured. "But I told you a long time ago that I can take care of myself just fine."

"And I told *you*, I could take care of you much better."

Clara Treadwell believed it was always necessary to have a powerful man in her life: One never knew what kind of assistance one was going to need down the road. But this kind of talk made her wary. Arch was very possessive. He liked being in control. She suspected he already had someone keeping an eye on her. That didn't exactly worry her, but she wouldn't be able to tolerate it for long.

The doorbell rang again, more insistently now.

"I've got to go."

Reluctantly she climbed out of the tub, grabbing her thick white terry-cloth robe. Dripping, she wrapped it around her and headed out to the entrance. Through the peephole she saw Harold Dickey in his ancient Burberry raincoat standing at her door.

She opened the door a crack. "What are you doing here?"

"Ask me in, Clara."

"I was in the bath, Hal."

"Is that where you were waiting for me?" He smiled the old smile as if they were lovers still and nothing had changed.

"What?" Her scalp tingled. The wet tendrils of hair on her neck felt like ice. Since when had old Harold Dickey started giving her the creeps?

"You asked me over for a drink before the meeting. I'm here. Aren't you going to let me in?" Harold still smiled the old smile.

Clara knew she hadn't done that. She'd never have him here alone. She didn't exactly feel any pressure on the door. But almost immediately it was wide open, and Harold was inside. They were standing in the foyer of her new life face-to-face, she in a robe he'd seen before and he in the raincoat that had been a joke between them eighteen years ago. She'd forgotten how deep and powerful the relationship between them had been. Student and teacher, lover and lover. Now she stepped back involuntarily, shocked that the past seemed to be breathing on her, still very much alive.

"Lovely home," Harold was saying. "I don't get to see it as often as I'd like, or even as often as I used to. You smell good. Same bubble bath?"

Clara pulled the robe tighter. Her fingers traveled up to the wet underlayer of hair clinging to her neck. She had always chosen her lovers so carefully—independent males with powerful egos who were just as happy to move on to other pastures as stick around with her. If they behaved well after it was over, she retained a warm feeling for them. If not, she cut them off. Life was too short for turmoil. But this was an old, old lover, and he had picked her, not the other way around.

"Hal, how did you get up here?"

He studied her face admiringly. "Lawrence was a close friend of mine, in case you've forgotten, Clara. I believe he was instrumental in getting you that first—"

"I remember."

"I told Tom I was expected. You know Tom, don't you? I thought I was expected." Harold took off his old raincoat and dropped it on a stool.

Tom was her doorman. Of course, he'd know Harold from the old days. The tic throbbed in Clara's cheek: Tom would be hearing from her about this. No visitors without her permission meant *no visitors.*

Harold stopped in the center of her living room and shook his head, admiring this, too. "Nice place. You've made it warmer and more inviting, of course. . . . You've certainly come up in the world, Clara."

"Do you have a problem with it, old friend?" Clara asked, feeling more secure now, and finally smiling a little.

The older Texan gentleman of sixty-something, with his nondescript suit, thickened waist, and white, white hair demurred convincingly.

"No, no. I'm proud of you at the head of the table. You're the mommy of us all, and you do it very well, Clara."

But he was the daddy no more. Maybe he couldn't handle it. "You really mean that?" she asked. Did anybody ever mean anything?

"Of course I mean it. I'm absolutely bursting with pride in you, you know that."

Clara had heard those words from him before. Years ago, they'd fed and fired her. Now they warmed her more than her hot bath. She realized he could still make her hold her breath. For a second, she tried to look deep inside him to see if what he said was true. He appeared admiring and full of pride. She decided she could handle him alone.

"I'm glad, because it's taken a long time, Harold, and I've worked very hard to get here. . . . Look, why don't you help yourself to a drink while I get dressed."

He nodded. "Thanks."

Clara wandered back into her room, where her navy suit was a mess on the bed. She decided to change her underwear and put the suit back on. When she returned to the living room, Harold sat in the wing chair by the fireplace that had no fire in it, sipping scotch with no ice. She sat in the chair opposite. She'd give him five minutes and no more.

"So, what's happening with you, Harold?" she said softly.

"Is it unusual for old friends to meet, spend time together?" Harold cocked his head, trying to look jaunty and not nearly as old as he was.

"It is when they haven't been close in many years. There's been a lot of water under the bridge since—"

"Of course the water is always flowing, Clara; but when two people were as close as we were, some things don't change. I still care about you. I still worry about you. There's not a lot I don't know about what's going on here. I could help you."

"I don't need help."

"That isn't what you used to say." Harold smiled.

"I've changed."

Harold shook his head. "No, Clara, you still need my help. I can still make things go right for you if you'll let me."

Clara made a noise.

"Don't scoff at me," he said sharply.

"I wasn't scoffing." She stared at him coldly. He had a lot of nerve making trouble for her, then offering to fix it.

"I hear you had a visit from the police today." He changed the subject and took a sip of his drink.

She nodded, her face tight. "Who told you?"

"I had one, too."

"You did?" Clara was appalled.

"Didn't the two detectives tell you they . . . uh, interviewed me first?"

"What did you tell them?"

"What do you think?"

"Don't play games with me, Hal. I have no idea what you told them."

"Do you know why they visited me first?"

"No."

"Oh, baby, don't play games with me, either."

"I'm not playing games with you. I don't know what's going on. They didn't tell me."

"What have you been up to, Clara?" Hal was irritatingly serene. "Why would that young man commit suicide? Did you seduce him, too?"

"Jesus, Harold, don't get on my case about this. I don't sleep with my patients."

He shrugged. "If you say so."

"I don't sleep with my patients!" she hissed. "That's a horrible thing to say. How could you suggest such a wicked thing?"

"It happens. It's unethical, but it happens. Occasionally one even commits suicide. . . ."

"Hal, I get the feeling you're threatening me."

"You're in trouble. You need help. I'll help you." He shrugged again. "It's not a hard one. I'll conduct the review for you. We could spend some evenings going over it, maybe take a weekend. . . . I'm sure the Quality Assurance Committee will—"

"Harold, no! You're the last person in the world who could review this case. You were my supervisor."

He smiled. "It went very well, as I remember."

"You know perfectly well I can't be held responsible for anything that happens to a patient fourteen years after I stopped treating him."

"You can if you were still seeing him."

"I wasn't *seeing* him!"

"Well, Clara, as the police will tell you, all this is extremely easy to establish. The question is: What game are you playing with me?"

She froze. "Hal, I have no idea what you're talking about."

"Clara, you must know perfectly well why the police came to me first."

Her face was blank. "No, I don't."

"My name and telephone number were found next to the dead man's body."

"Oh, my." Clara took a deep breath and was instantly calm. She almost clapped her hands with joy. Hal was on the hook, and she was off.

"I gather you gave my number to him." Harold put his drink down on the table beside his chair and his two palms on his knees. "Never mind. We can work it out. I've missed you, Clara. I know it'll be great working together again."

Clara smiled. She knew if she opened her mouth right now she'd say he was a dead man.

nineteen

Around eleven-thirty A.M. on November 2, April Woo paid a visit to the Fifth Precinct on Elizabeth Street, which now had its first Chinese commander. The first person she saw in the detective squad room was Lieutenant Alfredo Bernadino. The wiry Italian had a huge nose that had been broken more than once and looked as if he'd been born on the wrong side of the Mob fence. Smooth as the roughest grade of sandpaper, Lieutenant Bernadino was very popular in Chinatown. People believed he was fair in the right kind of way. The Lieutenant kept one eye open to the big things and the other eye closed to the little things.

"How ya doing, Alfie?"

"*Dio mio,* it's April Woo, as I live and breathe. How's life in the Two-O?"

Her former supervisor and head of the squad gave her the high-five, then settled down to talk in the metal visitor's chair of Detective Francis Harding, who was out on a call.

"Busy."

Different. Down here they were Alfie and April and Frank and Carlin, they high-fived each other and didn't stand on too much ceremony. Uptown was kind of starchy. If somebody tried to call Sergeant Joyce Margret Mary or MM or anything cute like that, she'd take his head off. Which was one of the many reasons April didn't appreciate the serious etiquette breach of Sergeant Sanchez calling her *querida* as if they were high school sweethearts.

"Or is it sergeant now?" Alfie chewed on a wad of gum at the same time as an unlit cigarette hung from the corner of his mouth. From the mangled and soggy condition of the filter tip on the cigarette, it looked as if the Camel had been lodged there since April left a year ago.

April smiled modestly. "I guess you saw the list."

"Congratulations." Deadpan, Alfie held out a small hairy paw.

April shook it, a little embarrassed. Maybe he could forget how she got her first promotion, but she never would. Four years ago she'd cuffed a gang member on the street and brought the sullen kid to the holding cell in the detective squad room. She'd been in uniform then, and the kid was having trouble with a triple loss of face. First, he was arrested.

Second, he was arrested by a woman cop who'd had no trouble getting his Glock automatic away from him. And worst of all, she was a Chinese woman cop.

The kid had a gang-member tattoo on his right hand that was brand-new to them, and he had no doubt already killed a number of people in Taiwan before he turned up in the Chinatown bean-curd factory where April and two other uniforms found him threatening the manager and four employees with his Glock.

Up in the interview room Alfie had asked the kid a lot of questions with April translating for him. After a while they left the kid to think things over. As April got ready to head back downstairs, out to the street, Captain Marcello Malacarne, the precinct commanding officer, wandered in. He nodded at her, then held out a piece of paper to Alfie. Alfie wiggled his finger at April as if he had a thought, then reached for the paper. April was required to stand there deaf and dumb, but there was nothing new about that. She was used to it.

Captain Malacarne, another mean-faced Italian with a long history in Chinatown, said, "This just came to my attention. What do you want to do about it?"

Alfie scanned the piece of paper. "Yeah. Sandford. Order to appear for promotion." He made a so-what gesture.

"Sandford retired last month."

"Ah, yes." Alfie remembered. He nodded solemnly, considering the situation. Guy had been in uniform twenty-two years, and they got around to promoting him two months after he retired. Somehow, the report of the retirement hadn't reached the Personal Orders department.

Lucky for them the Fifth was being assigned another detective. Unlucky for them they had no such officer to report for the promotion. Problem was that if the Fifth happened to report that little detail, the whole situation would be thrown into question. Another precinct could very well end up with the extra detective.

A few seconds later, with no more words having been said, the Captain had departed. Lieutenant Bernadino turned to April. "You want to be a detective, Officer?"

"Yes, sir," April replied.

"Then report for promotion first of the month, ten A.M." He handed her the paper so she would know where to go.

"Yes, sir," she said, taking it.

She often wondered how she had been assigned to the Two-O, where Chinese-speaking detectives were not exactly in the highest demand.

"I was hoping to meet the new C.O.," she said now.

"Good man," Alfie said, nodding and chewing. He wouldn't comment either way. Didn't matter to him who came and went; things didn't change much in the detective squad. He didn't say that Captain Chew might very well be out at one of the three thousand and two meetings and social events at which the Chinatown leaders expected their top man police chief to be in attendance every month. Nor did he ask April why she wanted to see the captain, or what was up with her. "What goes around comes around," he said after a moment.

"That's what I was thinking," she murmured. Her watch read 11:55. George Dong closed his office from twelve to one. "Well, I got to go."

Alfie smiled and took the cigarette out of his mouth. "Thanks for dropping by," he said.

The offices of Dr. George Dong were in a new building right across the square from 1 Police Plaza. He was on the second floor, facing south. In fact, every time he came out of his office, rain or shine, the very first thing George Dong saw was the prisonlike brick structure of police headquarters. April noticed this as she waited for him downstairs.

Three days a week George Dong operated on eyes in the morning and had office hours from three to six in the afternoon. Two days a week he was in his office all day except from twelve to one, when he shut the office for lunch. He had told April his schedule to indicate how well-ordered a person he was, balanced and in control of his life. Worthy of attention and respect.

This was the kind of information that was guaranteed to throw April into the slippery bog of despair about herself. Although she had mastered her facial muscles about the same time as she learned to read, she was in control of absolutely no aspect of her own life. There was nothing orderly about her life except the inevitability of chaos and the dense fog that surrounded nearly all of her cases as she walked into them.

"You could have come upstairs." George pushed out of his building's entrance at exactly 12:02.

"I just got here," she murmured.

So much for greetings. They were in the very early stages of getting to know each other and did not shake hands or kiss. In fact, neither April Woo's or George Dong's face revealed anything at all. Their Confucian heritage had taught them the essential rules on the cultivation of mind and heart. In this case, *wu wei* (nondoing and knowing you're not doing it) was an absolute necessity.

The first time April met George he'd been carrying a Wilson tennis bag and wearing a navy warm-up suit with red stripes down the legs. He had a round moon face studded with small, nondescript features. Not exactly chubby, but in no way well formed by Western standards, George reminded April of a Cantonese dumpling to which all spices had been added, then erased. Garlic is smashed and placed in the pan, swirled around in peanut oil for thirty seconds, then carefully removed so that no traces whatsoever remained in the sauce. The idea was blandness made your tongue work to find the flavors.

George was like that. April did not know whether the tennis racket was for real or for show, but she did not miss the meaning of the warm-up suit at their first meeting. He was reserving judgment on her. For the office, however, his attire was a different matter. Today George was wearing an excellent English tweed jacket of the sort April had seen on Jason Frank, the other doctor she knew. And gray slacks and a crisp blue shirt with white collar and cuffs. He looked every inch the successful professional. Without further ado he started walking, thus commanding April to follow.

Today he was going west two blocks to his newest favorite restaurant. Inside the crowded restaurant was an empty table in the window that seemed to have been reserved for him. When they were seated at it, without asking for the menu, he ordered in Chinese.

"That okay with you?" he asked April when the waitress was gone.

She nodded and told her first lie. "Sounds great."

"Good." He twisted his gold signet ring around his finger, studying her speculatively. "Have you ever had a permanent?" he asked suddenly.

"What?"

He pointed to the top of her head.

Ah, one of those frizzy jobs that always looked so wrong to April on Asians.

"No. Have you?"

"You should consider it. Curly hair would look great on you."

Her mother had curly hair. It looked shitty on her. April nodded a second time. Her training told her a low-class person speaks and reveals his immaturity. The perfect Confucian model is a person who does not speak and lets his silence reflect his wisdom. Mike called this restraint of feeling and passion *passivity* and told April he sometimes felt like slapping her for being like a stone. Even now, in a Chinese restaurant with George, she felt her sluggish blood stirring, just thinking about Sanchez's perverse opinions.

She realized she had tuned George out. He was telling her how a few weeks ago he did laser surgery on the cataracts of the grandmother of the owner of this restaurant, and now the ancient *zumu* could see better than when she was a girl. The old woman's children and grandchildren were so impressed that she no longer needed her glasses, they thought the three thousand dollars was a small price to pay. George never got a bill for any of the meals he ate there.

"Wow," April murmured; "must be nice."

"There's nothing nice about it. I feel good helping people," George said importantly.

April played with her chopsticks. Her mother believed George Dong was the ideal candidate for marriage and wanted her to close on the deal soon. She was having trouble working up an interest.

"But then there's a downside to everything." George looked at her gravely.

"What's the downside?" April piped up dutifully.

"The family thought it was such a miracle that their blind *zumu* could suddenly see without her glasses, they all wanted the surgery."

April didn't laugh. She could see how that could be awkward. "How did you manage that situation?"

"Twelve pairs of contact lenses." Now he laughed.

And now April understood why an American-born Asian like George, who had grown up in Queens and attended Columbia University and Columbia Medical School, would come down to Chinatown to practice medicine. Here, his patients never questioned his fees, didn't rely on insurance to pay their bills, and thought he was a god.

She laughed, too. "That's a lot of contact lenses."

"The disposable kind."

"Ah. Makes a difference."

"Indeed it does."

He fell silent as April poured the tea. It was the right kind, with the leaves floating around in the pot. George watched her.

"Can you cook as well as you pour?"

April moved one of the tiny cups to his side of the table. Her father was a chef. George had to know that. "I know how," she said, raising her eyes to look at him directly. She didn't have a whole lot of time to hang around the house chopping, though.

"I like a woman who can cook."

"And has curly hair. Any particular color?"

George flushed. "So you know," he said.

April nodded. It was a common police technique to make the person on the other side of the table think you already have the whole story even when you don't have a clue. The waitress deposited some metal serving dishes on the table and removed their covers. On the one closest to her, wrinkled gray sea slugs and smooth white squid lazed around in brown oyster sauce. April repressed a shudder.

"My mother told your mother, right?" George asked.

Again April nodded. George shrugged and immediately launched into the story of the lost love who'd broken his heart. A girl with curly yellow hair from Philadelphia who played the violin and was a Catholic. Apparently the affair had gone on for a long time although neither family approved. Religion was the issue with his. Anyway, by the time they both graduated from medical school, the girl had left him for an Indian anesthetist. Seemed pretty clear to April that George would enjoy never getting over it for the rest of his life.

"What about you?" he asked.

"What about me?" April hid a sea slug under a piece of lettuce on her plate and delicately picked up a piece of lemon chicken.

"You're very old. Why aren't you married?"

April was twenty-nine. She raised the piece of lemon chicken to her mouth and held it there, perfectly balanced in the chopsticks, while she delicately took a tiny bite. Twenty-nine was not so old, certainly not *very* old. Then she took another bite and another until there was nothing left. She was trying to think of something to say that would not damage either George or herself. Finally she put the chopsticks down and answered.

"Heaven does not speak, but the four seasons proceed on their course," she murmured.

"No kidding. *That* bad." George propped a tweed elbow on the table to support his chin while he gazed at her with interest. "I think we may have something going here. What do you think?"

April dabbed her lips with the stiff white napkin. She did not want to tell another lie. So she poured another cup of tea and looked remote.

twenty

At four P.M. on the second day of the Raymond Cowles case all the phones were ringing at once. Some of the second tour was hanging around chewing the fat, ignoring the tinkling bells. The third tour was half in, half out. Mike Sanchez wandered into the squad room looking queasy.

As he sank into his chair at the desk next to April's, she leaned across the notes she'd been reviewing and wrinkled her nose to sniff at him.

"What's the matter?" he demanded.

April closed her eyes, trying to identify the odd odor that clung to his leather jacket and the front of his shirt. It was a familiar scent, but one she had never before associated with him. In her mind's eye she saw gold and red, coins and ribbons, knew what it was. She opened her eyes. Got it.

Mike was frowning at her. "I smell or something?"

"Just a scientific experiment," she murmured.

"Oh, yeah?" Now he was sniffing at his armpits. "What?"

"I told you. I was just trying to figure something out."

"I never tell who I've been with. It's nobody's business."

"What are you talking about? You don't have to tell me. I know *where* you've been, so I know *who* you've been with."

"Oh, yeah? Where and who?"

"Well, could be one of two places." She ticked them off. "You've either been to a Buddhist funeral or a Catholic church."

"Uh-huh, and how do you know that?"

"Incense," she said triumphantly. "And you're no Buddhist. So that means you went to church with your mother, had a lot to eat, and feel like throwing up now."

"You knew that," he protested. "I already told you that."

She shook her head. "You didn't."

"Yes, I told you yesterday. You told me you had a date with that asshole Ding Dong, and I told you I was going to Mass with my mother on account of its being the Mexican Day of the Dead."

"Shit, Mike, I did *not* tell you that." April slammed the flat of her hand on the papers, then looked at it because it stung like a son of a bitch.

"Ha," he said. "Ha."

Now he thought he was speaking Chinese. *"Wǒ ni hèn,"* she spit out.

"Oh, no, you *love* me. You just don't know it yet."

Sergeant Joyce hated it when anyone had a happy moment. Now she stomped over and stood looking from one to the other. "What's going on?" she demanded, hands on chunky hips.

"The regular doorman's on at Cowles's building. I was just going over to question him."

"Yeah," Mike said. "And we're going to have another chat with Mrs. Cowles."

"Fine, then stop playing and get the fuck out of here. Check when the autopsy's scheduled and see what they've got in the way of prints while you're at it."

"I checked on the prints already," April said, glad to have a bomb to toss at them. "Two sets of prints all over the apartment. Raymond's and someone else's."

"Oh, anything else you'd like to tell us this year, like whose they are?" Joyce shrilled.

"They're running a computer check." April's eyes were innocent. "Maybe we'll know something tomorrow. Maybe next week." She shrugged. "You know how it is."

"What about the plastic bag and the masking tape? Anything on that?" Mike asked.

April shook her head. "Raymond's prints, only Raymond's. Looks like it just might be a suicide."

Joyce raked her fingers through her hair. "Okay, get going."

Mike got up, the grin still on his face.

Joyce hit him with one of her paranoid stares. "What's so fucking funny? Want to share the joke?"

"No joke, Sergeant. Just indigestion. You wouldn't believe what I had for lunch."

April reached for her bag. She didn't think they'd believe what she'd had for lunch either.

The sun made a stunning show of an autumn afternoon as they emerged from the precinct. It was warmer today, almost springlike.

"Let's walk. I could use the exercise," Mike said.

"Fine." They turned right and strolled slowly to the corner.

"You have only one day of the dead?" April asked as they waited for the light.

"Nah, there are a ton of obligations. Every family member has a saint's day. Even when they're dead you've got to remember them all. Aunts, uncles—you name it. Then there's birthdays. You've got to remember those, too, even after they're dead. Also the day they died. Day of the Dead, that's kind of like All Saints' Day."

The day before yesterday. April turned her face to the warmth. "You have a saint?"

"Saint April." He laughed. "How's Dong doing, any better than me?"

The light changed. They crossed the street to the east side, where the sun slanted from the west, warming the sidewalk and obscuring the view into store windows with its glare.

April squinted through the sunlight. "In Chinese, you know, every day is the day of the dead, kind of makes being alive torture. You mess up and every ancestor back to creation curses you."

"Why?"

"Because the responsibility of doing the right thing keeps going from one generation to the next. They think when you lose the fear of angering the ones who came before, you have no reason to be honorable. You can do anything, like the kids in the gangs, kill anybody."

Mike was thoughtful. "Isn't there such a thing as forgiveness?"

"Nope. You mess up, and you have to kill yourself."

"That's it?"

"That's it. Right now it looks like suicide. You think that's what happened to Raymond?" They reached Seventy-ninth Street and crossed to Raymond's corner.

"You believe in all that honor stuff?" Mike shook his head incredulously.

April gave him a hard look. Mike hadn't divorced his wife after she'd left him years ago. And today he'd gone to church with his mother to pray for relatives he'd never met and eaten the Day of the Dead foods she'd been cooking for him all week, enough of them to make him sick. "A lot of people do. What about you?"

"I never think about it," he said.

The regular afternoon doorman was nut-colored, middle-aged, scrawny. His cap of black hair had white patches all around the edges. He shot them an inquiring look as he opened the door for them. April pulled her ID out of her shoulder bag.

"Are you Tomas Torres?"

He dipped his head.

"Detective Woo." She pointed at Mike. "Sergeant Sanchez."

Torres dipped his head again.

"We're here about Raymond Cowles. He died on Sunday night. You hear about that?"

Torres let his head bob some more.

"You remember anything about him?"

"Like what?" The voice was soft and wary.

Ah, he could speak. "Like his habits, who came to visit him, things like that."

Torres glanced at Sanchez. *"Por lo visto está una mariposa,"* he told Mike.

Sanchez smiled at April. She frowned. *He looked like a butterfly?*

"You want to say that in English for the lady?" Mike said.

The doorman turned to April. "He was a very exactly man, kept to himself."

Not an exact translation. "Visitors?" she asked.

"One visitor."

"Only one?" That narrowed things down.

"Yeah, name was Tom, like mine. That's why I remember."

April's brow cleared. Oh, a *butterfly*. Raymond Cowles was a butterfly. That clarified things.

"Know this Tom's last name?" Mike asked.

With a little smile, Torres shook his head. "He only had the one name. *Tom's coming up*. That was his name."

Mike asked for a description. Torres gave them one. Tall, dark, handsome in an effeminate kind of way. The two guys looked like two peas in a pod, almost like brothers.

"Maybe Tom was Raymond's brother," April said as they headed back to the police lot to pick up a unit.

"Sure, and maybe they came out of the closet together. Maybe Tom didn't like the result and whacked Raymond for messing with him."

April shook her head. "Only Ray's prints were on the plastic bag."

"So maybe the other guy wiped his off."

"Then they'd *all* be gone. Anyway, this doesn't have the look of a gay killing. Sounds like Tom seduced Raymond and Raymond couldn't handle it. How about that?"

Mike shrugged and went in for the car keys.

Next stop, Raymond's wife.

Lorna Cowles lived on East Seventy-fourth Street in a smallish building not unlike the one to which her husband had moved when he'd left her. The second coincidence was that she also lived in 5E. This doorman, a rotund person with a German accent and powerful B.O., said he'd just come on and didn't know if she was there or not. He rang up on the intercom to find out.

"Mrs. Cowles." The doorman kept his eyes on April as he spoke into the intercom. "There's a foreign lady here to see you."

"Detective Woo," April prompted.

The doorman shook his head at her. "She says she already has a maid," he told April.

April flushed. This was the first time she'd been taken for a maid. "*Woo,* tell her it's Detective *Woo.*"

"Foo," he said into the receiver.

April took it out of his hand. "Mrs. Cowles. It's Detective April Woo from the police, remember we talked with you yesterday? Sergeant Sanchez and I want to talk with you for a moment. . . . Thank you."

April scowled all the way up in the elevator. At the end of the hall, Lorna waited for them by her open door, a tiny, snow-white Maltese in her arms. The dog reminded April of Dim Sum when she first saw her. The poodle puppy had been so beautiful, she had lured two young women to their deaths. She sneaked a look at Sanchez. His mustache twitched at her. She wondered if they'd ever feel quite the same about dog lovers.

Lorna studied them anxiously. "Did you find something out?" she demanded.

"Nice dog," Mike said. "May we come in?"

Lorna led the way to her living room. It was in the back, its windows facing a garden where a number of trees had grown so tall their leafless branches reached past the fifth floor.

As a cop, April wasn't supposed to feel anything, either pleasure or pain, so she tried to calm down, to listen to her instincts. The woman was a jerk, but her husband most likely had left her for another man, and now he was dead. Looking around, she was startled to see a style of decor she'd never encountered before. The room to which Lorna Cowles had led them was painted deep orange and had an unusual array of plants in it. A bamboo tree spread out from the corner and rose so high it brushed the ceiling. Around it were potted ferns and spiky bromeliads. African violets in deep purple, lavender, and white sat on tiered trays filled with wet pebbles. Pink begonias layered a baker's rack. A humidifier whirred mist into the air around a camellia bush bursting with sweet white flowers. It was hard to imagine a man living there.

The furniture consisted of undulating wicker chairs and love seats that looked as if they had come from colonial Vietnam or Egypt or India a century ago. An elephant's foot served as a footstool. April checked the corners for snakes.

"Nice place," Mike remarked.

Today Lorna Cowles was wearing a tweed skirt, gray with flecks of pink in it. Her blouse was pink silk. The pearls around her neck were the size of mothballs. She stroked her dog.

"I didn't want it to look like a New York apartment," she answered distractedly, making a motion for them to sit.

Well, she had nothing to worry about on that score. April regarded the low seat of the nearest wicker chair, then decided to remain standing. Mike made the same choice. They stood there in a tight circle facing one another as if about to play ring-around-the-rosy.

"What have you found out? When can I bury him?"

Mike raised his chin a fraction. This one was for April, his gesture told her. She took a breath and decided they had all better sit after all. She slid into one of the chairs, her bottom finally coming to a stop a few inches from the floor.

"Mrs. Cowles," she began, "how well did you know your husband?"

"What? What do you mean?" she demanded.

"Well, you had some marital problems. What were those problems about?"

"We had a wonderful marriage," Lorna said stiffly. "We loved all the same things."

"You don't have children?"

"No, we didn't want children. We had each other. Why are you asking me these questions?"

"Marriage problems usually center around certain issues: money, sex, religion, jealousy." April said it as gently as she could.

"We didn't have any of that," Lorna said flatly, pressing her lips into the soft fur on her dog's head.

"Good. We need to rule some things out. So I'm going to ask you what kind of person he was, the kind of friends he had, his habits."

Lorna settled the fluffy creature on her lap and began stroking it from head to tail. Her fingers were long and thin. She was still wearing a modest diamond solitaire and a gold wedding band. "All right. Money.

I have some money of my own. He earned a good salary. We attend St. Stephen's. Ray was in the choir. Is that what you want to know?"

"Yes." April opened her notebook and made a note.

"St. Stephen's—the Episcopalian church around the corner on Lexington?" Mike asked.

Lorna looked at him. "Yes."

"What about family?" April asked.

"We're both estranged from our families," she said softly.

"What about his friends? Did he have any special friends?" Mike this time.

"Friends . . . you mean women friends?"

"Or male friends. What about male friends? People from church, from the choir."

"I don't think he had any. He may have been friendly with some people in the choir. And Father Hartman. He called on us. But close friends . . ." She shook her head.

"What about work? Any special friends at work?"

"Ray never talked about work."

Now April. "Your husband moved out. Did he give you a reason?"

"I told the other lady yesterday. Ray was unhappy. It had nothing to do with me. He said he loved me, but he felt something was missing."

"Did he tell you what?"

"He didn't *know*. Look, I've been doing all the talking. What's going on? What have you found out?"

"The postmortem report hasn't come in yet, so we can't rule out foul play completely," April answered. "But our preliminary findings seem to indicate that your husband took his own life."

Lorna was confused. "But what about the woman who was with him? I saw the food, the wineglasses . . ."

"The doorman said Raymond had a frequent visitor—a tall, dark-haired man called Tom. Do you know somebody by that name?"

"A man?"

Mike nodded.

"A man?" Lorna looked puzzled. "Tom Hartman?"

"The minister?"

"He's not tall and he's not dark." Still puzzled. "Are you telling me you think Ray was a fag?" She didn't have to think about it, got it right away.

"Is that possible?"

"No! Ray hated fags, *hated* them. He thought there was no place for gays in the church. He *hated* them, I'm telling you." Lorna's voice had become shrill with rage.

"Well, thank you for clearing that up, for being so open with us." Mike struggled to get out of his chair, had to make two attempts. He was quiet all the way back to the station.

twenty-one

At six P.M. on Tuesday, November 2, Jason Frank had two unexpected messages on his answering machine. The first was from Clara Treadwell, the last person he'd have thought would want to consult him. Four years ago in California Jason had been the presenter of a paper, and Clara had been the discussant. She'd attempted to take him apart in front of two hundred colleagues with a stunning verbal assault that was completely unsubstantiated by any scientific or clinical evidence. After Jason provided a strong and compelling rebuttal, she'd asked him to lunch. She was a big deal at the hospital out there and gracious in defeat, so he'd accepted the invitation.

Then, in a dining room filled with a group of colleagues so finely tuned to nuance they wouldn't miss a skipped heartbeat through a brick wall, she started massaging his knee under the table and suggested they work together. She was unapologetic for her earlier verbal attack on him and completely unconcerned about creating gossip in a public place. She had the supreme confidence of someone who had no fear of rejection or consequences. Jason realized that she was testing her power like a sport fisherman with a swordfish on the line. He'd been thirty-five then, only a year married to Emma, and might have been a bit too vehement about his refusal. After she returned to New York as head of the Centre, Clara Treadwell showed Jason that she was in a position to make things uncomfortable for him: She did not hesitate to do so whenever she had the chance.

So he was surprised to hear the warm voice on his answering machine asking him to be the consultant on a personal case of hers involving the mysterious death of a former patient. Clara said she thought he was particularly suitable in light of his knowledge of police procedure. She ended by giving him her office and home numbers. He wrote them down and let the tape run on to the next message.

The second unexpected message was from his wife, asking if he minded if she came home for a few days. She was auditioning for a play in New York, Emma said, and needed a place to stay. This message cheered Jason so much that for a few minutes he refused to worry about who Clara Treadwell's dead patient was, what she really wanted him to do, or what helping her out would cost him. He checked his watch. It was seven minutes past the hour. He dialed Emma in California. It was 3:07 there.

Emma picked up on the third ring. "Hello?"

"Hi, it's me." Jason's voice was as warm as he knew how to make it.

"Hi." Hers was a little hesitant and distrustful. He believed he loved her a lot and was a uniformly nice guy. He didn't understand where the distrust came from.

"How's the weather?" he asked.

"If you called me for the temperature in Southern California, you could have gotten it on CNN."

He sighed. The temperature had dropped twenty degrees in one sentence, and once again he'd blown it, whatever "it" was. "I just said hello. Why be so testy?"

"Darling, men who love their women say: 'I got your message. I'm dying to see you, and I hope you get the part.' *You* say, 'How's the weather?' What am I supposed to think?"

Jason was silent as he struggled with gender differences that sometimes seemed unbridgeable. Was he really so evil if the right words to him were not the right words to her? Wasn't it the essence of feeling that mattered, the things that *weren't* said and *couldn't* really be said? Or was he just a caveman, no better than a scruffy, disorganized seventeen-year-old with a Walkman plugged into his ears, who just couldn't deal, man, with anything else but lust? The silence led him into a contemplation of his working space.

Jason's office had bookshelves up to the ceiling on two walls. The third wall had two windows facing the side street high above the entrance to the building. These windows were covered with shutters so that no patient attempting to resist treatment could see out and thus be distracted by the weather or the view. There were five clocks in the office. None had chimes. In this room, everything else was told, but time passed without comment.

In spite of the odd array on the shelves and tables of the usually tasteless gifts from patients' vacations—needlepoint pillows, painted rocks, sculptures made from colored seashells, watercolor landscapes, and his burgeoning collection of books and medical journals—Jason's office had an ascetic, almost hermetical, feeling to it. The two doors that sealed the office off from the waiting room didn't help. Sometimes even Jason had the feeling of being locked inside. His tour completed, he repressed a sigh.

"You there?" Emma asked after a minute.

"Where else," he murmured, leaning forward to adjust the minute hand on the nearest clock. "Shall we try again?"

"Good idea."

"I got your message."

"Good. What do you think?"

"I think it's great, Em, really great. You've always wanted to work on the stage."

"It's a good play."

"I'm sure it's a good play, otherwise you wouldn't want to do it." He doodled on his appointment book. It was the official one of the APA, with enough lines for every hour of the day. He could see that tomorrow was completely booked, and so was the day after.

"It's really a comedy. I probably won't get it," Emma said.

Jason didn't counter with his belief that she would get it. For many years Emma had auditioned relentlessly for every part in every play that was remotely appropriate for her, as well as every commercial in New York. She never got anything except voice-overs. She had a great voice and did a lot of voice-overs for people who looked right for such things as Excedrin headaches but didn't sound right for them. He didn't dare ask Emma to show him the play script, either. He'd abdicated that particular right when he neglected to read the script of *Serpent's Teeth,* the film that brought about her kidnapping and their estrangement six months ago.

"What's it called?" he asked finally. "The play."

"Strokes."

"Ah, another *S* title. Who's the author?"

Her triumph traveled east across the country with the speed of sound. "Simon Beak."

"Wow, no kidding." Now Jason's voice registered real excitement. "Jesus, Emma, that's thrilling. That's Broadway. That's—" *Big time.*

"Look, don't get too excited. I probably won't get it."

"So what. I'm impressed," he breathed. "I'm really impressed."

"You didn't think I was up to it, did you?"

"Yes, I did. You didn't think you were."

She didn't say it took a far-out, trashy vehicle like *Serpent's Teeth* for her to get noticed, and he didn't say it, either. What people had to do to get what they wanted—well, it was more complicated than either had thought. They both knew more about ambition and drive now. Getting ahead in any field was no picnic.

"So, do you have to clear someone out of my bed? Or should I stay in a hotel?" Emma's voice was light, but she meant it. She could take her lumps. That's what got her through ordeals that shoved other people into the shredder.

"That's a joke, right?"

"No. That's not a joke. It's no secret that they're lining up for you, Jason. All those lovely ladies in the caring profession."

"Ah, now you sound bitter," Jason said, a little pleased that the wife who wandered away from him was jealous. Many wives of psychiatrists were psychologists or social workers or teachers, sweet, understanding women who didn't make too many demands lest their busy husbands slap them down.

Whenever Emma met one of these wives, they always asked her if she was in the caring profession. And she always replied, "No, I'm in the uncaring profession." To which no one ever reacted negatively because that would be aggressive and judgmental. Aggressive and judgmental weren't politically correct in his field.

"Are we bitter?" Jason asked.

"Just a little. So what's the story on the bedroom?"

"The story is the sheets are clean. You have nothing to fear on that score. I've been saving it all for you."

"Oh, and what if I didn't come back? What would happen to it then?"

"Baby, you know what you have to do. Move your things out and tell me it's over. After that what I do is none of your business. Until then I'm yours."

"Good, I'll be home Saturday."

Jason flipped to Saturday in his appointment book. "Any particular time?"

"I'll let you know."

There was nothing written down for Saturday. He scratched at his beard. Emma hadn't seen it yet. Maybe he should get a haircut and a shave, but maybe he shouldn't. He pondered: To shave or not to shave, that was the question. "I'll be here," he told her.

twenty-two

"Bobbie . . ."

Bobbie Boudreau heard the soft, muted cry and swung his body around to look for trouble behind him, his hands curling instinctively into fists. Half a block south on Broadway little Gunn Tram was hurrying after him, calling out his name in the noisy, densely populated, brightly lit rush-hour dusk. Bobbie had turned into the wind off the river and now felt the bite of approaching winter on his face. He had important business on his mind, scowled at having to be distracted.

Gunn quickened her small steps. For a second, she looked to Bobbie like an aging dachshund. Her big head and thickening body teetered precariously along Broadway on stubby legs and tiny black-sneakered feet. He didn't call out to her but remained rooted where he'd stopped so she wouldn't scream louder and draw more attention to herself.

Finally within hailing distance, she called out to him: "Going to the house?"

"Maybe," he said slowly.

"Walk with me? I have news."

"All right." His eyes wrenched away from her, and he started moving again. He was pained to see this so-called *friend* in a shapeless pants suit and sneakers. It was embarrassing. It occurred to him that Gunn was letting herself go, was getting to be an old woman now, no longer bothering even with the pretense of carrying a good pair of shoes back and forth to her job in the personnel department at the Centre.

Gunn was sixty-two on her last birthday and joked about changing the dates in her own file so she couldn't be retired. Not that anyone would think of retiring her, she said comfortably. "I'm the heart of the Centre, the *human* resource," she liked to say.

Until recently, Bobbie had always thought so, too. Gunn was kind of saintly, soft on people. She was an optimist, she said, liked fixing bad situations. And she had the tools to do it. She had access to the computers with the business information, to the color-coded files on the shelves that had the personal stuff, to the progress and evaluation reports. Gunn knew almost everything there was to know about everybody who worked at the Centre, including the doctors and administrators. And she cared about everybody, especially him.

Bobbie had believed in Gunn all the way until he was fired last year and lost his insurance just when his mother got so sick. Gunn paid for the old lady to come north and told Bobbie how to get the maintenance job in the Stone Pavilion, but Bobbie still felt it was Gunn's fault his mother had died. Gunn told him he couldn't ever apply for another nursing job. Bobbie was bitter about that, too.

And now it was worse. He'd never minded the twelve years' age difference between them. Gunn had been twelve years older than him all along, all the years he'd worked there. She wasn't another white bitch out to get him, was Swedish and didn't know how to be mean. He didn't know why she was the way she was, maybe because she'd come from somewhere else, though you could hardly hear it in her voice anymore. She was bubbly and enthusiastic, never saw the bad in anybody. He liked her in spite of the annoyance of having to listen to her foreign ideas. Real good-looking never mattered much to him, anyway. He never spent any time looking at anybody, and fucking was just—fucking.

No, older had never bothered him, but *old* was beginning to get to him. Bobbie still felt like a *young* man, like the boy who'd gone off to the Army and still had opportunity in front of him. He still had the juice, expected to inherit the earth sometime soon. But more and more these days when Gunn bugged him about keeping his head down and holding his temper—when he looked at the strange, frightened old woman she was becoming—he felt he was history like Gunn and wanted to howl like a dog.

"The police came to the Centre today," Gunn said as soon as she calmed down and caught her breath.

"Yeah, what for?" Bobbie didn't slow his pace for her even though she had to struggle to keep up.

"You'll never guess what."

"A patient death." He guessed what. What else was there?

"How did you know, Bobbie, you sly old fox? Have you heard already?" Her hand bunched into a tiny fist to punch playfully at his massive arm. He stood way over a foot taller than she, wore a baseball cap pulled low over his forehead, and had the tight, mean look that made cautious people make a wide berth around him. She changed her mind and put her hand back in her pocket.

"It's not a hard one. Accidents happen all the time. Who's taking the fall this time?"

"Oh, Bobbie, I'm sorry. I shouldn't have brought it up. . . . I just thought you'd like to know, that's all."

"What then?" He spat out the words, didn't give a shit.

"Clara Treadwell, that's whose patient." Gunn said it with great satisfaction. "Rumor is she was sleeping with him."

"And she killed him for that? Overprescribed? The old cow should have been grateful."

Gunn laughed. "She didn't kill him. It was a suicide. She didn't hand him the *cup*—"

"*I* didn't do that." Bobbie interrupted her furiously. "*Alice* gave him the stuff. Fuck, why did you say that, Gunn? I'd never hurt a patient, never."

"Sorry—I'm sorry, Bobbie." Gunn's face was instantly repentant.

"I should take your head off for that," he fumed, stomping along the sidewalk punching the air.

"I know. It just slipped out, I don't know why. Forgive me?" She shook her head hard, pumping her own legs faster to get out of a bad situation. "I know you had nothing to do with it."

"The resident gave him the wrong prescription," Bobbie raged.

"I know, Bobbie. Everybody knows that. You weren't responsible."

"And *Alice* handed it to him."

"I know, you're right."

"So why did I have to take the fall? You tell me that!"

"I don't know, Bobbie." She didn't remind him about his knocking out an attending physician—not even a full-time member of the staff—after the patient's death. Or that the committee had concluded he was a danger to the community, quite apart from the question of his guilt or innocence in the matter at hand.

"Bastards." He strode north toward the brownstone on Ninety-ninth Street, where Gunn lived on the fourth floor. He had moved into the basement flat occupied by his mother the last year of her life. It did not surprise him at all that the head of the hospital was being questioned in a patient death. That bitch Clara Treadwell ruined people's lives every day. She'd ruined his life. It was about time someone got on her case.

"Bobbie?"

"They won't get her for it," he muttered angrily.

"No," she agreed.

"There's no justice."

"No . . . Bobbie?"

They were nearing Ninety-ninth Street. “What?”

“Will you eat with me?” Gunn asked softly.

He hesitated, chugging along for almost a block before he answered. “I don’t know. Maybe. If it don’t take too long.”

“It won’t take long,” Gunn promised eagerly.

twenty-three

Jason first heard about the death of Raymond Cowles from his friend Charles, who was in private practice all the way across town on East Seventy-ninth Street. Charles hadn't heard it from a colleague. He'd heard it from his wife, Brenda, who was the chair of some fund-raising benefit for the Centre. Brenda came back from a meeting on Tuesday with the news that the great goddess Clara Treadwell had been sleeping with one of her patients, that the patient had killed himself, and they had all better fasten their seat belts for the rough ride ahead. Jason fastened his seat belt.

"I'm sorry to get you in here so early" was the first thing Clara Treadwell said to Jason when they met at the elevators on the twentieth floor at two minutes to eight on Wednesday.

"No problem," Jason replied, although to meet Clara's urgent request he'd had to cancel a patient he'd been seeing at that hour for the past three years.

"Thank you, anyway." Clara extended her gloved hand with a small smile that acknowledged her advantage.

Jason offered his hand, only to have his bones crunched in a powerful grip. He had a good six inches on her, at least seventy pounds, and was surprised by her strength. Another smile curved Clara's lips as she turned down the long hall to lead him to the one place in the hospital he rarely saw. Jason knew all the other floors in the Centre as well as he knew his own apartment. He had done his three-year training there, qualified as a psychoanalyst, and had been invited to teach there long before anyone in his class. If he had been chief resident, he would have had an office in the executive suite on the twentieth floor and been at home there, too. But he hadn't been chief resident. His year the post had gone to the first Latino. Now the chief resident was a Hasidic Jew with tight little curls around his ears, a belly so big he didn't know where to wear his pants, and a leather yarmulke.

Jason scratched his beard as he watched Clara unlock two separate locks in the door of the executive suite. Inside, she hit a few light switches, then led the way to her office. She had to find another key to unlock the door there, too.

"I didn't realize security was so tight up here," Jason remarked.

"Oh, we've had to tighten up in the last year. There have been some incidents. . . . Just mischief." Clara shrugged out of her cashmere coat, unlocking yet another door and disappearing into the closet. After a moment, she came out wearing a pale green suit, the color of spring moss, tightly fitted over her breasts and hips.

"Please sit down," she said formally. She indicated a leather tub chair opposite the vast expanse of polished cherry and tooled leather that was her desk.

Jason sat and studied the view of the river. It was a sparkling November morning. The rushing water twenty stories below shimmered in the early light. "How can I help you?" he asked.

Clara's smile reappeared. The curve of her too-red lips sought to inspire closeness and confidence but lacked the warmth that might convince someone as sensitive to manipulation as Jason. His parents had been chilly masters of guilt and control when he was a child. Emma told him he could be pretty good at it himself. She didn't mean it as a compliment.

"You've come a long way in a short period of time, Jason," Clara said, studying him intently. She didn't answer his question. "I've heard you speak, of course. I've read your papers. You get the highest marks as a teacher, both from the residents and medical students." She smiled. "It's apparent you're our best teacher. And of course as a supervisor, you're very sought-after. No one feels his training here is complete without working with you."

Jason shrugged modestly. "Well, that's very flattering," he murmured.

"It's more than flattering; it's the truth. I've decided we can't let you get away."

"Oh?" Jason laughed. "Where exactly was I going?"

"You're going places, there's no question about *that.* A person of your gifts, your teaching abilities, your integrity . . ." Clara smiled again.

It wasn't clear to Jason what was in the air, so he crossed his legs and smiled back.

"It's people like you and me, Jason, who are going to be the leaders of our field in the new century. Yes, it's true. I want you there with me, at the top of this institution, in Washington—wherever I go."

Jason was taken aback. He was no follower. "I—"

"No, don't thank me," Clara interrupted smoothly. "Every gifted person needs a mentor and promotor. I'm going to be yours, that's all there is to it." The smile faded from Clara's face as she lifted her eyes to the ceiling. Her voice took on a musing tone. "I'm going to tell you a little story, Jason. My first analysand was a young man named Raymond Cowles. My supervisor was Harold Dickey. At the time, Harold was the head of the genetics department, was on the executive committee, president of associations. A really big cheese." Another faint smile. "He was the best, and so was I."

No response from Jason. He was the best, too.

"I don't suppose you ever forget your first patient in analysis. Raymond was a student in his early twenties when he came into Student Services and was worked up by Intake. He was considered for disposition as an appropriate patient for psychoanalysis and accepted by the Centre, all in the usual way. He was offered to me, and I accepted him with a good deal of excitement.

"Ray was everything a young analyst could hope for. He was highly motivated, highly intelligent. He had the capacity to maintain an observing ego, the capacity to free-associate. He even dreamed. He was handsome, well educated, knew literature and music, liked good food. His problem was persistent, recurrent homosexual fantasies that had resisted his efforts to suppress them by concentration and willpower. His was a clear case of homosexual fantasies as a defense against unconscious anxieties over heterosexual impulses. I thought it would be an interesting and profitable case. And it was."

Jason said nothing.

"Last Sunday Raymond Cowles died under mysterious circumstances. The police are looking into it. They suspect he committed suicide." She shook her head, disagreeing. "I presented the case at meetings. It was a classic case. A successful case. I doubt Ray committed suicide."

Clara checked her watch. "I have a meeting soon."

Jason shifted in his chair. He had to leave soon, too, and now it was clear to him what was coming.

"I want you to review Ray's case," Clara said suddenly.

"Why me?" Jason asked.

"You're an assistant professor without any administration duties, is that correct?"

Jason nodded. Yes, he was an attending physician there, not on staff.

"You are a supervisor?"

Again Jason nodded.

"Long hours, a lot of responsibility. No pay for any of it, correct?"

Jason watched her face. *So?*

"Well, you'd like that to change, wouldn't you? A full professorship, a big job at the Centre, more time to do your own work?"

"I wasn't aware there were any openings." Jason scratched his beard.

"Well, something's coming up, but I'm not really at liberty to discuss it at this time. . . . I have copies of the intake notes, my notes, Harold's notes. The paper I presented on the case."

"Ah . . ." That sounded like a lot. Why so much documentation on such an old case? Jason hesitated.

"I believe you know the police." Clara glanced at her watch, impatient now.

Her statement startled Jason. "What if it was a suicide?" he asked Clara, keeping his voice impassive.

"Ben Hartley called me at home last night. He's counsel for the hospital, as you know. Ben got a call yesterday from the lawyer of the insurance company that employed and insured Raymond. He was most upset about it. The bottom line is that if Ray Cowles was murdered, the insurance company has to pay a million dollars to his widow. There's no out for them. If Ray was a suicide, they still pay, but they see a window of opportunity for getting their money back and more. Hartley told me the company and the widow intend to sue the Centre for malpractice. And I'm named in the suit, too." A tic in Clara's cheek that Jason hadn't noticed before began to jump around when she said the doctor's nightmare word: *malpractice.*

"But certainly many years have passed since the patient's analysis and termination with you. How could it possibly have any bearing on his suicide now?" Jason was puzzled.

"I put the file together for you. I want you to take it."

"Clara, what exactly am I looking for?"

"I started treatment with him eighteen years ago. I handled the case correctly. Hal was my supervisor throughout. I did nothing without his approval. We did everything by the book. You have no conflict of interest here, no axe to grind. You're respected. I have confidence in you." She spread her hands out palms-up on the desk, as if she had answered his question.

"What is there for the insurance company to hang their case on? I can't help you unless I know what the issue is," Jason insisted.

Clara turned her hands over and studied her manicure. "All I want is for you to review the original file. It's not a hard one, Jason. I want you to sit in on the meetings with the lawyers as my consultant, take Dickey's place as Quality Assurance in this matter, be my liaison with the police. If it all works out well, as I expect it will, you'll be in an excellent position for—well, we'll talk about that later."

"I'll review your old file and examine the case. . . ." Jason said slowly.

"And talk to the police?" Clara asked. "My office has put in several calls, but they haven't been returned." Clara's eyes were on him, bright with her conviction that he could straighten out this mess.

"I will call the police," he heard himself promising.

"I'm counting on you, Jason. I know you're good."

Jason's empty stomach heaved. There had to be more to this than Clara told him. Maybe the gossip that Clara had been sleeping with Cowles was true. Jason's instincts told him to avoid the whole thing. He longed for escape from another police investigation and direct involvement in a messy hospital scandal. All he wanted was to do things New Yorkers never do. He wanted to meet his wife at the airport, make love to her, have a normal life.

Clara pushed her chair back and pulled open her desk drawer. Eyes still on Jason, she reached inside. Then she screamed and snatched her hand back.

"Oh, my *God*!" She held her hand out, staring in shock at the deep cut in the fleshy part of her palm. Blood dripped all over her green blotter.

Jason lurched to his feet. "What—?"

"I've been stabbed. Get me some water," Clara commanded, pointing at a door. She kept her bleeding hand extended.

Behind the door, Jason found a small kitchen and filled a glass for her. He grabbed some paper towels. When he returned to her office, there was blood all over Clara's desk and she was raging at the device that had cut her.

"Look at this. Will you *look* at this!" she hissed. The file she'd been looking for was on her desk now. On top of it was a scalpel plunged from below through a condom so the deadly blade faced up.

"Let's see. How bad is it?" Jason addressed his attention to the wound first.

"It's nothing, just a scratch." Impatiently, Clara grabbed the paper towels from him and pressed them to her hand, her attention fixed on the item on her desk.

"What's that?" Jason leaned over.

Shocked, Clara was staring at the message, on hospital stationery, that lay under the now-bloodied scalpel and condom. In words sliced and pasted together from newspaper cutouts it said: YOU'LL PAY FOR THE BLOOD ON YOUR HANDS.

"This is really sick."

Yes, it was, and very cleverly done. "How's your hand?"

Clara shook her head, uninterested in the gash. "Look at this mess—my desk, my suit, everything."

"I think we'd better call the police."

"No! I'm going to have to deal with it." Clara checked her watch and pushed her chair back. "Jason, I'd like to talk further with you, but I must get myself cleaned up." Her eyes measured him coolly, then she added, "Look, I'd like you to keep this in confidence for the time being."

Jason shook his head. "Does this have anything to do with the Cowles death?"

"No!" Clara's eyes shot down to the smeared blood on her hands. "No!" she cried again. "No, absolutely not. This is—"

"Clara, someone is obviously trying to hurt you. You're going to have to bring the police into the picture."

"I can handle it. I don't want the police involved in this." Her expression hardened. "This isn't going to happen again."

"You know who it is?"

"I have a good idea." With no sign of repugnance, she removed the device that had cut her and the stained message below it, slid them into the top drawer of her desk. Surprisingly, no blood had fallen on the Cowles file. She held it out to Jason. "Thank you for coming. I'm counting on you," she said, handing him the file, then rising to walk him to the door.

Once again, Jason was taken aback. "But what are you going to do about this?" he asked. He gestured to her swaddled hand. Blood had soaked through the wad of towels. One drop soon slid down her wrist, toward her pale green cuff.

"I'm going to take care of it," she said.

Jason had to leave. He had a patient waiting. But all morning he worried about whose blood was on Clara's hands.

twenty-four

On Thursday, a match came in for the second set of fingerprints found in Raymond Cowles's apartment. The ID slid out of the fax machine downstairs in the precinct around one P.M. A female uniform brought it up to the squad room and handed it to Sanchez.

April was on the phone with Lorna Cowles, who had already called and been put off twice that day.

"Ray died *four* days ago," the widow complained. "And what are you doing about it? Nothing. I can't give him a decent burial. You just put him in an icebox and left him there. You keep telling me you don't have an autopsy report. *Almost a week later* and you don't even know what happened to him. What's the matter with you people? The insurance company wants to know the cause of death. What's taking so long?"

Mike read the fax and swiveled in his chair to face April. He waved it in her face. She ignored him.

"Look, Mrs. Cowles. I have reason to believe we'll have the postmortem report this afternoon."

"Will you know who killed him then?" Lorna shrilled. On each of the three previous days April had told her there was no reason to believe anybody had killed him. But Lorna still wasn't buying it. Maybe the insurance company wouldn't pay up on a suicide. April couldn't get a fix on Lorna. But who knew—maybe she was just piqued because her husband had jilted her for a man.

"I told you Ray was a devout Christian," Lorna went on when April didn't answer. "He couldn't have killed himself; suicide was against everything he believed."

"Well, look, that's not for me to say. All I can tell you is I expect to have the M.E.'s report by the end of the day. I can let you know then." She hung up.

"Look who our little computer check came up with."

April took the fax from Mike and read it.

"Tom White?" she said, frowning.

"You know him?" Mike asked. "He was printed as an A.D.A."

April wrinkled her nose. An Assistant District Attorney and a suicide that could be murder. She had just been getting to think nothing in this life could surprise her.

Mike looked smug. "Nice, huh?"

"An A.D.A. was with Raymond the night he died?"

"Looks like it." Mike had a wolfish grin on his face.

"I don't know him, do you?" April said. They worked with a lot of the D.A.s, knew many of them pretty well.

"Nope, but he didn't come in to chat with us. That's interesting, don't you think?"

"You going to talk with him?"

"Yes. Want to come along?"

"No, you boys might do better alone. I'll go down to the M.E.'s office to get the autopsy report." April reached in her drawer for her shoulder bag.

"What makes you think it's ready?"

April knew it was ready because someone in the M.E.'s office had promised her it would be finished around now. She shrugged. "I have a feeling it's ready."

Nothing got past him. He smiled. "Fine, I'll give you a ride."

A quick check of the D.A.'s office indicated that Thomas Neale White had moved into the private sector two years ago. The D.A.'s office was happy to give out the information that Thomas N. White was currently employed at Unified Agencies in the tower at Forty-second and Lexington. That just happened to be the insurance company that had employed Raymond Cowles and which had carried his life insurance policy.

The huge agency occupied five floors. On White's floor there was no receptionist. The elevator hall was separated from the banks of offices on two sides by a locked glass door. If you didn't happen to have a plastic card to slip into the lock, you couldn't get in. There was a phone by the door for people to call, but there was no operator to give assistance. The phone was useful only if you knew the extension of the person you were visiting. Mike didn't.

He'd located Tom White's floor on the directory in the lobby. Upstairs he played with the phone by the glass door to no avail for a few minutes before somebody came out. Then he caught the door before it closed and went in. On the other side of the glass door there were miles of desks with no identifying names on them. There were no names by the doors of the offices extending along the corridors, either. It seemed that the people who ran the place didn't want anybody to know who worked there.

Mike stopped at the first desk he came to and asked for Tom White.

"Last door on the left," the woman replied without looking up.

At 2:07 P.M. Sanchez found the former assistant district attorney in his office. Tom White was a thin, dark-haired, youngish man as regular and conservative-looking as they come, with a gray suit, white shirt, navy-and-white-striped tie, and short haircut. White sat at his desk with his back to the window, motionless and staring at an untouched thick sandwich on a paper plate. From the smell of it, the white pasty stuff inside was tunafish.

The office was decorated with law books and files. The nondescript credenza and bookcase were loaded with them. So was the desk and one of the two chairs. The door was open. Mike wandered in.

White looked up. "Cop," he said wearily as if he saw hundreds of plainclothes detectives every day.

Mike nodded. "Sergeant Sanchez." He pulled out his ID. "I guess you were expecting me."

White took the ID and studied it, then handed it back. He didn't appear alarmed, just tired. "What can I do for you, Sergeant?"

Mike studied him before replying. A man in his middle to late thirties, just slightly leaner than a healthy person his age should be. His dark eyes were sunk deep and ringed with purple. His long face, with its good patrician cheekbones and strong chin, was colorless. White didn't look particularly gay, but he did look haunted.

"You can tell me what happened between you and Raymond Cowles on the evening of October thirty-first," Mike said. He was neither hard nor soft, just matter-of-fact.

White swallowed and pushed the paper plate across the desk. "Want some? I'm not hungry."

"No thanks."

"I didn't think so. No one does. I've been trying to get rid of it for hours."

Mike decided this was going to take a while. He sat in the empty chair and unbuttoned his jacket. The very first domestic violence call he'd gotten as a young cop had been between two men. Their yelling and screaming had compelled a neighbor to call the police. When Sanchez rang the doorbell, a young man in a flowered negligee and nothing else had answered the door. The young man had a black eye and blood pouring from his nose but he didn't want any assistance from the police.

"Men," he'd sobbed. "Can't live with them, can't live without them. Go home, honey, I love him."

It was the first time, but it wasn't the last. Mike Sanchez knew gay guys could get as attached to each other as normal guys did to women, but it made him uncomfortable to imagine it. He also knew it wasn't politically correct to make any distinctions between gay and normal. For gays it was normal to be gay. But it wasn't normal to him. As he sat in Tom White's office, he was made even more uneasy by the distinct feeling Cowles's lover was more bereaved about his loss than his wife was.

That didn't make White any less the sharp-eyed lawyer, though. And he knew cops. Mike was always just a little chagrined when people picked up so fast on the fact that he was a cop.

"You know Raymond Cowles is dead?" he asked.

White picked up a pen and played with it. "Yes, it's common knowledge in the office."

"You knew him well."

"Yes."

"You want to tell me about it?"

"Sure. As you can probably tell, this is the legal department. Ray was in Actuarial. Normally we wouldn't work together, but six months ago we were assigned a special project."

"Oh, what was that?"

"Ah, addressing the issue of underwriting risks for lethal illnesses. Ray provided the statistical input. I was involved in several areas—drafting policy language, legislative, statutory, and other legal issues."

Mike raised his eyebrow. "Is that for or against?"

"What?"

"Insuring potential AIDS victims."

White's pale face colored slightly. "It's an issue. We don't want to discriminate. We can't lawfully discriminate. But the statistics show that insuring certain groups of high-risk individuals for lethal illnesses without establishing appropriate reserves and some spreading of the risk—for example, through a government-supported pool—can bankrupt a company. We were working on that."

Uh-huh. "So you knew Ray pretty well."

"We put a lot of time in on that project. In fact, it's still in the works." White's voice wavered. He glanced down at the pen.

"Did you see him out of the office?"

"We had lunch together occasionally."

"What about dinner?"

"We may have, a few times. I'm not married. I eat out a lot."

"Did you know his wife?"

White looked blank. "No. I didn't know he was married." He shrugged. "Maybe he was married. I don't recall."

"Was Ray disturbed about anything recently?"

"No. I don't know."

"He didn't talk to you?"

"No, we had a business relationship. We didn't talk about personal things."

"So you didn't know he was depressed, worried, troubled about—anything?"

"No, I didn't know."

"What about his homosexuality? Did you know anything about that?"

"What?"

"Ray was a homosexual. You didn't know that?"

Tom White studied the pen in his hands. It was a Montblanc, fat and black. "Yeah, I guess I did."

"And you were having a relationship with him."

"Look, I'm going to deny anything you suggest. So—"

Mike took a breath and let it out. "No, you look, Mr. White. We're investigating a death. You've been in the D.A.'s office. You know how that is. We're going to keep at it until we know what happened. Here are the facts. Ray died. You were with him the night he died. We know that."

Actually, they didn't know that, but his words had a certain effect. Tom White shuddered. For several seconds his long body jerked as if he were on the edge of an epileptic fit. But before Mike had a chance to offer assistance, the attorney had regained control of himself. He smiled grimly. "I have the right to remain silent," he said.

"Look, your private life is your own business," Mike countered. "All I want to know is what happened. If you didn't kill him, it won't go any further than this."

"I didn't kill him."

"Okay, was it an accident then?"

"What? Was *what* an accident? I don't even know how Ray died. Maybe you'd like to tell me."

"He was found with a plastic bag over his head," Mike said carefully.

Tom White closed his eyes. "I've been wondering," he said to the dark.

"You could have paid us a visit. We would have filled you in."

"You know I couldn't do that." White's eyes popped open. He was back on the scene. "So a plastic bag was over his head. You don't have a cause yet?"

"This afternoon."

"I'd like to see the report."

"I'm sure you would, but you're not in the D.A.'s office anymore. And it would be pretty hard to pull strings over there without drawing attention to the case and your involvement in it. Unless you have another very good friend, someone might get interested in your interest and start looking into it." Mike paused. "You seem to be stuck between a rock and a hard place."

That's what happened to people who lived secret lives. There was no place to go when the shit hit the fan. Mike almost felt sorry for him. "Look, I have no vested interest in this. You're probably safest telling me."

White shook his head. "I don't have anything to tell you. I wasn't there when he died. I worked with him. He was my friend. . . ." He passed his hand over his eyes. "How could I—let him hurt himself?"

"Maybe you two were getting into things he couldn't handle."

"I told you I wasn't there."

"And I told you I know you were." Mike had pulled some strings himself. The police labs were so backed up that hundreds of rape kits hadn't been tested against the semen of the accused rapers in the last year or so; but on Wednesday, in between following leads on an apartment in Queens, Mike had wandered over to the lab on Twentieth Street and got a friend to test the sheets from Raymond Cowles's bed just in case they got an ID on the prints. Turned out there were two different blood types in the semen stains. Which meant two men had ejaculated. It would not be difficult to prove one of them was Tom White.

"Your prints are all over his place."

"That's how you located me. . . ."

Mike didn't answer. White's exhaustion and grief were beginning to wear on him. It was warm in the office. Mike felt hot, and a little sickened by the smell of tunafish. He decided to make a hypothesis.

"The two of you had dinner together on Sunday night. You partied together. You left. He was alive. Is that your story?"

"We had dinner together. I left. He was alive."

"So he partied with someone else after you left?"

"What? What makes you think Ray *partied,* as you put it, with anyone?"

"Well, he didn't party alone. There were semen stains from two different people on his sheets."

"Jesus." Tom closed his eyes again.

"You're all over the scene, pal."

The dark eyes opened. They were filled with tears. "Ray was alive when I left. We were talking about living together. He was euphoric. *Euphoric.*" He said it again to feel the word in his mouth. "Do you know what it feels like to be completely happy?" he demanded.

Mike wasn't sure that he did, so he didn't answer.

"Well, that's how Ray was when I left. I can't imagine what happened after that." He tried to shake away his tears, but they kept coming. "I just can't imagine."

"Thanks. I'll try to find out." Mike got up to leave.

The former assistant district attorney who had sought out a quieter life in the back office of an insurance company let his head fall into his hands and gave himself up to his sorrow. When Mike left, he didn't say good-bye.

twenty-five

Sergeant Joyce grabbed a fistful of hair with one hand as she studied the top piece of paper on the mountain of number-coded forms on her desk. She was wearing a short-sleeved green shirt with plump black hippopotamuses on it similar to the hippos on a tie often worn by the Police Commissioner at important news conferences. She appeared to be pulling the clump of hair out of her head as April arrived at her door.

April cleared her throat to get the Sergeant's attention. Joyce glanced up, letting go of the yellow bundle, which did not flop down as normal hair would do but continued to stand straight out as if the woman were electrified.

"Got it?" she demanded.

"Yes." April held out the envelope with the M.E.'s report on the cause of death of Raymond Cowles in it but remained in the doorway. She didn't exactly trust her supervisor and wished Sanchez would hurry it up in the men's room so they could do this thing together and get it over with. She edged her arm around so she had a view of her watch without seeming to be anxious about time. Fifteen minutes it took him. What was he doing? The man took longer in the bathroom than she did.

"Useful?" Joyce demanded, eyes on the envelope.

April nodded. Very useful. "I think you'll be pleased."

"Come in then and give it over."

The furrows between Sergeant Joyce's drawn-on eyebrows eased up on her a little and her small grim mouth curled into something resembling a smile. Clearing the Cowles case in less than a week would be a very good thing. She waved her hand toward the two empty chairs in front of her desk, but April preferred her usual spot by the window. She handed over the manila envelope as she headed across the tiny office to the window, where she checked out the vital signs of the three plants spread across the sill.

Recently Sergeant Joyce had added a new plant to the two dusty ivies. It was a fernlike thing that had started to die almost the minute it arrived. The length of brown on the spiky ends increased every day. April saw that soon it would be as dead as Raymond Cowles. She edged her finger into the dirt, thinking of Lorna Cowles's lush, moist garden. Lorna sure knew a lot more about plants than men. The dirt in the asparagus fern was dry as a desert and filled with cigarette butts. April withdrew her finger hastily.

Mike slipped in while the Sergeant was reading. He sat in the chair closest to the door, his face thoughtful. Sergeant Joyce got to the relevant parts and started to mutter.

"Perianal scarring, evidence of perianal infection. Looks like he was into it for a while. Broken collarbone, very old, possibly a childhood injury. Hah, his arteries were not in good shape." Sergeant Joyce had the front clump of hair back in her fist.

"Look at the alcohol and Kaminex levels in his blood," Mike said.

"Uh-huh. Certainly could be a suicide. He had enough to relax, but probably not enough to pass out before he got the job done."

"He was HIV negative," April threw in. Which meant Cowles hadn't been motivated by the fear of a long and nasty decline followed by a horrible death.

"Yeah." Sergeant Joyce threw down the report. "No evidence of foul play." She glared at them. "Doesn't mean someone didn't help him out, though. What do you say?"

Mike stroked his mustache, doubtful. "His boyfriend, Tom White, swears Cowles was euphoric when he left Sunday night. Said they were making plans to live together." He raised a crooked eyebrow. "Come out of the closet."

"Maybe he couldn't handle that." April tapped her foot, eager to get away.

Mike shrugged.

"What about the wife?"

"There's no evidence she was involved in any way. No witness to say she was ever in his apartment," April said. "There's nothing on her." She went over it again, reviewing Lorna's behavior in the light of her husband's homosexuality, wondering as she did so how it must feel to be married to someone who preferred his physical life with a person of his own sex. She thought of the scarring and infection in Cowles's anus, the stains on the sheets. The second was the giveaway of two men engaged in mutual masturbation. He clearly had done it before. Why end it this time? Shame? Had White been threatening to expose him if he didn't come out of the closet? Did it matter?

She turned to Sanchez. He was gazing at her with the familiar pirate's smile that said "I've got what you want and I'm waiting to give it to you." Her stomach lurched and the blood rose to her cheeks. Sometimes Mike's eyes became liquid smoke. Inside was an evil spirit that distracted her, made her wonder about things like her parents all those years ago in China. How did they choose each other and how did they feel, those two skinny people, modest as monks?

The Chinese were prudish, no doubt about that. They were too busy trying to survive to have much tolerance for the concept of love or romance. Marriage was business. For women, anyway. In old China men got to marry as many women as they could afford, do whatever they wanted to them. And the great reformer Chairman Mao had had no qualms about carrying on the tradition. He had hundreds of girls, liked them young, tired of them quickly, and needed new ones all the time. American Presidents seemed to be like that, too. Nobody bothered about love, and nobody ever died of shame. Why had Raymond Cowles done so in this day and age? And why did she have to be so tough?

Sergeant Joyce had caught her blush and was smirking. She enjoyed watching April squirm. Joyce returned to the question at hand. "So, Raymond dies around ten P.M. What time did the boyfriend leave?"

"He told me he left around nine. He had work to do."

"So Raymond places a call to his shrink, either to tell her he's getting married to a guy or to say he's checking out. Did he speak to her?" Joyce demanded.

Mike and April exchanged glances. They hadn't told Treadwell that her number was the last one Cowles had dialed. They purposely held back everything but the news he was dead.

"It doesn't change the case for us, does it?" April asked.

Mike shook his head. "No, Forensics says he definitely prepared the bag by himself. His prints were on the inside and the outside, and there were some partials on the tape. He was really cool when he did it. He knew what he was doing, pleated it up all nice and tight, made it airtight. Then he must have taken the Kaminex. After a while he put the bag on his head, lay down on the bed, and went to sleep."

Sergeant Joyce pursed her lips. "Anything we might have missed that could come back and bite us on the tail later?"

Mike shook his head again.

Joyce sighed. "Fine, that about ties it up on Cowles, then. Get the report in by tomorrow."

April waited until Sanchez was out of the room before she pushed herself off the windowsill. Sergeant Joyce bent her head over her mountain of paperwork. April could see the Sergeant had moved on to something else. As far as she was concerned, the Raymond Cowles case was closed.

twenty-six

At eight-forty-five on Friday morning, Clara Treadwell entered the executive conference room next door to her office. She was as prepared as she would ever be for the meeting Ben Hartley had called to discuss the Raymond Cowles death. She set her leather folder with its datebook and notepad at her place at the head of the table. As she sat, she curled the tips of her fingers into a half-fist to test the cut in her palm.

The point of the sharp surgical knife had dug deep, and the wound still ached, but the real damage of the incident had gone much deeper. Clara was sure the scalpel and the condom—those profoundly symbolic objects, one slashed through the other—related directly to her intimate relationship years ago with Harold Dickey. Like most men of his generation, Harold had hated condoms, couldn't stand having his manhood sheathed and had said so often. As for the scalpel, Harold liked to tell his students their most sacred duty was to scrape away the patient's carefully built-up defenses *with the lightest possible touch of the scalpel.*

Now, this insane act of his seemed to be a direct accusation that Clara had wielded her doctor's scalpel like a dagger and was personally responsible for a patient's death. After all the opposition and difficulty Clara had experienced over the years as a chief executive, and as a beautiful and desirable woman endlessly bothered by lovers and husbands who wanted too much, never had anyone physically hurt her. And never had anyone made her so deeply furious. She could hardly bear to be in the same room with him.

And just on this Friday morning, when Clara was scheduled to get out of there, to leave for a Commission meeting in Washington and then have a quiet weekend in Sarasota with the Senator, Ben Hartley had to call this idiotic meeting. Clara pulled her tiny tape recorder out of her purse and fiddled with it. She carried it with her everywhere and always took it out at the beginning of meetings. It amused her that no one knew when the recorder was on and when it was off, and no one ever dared to ask.

Ready, she glanced around the table at the three useless men whose jobs were to advise her. Max Goodrich, Vice Chairman of the Centre, who had been lurking outside her office when the police called on her and who now seemed dazed and unsure which way to blow in the wind; Ben Hartley, General Counsel, an inflated, elegantly dressed, silver-haired gentleman who looked as if he belonged in the State Department; and Harold Dickey, extravagantly pompous in his lack of importance, who had somehow invited himself. The fourth man at the table was the only one she had invited. Jason Frank had something to gain, so Clara felt he was the one she could count on.

Seething, Hartley stared at her, waiting for her nod to begin. She smiled at him.

"Calm down, Ben. Whatever's bugging you can be dealt with," she said soothingly.

"I don't like surprises, Clara. You've thrown me some curves before, but this is a doozy."

"Oh, come now, Ben. When has life at the Centre ever been anything but fat sizzling in the fire?"

"Clara, when a man I went to Harvard with thirty years ago calls me to tell me the chief administrator of my organization is being hounded by the police for a possible suicide in which she seems to be implicated—and this old friend's company is about to sue the Centre, and you, for malpractice—and I don't know a single thing about it . . . Well, I'd say that's more than fat in the fire."

"Now just a minute, Ben. I wasn't *hounded.* The police came here to *inform* me of a death, and there's absolutely no evidence at this time it was a suicide. It could have been accidental, it could have been a homicide. But whatever it was, I'm not in any way implicated. So let's get the facts straight."

"If you're not implicated, what was your number doing in the memory of the dead man's telephone?"

Clara frowned. "What are you talking about, Ben?"

"Didn't the police tell you the last call made from Raymond Cowles's apartment was to your home number?"

No, they hadn't told her that. She didn't know that, so how could he? Clara felt Harold's accusing eyes burn her cheeks. She felt Ben was bluffing about the telephone thing and refused to let it intimidate her. "No. No one told me that. But there's another false note right there. I never heard any such thing. It's just not true."

Max Goodrich looked appalled. "Let's fix an agenda here. What are we here to talk—"

Hartley interrupted him. "Look, my job is to protect the hospital—and to protect Clara insofar as she is acting in the lawful course of her employment as an officer."

Clara stared at him. "We're aware of that, Ben. What's your point?"

"Well, let's put it this way. First scenario: The director of a hospital, driving a hospital-owned car on hospital business, hits a pedestrian. Second scenario: Clara Treadwell, who is the director of the hospital, drives her own car to the country for a weekend tryst with her lover and hits a pedestrian. In scenario one, the pedestrian may sue and recover from the hospital. In scenario two, the director is on her own."

Clara touched her nails to her top lip. It was amazing how no matter how high a person climbed, and how big the support system for her seemed, none of it counted when there was a problem. She dropped her hand.

"I take your point, Counselor," she said coldly.

"Now let me make this very plain. This is not a meeting of the Quality Assurance Committee."

"Why not?" Max asked. "I thought that's what we're here for."

"Because if there are complaints concerning the members of this committee or officers of the Centre, we have to consider very carefully questions of conflict of interest as well as the rule, which I believe even psychiatrists accept, that investigators may not investigate themselves."

"Look, there's nothing here that deserves any attention out of the ordinary," Clara interjected smoothly. "Raymond Cowles was a patient of mine when I was a resident here eighteen years ago. Harold Dickey was my supervisor. The patient's treatment lasted for a period of nearly four years, was terminated in the normal way, and was successful in every respect."

"Except the patient died." Hartley said it coldly.

"That was uncalled for," Dickey snapped angrily.

"Harold's right," Max chimed in. "Let's keep our cool."

"I'm sorry," Ben Hartley said softly. "But I'm concerned."

"We don't know what happened to Raymond," Clara said firmly. "We probably never will. Several months ago, he called me and said he was having trouble sleeping. I spoke with him once or twice. I prescribed a mild tranquilizer and told him I would refer him to another psychiatrist if he wanted to return to treatment. That's all there is to it."

Harold Dickey shifted in his seat, coughing for attention. Clara ignored him. "I would be happy to investigate," he said suddenly.

Hartley jammed his fists into his eyes. "Harold, you amaze me. If you are being investigated, you cannot be the investigator. If we are sued—and I sincerely hope we aren't—you and Clara will be the subjects of more than one investigation. It's that simple. Now that leaves this committee with only two functional members."

"Hold on, Ben," Clara broke in. "Of course the subject of an investigation cannot be the investigator. That's precisely why I've asked Dr. Frank to become involved and to review the matter for us. I've already turned the file in this matter over to him." She did not glance in Harold Dickey's direction, but the heat of his rage spread around the room. Only Hartley seemed unaware of it.

Hartley turned to Jason for the first time. Clara bent toward him, smiling encouragingly. Jason said nothing.

"Dr. Frank, what is your connection to the Centre?" Hartley asked.

"I did my training here. I'm an attending. My teaching title is lecturer at the medical school. I supervise residents. My other associations include—"

"Thank you. You seem to be sufficiently well qualified, and unconnected to the administration of the Centre, to review the case and make inquiries where necessary. I suggest we set up an ad hoc Quality Assurance Committee headed by you to oversee our internal handling of this matter." Hartley rubbed his hands together as if relieved to find a solution.

"You'll write a report, of course, and keep us informed of your progress," he added, almost smiling.

"Good work, Ben. Then we'll be relying on Jason to give us a preliminary take on the case." Clara glanced at her watch. Done and done, and she was free to go.

"All that leaves us is to agree on a date and time to meet again. Dr. Frank, what day and time next week would be good for you?"

For the first time that day, Clara flipped open the expensive burgundy leather folder with her name embossed in gold. Inside, a used and leaking condom was stuck to her datebook. She slapped the folder closed, but not before everyone around the table had a chance to see what was inside it.

For several seconds there was shocked silence. Clara felt the public humiliation as violently as if she had taken a direct hit from a heat-seeking missile. Her vision blurred with the impact, and she was afraid she was losing consciousness.

Just then, Hartley snickered, and her vision cleared. Her eyes locked ferociously on Dickey. "Harold, I need to see you before I leave," Clara said. "Gentlemen—this meeting is adjourned."

harold

twenty-seven

Harold Dickey left Clara's office with a pain in his chest. If he hadn't been a doctor, he might have believed he was having a heart attack. The blood had drained from his face, robbing his cheeks of their healthy pink appearance. His skin was clammy and cold, gray as a filleted sole. He could feel the soft jowls under his chin jiggling with the slight tremor of his head that moved from side to side just the tiniest bit, out of his control. His eyes, sunk deep in pouchy purplish bags, burned with humiliation and distress. It hurt to be alive, to breathe, to think. The worst was it hurt to think.

Outside the executive suite, he stood leaning against the wall waiting for an elevator for a long time, for many minutes. No one passed by to ask him if he was all right. He wasn't all right. He could feel the icy perspiration on his forehead, on his chest, under his arms. The tightness in his chest was an iron grip that wouldn't let up. He punched the button for the elevator but nothing happened, punched it again. He was not having a heart attack, would not accept a heart attack. He'd always been careful about what he ate, walked four miles a day, and still played tennis with a few chosen residents. He could still beat many of them.

This was simply an attack of impotent rage to which the unfortunate reaction was a somatical imitation of a heart losing its rhythm, failing to pump oxygen into his lungs and brain and creating an unbearable pressure, a drop in body temperature. Cold sweats. It was not a heart attack. He was sure it was not. It was anger blocked at its source, white-hot and inexpressible, with nowhere to go but deeper inside.

How *dare* Clara blame him for humiliating her by putting a used condom in her appointment book? It was appalling, paranoid. Where would she get such a crazy idea? Why would he want to humiliate her—he loved her. All Harold wanted was to be loved by Clara Treadwell as he should be loved by her. That was all he wanted. He'd never humiliate her, never hurt her.

How could she jump to such an appalling conclusion and tell him he was through at the Centre? He'd been at the Centre all his adult life, had been the lifeblood and inspiration of the place for over thirty years. He was not only her teacher, her mentor. He was everybody's mentor. But most particularly he was hers. Clara Treadwell would have been a nobody without him. She *was* him; even her hopes had sprung from his ambitions for her. He had taught her everything he knew. Harold felt sick. But it was betrayal, not a heart attack.

He couldn't get the image of her standing behind her desk in her office out of his mind. Now he would always see her like that, palms on the polished surface, leaning forward slightly, a look of utter conviction on her face. That expression of self-righteous hostility must be what judges, prosecutors, executioners wore. People who ended lives for the "public good."

"Harold, you've gone too far. It's over" was how she had started on him.

He was struck dumb. He didn't get it. "What, my dear? What's over?" They'd had a pleasant evening together Monday night. They'd had several amicable communications since. Until the meeting this morning, Harold had thought things were improving between them. He was the one who should be hurt and angry. He'd been advising Clara on the Cowles matter. And today she had publicly cut him out and replaced him with Jason Frank without even telling him first. It was outrageous.

Clara flipped open the folder. The condom still lay inside.

In the sudden movement he saw for the first time the bandage on her hand. "What happened to your hand?"

She didn't answer.

"What's the meaning of this? What's going *on,* Clara?" he demanded.

She glared at him, the friendly old tic from her childhood leaping around in her cheek, signaling him that something was very wrong and that she blamed him for whatever it was.

"Where did this come from? What's it about?" Harold was confused, couldn't guess the meaning of her stance, of the expression on her face. Frigid rage.

"Don't play the innocent with me, Harold." Suddenly she began jabbing the air with her finger. "I know you too well."

He could smell her perfume, Paris. The odor exuded from the scarf around her neck, from the deep purple wool of her suit. The pain began in his chest. Clara seemed disturbed, out of control. He'd never seen her like this.

"Don't fuck around with me, Harold. I've been patient with you so far, extremely patient. But I've had it. I can't tolerate this anymore. You'll have to leave, retire. You decide how you want to do it. You can't stay any longer."

"What? Why?"

"Because you've been harassing me. You won't let go." She slapped shut the folder with its obscene contents. "You're through, Harold."

"Clara, I can't even begin to imagine what—"

"I'm talking about what's been going on up here. The vandalism, the thefts. The mysterious little things going wrong, things that only someone who knew this place very well could pull off. The threats on my life. The cut on my hand. And now—*this*! This is sick. What do you want to happen? Don't you understand how dreadful this is? You'll have to leave. That's all there is to it."

"Sit down, Clara, and pull yourself together. You're not making sense."

"No, I will not sit down. I'm not some insecure resident. I'm not under your thumb. I'm all grown up now. You can't hurt me anymore." Her face was distorted, cold with rage.

"Clara, I would never hurt you. I care about you much too much. In fact I—love you. I've always loved you. You know that." His hand went to his chest. The pain was intolerable.

"I didn't want to have to take any action, you understand that? I didn't want to involve you or damage you in any way, Harold. You *made* me do this. It's your fault. You wouldn't stop."

"What is going on? Stop and tell me. What and when and how long?"

"You know what I'm talking about. You've as much as told me you know everything that's going on here." She spoke bitterly now.

"You said there have been other incidents. You've been stabbed in the *hand*, and you think I did that? Clara, I'm really worried about you. You think I *stabbed* you? How could I possibly have stabbed you? With what? When?"

"Don't patronize me," she snapped.

His eyes moved from the closed folder to the bandage. Either somebody was harassing Clara or she was setting him up for a very big fall. He shook his head, unsure of what to think. Would Clara do these terrible things to destroy him?

Harold couldn't imagine it. All their adult lives he and Clara had lived among the mentally ill, trying to understand and help them. Would Clara, this gifted, dedicated woman, this superb administrator—his darling of so many years—coldheartedly use their environment to ruin him?

"This is very serious," he said softly.

"Yes."

No, not even Clara/Carmen could do this to him. Harold made a leap of faith and decided to believe Clara was innocent, that she was being harassed and was in real peril.

"This is very dangerous, Clara. How long have these incidents been going on?"

Clara took an impatient breath. "Harold, don't play games with me. I know what you've been doing. And you haven't hurt me. You haven't scared me. You've only hurt yourself."

Again the wave of shock. "How could you suggest such a thing? I couldn't do anything like this. Stab you, humiliate you? I've always been on your side—even when you're wrong, I support you. I support you now."

Clara's eyes flickered. "Wrong? When was I wrong?"

"You're often wrong. You're wrong now. You're delusional if you think I am capable of doing something like this—" He pointed to the closed folder, sputtering in his anger.

"Don't start that," Clara warned.

"For what *possible* reason would I want to hurt you?"

"I don't wish to get into it, Hal. Our relationship has changed. My position has changed. It's time for you to retire."

"I haven't done anything *wrong.*"

"I don't want to get into that. I don't want to point fingers. I don't want to debate. I have to catch a plane."

"I haven't done anything wrong."

She looked down at the folder. "I don't want to hear this anymore. I'm having this . . . *thing* tested. Hal, I'm warning you. Don't make me hang you."

His heart pounded, his head, too. Hang him? *Hang him?* For what? For loving her, for protecting her, for wanting to be close to her?

His body felt broken, but his voice was firm when he spoke. "Clara, you're in too much trouble to hang anybody right now. You've been threatened with a malpractice suit that will swallow you whole, muddy you so badly and suck you down so deep you won't see sky for a long, long time. And it looks like you have someone else, someone right here in the Centre who can put anything he wants into your private spaces. That's a pretty fearsome thought. If I were you I'd think about those things. I'd prepare for a legal battle. I'd want to find the *right* culprit."

"You're threatening me. Everything you say makes it worse."

He shook his head, his face as gray as that of a dead man. "You're making a big mistake here. Somebody wants you in trouble, honey, but it isn't me."

"Who then? You tell me, *who*? Who has access to my office, my desk?—" She stopped talking. Her lips closed. She would tell him no more.

"Give me that thing. I'll find out who put it there. And when I do, you'll have to apologize to me, Clara. This place is full of paranoid, psychotic, unstable people. Have you even bothered to question the staff? The night staff, the cleaning people, the security people? Have you checked them out? One of them has a grudge against you. You've been very, very bad to think it's me. I don't take this kind of abuse from anybody. I will not take abuse." He repeated the last sentence, holding his hand over his heart as if reciting the Pledge of Allegiance.

But Clara didn't give the folder to him. She turned her back on him, stared out of the window at the Hudson River and stayed that way until he left. Somehow he got to his office, where the pain refused to ease. Instead it settled in, a steady agonizing pressure that began to alert him to the possibility of a real problem. He was a doctor, though, had to go about his business and shrug the pain off. He couldn't afford a life-threatening event right now.

Clara was stubborn and foolish; she was not dealing correctly with any of her problems. Her secrecy about the harassment incidents was particularly worrying. How could someone do these things without getting caught? Harold sat in his office, trying to pull himself together to form a plan of action. He could not allow himself to have a heart attack. Clara was surrounded by idiots—Ben Hartley, Max Goodrich, the entire board of directors. They would skin her alive to avoid controversy. Harold was overwhelmed with fear and anxiety, terrified that if he didn't deal with Clara's problems, if something happened to him, Clara would have no one to protect her. He went down to the third floor to see Gunn Tram.

twenty-eight

"Hi, Jason, it's Friday around three-thirty. April Woo returning your call. Long time no see, huh? I'll bet you called about the case at your shop, Cowles—or has something else come up? I'm here for a half an hour or so. Saturday I'm working four to one. Sunday I'm off."

That was your last message. Doodle oodle oo.

Jason hung up and glanced at the brass bull with the clock on its back on the bottom shelf of the bookcase, between a glass paperweight in the shape of an apple and a stack of *JAPA* journals. Jason knew the clock was at least two minutes slow. That made it three-forty-seven. He'd had back-to-back patients since the meeting at the Centre that morning. At the best of times it was exhausting having to figure out what was going on with each patient every moment so he wouldn't slip up and make a fatal mistake about what he or she might really be saying. At the worst of times—when he had more than the needs of his patients on his mind—he felt overwhelmed.

Today, he had wanted to think only of his patients and getting some groceries in the house so that when Emma returned tomorrow from her six-month absence, she wouldn't have to indict him for domestic incompetence. Instead, Clara Treadwell had cleverly maneuvered him into the seething cauldron of hospital politics where he'd never, ever wanted to go. He had to hand it to her. Two days ago Clara had gotten him to agree to review the Cowles case. Now, as a result of this morning's highly unpleasant meeting, he was suddenly chair of an "ad hoc Quality Assurance Committee" with the responsibility of investigating the Director of the Centre, the person who claimed to want to be his mentor.

Jason snorted at the thought. He was supervisor, and maybe mentor, to several residents every year; but he'd never actually had a mentor himself. He hadn't wanted to be constrained in his thinking and loyalties, so he'd trudged along, with no advice or support, his parents telling him he was crazy to go into psychiatry instead of becoming a heart or brain surgeon where the money was.

Jason glanced at his watch. The second hand advanced painstakingly around its face, reminding him of himself, trudging along all those years, listening to his own counsel every step along the way, making his own choices and his own mistakes. He had to laugh at Clara Treadwell's arrogance. It was too late to mold him. He was already formed; she could worry and disturb him, but she couldn't influence his findings.

The clocks ticked, and time was passing. Jason wanted to try April before his next patient arrived. He heard the door to his waiting room open and close. After a cooling-off period in his waiting room, his last patient was finally leaving. Jeannie had sobbed nonstop for forty-five minutes, apologizing the whole time. "I'm so sorry. I just can't stop. I don't know what's wrong with me."

Jason knew what was wrong. The poor woman's husband was selfish and no longer loved her. He'd told her he needed time to relax and was insisting on the freedom to do his thing. Jeannie had long ago given up her career and earning power to care for the two tiny children her husband had wanted and now expected her to care for. She felt heavily burdened with the responsibility for everything since her husband was the kind of man who thought his time was too precious for any kind of domestic endeavor. She starved herself in her misery and apologized for her anguish as if only she were at fault for her loneliness and pain. Twice a week when Jason met with her, he appeared solid as a rock, unemotional and calm. She had no idea that every muscle in his body ached from the tension of restraining his impulse to hug her.

Thinking of Jeannie's tiny wrists and puffy eyes, Jason flipped open his address book to April Woo's number. He didn't really have to look it up. They'd worked two cases together: Emma's kidnapping six months before and the Honiger-Stanton sisters case three months later. By now the precinct number was burned in his memory. He smiled grimly at the thought that his quiet analyst's life had changed so dramatically that he was suddenly the Psychiatric Centre's crime expert. And not only that, it seemed a New York cop thought a few weeks of their not seeing each other was a long time.

As he reached for the phone, Jason heard the door of his waiting room open and close again. His next patient had arrived. That reminded him of the moment April had told him she was more scared of a closed door than a handgun with a cocked trigger aimed at her head.

"Behind the door could be anything. With a nine-millimeter at least I know what I'm up against." He remembered her smile. "Sometimes they jam."

April had also told Jason it took a pressure of between eight and twelve pounds to pull a trigger, depending on the gun. "But in the heat of the moment, all it really takes is a tiny little squeeze. If you have to shoot at somebody, afterwards your hand shakes for about a week."

Things like that Jason hadn't known before meeting April Woo and probably would never have known. He may have been a streetwise kind of kid, growing up in the Bronx with a basketball never long out of his hands, but he'd never held a gun, never had a cop on his side. Never been involved with the investigation of criminals, let alone his colleagues and peers. All this was new.

Jason had always left the door to his waiting room unlocked so his patients could come in and out. The two doors to his office were closed. His patients came in and then waited for him to open the door to his inner sanctum. He used to take comfort in the fact that he knew who was out there, but they never knew who was inside with him or what he was doing when he was alone. Now he was more like April. He couldn't be so confident anymore about anything he couldn't see with his own eyes. He needed to urinate, needed to reach April before she went home.

He considered taking his portable phone into the bathroom to talk to April while he was relieving himself, decided against it. He dialed her number. This time she picked up.

"Hi, it's Jason. I don't mean to be abrupt, but I only have a minute. What can you tell me about Raymond Cowles?"

She didn't hesitate before replying. "The death report came in yesterday afternoon. The M.E. says there's no indication of foul play. As far as he's concerned, Cowles's death is consistent with suicide. We closed the case." April did not waste words in the telling.

Jason let out a small groan. "Suicide" was not the word he'd wanted to hear. He said, "I'd like to chat with you about it."

"Fine. Tomorrow?"

Emma was coming home tomorrow. "How about early next week?"

"Okay by me."

They scheduled a time. Jason replaced the phone in its cradle, then took a moment to urinate before opening the door to his next patient.

twenty-nine

"Bobbie, what are you up to?" Gunn Tram scolded the ringing telephone in Bobbie's apartment as if it could hear her and pick up. "Dr. Dickey was asking about you today. Bobbie, don't you try to hide from me. If you're in trouble, I got to know."

The phone didn't care. It just rang on and on, as if mocking her distress. "Come on, Bobbie, pick up."

He wasn't picking up, but that didn't mean he wasn't there. Gunn Tram trudged up and down the three flights of creaking stairs between their apartments all Friday evening looking for him.

"Just because I have a phone doesn't mean I have to use it," he had told her on the other occasions when she complained about having to come down the stairs to find him. "Maybe I don't want to be found."

That night he didn't want to be found. Even if Dr. Dickey hadn't come down to her office asking a lot of questions about "people who had grudges against the Centre," Gunn would have been worried. Bobbie had the look in his eye that something was bothering him. When something was bothering Bobbie, Gunn knew, he usually did something about it that bothered other people.

Gunn was scared for him. Bobbie didn't mean to get in trouble. But like today, when Dr. Dickey asked if Bobbie could possibly still be hanging around the Centre—well, trouble just seemed to come to him. It hurt Gunn that Bobbie made people mad when he hadn't done a thing. He was like a magnet for bad luck. She didn't understand why the doctors cared so much about crazy people they couldn't even help, and didn't try to help Bobbie who'd been such a good nurse to them.

Around eleven Gunn walked over to the French Quarter bar on Broadway looking for him. Brian said he hadn't been in. She sat drinking beer at the bar until midnight. At midnight she walked home slowly.

Bobbie's apartment was in the space that used to be the kitchen when the brownstone was a private home. It was just below ground level at the back of the building. Steps up to the back door led to a long-unused garden. His two windows were not visible from the street.

Gunn knew, from the long list of grievances about him, that Bobbie often came in and out the back way, frightening the neighbors at odd hours. And she had to agree with them that the way Bobbie did things was a little peculiar. Often when he came to see her, he climbed the fire escape and entered through an open window. Gunn saw him as eccentric and attributed his strangeness to his unusual childhood in Louisiana and the terrible things he had witnessed in Vietnam.

All her life, Gunn had been interested in people. The sameness of the population in Sweden had been the real reason she left home at sixteen, all alone, to come to America. She had wanted a different kind of life from her parents' dull repetition of their parents. Even then, she had liked all kinds of people. Their stories fascinated her, especially the sad ones. She felt she could be any one of them and her heart was filled with a powerful desire to help. Gunn worked at the Psychiatric Centre because she craved the tragedy and disappointed dreams she found there. So many sad stories made her own uneventful life seem almost joyful. At the Centre, there were very few happy stories, many damaged people. Gunn had loved Bobbie from the first conversation she'd had with him over fifteen years ago. He had come to work at the Centre with the same wish to help she had. He was good to those poor mad creatures on the locked wards, people Gunn was afraid of being too close to even though the shrinks taught tolerance, and Gunn had tried hard to learn their lessons. Bobbie cared about the little people, and so did she.

All the thirty years Gunn had worked at the Centre the docs had joked about how everybody was crazy, how it was all right to be crazy. Over the years, Gunn had watched the degree of craziness escalate. Now it was spilling out all over the place, and it was still all right. The docs, the patients, the residents—nobody complained about anybody. Even Gunn could tell that some of the young women residents coming in were very strange, very strange indeed.

In the old days, all the iffy things like attitude and sexual preference were watched very carefully. In those days, a person couldn't be too strange and still qualify as a doc. Supervisors were informed about every little thing every resident did. It was hard to get into the Centre, and even after they were in, residents were carefully screened during all the years of their training. Gunn had loved working in Personnel in those days. Little notes about any peculiarity were added to everyone's files. But not anymore. PCness decreed that everybody had a right to keep whatever baggage they came in with and never mind how it affected the patients or the system. It was scary what people got away with now. Gunn knew for a fact that many of the doctors took a wide range of painkillers; even the great Harold Dickey himself had a weakness for Johnnie Walker that he indulged in in his office throughout the afternoon following lunch. There were a lot of things going wrong that Gunn had to worry about.

The light was on under Bobbie's door when Gunn returned to the brownstone. She stood in the dim, cramped hallway outside his apartment and knocked timidly.

"Bobbie?"

Inside, she could hear movement, but he didn't answer. "Bobbie, you in there? I got to talk to you."

Sounds of the toilet flushing upstairs, then a slammed door. Gunn put her face so close to Bobbie's door her lips almost touched the faded paint. She whispered urgently, "Bobbie, you remember Dr. Dickey, don't you? . . . Dr. Dickey came to see me today. He asked about people with grudges against the Centre, people who hated Dr. Treadwell. . . . Bobbie, you don't hate Dr. Treadwell, do you?"

No answer from inside. Gunn felt dizzy in the gloomy silence, but she had something to say, and she was going to finish no matter what. "Of course, I didn't tell him anything—I didn't know anything—Bobbie, Dr. Dickey took the files, lots of files. He said he wanted to check out all the disciplinary actions taken against staff for patient errors. He took some patient files, too. . . .

"Bobbie, he took the files, and there wasn't a thing I could do to stop him. You know he's the head of the Committee. He wanted them, and everybody from upstairs was already gone. There wasn't even anybody to ask if it was all right."

Gunn could hear Bobbie breathing on the other side of the door, but he didn't open up. She said, "Something's going on, Bobbie. Dr. Dickey told me somebody wants to hurt Dr. Treadwell. I feel so bad about it. I didn't know what to say." There was a pause while Bobbie, unseen behind his door, breathed in and out.

"Oh, Bobbie, I'm afraid. Please . . . Tell me you don't hate Dr. Treadwell. You wouldn't do anything to hurt her, would you?"

Gunn did not like the dark, the tight space, the dense stillness in the decaying building, the slight wheeze at the end of Bobbie's exhalations. She knew him, knew he sat on her fire escape sometimes in the middle of the night, not doing anything at all except breathing in and out just like this. She remembered Dr. Dickey's own words so many times over the years: "We're all a little crazy, Gunn. Don't let it worry you one little bit. Most crazy people never hurt anyone but themselves." Gunn had tried not to let the crazy things worry her.

Suddenly the light went off under Bobbie's door, and his voice came out of the dark. "Go away, old woman. The bastard is looking for someone else, not me."

Now she breathed a sigh of relief. "I'm glad, sweetheart, because your file was one of the ones he took."

"Fuck!" Some heavy object crashed against the flimsy wooden door, stressing the lock and cracking the wood. Gunn jumped back, cringing.

"Bobbie? Bobbie, don't get upset, please don't get upset. We can talk about this—"

But Bobbie didn't want to talk about it. Gunn heard him slam the door to the garden and knew he'd gone out again. She started worrying again, this time that he'd go out drinking and get into another fight. She felt real bad about upsetting him.

thirty

A slick of sweat gathered on Clara's upper lip and between her breasts and thighs as she brooded about Hal's many betrayals in the hot sun by the pool at Arch Candel's beach house on Sleepy Key, a prime spot in the Gulf of Mexico off the coast of Sarasota, Florida. She had considered the situation with Hal on the plane from New York to Florida and was sure she was doing the right thing, wondered how long it would take to end. In front of her, thousands of diamond lights from the Gulf winked between the palms that studded the thick green lawn bordering the beach.

Senator Candel himself sat farther back on the patio at an antique iron table that had been made for his family at the turn of the century. The valuable table with the signs of the zodiac arranged in a circle around its top was badly rusted from the salt and humidity and heavy rains of many summers. Its owner showed the same signs of wear. Born fair, Arch Candel was permanently reddened and freckled from a lifetime of deep and dangerous sunburns. Even now he was indifferent to the hazards of sun worship. He was shirtless at noon, wore only a pair of navy swimming trunks with a Polo insignia on them. Beneath his shrewd and penetrating blue eyes, the sun damage could be seen on jowly cheeks and a red nose that was needle-thin and peeling. His long bony legs supported a thick upper body that had begun softening many years ago. A substantial slab of gut spilled over the edge of the waistband of his trunks.

Clara studied him reading at his rusty table.

He felt her gaze and looked up. "What?"

She was mentally reliving her old grievances about Hal when she thought she loved him, and the recent incidents of Hal's harassment now that he wanted her back. The complete *bastard*! The arrogant old *fool* to think he could get away with this. She pumped up her outrage and didn't even hear Arch speak.

The first message she'd received had come nearly six months ago. It was composed of letters cut from newspaper headlines and pasted on a piece of hospital stationery. The neatly folded paper had been on the podium when she'd gone up to introduce a seminar. She'd silently read the words *Someone you love is going to die* standing in front of an auditorium full of people, then had crumpled up the paper and begun her welcome speech. At the time the episode passed immediately from her mind. She'd thought the thing was a joke, possibly not even meant for her. *Someone you love is going to die.* Clara had a literal mind; she didn't love anyone, so she wasn't vulnerable in that way, therefore, the note probably was intended for someone else, another speaker. Only after, when there had been several more nasty threats, had she become annoyed.

"Darlin'?"

Clara shook her head, adjusting the brim of her straw hat to hide her face. She was lying on a chaise with a green-and-white-striped mattress under an umbrella by the pool. Her bathing suit was basic black, cut low in the bosom and high on the hips. She crossed her legs the other way to even her tan.

Distracted, Arch removed the reading glasses from the end of his sharp nose and twirled them between two fingers. For the last two hours he'd been studying the thousand-page committee report he'd have to debate in Senate hearings the following week. Without the ballast of his elbows, the sheaf of printed pages fell shut from its own weight, closing on his notes and the list of questions he was preparing to ask Clara to get her opinion on the issues.

"Darlin', I know something's bothering you. And whatever bothers you bothers me." His soft lazy voice came from between thin chapped lips, but no one who heard it was ever fooled. Arch Candel was as tough as the 'gators he grew up with.

He was also a man who knew what he wanted. When he met Clara Treadwell, he was still reeling from the long decline and death from cancer of his wife of twenty-eight years. He had been instantly impressed by Clara's energy, her electric smile and shrewd intelligence. He'd wanted to marry her immediately despite the undisguised misgivings of his two grown children. He'd shown Clara his houses in Florida and Washington and told her she could redecorate them as she wished, she would be the mistress of all he owned.

At the time Clara had just emerged from her second divorce, still childless and with nearly a million dollars in her pockets. Her mother, like Arch's wife only a few months before, was in the final stages of cancer and not taking it well. On her deathbed, she reviled her daughter for abandoning her years ago, then for using one man after another to get ahead. Clara's dying mother repeatedly called her a slut and a whore. Her mother's words never touched Clara. She knew it wasn't any parade of men that enraged her mother. What her mother bitterly resented was that Clara had succeeded and succeeded on her own terms.

Clara was successful, but she had also been burned a few times in her rise to power. Though she would not admit it in any conscious way, deep inside she felt she had been hurt, even abused, by the men in her life. She touched the bandage covering the cut on her hand. The cut was healing and now itched unbearably. Clara knew she had reached the top of her profession. She knew there were people out there who could hurt her if she wasn't constantly vigilant. She also knew she had to be careful who she married next. Arch was almost too eager to get her. He was crowding her, pushing.

Arch stood up, patted his belly, and stretched. Then he crossed the mossy stone patio to the pool area where Clara lay. "You're awful quiet, gorgeous." He lowered his bulk to the edge of her recliner and began stroking Clara's carefully tanned thighs.

This close she could see the telltale dry patches on his leathery skin and the sweat trickling down his sagging breasts, tiny rivulets catching in his graying chest hairs. "Come on, baby, tell Daddy what's bothering you." Arch's freckled hands traveled up her leg, two fingers heading toward the tight elastic bands of her bathing suit.

This one liked tight places—elevators, backseats of cars. His fantasy was pretending he was still a boy who had to grab any opportunity he could get, fight the good battle with unyielding undergarments so he could get to the magic buttons with his fingers and his tongue and hit the jackpot. Clara knew what he liked. At the moment the trusty appendage he called his dick—which hadn't been much in use for the previous several years—was already straining against the confines of his swim trunks. Arch believed that Clara made him young again, and for that he was excessively grateful. He leaned over her, heavy and hot, his chapped thin lips and peeling nose diving first into her perfumed cleavage.

He smelled of soap and shaving cream, for he didn't even bother to use suntan lotion or sunblock. Clara closed her eyes against the insult of his ruined skin and saw behind her eyes the mountain of edema that had been her mother in those final appalling days. Lying in her hospital bed with a hugely swollen belly and legs, cadaverous arms and face, and hair falling out by the fistful, she'd bitterly predicted Clara's own end. "You've never cared about anybody but yourself," she'd shrilled. "When you die no one will care about you." Her mother's last words had been a curse; Clara did not grieve for her.

She did worry about Arch, though. Clara had warned him many

times to see a doctor and have his skin examined, to stop sitting like this in the sun. But the Senator was a stubborn man, focused only on what interested him, and what interested him now was a foray into the damp and musky depths of her body.

Sucking on a freed nipple, he was simultaneously working his way into the crotch of her bathing suit with two fingers and moaning deep in his throat. His concentration was complete. He was indifferent to the possibility that anyone walking on the beach and pausing to look at the splendid house through the trees could see them.

Clara squeezed her eyes shut. She allowed the familiar sensations of a man's overwhelming and reckless lust to soothe her. She let her body take over and provide him with a feast of the senses he couldn't resist. He loved her body, the tempting contours of her breasts, her neck and shoulders, her hips and belly unblemished by the ravages of procreation or illness. He loved the expert suppleness of her female parts well-lubricated and used to pleasure, and so did she. None of it ever failed her. She was a sex queen, a goddess meant for adoration. This old Lothario groaned and panted, another middle-aged man out of control. The excitement of his ardor enflamed her from crotch to belly. She roiled at his probing of her slippery labia, demanding more than fingerplay.

"Let's go inside," she murmured.

An hour later, lying on the bed he had shared for so many years with his wife, Arch Candel gazed at his beloved with the devotion she had come to expect from her lovers.

"Darlin', let's not wait anymore. Let's tie the knot."

Clara pulled up the sheet. "It's not that simple, Arch."

"We're two mature adults in love. What could be more simple?"

Crows screamed in the Australian pines outside. Clara shook her head. She had to be careful, real careful, now. She had a feeling Arch had her under some kind of surveillance. He was interested in that kind of thing, talked about having friends in the FBI.

"Oh, I know you've been married before. I know some old patient of yours died this week. In fact, I know your whole history." Arch waved the history away.

Clara pushed some air through her nose. "How?"

"Never you mind how."

"What do you know about me, Arch? Tell me."

"Darlin', don't argue with me. I said I know your history—let's leave it at that."

"You had me investigated?" Silently she dared him to admit he had.

"No, darlin', nothing big like that. I just have some sources. Wouldn't want you to marry me for my groves, would I?"

His orange groves? Clara laughed out loud.

"Or my money." He laced his fingers across his stomach. "So what's bothering you? If you can't trust me with it, who can you trust?"

She could trust *no one* with all of her. But maybe she could trust Arch with a few pieces. What the hell, maybe he'd be useful. Clara cocked her head to one side and caught sight of a storm cloud gathering in the Gulf.

"Oh, I'm dealing with someone who used to be a nuisance and now is"—she pursed her lips—"getting dangerous."

"Politically?"

"No, physically." She sighed with irritation, her mood plunging again.

"Somebody threatening the hospital?"

"Not like that case out West."

"What was that?"

"There were incidents in one of the genetics labs out there. Did you read about it?"

Arch shook his head. "No, what happened?"

"Well, it's everybody's nightmare in every institution—sabotages that could end in tragedy. In hospitals, it's staff that could hurt a patient. In pharmaceutical companies it's someone contaminating the medication. In the government it's the fired employee who comes back with an assault weapon or a bomb. In this case it was threatening notes, a birthday cake with poisoned frosting, slashed tires."

"Who was doing it?"

"Oh, they couldn't prove it. They thought it was a midlevel associate who was in love with one of the women he worked with. She had slept with him once, then decided he wasn't for her. Apparently, he didn't take rejection well. But they never proved it was him." Clara chewed on her lip, thoughtfully. "It was the genetics lab."

"Clara, honey, you're losing me here."

"They couldn't get him. They just couldn't catch this guy. He was brilliant, after all. They tried everything, put in surveillance cameras everywhere, even hired a DNA expert to test the saliva on the flap of the envelopes he was using for his threatening notes."

"How would that help?" Arch was bewildered.

"They had the DNA from the saliva. They made everybody on the staff give a saliva sample. They thought with a match, they would have cause to get rid of the guy."

"And?"

"That's the irony. It was a genetics lab, so the guy fooled them. He contaminated everything he touched with genetic material from a dozen different sources. The saliva on the envelopes they tested came from a dog. So they couldn't nail him. The incidents stopped, and for all I know he's still there."

"How does this relate, baby? You got some genetic material you want to test?"

Clara stared at him, stunned. How could he know about the week when she got back to New York? "You know all this already?"

The Senator smiled. "No, sweetheart, you're telling a story, I'm just trying to see where it's heading."

Clara watched a trio of dolphins out in the Gulf playing in the wake of two Jet Skis before replying. "For a while it was just stupid stuff—someone trying to scare me. I knew who it was. I thought he'd get tired of it."

"Who?" Arch indicated the dolphins with a finger. "Nice, huh?"

Clara clicked her tongue against the roof of her mouth. "Somebody pretty high up. He was my supervisor when I was a resident. We had an affair." She looked at Arch quickly.

He leaned over to scratch a mosquito bite on his thigh.

"He's nobody now," she added quickly.

He sat back, didn't say anything.

"Ray got married. I got married. Hal lost his clout at the Centre when biology took over the field."

Arch rubbed his lips with the backs of two fingers. "Who's Ray?"

"Ray's the patient who died this week."

"Did you have an affair with him, too?"

"No!" Clara exploded like a flare. "He was my patient!"

"And the other guy was your supervisor. You had an affair with him." Arch frowned. "Was he your supervisor with this particular patient? With Ray?"

Clara nodded again.

The dolphins were gone. Arch concentrated on Clara's face. "Now, this . . . former patient, is there any relation between his death and your—"

"Harold?" She stared back at Arch, suddenly uncomfortable, screwed up her face. "It's possible," she said slowly. "Yes, I would say anything is possible."

"So it's muddy, my dear."

"Yes. Because any investigation into Ray's treatment will involve Harold. He was my supervisor. He studied my notes and determined the course of the therapy. I suspect he's involved in Ray's death because he was the first person the police questioned after they found the body."

"Darlin', *is* this a suicide?"

Clara closed her eyes. "It could be."

"So you're in a pickle." Arch tapped his lips and thought for a while. "How does it stand with this Harold . . . ?"

"Dickey. I, uh, told him he had to leave."

"I thought it was practically impossible to fire people in these institutions."

"It is, unless they're in administration. *I* could be fired in a second," she said bitterly. "But he's a tenured professor. The committee will have to meet, determine he's unfit to hold his position . . ."

Arch slapped his thigh. "I think you have to do what they did at the lab out West, put the surveillance in all over the place. If this guy does anything else, you'll catch him in the act."

"Oh, he'd know. He'd stop."

"Fine, then he stops."

"But that wouldn't be the end of it. He's insane. He wants *me.* He'll think of some other way to get me. He has to be let go on the basis of his mental fitness."

"Fine, then we'll bring in the FBI. That's what they're there for. Leave this Harold alone, baby. In the end he'll hang himself."

"I'm counting on it." Clara smiled. So Arch did have the FBI watching her.

He tossed her a towel. "Let's go get some lunch, honey—and stick with me; there are ways of dealing with everything."

Clara nodded solemnly. "I've always thought so," she said.

thirty-one

Mike Sanchez and April Woo were due at work at four P.M. on Saturday. At exactly nine A.M. Mike took a calculated risk. He pulled his red Camaro into an empty spot in front of the neat brick house in Astoria where April lived with her parents. The house had green fiberglass awnings in the shape of fans over each window. April had once told him the awnings made every raindrop sound like thunder.

"What are they good for?" he'd asked.

"For show."

She told him the decoration had been installed by the previous owners and the Woos had decided not to waste the cost of the improvement by removing it, even though they themselves did not like them. Mike had pondered their reasoning for a long time. He was beginning to understand how he might solve his problem.

His problem was the porcupine living inside him in the soft, vulnerable parts of his body. The porcupine was April Woo. He wasn't exactly sure how she had moved from the outside of him to the inside of him. But there she was. When he wasn't with her, he thought about her. When he was with her, he couldn't stop looking at her. Sometimes he wanted to touch her so badly that holding back felt like too much steam in a turned-off radiator. This was one of the many kinds of Chinese torture.

April had told him in old China the death sentence was never only death. Sometimes the guilty party was pulled apart by four horses, then hacked into pieces, the cut-off head paraded around on a stick. Sometimes the condemned man was skinned alive. And people thought the violence in New York was bad. Mike had no doubt April was capable of a similar lack of forgiveness if he dared to touch her where she didn't want to be touched. Which was everywhere.

Sometimes his desire for her took his breath away. It occurred to him that she was rendering him brain-dead and helpless by extracting his oxygen from the air. He'd had many women in his thirty-four years. Not one of them, not even the girl he'd married, had ever taken his breath away. Well, certainly not on a regular basis with no physical contact. And now he was too preoccupied with April to get relief from other women. He was concerned that her scorn was powerful enough to cause his dick to wither away and die. He worked out a lot, smelled other women's perfume and their sweat, and was not interested. He figured this was the way homos felt about women and worried that April was making him gay.

From Mike's point of view, wanting April Woo was stupid, wasteful, irritating, and dangerous. Dangerous because whenever he let her know, she raised the spines on her back and tore at his gut. But he was beginning to see a way out. April was a person of quality, of character. To get her he was going to have to get the approval of her mother, her father, and quite possibly her entire community. When he got that, he'd have her.

He got out of the car and stretched. Busy by the front door was a thin man of indeterminate age with his very little hair cut so short his head looked like an unadorned skull. The man wore a white shirt much too large for him and black trousers, black Chinese canvas shoes—the newest version with rubber soles. At the moment he was carefully trimming a dense, prickly bush with shiny dark green leaves and red berries on it, attaching the shoots to a trellis that curved up and over the front door, and peering at his work through black frames with thick lenses. There was a similar untamed bush on the other side he hadn't gotten to yet. It would be a while before the two bushes met above the door.

Mike guessed the man was April's father, Ja Fo Woo, making his own improvements to the house. The trellis had not been there the last time Mike had seen the house. Neither had the tiny apricot poodle sitting at attention at the top of the three steps that led to the front door, watching the thin man's every move.

For a few seconds, Mike, too, watched the man's every move. The man continued snipping and tying, but the dog jumped up and began barking excitedly. The sudden racket of yips and yaps brought two faces to the windows. Upstairs, between a parting of white curtains, April's face appeared. At precisely the same position in the window below it, her mother's head came into view.

The man spoke in Chinese to the dog, but he didn't turn his head as Mike advanced up the path toward the house. This ignoring of him forced Mike to speak first.

"Morning, sir," he said. "I'm Mike Sanchez."

"Know who you are." Now the man turned his head to look at him. On display between big teeth was suspended a slender gold toothpick. "Sergeant."

"Yes, sir." Mike was wearing cowboy boots and the leather jacket that made him look like a drug dealer. He'd combed his hair four or five times, trimmed his mustache, splashed his body with cologne, and gargled with Scope. "Very nice to meet you," he offered.

Woo's father shifted the toothpick to one side of his mouth and elaborately sniffed at Mike's collection of strong odors. He himself smelled of shirt starch, garlic, and cigarettes. "Not here, went out."

"Ahh . . . April?"

No, she hadn't. She was in the house, now on the first floor conversing with her mother in Chinese, probably caught on the way out. It sounded as if the two women were in something of a dispute. In fact, if Mike had to interpret their noises, he'd have to conclude they were screaming at each other.

The dog became more excited, jumped up on him. Mike leaned over to pet it. "Hi, guy, uh, girl."

"Dmsm!" Woo's father barked.

"Ah, excuse me?"

"Dog name Dmsm."

"Yes, April told me that. She's very cute. The dog, that is." Mike patted the dog, then straightened up as the front door swung open.

April came out in jeans and a sweatshirt. She didn't look happy to see him.

He gave her a big smile. "April, you came back."

She clashed eyes with her father. Ja Fo Woo coughed and spit into a patch of lilies. After a brief, awkward silence, April mumbled, "This is my father . . . Sergeant Sanchez." End of introduction.

"We've already met," Mike replied.

Two seconds later, April's mother appeared at the door. Sai Woo wore a brown Chinese dress and a blue padded jacket. Her hair was black as shoe polish, tightly curled all over her head. Her body was as thin as the toothpick still on steady exhibit in her husband's mouth.

She glanced at April and snapped out something in Chinese.

"And this is my mother," April said dutifully. "Sergeant Sanchez."

Sai Woo looked him over, frowned a little at the leather jacket. "Why Sergeant? Why not Captain?" she demanded. She, too, sniffed the air around him, trying to get the hang of it.

"Mom!" April protested.

"You not pass test?" Sai demanded.

Mike scuffed a boot on the sidewalk sheepishly, like a kid confronted by an important teacher who was hoping to stick him with a *D.* "Ahh, I didn't take the test," he admitted.

"Mebbe next time take test. Betta for you."

"Maybe I will. Thank you for thinking of it," Mike muttered.

"Think of everything."

"Good. That's good." He nodded at how good thinking was.

"Well, thanks for dropping by." April jerked her head at Mike and headed down the walk toward his car.

"Where go?"

"Just over there to the car, Mom. Mike has to go."

"Dmsm!" Sai said sharply.

"What?"

Sai pointed at the dog.

"Oh, and this is *Dim Sum,*" April said, enunciating carefully. "Remember Dim Sum, Mike?"

"Yes, I do. She seems very happy here." He was breathing a little easier now that his rank in the Department was no longer an issue, patted the dog that jumped up on his leg again.

"Velly rucky dog." Sai made a strange noise. Instantly the little dog let go of Mike's leg and sat, cocking its head to one side for praise.

"Wow, it sat. I'm impressed. Good *girl,* Dim Sum."

"Say good-bye, Mike."

Figuring he'd accomplished his goal, Mike took a few seconds to say his good-byes and admire the tiny yard.

"They talked to me," he said triumphantly when he joined her. "I was kind of worried, but it went great. What do you think?"

"Well, they may have talked to you," April conceded. "But don't get any ideas that they *like* you. They don't like you. What's up?"

"They have someone better in mind? Huh?"

"What's up, Mike?" April tapped her foot irritably, one eye on her parents, both dead silent by the front door, watching them.

Mike waved at them. "Next time they'll ask me in."

"Trust me, they will *never* ask you in."

"What makes you so sure, *querida*?"

"You smell too sweet for a man."

He stared at them, smiling affably. They did not smile back. "That's pretty bigoted."

"Well, they have their own ideas about things. What are you doing here anyway?"

He shrugged and turned to her. She sounded annoyed but was leaning against his car with a smile that lit up her face and cut right through him.

"I was in the neighborhood and thought I'd stop by and—" He shrugged. "You know, meet the family."

"Well, you met the family. Happy now?"

He nodded. "Now maybe you'd like to come with me to check out this place I'm supposed to look at."

The smile vanished. "Oh, come on, Mike. I can't go looking at apartments with you." April shook her head. "I already told you. You *know* I can't do that."

"It's a house."

"Oh, yeah? Aren't you in the wrong borough?"

"It's nice in Queens. I like it here. Come on, get in. It'll only take a few minutes." He opened the passenger door for her. "I need some expert advice. Come on, you know I'd do the same for you."

April glanced at her parents, then down at her jeans and sneakers. It was about 9:20. They didn't have to be at work until four. Mike smiled and tried to keep his mustache from quivering.

"Damn you," she muttered. Then, after a second, she screamed something out in Chinese, shattering his eardrums.

"What did you say?" He banged the side of his head to stop the ringing.

"I told them there's been a triple homicide and I'll be back in an hour."

"Good thinking, *querida.* But a triple homicide will take a lot more time to clean up than an hour."

"True. I better get my bag." April ran up the walk and into the house. The dog and her mother followed her, slamming the door. Two minutes later April was back with red lipstick on her lips and the handbag slung over her shoulder. By then her father had resumed his pruning.

thirty-two

Harold Dickey had until Monday morning to clear up this problem of Clara's, and not a second longer. That meant he had two days—Saturday and Sunday—to sort through the hospital dirt. Dickey had been surprised that little Gunn Tram, who had always been so eager to be helpful whenever he needed information, suddenly got quiet when he asked about dissatisfied employees. After three decades of knowing every kink, every whisper of discontent from everyone on the payroll, Gunn suddenly could think of no one who had a problem of any kind with the Centre.

"Why are you asking?" she wanted to know.

"Because there's some mischief going on, and I intend to find out who's behind it. Have any ideas, Gunn?"

She shook her head so hard her double chins wobbled. "No, no idea. I haven't heard a thing."

Later, she actually claimed not to remember the tragic case the year before when a male nurse had given the wrong medication to a new inpatient and the patient had jumped off a terrace, impaling himself on the fence around a terrace several floors below. Harold remembered how angry the nurse had been when he was fired. His name was Bobbie something, and he'd been working at the Centre for many years. He claimed he'd been framed.

When Harold asked Gunn whatever happened to Bobbie, Gunn was almost hostile. "How should I know?" she replied angrily.

How indeed? The same way Gunn knew everything else. She was constantly asking questions and following up. She claimed it was her job to know things. She certainly must have known that Harold had had more than one run-in with Bobbie before the tragedy, when the Centre had had no choice but to terminate the man's employment. Bobbie had a problem with authority, and probably with women, too. It was easy to imagine Bobbie harassing Clara. And Gunn didn't want to hand over Bobbie's file. To Harold, that was significant.

"Why won't you leave him alone? He's not even here anymore," Gunn told Dickey. "How could he be the one you're looking for?"

"All the same, Gunn . . ." Harold gave her a sharp look, and she quickly produced what he wanted.

On Saturday, Harold left Westchester before nine and was in his office on the nineteenth floor of the Centre by 9:45. He was fueled by the need to spare Clara the tremendous damage to herself that would result in her trying to force him out. Clara had made many mistakes. Harold knew he was loved and revered at the Centre, and Clara was not. If she foolishly tried to create bad feelings about him, there'd be a backlash. Clara would be the one to fall down like a house of cards, like a sun-dried sand castle hit by a tiny wave on the beach. He could not allow his own protégée to make a fool of herself and polarize the Centre in this way.

Harold carried up coffee from the cafeteria and began concentrating on the histories in the files Gunn had given him. There were so many incidents and problems with staff, every single one documented. The files he had collected contained case accidents of varying degrees of seriousness. And Harold's committee had investigated every one.

Emily, a seventeen-year-old affective-schizophrenic girl on a locked ward with a special precaution re: sharps, had been confused with another female locked in for a food disorder. Emily asked for a razor to shave her legs, was allowed one by a nurse who thought she needed only arm's-length supervision, then failed to provide that. The nurse went to the bathroom. Emily slashed her own arms and legs in a dozen places, started screaming, then attacked the orderly who heard her screams and tried to take the razor away.

Patrick, a thirty-eight-year-old paranoid epileptic male, had been put in restraints with the special precaution of checking vital signs every fifteen minutes. The man had a seizure and suffered brain damage during the twelve-hour period when no one had checked on him.

Martha, a sixty-five-year-old depressed woman on a weekend pass, was delivered by a nurse to the wrong house. The disoriented patient didn't know where she lived and the nurse's error was discovered only when the woman's family called to find out why she was three hours late.

An adolescent male recovering from a psychotic episode was given an "arm's-length" pass to buy a pair of shoes and get a Big Mac. The aide taking him out stopped at a newsstand to look at the sports headlines in the *Daily News.* Believing he was invisible, the boy walked out into oncoming traffic and was struck by a bus.

There were also cases of elopements—patients walking off locked wards and disappearing for days at a time, or forever. Patients getting off their floors and wandering around the hospital wreaking one kind of havoc or another. Nurses who didn't show up, or who showed up and did the wrong thing. There were a lot of cases of screwups, many, many cases of poor judgment where self-destructive patients had opportunities to harm themselves or others.

As Harold reviewed case after case, the pain slowly receded from his head and chest. He could not allow Clara's vicious attack of Friday morning to defeat him. He would not let it hurt him. He had no doubt that Clara would love him again, as she had loved him before—as soon as he uncovered the true culprit of everything she now blamed him for, all those evil pranks. He had no doubt of it.

All he had to do was find the rotten egg. Harold knew it could not be a member of the faculty or a senior administrator. At that level they were all too well screened for this kind of disorder. If it was not one of them, it had to be somebody who had access to the keys, someone who could wander around on all of the floors without attracting notice. It was somebody from the inside, but not one of *them*. He would find the person, was in control again.

All Saturday he felt better. To further assert his control, he took the bottle of Johnnie Walker out of his desk drawer and set it out where he could see it. He would not drink a drop until he had solved his problem and restored order to his life. The bottle was half full. That perplexed him. He remembered a nearly full bottle, with maybe an ounce missing at most. He drank a bottle a week in his office. Not a drop more. He was certain he'd replaced a full bottle on Friday morning, had only the tiniest sip on Friday afternoon. Yes, he was certain of it. He hadn't felt well on Friday, didn't want to drink.

From time to time he glanced at the bottle. Was he kidding himself about his consumption? He badly wanted a drink, particularly by late afternoon, when he was used to having one. He put it off and put it off, telling himself he was in control. He didn't find what he was looking for in the files.

By Sunday he'd thrust them aside and opened his own files in the computer. It was there in his computer that he found his graphic notes on Bobbie—Bobbie Boudreau—and remembered the kinds of stunts the male nurse had pulled before they were finally forced to fire him. There was no question in Harold's mind. Bobbie was Clara's harasser.

The first thing Harold did was to leave a message for Clara. The second thing he did was have a celebratory drink while he waited for Clara to return from wherever she was and call him back.

thirty-three

On Sunday Clara caught the nonstop noon flight from Sarasota to Newark. She was back in her apartment by four, clearheaded and confident. She hit the play button on her answering machine and heard Harold's voice.

"Darling, it's Sunday around two o'clock. I'm in my office. I've got the solution to your little problem, so please give me a call and let me know what time you'll be here."

Clara shook her head and erased the message. The next one was Harold again, more urgent this time.

"Clara, darling." Pause. *"True love, great love, can always be renewed no matter how long the break. It can be refreshed, nourished, made to bloom again. You know no man has ever been for you what I am. Maybe you thought you could love another man, but you can't, not after me."* His voice was the teacher's voice, persuasive, urgent.

"Our love was the model that could never be duplicated. All the others are failures. Only our love and what we accomplished together have endured, Clara. The older and wiser I become, the more I understand how deep and persistent our connection is. Darling, my heart is full of you. I have the answer. Hurry! Hurry."

For a moment Clara was puzzled, then she punched the button and listened to the message again. Between the first and the second time he had called, Harold had lost his anchor to reality and spun out into space. All semblance of normalcy had vanished. Here was the proof she'd needed. The last two incidents were truly disorganizing acts, probably as disorganizing for Harold as a second or third murder would be to a serial killer. He was hanging himself. With some satisfaction, she pushed the button to hear the next message.

"Clara, our love is still here, whole and unsullied, as we used to talk of it. Remember? How the passionate merger of man and woman puts them in touch with all the beauty and nobility of the world? The history of art, the paintings, the statues, the poetry? Both partners flooded, in touch with it all. A transcending experience that can never, ever be erased. The merger of body and soul is always there, and the feelings can be recovered at any time. In a glance, in a touch, in a kiss. Only mistrust, only suspicion can destroy it. Clara, I'm waiting for you. I have the answer."

Clara closed her eyes as the fourth message played. *"I have been waiting for you all weekend! Carmen, you filthy slut. You accused the wrong man. I spent my whole weekend working for you, and you're not here . . . you selfish bitch . . . The guilty man is that nurse we had all the trouble with last year, that Boudreau. You've gone over the line with this, Clara. I warn you, I'm not putting up with it any longer."*

Boudreau . . . Hal was blaming Boudreau, that crazy nurse who'd overdosed a patient last year? Clara sat on the edge of her bed, trying to think. Could she have been wrong about this all along? Could she possibly have made a fatal mistake? She punched out Arch's number, first in Sarasota, then in Washington. He wasn't in either place. Then she went into the bathroom and threw up the sandwich she'd eaten on the plane, peered at herself in the mirror, shaking her head at the attractive, dark-haired woman she saw reflected there. She'd come so far from the ugly duckling she'd been. Poor, fatherless, without any resources beyond her own intelligence and will. Tears stung her eyes.

"Why? Why me?" she asked her reflection plaintively. "What have I done to deserve this?" She suddenly felt old, vulnerable. She should be the reigning queen now, a woman in her prime, not a victim plagued by an elderly, obsessed former lover. The irony was more bitter still, since it was Harold all those years ago who had refused to marry her. She had wanted him even though he was almost fifteen years older than she and not by any means the most powerful man in their world. But Harold hadn't wanted to divorce his wife after so many years. He refused to bear the stigma of disloyalty.

He was the one who told her "all things must end" when she finished her residency and wanted to stay on at the Centre. He even set up a new post for her far away and sent her off. *They* hadn't agreed to end it. He hadn't wanted the scandal of a permanent relationship, so *he* had ended it. Clara had been analyzed for many years while she was in training. She knew that her father's abandonment of her and her mother had made it hard for her to trust any man. But it was her experience with Harold that had shaped all her other relationships with men. Clara's defeat with Harold had never been analyzed. Harold had taken advantage of his position and used her. And now he was muddying the waters, confusing the truth, again.

Clara decided if she'd made a mistake and accused the wrong man, she could not blame herself. It would be a perfectly reasonable error, stemming directly from Hal's betrayal of her trust years ago, and his attempt to carry that treachery forward into the present as if she were still a defenseless resident, his adoring pupil. It was intolerable. Without changing from the khaki trousers and cashmere jacket she'd traveled home in, Clara tucked a clean handkerchief in her breast pocket, picked up her purse, and went to meet Harold in his office.

She heard his voice the moment she got off the elevator.

"I told you. I told you. You're supposed to listen to me, and you didn't listen. Why didn't you listen to me? We could have avoided all these . . . people descending on us."

Clara stopped to listen. Her footsteps clacking on the stone floor suddenly went silent.

"They're going to know, and I'm not going to keep it a secret. You think this is a secret. Well, this is no secret. They know. They know all about us."

Harold's voice was both conspiratorial and threatening, but he was making no effort to keep it down. That was significant because people were careful there, even on Sundays. No one liked his paranoia to show. Clara approached like a hunter now, silent and wary.

The doctors' academic offices were lined up, one after another, on the nineteenth floor. Up here there were no waiting rooms or secretarial areas. Just doors that opened into identical, unremarkable rooms all dominated by large institutional radiators that always seemed to work in opposition to the season. Today it was chilly in the building, but there was no sound of any of them clanking now. All the other doors on the hall were closed. For a second it was quiet. Clara picked up her pace.

"Clara, show yourself! I know you're there."

She pushed open the door.

"Aaahh." Harold gave a little cry and lunged behind his desk. "Clara!"

"Hi," she said softly, halting in the doorway. "What's up?"

He raised his hands to protect his body, cowered behind his desk, gaping at her with wild eyes. "What are you doing here?" he cried.

"You called, Harold. What's going on?"

She took in the room without turning her head. Harold was alone, surrounded by dozens of files. The files were scattered all over the desk and piled on the floor. His laptop computer was in the middle of his desk, half covered by files. The computer screen was blank, but the printer light was on.

"That's right, I did. Clara," he said sternly, suddenly moving out from behind his desk. His hand came up, finger pointed at her in a characteristic lecturing gesture. "The file has disappeared, but the answer is in here." He pointed at the computer.

"In here," he continued. "I told you not to ignore this, and you didn't listen to me. Now they're going to come down . . . on us." He put his finger to his lips, looking toward the door fearfully. "They're going to . . ." He came out from behind his desk, picking a path through the papers on the floor.

"Who?" Clara asked calmly.

Harold's head jerked toward the door. "Were you followed?" he demanded shrilly.

"What?"

"Did someone follow you?"

She didn't think so. Not today. "Why would someone follow me?" she asked.

"Did someone follow you here? Answer me. I'm asking a question."

"No." Coolly, she watched Harold slowly hang himself.

He was dressed as usual. He wore gray flannel slacks. His sports jacket hung on the back of his swivel chair. He wasn't wearing a tie, and the collar of his blue dress shirt was open, the sleeves unevenly rolled on his arms. But his white fringe of hair stuck straight up and his eyes were wild.

Clara's eyes moved back to his desk. On the wooden extension pulled out halfway sat a quart bottle of Johnnie Walker Black Label with a nearly empty glass beside it. The top was off the bottle and only about half an inch of the rich golden-brown liquid remained. Harold must have been drinking all afternoon.

"Oh, God!" He started screaming. He stared at the wall, shuddering and gasping. "Ahhhhhh. Oh, God. Ahhhhhh. Bugs. Ooooh. Bugs . . . eeeeee. Running up and down the wall . . . Eeeeee. Clara!!!! You brought bugs in here," he cried. "You brought the bugs."

"What bugs?" She twisted around to look at the wall where he pointed. There were the usual diplomas, awards, museum poster. Harold lurched toward her accusingly.

Clara held out her hand to stop him. "There aren't any bugs in here, Hal," she said evenly. "No recording devices. No crawlies. No FBI, no CIA coming after us. It's just us kids. Calm down, Hal. We're going to be just fine."

He stopped, stood still, and for a moment struggled to haul himself back into lucidity. "I'm . . . sorry, Clara . . . I don't know what's the matter with me." He shook his head, as if to push the crawlies out. "It must . . . be the summer heat."

"Hal, it's November. It's cool."

"That's right. August. Don't worry. I'm all right now." He raised his teaching finger, trembling all over, swaying on his feet. His face flushed cherry red.

"Hal—?"

The red in Harold's face darkened to purple. His body hurled backward, hitting the corner of his desk, knocking over a pile of files, and sending their contents in all directions as he fell heavily by the feet of his analyst's couch. He landed on his side, hitting his head with a sickening thud.

"Oh!" Surprised, Clara lunged toward him just as his back arched unnaturally and his legs started kicking out at the scattered papers. As he began writhing on the floor, she scrambled for the phone on his desk.

"This is Dr. Treadwell in 1917. I have an MI. Call the code. Nineteenth floor, room 17. Call the code!" she screamed. Then she slammed down the receiver and sank to her knees.

Hal's sphincters had let go, releasing the contents of his bowel and bladder. Foul foam-flecked vomit trickled everywhere. On the rug, on the papers, on her pants.

"Life is wet," Hal always used to say, laughing at how surprised, year after year, his students were to find out how messy every aspect of human existence was. "Love is wet. Life is wet. Death is, too."

"Oh, God, Hal." She began to work on him. He was still now, cyanotic.

She rolled him onto his back, opening his mouth and sticking her fingers in it to clear away the vomit and mucus. He was apneic, had stopped breathing. She struck his chest with both fists together, wiped his face and mouth with the handkerchief she'd snatched from her jacket pocket.

"Come on, get going." It was all automatic. She struck him again, then put her mouth to his. Struck him again and again, breathed into his foul mouth.

Two pants to fill his lungs and one strike to the chest. She didn't hear people running down the hall, rolling the gurney. *Breathe. Breathe. Strike.*

Guards tumbled into the room, trampling the files.

"Oh, shit, it's Dr. Dickey."

"Heart attack?"

Breathe. Breathe. Strike. Clara didn't answer. She made a motion with her hand and one of the guards took over the chest massage as the other brought the gurney as far into the room as it would go. Together they lifted him, continued to administer CPR.

Within seconds, the gurney was out in the hall and three paramedics from the main hospital building down the street ran toward them, pushing the crash cart from the closet on the end of the floor. Wordlessly, a young man with a ponytail found a vein in Harold's wrist and shoved the IV needle into him, so he could start a drip. Another opened Harold's mouth and inserted a short oral airway attached to a breathing bag.

The third set the defibrillator machine. He looked to Clara. "Juice him?"

Clara nodded.

He ripped open Harold's shirt, squirting contact jelly on the two steel paddles. He placed them under Harold's left arm and on his chest, looked to Clara again. Again she nodded.

"Get back, everyone," the paramedic said, and hit the buttons on the paddles.

Harold's arms shot up, fell down, and suddenly they were all running to the elevator as his chest heaved.

"Here, I got it. Move aside, please."

Silently they piled in. Gurney, guards, paramedics, Clara.

"Jesus. Who's that?" a white-suited aide said.

"Oh, my God. It's Dr. Dickey." A fat nurse cradling her take-out coffee and doughnuts started to cry, dribbling coffee down her pink angora sweater. "Oh, no, is he dead?"

"Shut up."

"Who said that? Who told me to shut up?"

The paramedic with a ponytail and two earrings that Clara hadn't noticed before shot the sobbing nurse a furious look, then went on with his work.

"Shit, don't stop," Clara cried as the doors slid open on the wrong floor.

"Sorry, Doctor."

The doors closed on the appalling stink. Everyone was panting, sweating. Someone swore softly. The patient wasn't responding. They couldn't shock him with the paddles again in this tiny, crowded space with no electricity. Clara's head pounded.

Finally they were at the front doors, rolling down a ramp out on the street. Then they were running with the gurney and the IV dripping an anti-arrhythmia drug, the breathing bag pumped by a paramedic. It was a block and a half to the emergency room. Traffic clogged the street around the ER entrance. None of it was going well. Everyone knew it. Harold wasn't coming around. They were silent, running, gasping.

Suddenly a car careened through the changing light at the corner and the gurney tipped off the curb as they frantically tried to stop it from rolling onto the street into the oncoming car.

"Oh, Christ, hang on."

Two paramedics held the patient as two pedestrians ran up to help the third right the gurney and get it going again. "Oh, man. Did you see that? Guy just kept going."

Through ER, they moved into a back treatment room and continued working. Clara silently watched procedures she'd seen a hundred times. The airway removed, Hal's mouth opened again, illuminated by a laryngoscope, a clear plastic tube was slid down into his trachea, then attached to a black ambu bag so that oxygen could be pumped into his lungs. Six, seven people were working on him now. He was hooked up to a respirator, an electrocardiogram. Adrenalin was shot directly into his heart. Clara stood back as they worked for the full required hour, trying desperately to resuscitate a man she knew had been dead almost from the moment he hit the floor.

Hal's internist finally strode in. He'd been called from a tennis game and was wearing a black warm-up suit. He was tall and young and fit, and seemed surprised to be there.

"Jesus, smells like someone's been hitting the bottle pretty bad," he said, even before he looked at the flat line on the EKG or picked up the chart.

"Yeah, the patient."

Dr. Chatman turned to Clara. "You're Dr. Treadwell?"

"Yes." She put out her hand and he shook it.

"Ivan Chatman. You were with him?"

She nodded.

"What happened?"

"He was in his office, pretty upset, I guess. He'd been drinking. He called me at home. I came over to check on him and almost the moment I arrived, he keeled over."

The young internist frowned. "I checked him out only a few weeks ago. He was in excellent condition—"

"A man over sixty, you never know," Clara said.

"I was fond of him." The internist shook his head and pronounced Harold Dickey dead. The machines were turned off.

The ER cardiologist turned to Dr. Chatman. "Ivan, we'd like permission to do an autopsy."

Chatman nodded. "Sure, I'll call his wife. I don't think it'll be a problem. She's a former nurse."

The oxygen mask was off the dead man's face now. The EKG and other machines were unhooked. The IV bag was detached, but the needle was still stuck in his hand with some tubing hanging from it. They had left it in him because they wouldn't be using it again. He was blue, his hands already slightly clawed. All the efforts to save him made him look as if he had been beaten to death.

"Problem?" The cardiologist watched Chatman.

Chatman moved to stand by the dead man's head. "I don't know," he murmured. "This doesn't feel right to me."

"Oh, for heaven's sake," Clara said.

"I knew him pretty well. He didn't take narcotics or any medication that I know of. He was fit as a horse. . . ." He frowned, then turned away from the body. "Oh, well."

"You want to run the toxes?" the ER cardiologist asked. "You never know. If there's a question later, I don't want any problems on this end."

"Yeah, okay. I'll speak to his wife. If she gives the okay, then go for it," Chatman said.

"Any ideas what we might be looking for?"

"Oh, for heaven's sake," Clara muttered again. "The man had a heart attack. This is absurd."

Chatman looked at the cardiologist, then shook his head. "I can't imagine him taking anything." He reached out and pulled a sheet over the dead man's face.

Clara stalked out. They were going to run toxes on Hal. She didn't want to hear Chatman's side of the conversation with Sally Ann, Harold's wax-museum figure of a wife. Or anything else, for that matter. Suddenly she was uneasy, deeply uneasy. Her mouth was dry and had a sour taste. Her whole body ached, smelled of sweat, vomit, and Hal's Johnnie Walker.

She remembered Hal's door had been left open. She had to go back to the Centre and secure his office. She didn't want to go through the front doors and answer a lot of questions. She thought about the questions and how she would answer them. Her head was down; her eyes were on her feet. She felt numb, queasy, didn't want to go back to the Centre. Had to. When she lifted her head, she was horrified to see the man Harold had mentioned in his message. Bobbie Boudreau was leaning against a tree across the street, smoking a cigarette, looking the other way. Clara had seen him many times on the locked ward, where he had been a nurse. She recognized him immediately.

thirty-four

"Aeiiiiii!" Sai Woo stood in the doorway of her daughter's apartment, screaming. The sound was shrill and piercing like the radio signal for disaster.

Startled, April swung around to face her, the dangerous new Glock 9mm automatic that could fire off sixteen rounds without reloading still level in her hand.

Skinny Dragon Mother clapped both hands to her head. "I mother," she shrieked. "No kirr me."

Disgusted, April lowered the gun. "Maaa, haven't you ever heard of knocking? I could have shot you."

"Go ahead, shoot me. I dead awleady." Sai's screams brought Dim Sum scampering up the stairs. When the dog saw her mistress, she crouched like a panther and jumped several feet straight up into Sai's arms, trembling all over.

"Oh, come on, Ma, give me a break."

"Rook," Sai said accusingly, "you scare *ying'er.*"

"Ma, I hate to tell you this. That thing is not a baby, it's a dog."

"Onny baby I eva see," Sai muttered angrily, hugging the puppy to her chest. "You no have baby. *Boo hao, ni.*"

"Oh, come on, Ma, don't start that." April swung around and put the gun on the table beside the couch in her living room, then hunkered down to unstrap the weights on her ankles.

She'd been exercising with the gun and the weights, trying to keep her forearms strong and develop some perceivable curvature in her butt. The last thing she needed at the moment was Chinese torture. Skinny Dragon Mother seemed to have other ideas.

"What kind dautta prays with gun?" She answered her own question. "Long kind dautta. *Boo hao* dautta. You hear me, *ni*? No good dautta."

Her mother sounded ready for a good long fight. Never mind that they lived in a free country, never mind that her U.S. citizenship papers said she was American now. Skinny Dragon Mother was old, old Chinese to the core. She believed giving birth to April made April hers forever. She also believed the path to heaven was paved with abuse and terror. She had crowded April's dreams with demons and ghosts and monsters so terrible April had to become a cop to defend herself. Out there she felt relatively safe; it was at home that she couldn't defend herself against the breaking and entering of her own mother.

This had not been the deal she had struck with her parents when they bought the house. The deal was April had the top floor, it was hers and she was supposed to be able to live as she wanted, come and go as she pleased. That was the deal. But not for a single day had it worked out that way. Although the second floor had a door and a lock, the two apartments shared the downstairs front door and front hallway. Sai not only knew the exact timing of her worm daughter's coming and going, she also had a key to worm daughter's apartment and dropped in whenever she felt like it. Now, as she studied April's living room with an expression of extreme disapproval on her suspicious, Skinny Dragon Mother face, she dangled the keys she had used to get in.

"I thought you had a date," she said in Chinese. "I came to help you get dressed."

April was clearly not getting dressed for a date. She was sweating freely in a ratty Police Academy tee shirt and shorts. She did not look her mother in the face as she went into the kitchen for some water.

"It was canceled," she answered in English.

Her kitchen was decorated with the same pea-green tiles as the bathroom. April had added many open shelves on which her collection of colorful ginger and pickle jars was displayed all the way up to the ceiling. Hung on hooks were two frying pans and two woks, many plastic bags of dried tree ear, dried mushrooms, dried lichees, tiny dried shrimp, gingko nuts, pickled radishes, and a dozen other items, all gifts from her father. Her collection of boning, hacking, carving, and chopping knives (and cleaver) was stuck on a magnet rack by the side of the door. They were the old-fashioned kind that rusted if they were not properly dried after each washing and had to be sharpened endlessly. These staining steel knives, too, were a gift from her father. April had known how to use her father's set by the time she was seven.

"Cancered? Why cancered?" her mother demanded.

April's favorite glass was sitting in the sink. It had the characters Good Luck and Long Life painted on the side. They were two of the five blessings the Chinese prayed for most. April filled the glass with tap water and swallowed half of it down. Please give me some good luck, she prayed silently.

"Ma, these things happen," she told Sai.

Grimacing at the decadent plushness of it, Sai sank into the soft pink satin sofa April had bought for even less than half price in Little Italy. The sofa was opposite two windows that looked out over the backyard, where the garden, invisible in the dark, was already mulched for the winter. It was around six in the evening.

"What happened? He no rike no more?"

April swigged down the rest of the water. In front of the sofa were two good-size Chinese stools that also served as tables. She sat on one. Her mother was talking about George Dong, her great Chinese Doctor hope for a son-in-law. And the probrem wasn't he no rike her. Probrem was she no rike him. April shrugged guiltily. It wasn't something she could easily explain.

"Ma. He wanted me to meet him in Chinatown."

"So?"

"So, it makes me lose face. He should pick me up. He should come here." She put the glass down on the other table.

Sai thought it over. Since when was her daughter so correct, her face said. *"Na bú shi gùyi de,"* she said finally.

"Well, I'm not so sure it's not an intentional thing," April said slowly. "You stick up for him without even knowing whether it's intentional or not. If he likes me, he should want to meet my parents." Touché.

Dead silence for a long time.

Ha, got her. April suppressed a smile. There was nothing her mother could say to that. She had drawn blood on the first parry and her mother was stopped cold. Should have been a Japanese samurai.

Finally, Skinny Dragon Mother's eyes narrowed to nothingness, and a clicking sound began at the back of her throat. This was a sound of pure rage that indicated soon Sai would spit out her true reason for being there.

"Why go to Mei Mei Chen?" Her voice got so cold and angry, the dog growled.

"Huh?" April was taken aback.

"You hear me, *ni*."

"Oh, that, that's nothing."

"No nothing. Sunsing."

April sighed.

"Terr."

April sighed again. She couldn't get out of it, had to tell. Damn Judy. "It's nothing, Ma. You know Sergeant Sanchez who was here yesterday."

"I know."

"He said you are very beautiful, Ma. He wants to take your advice."

Sai made another noise, something like a grunt that said "So?"

"So, he's looking for a better place to live. He couldn't find what he wanted, so I put him in touch with Judy."

"Hmmmmph. I cousin with Judy mother."

"I know that, Ma."

"Judy terr mother. Judy mother call me."

April shrugged. "So?"

"So she say mebbe you no mellee George. Mellee Spanish."

Furious, April scooped up the glass and headed for the kitchen for a refill. "Ma, Judy is a real estate agent. She finds places for people. I gave her some business. That's the beginning and end of the story."

"No berieve. Yestidday, no rook for monkey business with Spanish, have date with docta. Today monkey business with Spanish, no date with docta. *Boo hao ni.*"

April thought she was pretty no good herself. She came back to the living room, the blood hot in her face. "Don't call him Spanish. His name is Mike."

"He no Spanish?"

"He's American, like me."

"You Chinese."

"We're both American, Ma. Both our fathers cooked in restaurants for a living. We're both cops. Just the same."

"Cook Chinese?"

"Mike's father? No, Ma."

"Cook what?"

"Mexican," April admitted reluctantly.

"Ha," Sai said.

"Ha, what?" April demanded. She was furious at the way her mother sat on the beautiful pink sofa in her black pants and padded black jacket just like a mean old peasant woman about to deliver a curse. She wasn't going to choose a man to please her mother. It wasn't love. And it *wasn't* the American way.

"Ha Spanish," Sai said, triumphant. "He Spanish."

"Ethnically, Ma, he may be Spanish. He may even have some Indian in him."

"Aeiiiii. Indian?" Now Sai was really upset.

"Mayan Indian. They lived in Mexico thousands of years ago, intermarried with the Spanish. I think they drank the blood of their enemies."

"Aeiiiiiii." Worse and worse.

"They cut out their hearts, and they have ghosts, just as old as Chinese ghosts. You don't want to mess with these ghosts, you hear me? They're a mean set of ghosts. And you know what else? These people may *still* drink the blood of their enemies. So call him Mike, Ma, and treat him with the respect he deserves."

Sai glared at the gun, then away. April could see that her mother was fighting the urge to say something truly terrible, but for once she didn't dare. Watching the wrinkles in Sai's face close in around her rage, April realized that Skinny Dragon Mother was actually afraid of Mike Sanchez. She was afraid to say anything bad about him and push April into liking him even more. The thought that her mother was afraid of a friend of hers cheered April up quite a bit. "Come on, Ma. I'll get you some dinner," she offered. "You want to try some take-out chicken mole?"

thirty-five

Jason sat on the bed in his shorts and tee shirt, the Raymond Cowles file open on his knees. It was thick and quite detailed, and he wasn't much further along in it than he'd been when he set it aside to make love to Emma seven hours earlier. Since then they'd done a lot of talking. They'd had dinner, talked some more. Then she'd gone for a run on her treadmill in the tiny room behind the kitchen. Now he felt her eyes on him as she padded into the bedroom.

He looked up from the page he'd read four times. "Hi."

"Hi yourself." Her shorts and the white cropped shirt that showed half her abdomen were wet.

Emma had a beautiful body that Jason had never been able to resist, no matter how hurt or angry he was with her. Her hair was blonder now, short. She had real movie-star hair and a real movie-star body—not too thin. Her face could be anything. Now it was a little tense. She shook her hair out as he watched her. She'd had all day to run and finally gotten to it after dinner and half a bottle of wine. He didn't know how she could do it.

She spread out the towel on the floor, sat on it, and starting doing sit-ups. He figured she'd throw up soon, must be scared to death.

"What time is your audition?" he asked, watching her crunch and grimace.

"Really early," she grunted.

"How early is really?"

Grunt. "Eleven-thirty."

He laughed. For him, by eleven-thirty half the day was over. She had twelve hours to prepare. "Nervous?"

Grunt. "Always."

"You really want to do a play, the same thing over and over every night—and twice on Wednesday and Saturday?"

"You do the same thing over and over, with the same people year after year. Don't you get tired of it?"

"Mmmm, no."

"So, it's a night job instead of a day job. Might be fun for six months. Then I'll do another film."

Jason felt a chill and shivered. Six months. His wife planned on being around only six months. Thanks for letting me know, he didn't say. What did she think, that she could just come and go in the marriage without consulting him? What was he, a piece of furniture? His brows came together in a single angry line. Passivity wasn't exactly easy for him. A part of him wanted to throw the baggage out, let her have her brilliant career on her own. Fine.

Emma stopped midcrunch, staring at the fringe on the bedspread.

Fine. He could live without her. There were lots of women in the sea. He'd find another. His jaw set.

"What?" she murmured.

"What yourself?"

"You know, I've been thinking. How would you like a different look in here?"

He looked around at the cream-colored walls and tasteful prints, the teal bedspread and chair, the many coordinating pillows. "Why?"

"I don't know. Maybe it's time for a change."

"Humph." Jason went back to the file. He'd never really liked the strange blue-green bedspread and drapes she'd chosen when they married. But he didn't like change. He liked his life the way it had been *before.* He didn't want a new bedspread or a new and different wife. If Emma got the part in this Broadway play, she'd be an even bigger star. If she didn't get the part, she'd go back to California to her pretty rented house on the beach and make stupid movies, leaving him alone in limbo. The whole thing pissed him off.

Jason understood his ambivalence and conflicts about connection, but after all his training and two wives, at almost forty he still wasn't sure what made love sometimes conquer all. Was it a sensory thing that could be regenerated over and over by sight or touch or smell, or was love driven by fantasy, the secret things that happened in a person's head?

"Well, what do you think?" Emma said.

"About what?"

"Never mind." She pointed at the Cowles file he'd been lugging from one room to another all day. "What's the case?"

Jason was still on Intake's descriptive assessment of Raymond Cowles's analyzability. He'd noted in the part on family history that Ray's mother's father had been in and out of psychiatric hospitals for most of his life and had died under suspicious circumstances when Ray was two. Out of a lot of routine information, in the middle of his annoyance with his wife, that piece jumped out at him. It was important because it meant there was a possible history of suicide in Cowles's family. It also meant that his mother might well have experienced a profound depression herself when her father died. The grandfather's cause of death was unclear and was stated in the most perfunctory way in the assessment. No further questions about that seemed to have been asked because there was no elaboration.

The chart read:

> Diagnosis deferred in 20-year-old man with what appears to be a character neurosis and identity confusion. In addition, the patient has repetitive and recurrent ego dystonic homosexual fantasies that he has never acted on. Masturbation fantasies have been homosexual. Patient is likable, highly intelligent, responsible, and intends to stay in the area since he has a job waiting for him, and his fiancée is getting a doctoral degree at the same university. He has limited financial resources.

"Jason?"

"Huh?" Jason looked up. He realized Emma was waiting for an answer to something or other. He dropped the report guiltily.

"Plus ça change." She laughed.

"What does that mean?"

"Nothing, darling. I know. I know. If I want you, I have to take you the way you are."

"And it appears I have to do the same. Is that fair?"

She nodded. "You have your life. I have to have mine."

Is that *fair*? he wanted to whine. Was that the deal? Damn, she was gorgeous. "What'd you ask?" he muttered.

"Nothing. I just asked about the case. I can't know, right?"

"Wrong. I can tell you about this case. A former patient of Clara Treadwell committed suicide last week, and Clara asked me to review the file."

"Oh, my. *The* Clara Treadwell?" Emma pulled off the cropped shirt and the bicycle shorts, rolled them up in the towel for the laundry.

Her nudity was a conversation-stopper in more ways than one. The body was lovely, but around Emma's navel were the broken images of the tattoo started by her abductor. They were just bits of black now, more than half removed by the laser surgery she was having in California. It was no longer possible to decipher what the tattooed picture had been, but Jason had already seen it. The thing that really startled him was how his formerly modest and reserved wife—who used to hang back never wanting to annoy him with too much of herself—was now a bold temptress. He wanted to maintain his equilibrium and not be bowled over by it, but the balance was gone. A renewed surge of enthusiasm for the woman driving him crazy jolted through Jason.

"Very nice," he muttered. "Show off." He cleared his throat, wondering if she wanted more love—just at this moment. And if he was up to it. Yep, his body indicated he was up to it.

But Emma was just kidding. She grabbed a shirt, tugged it over her head, and perched on her side of the bed. No panties. She crossed her legs. Now he was sweating.

"Is this *the* Clara Treadwell, the one who once leaped upon you in Seattle—"

"Ah, it was L.A.," Jason said modestly.

"Wants *you* to review her case? After all the trouble she's made for you at the Centre? Why?"

Jason beamed. "You know. You remember. Darling, you're still jealous."

"And you're still mine," Emma said loftily. "Even with the beard."

He scratched the beard, pleased she was taking it seriously. "Hey, nobody owns anybody, you know that."

"So why did she come to you?"

"Clara? I have asked myself that question." He did not think it wise to say Clara wanted to be his mentor and improve the quality of his life. He smiled at the thought of anyone but Emma succeeding at that.

"What's the story? Is she responsible for this patient's death?"

"This is the question his wife and insurance company might ask a jury to consider."

"Malpractice." She shivered and was silent for a moment, then asked, "Why?"

Jason shrugged. "Money."

"What do *you* think?" Emma lay back against the pillows and considered the ceiling.

Jason shrugged again. "I have no idea. When Clara asked me to look at the file Wednesday, there was some doubt as to the cause of death—they thought it might be a homicide—and because of my ties to the police—"

"Ah. April Woo."

Jason nodded. "April Woo. But now they seem sure it's a suicide."

"So what now?"

The first of many clocks started chiming eleven.

"I missed the clocks," Emma murmured. "I didn't think I would. But it was so quiet at night. Sometimes I thought of getting a grandfather clock." She raised her hands in a helpless gesture. "But you know how they all have to be wound every five minutes . . ."

"I'm glad you came, Em. I missed you, too."

The phone joined in with the *ding-dong*s. Emma frowned. "Your girlfriend?"

"I don't have a girlfriend." He reached for the phone. "Dr. Frank."

"Oh, Jason, I'm so glad you're there. I hope I'm not disturbing you. This is Clara Treadwell."

"Oh, hello, Clara."

"Oh, my," Emma murmured.

"I'm sorry to call so late. But I have some bad news," Clara said.

"Oh?" Jason glanced at his wife. Emma raised an eyebrow.

"Yes. Harold Dickey died this afternoon."

"What?" Jason was stunned. He'd seen Dickey only two days ago at the meeting in Clara's conference room. He'd looked more than healthy then.

"I'm sorry to hear that," Jason said. "He looked so well. It's a shock."

"Yes, well, a man over sixty . . . I thought you should know."

"Thank you for calling. Can you tell me what happened?"

"It was very sudden, very sad." Another long pause. "It happened in his office at the Centre. Massive MI. Now we'll have to look for someone to take over his position."

There it was, the offer of a staff position, coming less than a week after Clara had raised the subject as a vague possibility.

"Thank you for calling me," Jason said again. He wondered what Harold had been doing in his office on a Sunday afternoon. Harold had never worked on Sunday, even in Jason's day. He played tennis on the weekends, was known for it. Everybody knew he liked his booze and his tennis on the weekends. Jason thought about that.

"Of course, you had to know. . . . Jason—?"

"Yes?"

"Um, did you hear from the police about Ray Cowles?"

Jason was surprised. "Yes, late Friday. Didn't they call you?"

"I've been out of town. Well—?"

"They've closed the case as a suicide."

There was a pause. "That's a real disappointment. Well, good night, Jason. We'll be in touch."

Clara hung up before he could say anything else. He put the receiver down thoughtfully.

"What's going on?" Emma asked.

"Harold Dickey died of a heart attack this afternoon."

"That's too bad. I'm sorry." Emma got up, heading for the bathroom, then stopped.

"Ah, are we heading toward a hospital appointment, or have you two"—she wrinkled her perfect nose—"just suddenly gotten very chummy for some reason?"

"God, you women are competitive. Clara's sixteen years older than you."

"And you rejected her once, Jason. Women don't forget things like that. Maybe she hasn't heard your wife is back." Emma disappeared into the bathroom and slammed the door.

Distracted by the memory of something April had once said, Jason scratched his beard. April once told him that in police work it helped always to think dirty because very little in life is really clean. Suddenly, the back of his neck prickled at the recollection of an old rumor about Dickey and Treadwell. Not to mention the possible job materializing almost instantly. He heard the shower come on and Emma begin to vocalize in the steam. Without meaning to, he was beginning to think dirty.

thirty-six

"What kind of car is it, Mr. . . ." April's eyes dropped to the complaint on her desk, but her mind was on the two young women grabbed off the street and raped in empty classrooms at the university on Monday at six P.M. and that morning at ten-thirty.

It was two P.M. on Wednesday, November 10. At three, she had an appointment with Jason Frank, but for the third time this week she didn't think she'd make it. Today she'd just spent two and a half hours in the emergency room with the second rape victim, an exquisite, espresso-colored, nineteen-year-old student from France. Nicole Amendonde had been raped, sodomized, beaten on the head, and bitten on the breasts and inner thighs.

A professor found the young woman naked and bleeding profusely and called for help. In the hospital, however, the girl refused to talk about what happened. She didn't want the police involved, didn't want her parents to know. She was terrified she'd be blamed for the attack and her parents would be angry at her. The hospital called the precinct for a female detective to come to the emergency room to talk to her.

April had encountered this kind of resistance before in Chinatown. She knew how to get Nicole to tell her what happened, and she knew how to persuade the girl to agree to let the ER doctor use the rape kit. Then, as soon as she'd gotten back to the precinct, before she'd even had time to grab a cup of coffee, Sergeant Joyce had sent her this clown.

"Dr. Lobrinsky." The plump, deeply tanned little man sitting by April's desk in a single-breasted camel hair coat buttoned all the way up was convulsed with rage. His yellow toupee, no longer straight on his head, had realigned his part so that now it seemed to originate from the top of one ear. Two tightly compressed fat lips busily worked their tension from one cheek to the other.

Absolutely furious at the perfunctory way he was being treated, the fat man thundered out his name in the crowded squad room as if it had the power to bring his case the deep respect he felt it deserved. No one, however, had ever heard the name, and no one turned a head in his direction.

The week had started badly and was getting worse. Sergeant Joyce had heard the rumor that she was about to be promoted to lieutenant after having made the short list nearly a year ago. That was the (maybe) good news. The bad news was the rumormonger either didn't know or wasn't telling where the assignment would take her. So the good Sergeant was in a state of partially preoccupied hysteria over her future. One just never knew until it happened what a promotion meant. It could just as easily signal the end of a career as the advancement of one. So far the Sergeant had nibbled away all the skin around both thumbnails and begun chewing on the nails themselves.

It didn't help that the neighborhood seemed to be having a rash of car thefts and two young women had been viciously raped with the same MO in a three-day period. Sergeant Joyce had once been in Sex Crimes and demanded a game plan on this even before the second case. The second case occurring that morning in a different building put the perp's cycle of recidivism at three days. Three days for gearing up to this kind of assault was a bad sign. It meant the guy was way out of control and would keep at it until he was stopped. Never mind that the sites he chose were well-peopled or that subconsciously he might want to be caught, the odds of his eluding them were still in his favor. And, of course, at any moment he could always get on a bus or a train and leave town.

In addition, the two victims were black college students and the rapist was white. This added a politically sensitive and potentially explosive element to the case. The Department didn't want another girl hurt. Already powers in the Department had sent word down from above that there would be no time or expense spared on this one.

No time spared on anything else with the exception of the time April had to waste on this Dr. Marcus Lobrinsky, who happened to be some kind of bigwig doctor from the hospital. It was unfortunate for him that his 1992 Mercedes 500SEL, double-parked in front of Zabar's at Eightieth and Broadway, was stolen when he went into the gourmet-food store for his weekly supply of smoked fish and caviar. And it had to happen just when the whole precinct was galvanized on a more pressing matter.

So when he bellowed his name, only April was available to nod respectfully. "Dr. Lobrinsky." As he jabbed a surprisingly slender finger at her, she wondered what kind of doctor he was.

"I want my car back immediately. The car cost me over eighty-five thousand dollars. And that was in '92," he said contentiously.

April pretended to study the complaint. The problem she had here was that Dr. whatever-he-did Lobrinsky had absolutely no chance of getting his car back. Not immediately or ever. It just didn't happen. No one got his car back anymore. Stolen cars weren't lost sheep that wandered home wagging their tails behind them. Neither were they taken for joy rides and abandoned on some quiet side street in Queens or New Jersey, where they sat waiting for recovery by alert police officers a couple of days later. They weren't snatched for resale in their present form, either.

Car theft had become very big business, was an organized-crime thing. Cars were taken for the sum of their parts. Twelve hundred dollars each for the airbags, thousands of dollars more for the radio, the tires, the seats, the bumpers, the wheels, the steel frames, the halogen lights, the muffler, the gas tank—every single part had a value and an outlet. And everybody profited—except maybe the people who lost their rides and the insurance companies who had to shell out for new ones. Dr. Lobrinsky's Mercedes had been gone for only an hour or so, but April had little doubt that it was already stripped to the ground and no longer a car. She sighed.

"I'm going to have to hook you up with Auto Theft," she told the doctor. "I'll give you the name of someone to contact down there."

"Shit," Lobrinsky exploded. "Down where?"

"I think the office is located at One Police Plaza."

"Downtown? Why the hell can't you take care of it up here?"

"Your car is not likely to be in the neighborhood any longer."

"You mean *you* can't take care of it." The look beamed at April was hateful and contemptuous in the extreme. It said that while the police in general might be stupid and inept, she, April Woo, personally had to be the most stupid and inept member of the whole Department. She'd seen it before.

Usually the next question was "Are you a real cop or what?" In this case, April was sitting at her desk in the detective squad room and there could be no doubt as to her status.

Whatever accusation the angry doctor was going to make next, however, was drowned out by an eruption of noise as two large police officers brought someone in. He was wearing a red baseball hat backward, dirty jeans, and a stained One World sweatshirt with holes in it. The guy was white, medium build, maybe an inch shy of six feet. His greasy brown hair hung below the baseball hat to his shoulders. He was held in an upright position by the two cops, seemed to have some fresh scratches on his pasty face, and his eyes gave the impression that his address was some other planet. Then it got quiet.

April strained to pick up the vibes that would tell her what was going on, but Dr. Lobrinsky, sitting in her metal visitor's chair with his expensive coat still buttoned over his chest and his hair on all wrong, was fully focused on his own problem. Completely unaware of the drop in air pressure, the doctor came to a decision. His fist hit the desk and he began to scream.

"I don't have time for this shit! It's not a hard one. Go out and find the fucking car. That's what you're here for. If you can't even locate a 1992 canary-yellow Mercedes—what the fuck are you good for?" His words hit the crowded room like the roar of an Uzi machine gun.

Sergeant Joyce popped out of her office with the speed of a Jack sprung from its box. *Her* yellow hair, only an inch longer than the doctor's, also seemed attached in the wrong place. The crowd of uniforms and detectives moved aside as she advanced toward April's desk. At the moment there were fewer than the usual number of coffee stains on her blouse, but she was frazzled and harried nonetheless. Her look said, Can't you see we're in the middle of something here? Can't you see we're *busy* and don't have time to take this kind of shit from anybody?

Her face also told April that she was deeply rattled by what had happened to those two girls and had changed her mind about wasting time on nasty, arrogant, disgruntled victims of auto theft. She cocked her head at April. *Get into my office.*

April excused herself and headed for Joyce's office. Thirty seconds later Sergeant Joyce stormed in and slammed the door. "I got a call from a path in the M.E.'s office," she announced, collapsing in her desk chair.

April leaned against the windowsill. What passed for heat in the precinct hadn't been turned on yet even though it had been a cold month. The air leaching in around the window frame was truly frigid. Already she could feel her fingers beginning to stiffen. Sergeant Joyce shuffled some papers around on her desk importantly.

"I'm not exactly clear on how this one came about," she muttered, looking for the note she had written to herself. She lifted one shoulder and let it drop as she shifted bits of paper from one untidy pile to another. She couldn't find the scrap she was looking for. "Tox screening of apparent heart attack DOA comes up with drug overdose. Check it out."

April frowned. What? With all that was going on right now? She jerked her thumb back toward the squad room. "What about Lobrinsky?" What about the rapist?

"I told him his yellow bird was a pile of scrap by now and it wasn't productive to talk to people like that."

"What was his response?"

"He went ballistic and his hair fell off." Sergeant Joyce's teeth clicked as she tore a chunk of nail from the top of her thumb. "Then he left."

Well, that wasn't surprising. Sergeant Joyce often had that effect. April changed the subject. "Who's the DOA?"

The Sergeant excavated a piece of lined paper covered with her scrawl. "Ah, here it is. Guess who? Dr. Harold Dickey. Age sixty-eight, apparent good health. No sign of heart disease, no embolism or anything like that. Unusually high blood levels of—*Ami*—" She squinted at her writing. "I don't know what this is, *tripty* something. The file isn't complete yet."

"Harold Dickey?" April frowned. "The shrink in the Cowles case?"

"The very one. Suddenly turns up dead."

"Dickey told me he didn't know Cowles, had never spoken to him," April said. But people lied. Maybe Dickey committed suicide because he had been involved. Would anybody do that in this day and age? She shook her head. Maybe it was a homicide.

"Check it out."

"Okay. Do you have the name of an officer at the scene I can talk to?" April asked.

"Apparently there wasn't one."

"What? Then how did the M.E.'s office get the case?"

"Don't fucking hock me, Woo. It's a little hazy, a little unclear, understand? Maybe somebody saw something and said something to somebody. Maybe the attending was nervous about signing the death certificate. How can I fucking know how the M.E. got involved? All I know is they took the case. And now they want to know how the Ami—whatever it is got into the guy."

April risked one more question. "Did you get the feeling there's any suspicion of—"

In her frustration, Joyce reached for a clump of hair to pull. "Christ on the Cross, April. It's just a routine fucking investigation. Could be the guy took the wrong medicine, could be he got too much of the right medicine. Could be an accidental overdose. Could be a suicide. It's just not a natural."

April didn't like having to go to the Psychiatric Centre again so soon. There was something not quite right about those people. The doctors were as creepy as the patients, and now another person was dead. "What about the rapist?" she asked finally.

"We're getting a profiler from downtown. Mike is talking to the university about warning the girls." Abruptly, Sergeant Joyce got tired of talking and closed her mouth around the next victim, her left pinky.

April pushed off from the windowsill. So the guy they just put in the pen was not a suspect in the raper case. She opened the office door. Out in the squad room there was a lot of noise and a number of plainclothes she'd never seen before. She stopped at her desk to grab her bag from the bottom drawer. It looked as if a lot of extra people were about to fan out on the streets looking for a squirrel, and she wasn't going to be one of them.

thirty-seven

At precisely three P.M. April hesitated by the two open doors to Jason Frank's inner office. She could see Jason sitting at his desk with his back to her. In spite of the number of clocks she knew were in there, none of them happened to be chiming the hour. She wondered if she was early.

He punched a button on his laptop and swiveled around. "Hey, April, you made it."

"Oh, my." She tried to keep a straight face. His new beard wasn't exactly the same length all over his face and wasn't the same color as his head hair. The beard and mustache were grizzled, made him look older than his thirty-nine years and blunted the good looks April had always admired.

"Smartest detective in New York. How are you?" Piercing through the ragged edges, though, Jason's dark eyes were as sharp and knowing as ever. He looked the detective over with obvious pleasure.

April was wearing black wool pants, ankle-high black boots, a red turtleneck sweater, and a black pea jacket. Her short layered haircut was a little longer and fuller now. She carried the same heavy shoulder bag with an extra gun, the handcuffs, and the Mace in it. She was the only woman Jason knew who carried around such things and never forgot what they were there for . . . the way he never forgot he was a doctor. The last time he saw April her lipstick was pink. Now it was fire-engine red, apparently to match the sweater. She looked good.

She looked even better when she smiled. "I'm tired, Doc. How about you?"

He nodded, raising his shoulders equivocally, shook the hand that could shoot a gun, let it go reluctantly. "It's a chronic condition."

"So?" she murmured. "What's with the beard? Are you Dr. Freud now?"

"Don't you like it? I'm taking a survey."

"It wasn't a bad face." April shrugged. "You undercover or something?"

Jason smiled. "Maybe."

April picked up on the smile. Things were going better for him.

Maybe he had a new girlfriend or his wife was back. "And the clocks. What happened to them?"

Jason swung around to check the bookcase. "Nothing. You're exactly on time."

"Why aren't they making a racket?" April pointed to the brass bull with the clock on his back. The minute hand jumped to five past.

"Oh, only the ones at home chime."

"Ah, silent clocks for patients." She fell silent herself, didn't want to ask about Emma, wasn't sure whether she should sit down. "Sorry I had to cancel out on you twice. You know how it is when something comes up. You had some questions for me?"

"Yes, thanks for coming. You want to sit down, go out for a coffee, or stand there?"

She was starved. "How much time do you have?"

"I have to be back at four-fifteen. I get the feeling you're hungry."

"I am," she admitted. The last thing she had had was scrambled egg fried rice at six, forced on her by her mother as she tried to sneak out of the house without engaging in another conversation about duty and marriage. It was the same breakfast her mother had served when she was a kid. And the same conversation they'd been having for the last nine years. Only now, thanks to Mike's turning up on Saturday and Alice Chen's intelligence on what had happened that afternoon, Skinny Dragon Mother had something new to obsess about. Finally getting a marriage but to the wrong kind of guy.

"It's been a long day." She didn't mention her morning with Nicole Amendonde, the rape victim in ER.

Twelve minutes later they were sitting in a coffee shop on Broadway. From where they sat they could see Zabar's, the site where Dr. Lobrinsky had so very recently lost his much-loved, canary-yellow ride. April didn't mention that, either.

"So fill me in," Jason said when she had put away half of her BLT and was working on a huge side of fries.

"I just got another unnatural from your shop. What's going on there? You got people dropping dead left and right."

"An inpatient? You going to eat all those?"

"Uh-uh." April pushed the fries in his direction. "I've had it."

"I'm not supposed to . . ." he muttered vaguely, tucking into them.

April dabbed her lips delicately with the paper napkin. "No, it's not a patient, actually. It's a doctor. Maybe you know him, guy named Dickey."

Jason's handful of french fries stopped halfway to his mouth. "Harold Dickey, an unnatural?"

"Yeah, that's the one."

"An unnatural, are you sure?"

"Well, the guy supposedly dropped dead of a heart attack, but it turns out he was full of Amitrip-ti-something."

"Amitriptyline?" Jason frowned and shook his head as the waiter offered him the last inch of muddy coffee in the pot.

"Yeah, what is it?"

Jason raked his beard unhappily. "It's a tricyclic."

April looked blank. "What would someone take it for?"

"It's an antidepressant. It's given for depressive neurosis, manic depression. Anxiety. You might know it by its trade name. Elavil."

April nodded. "What would Dickey have been taking it for?"

"I'm not sure. I wasn't aware that he was depressed." Jason raised his eyebrow, thinking it over. It was no secret that Harold liked his scotch. Maybe he'd slipped from social drinking to alcoholism, had gone on the wagon, and was taking Elavil to relieve withdrawal depression. Maybe he was self-medicating. A lot of doctors did that.

"What's the thought?" April asked.

Jason grimaced. "Nothing. It's complicated, that's all. Why are the police involved?"

"Yes, it is complicated. More than you might be aware of. Dickey's name and number were found beside the body of Raymond Cowles."

"What?"

April nodded. "I interviewed Dickey last week, and he said he didn't know Cowles and certainly hadn't spoken to him the night he died."

"That's . . ." Jason shook his head. "So what happened to Dickey? How did you get involved?"

"It's a little mysterious. Usually in cases like this, the ER doctors will sign off on the spot. Or the attending will sign the certificate. Dickey was sixty-eight, had a heart attack. It should have been straightforward enough. Buuut—I guess somebody didn't like the way it looked and didn't want trouble later. All I know is someone called the Medical Examiner, the office took the case, and the path found something." She watched Jason move in on the fries again, then said, "You know, the Cowles case looked like a clear-cut suicide, too. It turned out to be, but still, we have to check it out."

"Tell me about it." Jason licked a finger, then another one.

April wrinkled her nose. "Anybody ever teach you what napkins are for?"

"Nope." He finished licking his fingers and pushed the plate away. "So, what's the story on Cowles?" he asked, finally getting to his reason for wanting a meeting.

"What's your interest?"

Jason sighed. "I got sucked into reviewing the case as a consultant. There might be a lawsuit."

"From what I've seen of the widow, there will certainly be a lawsuit." April watched Jason catch sight of his image in the mirror behind the booth and look surprised, then refocus on the subject.

"On what grounds?" he asked.

"She was married to him for almost fifteen years, didn't know the guy was gay. Her story is they were the perfect couple. Then suddenly her husband needs space. Out of the blue he takes another apartment and returns to his former shrink, Dr. Treadwell. The doctor sees him a few times, prescribes tranquilizers. He uses them to kill himself. The widow thinks the shrink made him believe he was gay when he was in a vulnerable state. Then because it was against everything he believed, he freaks out and kills himself. Whatever the truth was, the medication she prescribed helped to kill him."

"Anything else?"

"The autopsy showed Cowles had a lot of perianal scarring and signs of long-term infection. The pathologist said it wasn't a new thing with him. He'd been into it for a long time."

"Probably all his adult life," Jason murmured.

"Another thing. Cowles was with someone just before he died. His lover was a lawyer from the insurance company where he worked. The night he died they cooked dinner together, had sex. The lover said Cowles was in a great mood. They were in love and planned to move in together. The lover went home to his own apartment about nine."

"When did Cowles die?"

"Not likely to have been before ten. Three trick-or-treaters rang his doorbell at nine-thirty. They said he complimented them on their costumes."

"So something happened after that. Any idea what?"

"Well, he placed a call to Dr. Treadwell at nine-thirty-eight. The phone company logged the time at six minutes."

"What?" Jason said, shocked again. "What did Dr. Treadwell have to say about that?"

"I didn't call her on it, Jason. It wasn't relevant to our investigation. We were looking for a homicide."

"It would be relevant to malpractice, though."

"Yeah, I guess in civil suits, sticks and stones can break your bones and words can also harm you." April glanced up at the clock over the counter. It read 4:02.

"Yeah, and sometimes words can even kill you." Jason raised his hand for the check.

"I'll take it," April said.

Jason shook his head. "Next time . . . So, there was a six-minute conversation between Dr. Treadwell's phone and Raymond Cowles's phone. And Cowles committed suicide almost immediately thereafter." Even if it could never be proved that Clara talked to Cowles, it was very nasty news. Jason rubbed his cheek.

"That's about the size of it." April reached for the check, but Jason got it first.

"I said next time."

"Thanks." April gathered up her jacket and bag. "What about this Dickey? You know of any reason he had to kill himself?"

Jason scratched his cheek. That morning he'd had a call from the head of the medical school asking him to take over Dickey's classes until they found a replacement. Oh, and by the way, was he interested in the job? Now Dickey turned out to be an unnatural. Had words harmed him, too?

Deeply disturbed, Jason took a deep breath and exhaled. "No, I wouldn't have said Harold Dickey was the type to commit suicide. Could it have been an accident?"

"That was my next question."

"People make fatal mistakes all the time. I know older heart patients who forget they've taken their medication and take it again. It's not supposed to happen, but it does." He counted out the bills and left them on the table with the check.

"I'll probably need your help with this hospital stuff," April said, out on the street, vaguely annoyed that he wouldn't let her pay and didn't even look like himself anymore.

"So will I," he said, smiling grimly. "Let's keep in touch."

thirty-eight

Clara Treadwell did not get up or say hello when April came into her office. She merely pointed to the tufted leather tub chair in front of her desk.

"Please sit down, Officer."

"Detective Woo," April corrected her.

"Yes, I remember. But there were two of you. Where's your partner?" The woman seemed annoyed that there was only one of them now. She also seemed much older than she had a week ago. Her skin had a dry and grayish cast under the tan, and the puffiness around her eyes made her look as if she'd been worrying a lot and not sleeping much.

"He's on another case." April did not bother to tell the doctor that precinct detectives sometimes worked together but did not have partners. She sat gingerly on the shiny tufts, which were so hard, they must have been designed to discourage visitors from staying too long.

On the Upper West Side she had worked on cases involving all kinds of women—homeless, hookers, students, housewives, store owners, and businesswomen. It was the people April considered rich who fascinated and intimidated her the most. Until she'd come uptown she'd never seen this kind of people up close before, the kind who looked like they walked out of TV shows and magazines. They lived in luxurious apartments with doormen and porters, who took out the garbage and hosed down the sidewalks every morning. They kept their cars in garages that cost what a one-bedroom apartment cost outside of Manhattan. They ate in restaurants with white tablecloths and worked in stores and offices that were attractive and clean and comfortable—unlike New York City precinct stations or anything April had ever encountered in Chinatown.

But privilege gave rich women more than luxury. April had noted the extra piece in their design over and over, wanted it and knew how hard it would be to achieve. No promotion would give it to her, and no amount of money could buy it. The posture of Clara Treadwell's body, the arch of her eyebrows, the set of her mouth as she sat at her desk exhausted but undaunted—her hands easy among expensive blotter, appointment book, and pen set—everything about her stated her confidence in herself, her certainty that she was right and could get that rightness across, her ability to intimidate without saying a word. Her lack of fear. April believed you had to be born with that lack of fear, educated to it, and Caucasian to carry it off.

"You're here to report your conclusions on the Raymond Cowles case," Dr. Treadwell said imperiously.

"I'm here on another matter, but I'd be glad to fill you in on that investigation if you'd like."

Clara nodded.

April quickly told her what they had discovered about Raymond Cowles's last night and what the forensic evidence had indicated about the manner and time of his death. Clara's face tightened as April described the dinner and sex with his lover. Otherwise she betrayed no emotion.

"Except for his phone call to you, there seems to be no mystery about it," April concluded.

The weariness and age dropped away from the hospital director's face as indignation animated it. "What makes you think I had a conversation with Ray that night?"

"We hit the redial button on his phone, Dr. Treadwell. Your number was the last one he called."

"That doesn't mean he reached me," Clara said angrily. "If he called the number, he must have gotten my answering machine and hung up."

No, that was not possible. The phone company had logged the call in at over six minutes. Clara's answering machine took messages of only two minutes in length. April knew that because the machine itself had given her the information when she called the number. Cowles and Treadwell had talked, but April decided to let it go. If Dr. Treadwell bore some responsibility for Cowles's mental state at the time he took his life, some other court would have to determine it.

"It's a mystery," April murmured.

"I'm a doctor. Do you think I would have hung up on him if I had known he was on the edge?" Clara persisted.

"You spoke to him," April said softly.

"No, of course I didn't. I'm saying it wouldn't have happened *if we had* spoken."

April's mouth went dry exactly the same way it had when she followed Mike to the door of Raymond's room and saw by his stance that Cowles was in there and he was dead. Clara had most certainly talked to him. The admission was there in her denial. It didn't change anything, though. Only that April could no longer believe any statement she made.

"Well." April backed off on Raymond. "I'm here to ask you a few questions about Dr. Harold Dickey. You were with him when he collapsed, I understand."

"Yes." Clara's eyes flared. "Has this become a police matter, too?"

April was surprised. "Haven't you been briefed on it yet?"

Clara shook her head, wary now. "What's going on?"

"The death file isn't complete yet, but the preliminary findings show no signs of heart disease or natural—"

"Then what killed him?" she demanded impatiently.

"According to the tox reports, he had very high levels of alcohol and Amitrip . . . ah, Elavil."

"Jesus." Clara's brow furrowed. "Amitriptyline? Are you sure?"

"Yes, ma'am."

"But he'd been drinking. He knew better than—" Clara Treadwell froze.

April pulled out her notepad. "Do you know of any reason *he* might have wanted to commit suicide?"

The doctor stared at April, clearly stunned. "Give me a minute, will you. This is . . ."

Pressed rigidly against the unyielding chair, April's back began to ache. She wanted to get up and walk around.

Clara pulled herself together. She could do it faster than anyone April had ever seen. In less than sixty seconds the imperiousness was back. "Detective, I'll have to talk to you some other time. I need to organize my thoughts about this."

"I won't take long," April said evenly. She didn't want Clara Treadwell organizing her thoughts. She wasn't getting a cozy feeling about this woman, who was already implicated in one death. This was her second death in little more than a week. April wanted to know what happened to Harold Dickey. It was her job to find out, and find out she would—no matter who the woman was or how intimidating she could be.

"I don't care how long it will take. I cannot do it now."

Clara stood up. April did not.

"I'd rather talk to you before you think about it, Doctor. It's an unnatural, that's all. We just have to establish whether it was an accident or Dr. Dickey took too much medicine on purpose."

"How can I know that?" Clara clenched her fists.

"You were there."

"Yes," Clara said, calmer now. "Harold asked me to come there. He was already ill when I arrived. At first I thought he was drunk." She shook her head. "Then I realized it was something more than that."

"What made you think so?"

"He was agitated, paranoid, raving, hallucinating. He was having a psychotic episode." She looked puzzled. "But I—"

"Did he ask for help?"

"He didn't know what was wrong with him. He didn't know. He would have told me." She shook her head again.

"When did you call for help?"

"He collapsed and had a seizure almost immediately. I was only there for a minute, maybe two minutes, before it happened. You can ask the guards. They saw me come in and they responded when the code was called."

"The code?"

"There's a code for medical emergency."

"When did you arrange to meet?"

"We didn't. He just asked me and I—" She froze again.

Another nerve. "When?"

Clara closed her eyes. "I don't remember. I just know he didn't take anything while I was there, and he was already very ill. If I'd gotten there five minutes later, he would have died alone." She fell silent.

"Was he depressed when you talked to him?"

"Not at that exact moment, no."

"Had he been depressed recently?"

"Well . . . yes. There was the Cowles suicide. He was upset about that."

"Oh? Did he know Raymond Cowles well?" April asked.

"Of course he did, he was the supervisor on Cowles's analysis. He directed every aspect of the case." Clara pursed her lips. "But I'm sure he told you that when you spoke with him."

Uh-uh. Dickey had told her he hadn't known Cowles.

"Dr. Dickey told me you found his number by Cowles's body. Maybe Dr. Dickey spoke to him," Clara speculated.

"Maybe." April nodded, wondering if the two deaths were connected or not. "Well, thank you for talking to me. I'll need to see his office. Has anyone been in it since—"

Again the eyes flared. "No. I locked it immediately. No one's been in that room or touched a thing."

"Good. I'll also need a list of his patients, people he worked with—colleagues, nurses—his relatives." April got up. Her back throbbed, and she had to pee.

"I'll have my assistant take care of everything." Clara Treadwell didn't say good-bye. She closed her eyes. When she opened them, the Chinese detective was gone.

thirty-nine

Dead leaves drifted over the paths of Riverside Park and brushed against Jason's pant legs as he hurried to the Psychiatric Centre to find Hal Dickey's course syllabus. It was Thursday, November 11, at 9:50 A.M. Emma had been with him for six days. In that time she'd been called back twice for the Simon Beak play. She was trying out for the part of the wife who finds out her husband had a secret life only after a stroke immobilizes him. The day he returns home from the hospital, a vegetable in a wheelchair, she finds out he cheated on his taxes and stole all their savings to set his girlfriend up in a house nicer than hers. Jason loved the play. Reading it, he almost fell off his chair laughing at the sexually repressed timid woman who revenges herself in a variety of ways. But he was ambivalent about Emma being in it. Anticipating domestic misery, he shuffled grumpily through the leaves.

Out in the Seventy-ninth Street Boat Basin, a number of sleek sailboats bobbed at their moorings in the sparkling river. Jason didn't notice the boats or the leaves or the sun glinting on the water. He was too busy juggling his thoughts about work and his wife. The movie role that had made Emma famous featured a smarmy shrink whose sexual interest in his female patient prompted her to act out sexually with a hoodlum. The film had humiliated and devastated him—in no small part because it had come as a complete surprise. Jason had been too busy with his own work at the time to bother reading the script and discussing it with her.

And now she had a vehicle that would allow her to vent her rage at him in a wholly different way. This time her role was funny, complicated, and so satisfying at the end that it demonstrated how perfectly theater could balance story and emotions that were utterly unmanageable in real life. In this part, Emma and all her voices would finally come together. Jason dreaded the possibility of her getting it. What would happen then?

He put his head down against the glare of the sun. What he did for a living was ease other people's pain. The way he did it was to work out the structures of people's minds in his head, using Tinkertoy parts with psychiatric labels. He made a weightless space for each one and created the Star Trek stations that incorporated each person's mental makeup.

He saw each space station of a human being as three-dimensional: the inside, crowded with booby-trapped baggage; the outside, bristling with antennae for picking up ever more hurt and disappointment. He was always working on what was really going on in a person's mind, not just what appeared to be happening in the room at the moment. His reserve made him seem to be holding back, waiting for the next piece of information, the next session, the next day. His analytic gifts didn't exactly help him with his own life. Emma wanted a husband with simple thoughts, thoughts that stayed in the room with her, preferably focused on her all the time. It wasn't going to happen.

Now he'd been drawn into hospital politics. He'd begun to study those first sessions between Clara Treadwell and Raymond Cowles eighteen years earlier and knew already that things about Cowles's treatment were disturbing. Without noticing, he'd left the path on Riverside Drive and crossed the street. As he approached the entrance to the Centre, he automatically drew his ID from his pocket and clipped it on his jacket pocket.

"Hey, Jason. Too bad about Dickey. I hear you're taking his spot." A colleague Jason had known since medical school spotted him waiting for the elevator and shouted over the crush of attendings, outpatients, social workers, secretaries, all craning their necks to catch a useful tidbit of gossip to trade later.

"Just filling in for a week or two, and it is too bad," he muttered in response.

He checked his watch. Two minutes for the elevator to come and four minutes of stopping and starting to get where he was going. While he waited, he thought of the young and powerfully magnetic Clara Treadwell in her first session with Raymond Cowles.

> I asked RC to lie down on the couch. He didn't want to. He said it made him nervous not to be able to see me. We talked about how the blank screen was part of the analytic process and would make it easier for him to say things without worrying what my reaction was going to be. He said it reminded him of the Wizard of Oz, who hid behind a screen and wasn't really a wizard. I remarked that wizard or not, he got the job done. RC seemed to accept that and lay down on the couch. Immediately he began to talk about how much he loved his fiancée, Lorna. How beautiful and sweet and gentle and understanding she was. How comfortable he felt

with her. I could see that he had begun to sweat. Then he said he didn't know why he kept having these fantasies about doing "things" with men. He wasn't a fag, couldn't imagine being a "fag, having intercourse with a man." He'd had sex with Lorna, his fiancée. He wanted to marry Lorna and be with her forever. But in his head it was like there was some kind of switch. Like the Devil or a demon distracted him. He said he didn't like thinking about Lorna's breasts, or touching them. He was terrified that wasn't normal. He said he had to imagine that she was a man in order to get excited enough to "get in her" . . . Then he stopped talking suddenly and turned around to look at me. I was sitting in the chair behind him. He looked at me in a very piercing way. I held his gaze and did not look away. After that, we made the treatment plan. RC agreed that he would not act on his homosexual impulses or marry until the treatment was complete. That night he cruised a gay bar, met an older man who took him home to his apartment. They had oral sex. Later in the evening he called Lorna and set a date for their marriage. This was the first thing he told me in our second session. I was stunned. We'd just started.

In his supervisory session Dickey had told his student Clara that her patient Ray had had his first homosexual experience the night following his first session with her because he was resisting his true heterosexuality. Jason shook his head as he got off the elevator.

Resistance to heterosexuality had been the classic diagnosis of homosexuality for almost a hundred years. Many people all over the world still believed a man wanting to have sex with another man, or a woman with a woman, was just being contrary and could change if he or she wanted to. Now a great deal of scientific data pointed to sexual preference being innate, already fixed at birth. Jason wondered what Dickey would say now if he read what he had said and Clara had carefully recorded eighteen years ago when the views he expressed were already out of date.

"Sorry, sir. You can't go in there." A stocky officer snaked out an arm the size of a watermain to stop him outside of Dickey's office.

"What's going on?"

"Room's been sealed."

"Why?"

"I really couldn't say."

April Woo opened the door and popped her head out. "Hi, Jason. I thought I heard your voice. What's up?"

"I could ask you the same thing." Jason cocked his head at the red-faced man blocking his way.

"Officer, would you mind giving us a little breathing space here? The doc is on our side." April smiled at the cop.

The uniform hesitated, then shuffled sideways two paces so Jason could get two steps closer. Slowly he took in the mess. Paper all over the place, documents from the spilled stacks of files, notes, reprints of articles. Spots on the floor by the green vinyl couch that looked like vomit and dried blood. A Brooks Brothers jacket hung on the back of the chair. Abandoned lengths of plastic tubes, torn packaging of disposable needles, sterile wipes, and other medical detritus left where they'd been dropped. More files were stacked on Dickey's desk next to a laptop computer with a portable printer attached to it. There was nothing on the pull-out board except a nearly empty glass with a small quantity of brown liquid with a greasy film around the sides. The rest of the room seemed untouched, the bookcases with plaques and knickknacks, the table by the window with small, fragile decorative objects on it.

"It's peculiar," April told Jason. "I've gone over the place pretty carefully, and there's no sign of medications of any kind. No aspirin, no cough medicine. Guy didn't even take antacids. That's unusual. Another thing. In suicides, the pill containers are on the scene. They don't just walk away after the guy drops dead. How did the Elavil get into him?"

"He has another office. Maybe he kept his medications over there."

"Well, Jason, if he took the stuff in his other office, wouldn't he have died over there?"

"Not necessarily. It might have taken several hours for him to get really sick. If he ingested the Elavil by accident somewhere else, he might have felt fine for a while and gone about his business." Jason scratched his beard. "What was he doing with all these files on a Sunday? Do you know?"

"All I know is the lady with him at the time says she locked the door after they took him away and no one touched a thing. Does she always tell the truth?"

"There was a lady with him?" Jason asked.

"Yeah, Dr. Treadwell."

"Really." Jason remembered Clara's phone call on Sunday night telling him Harold had died. Clara always seemed to leave a few key items out of every story. This time it was the fact that she had been with Harold when he had his seizure. What had she been doing with him? He let his breath out in a rush, didn't want to think about it.

"The woman in Personnel is real upset. She says there's going to be hell to pay if she doesn't get her files back where they belong. She's in quite a panic about it."

Jason smiled. "Gunn's an anxious person. So, what's the procedure for investigation here?"

"I'm waiting for my supervisor. By the way, where's that other office of his?"

Jason took her arm and moved down the hall away from the uniform. "It's in the doctors' office building. That's where he saw patients."

"So what did he do *here*?"

"This is his academic office."

"Yeah?" April deadpanned. She didn't even have her own desk, not even a drawer of her own. Academic office, patient office. What'd these doctors need two offices for, her face said clearly.

"Yeah." Jason smiled. She was cute.

"You got two offices, too, Doc?"

"Uh-uh, only the one." He scratched his face.

"So what'd Dickey do in *this* office?"

"This was where he did the administration side of his job. Harold was on hospital committees, taught classes, supervised residents. He wrote articles for journals, spoke at conferences. Maybe he was working on some kind of patient follow-up project with those files."

"Like what kind?"

"Like I don't know what kind, April. Like to make statistics, see how patients were doing five years later, ten years later. Something like that." He checked his watch, was certain that was not what Dickey had been doing with the files.

They'd arrived at the elevator bank. Miraculously, no one else was around. "A patient like Raymond Cowles committing suicide fourteen years after treatment ended?" April asked. "Are you suggesting Dickey was working on that?"

"Huh? No . . . Look, April, a certain percentage of the borderlines commit suicide no matter what you do to help them. It's a fact of life. If they want to die, they find a way."

"Oh, I didn't know Cowles was a borderline personality," April murmured.

Jason *tsk*ed. "You know what I mean. I'm just saying don't jump to conclusions. There may be no connection between the two deaths."

"Maybe not. This one might not be a suicide. I don't see a note. I don't see a container of pills. I smell liquor, I see a glass, but I don't see a liquor bottle or a flask. Where did it come from? Where did it go? . . . Anyway, Jason, the files Dickey was working on are employee files. Very few are patient files."

Jason's brow furrowed. He had to talk to Clara. Maybe Hal had been working on the condom thing and the person he'd been looking for somehow . . . "Look, April, I've got to go. I have a patient waiting for me."

"Yeah, well, what did you come here for, anyway?" April's face stayed blank.

"It'll have to wait. Will you keep me posted on this?"

She smiled suddenly, as if he'd told her something important. "Well, thanks for the input."

"So keep me posted," he said again.

"Hey, I'll level with you as long as you level with me."

"Oh, come on, April. When have I ever not leveled with you?" He'd punched the button twice for the elevator. It didn't light up. He punched it again.

"Oh, Jason, this is something different. This is your turf. I'm not feeding you information so you can house-clean before we get the facts."

Would he do that? He opened his mouth to protest. The elevator doors slid open. The elevator was full of people.

"Hey, Jason. Good to see you. I heard you're—"

Jason pushed in. "Is this a down? Oh, sorry, getting out."

Too late. The doors slid shut.

forty

"Anything?" Sergeant Joyce stormed into the empty squad room as Mike Sanchez was on his way out. There was no question she was pissed. A case from when she was in Sex Crimes three years ago had finally come to trial, and the A.D.A. had promised her she'd be up and could testify first thing.

"What took so long?" Mike asked. It was already after one.

"Some damn thing with the judge. The opening of the trial kept getting delayed and delayed. Bailiff wouldn't let me go, and I wasn't called until eleven-forty-five. What's new?"

"Your unnatural at the Psychiatric Centre left a mess in his office."

"What kind of mess?" Sergeant Joyce was something of a mess herself. First thing in the morning, in her black suit with the wraparound skirt that just grazed the top of her chubby knees and apple-green blouse, she must have looked pretty put-together for her court appearance. Now the four-leaf clover pin with a tiny green stone in the center, which may or may not have been an emerald, was the only thing about her still on straight. Everything else looked like yesterday's well-thumbed newspaper. Almost the whole of her blouse had worked its way out of the wrinkled skirt. Her hair was wild, her eyes were watery, and her upturned Irish nose was red and raw. Balled up in her fist was a green handkerchief, which she clapped to her face suddenly but too late to stop the explosion.

"Achoo!"

"*¡Válgame Dios!*" Mike said.

"Thanks. Both my kids are sick," she muttered, snuffling angrily as if illness, too, were a purposeful act intended to further complicate her life. "Can you believe that? Both of them at home with flus and fever, and I don't feel so hot myself."

"Too bad," Mike said. "Have you taken anything?"

"Nah." She shrugged it off. "Where are you going?"

"I'm on my way over to see what's up with Woo. Seems this guy Dickey took a lot of files over the weekend when they were supposed to be secured, and the hospital wants them back."

"Uh-huh. What's the problem?"

"April says there's something wrong."

"Yeah, so what's wrong?"

"Lot of mess in there, but the doc was known for never working on the weekends. Something was up with him. Also there were no medications of any kind on the scene."

"So he swallowed the pills somewhere else. Anybody check on what medications he took? Guy was in his sixties, wasn't he? Maybe he took his medication, forgot he'd taken it, and took it again." She edged the side of her thumb into her mouth and started nibbling at it, her red nose leaking. She didn't want a homicide here.

Mike looked away. "We're checking on it."

"Aw, shit. Let's take a look." She sneezed again. "Anything new on the rapes?"

"No. Squirrel must be new in the area. No one knows him."

"What about the street people?" Joyce sloped reluctantly out into the hall.

Mike followed her at a distance. Suddenly his throat felt a little scratchy. "Yeah, well, we got a few of the street people say they saw someone who looked kind of like the guy in the sketch hanging around earlier this week. But we have no leads on who he is."

"I don't want any uniforms out there. We have to let him think he got away with it."

"No uniforms," Mike confirmed. A lot of people, but no uniforms. He put his hand over his mouth and coughed, testing. Now he had to get in the car with her. All he needed was a bad cold. The temperature had gone up again. Maybe that was the problem. Hot, cold. Everybody wore the wrong thing, got sick, passed it along.

In the lot Sergeant Joyce headed for the navy unit she'd used that morning to go to court. With her there was never any argument about who drove. She always sat on the passenger side and told whoever was at the wheel how to drive. Mike got in and opened his window all the way. It was only a few blocks to the Psychiatric Centre. Today Joyce clearly didn't feel well enough to tell him how to get there.

Instead she sneezed and complained all the way, didn't like being pressured into a big investigation at the Centre when young girls were getting brutally raped a few blocks away on their college campus, didn't like the way she felt, didn't appreciate spending the morning in a closed witness room waiting for a case three years old to come to trial. Then she started all over again. Without exactly saying it, mostly Sergeant Joyce seemed uncomfortable about going into the Psychiatric Centre, where cops had to hand over the bullets in their guns and walk around with the anxious feeling they were buck naked.

The hospital parking lot was down the hill nearly two blocks away from the Centre. In the interest of time, Mike parked inside the white diagonal lines a few feet from the entrance. And still it was twenty minutes before they found April and Serge on the nineteenth floor. The ritual of finding the head nurse on the third floor, emptying their guns and turning them over to her, did indeed worsen Sergeant Joyce's mood. She headed for the uniform, drew him aside, and talked to him for a few heated minutes.

"Yo, *querida*." Mike smiled at April. "What's up?"

"Nothing's up." April was cool. "What's going on? You said in ten minutes two hours ago."

Another angry woman. He shrugged. "Unavoidable delay."

"Oh, yeah? What kind?"

He cocked his head toward the uniform, who was suddenly galloping off down the hall toward the elevator bank. Sergeant Joyce turned to them, honking into her handkerchief. "So what am I doing here?" she demanded.

April closed her mouth and led the way to the late Harold Dickey's office. She repeated the facts as she knew them while the two Sergeants looked around.

"Dr. Treadwell told me she locked the office after Dickey died, and no one's been in here since. No way to know, though."

April pointed out the almost empty glass with its greasy coating. They all crouched around the glass studying it.

"Smells like scotch," April said. "So where's the bottle?"

Joyce turned away to sneeze on a stack of spilled files.

"*¡Válgame Dios!*" Mike said automatically. He caught April's eye, then smiled. Nice, huh? The place had probably been contaminated thirty different ways to Christmas before. Now they had a whole new set of genetic markers and a germ farm. A tiny jerk of April's chin indicated a slight thaw.

Joyce finished mopping her face. "Bag it."

"You want the place dusted, sealed?" Reluctantly, Mike turned his attention to her.

Joyce shook her head, rolling her watery eyes. "How many people were in this room when the guy collapsed? What, ten, fifteen?"

"Probably not that many. Maybe seven," April said.

"I got a call on this last night." Joyce wiped her eyes. "Seems this Dr. Dickey treated a lot of important people in his day. One of the trustees claims Dickey saved his kid's life when she had a breakdown a few years ago. Three or four seem highly motivated to know what happened to him."

Mike's scrutiny focused on the laptop. He could feel April looking at him.

"So it's not going to go away," she said.

"That's right. They want it clean. No mystery," Joyce said.

So the Sergeant had known it before they even met in the squad room. Known she was coming here and there was cause to investigate further. Mike chewed on the end of his mustache. Nice of her to tell him.

"So you want the place gone over."

"Yeah. And don't release the files."

Mike pointed at the laptop. "You been into that yet?" he asked April.

She shook her head. "Didn't want to touch it."

Suddenly Joyce fixed her attention on April. "You been here all morning?"

"Since nine-thirty."

"You haven't interviewed the wife?" the Sergeant demanded accusingly.

"No, ma'am."

"Why didn't you go interview her?"

"Ah, I was concerned about leaving the scene. I've had two requests for the return of the files," April replied evenly. "The hospital lawyer was down here. He told me we couldn't have access to them. Said they've been patient with us so far. But the files are confidential and have to be returned today. As far as I can tell, nobody'd given them a thought until this morning, when we turned up. There seems to be a lot of anxiety around here."

"What's his name?"

"The lawyer? Hartley."

"Fine, I'll talk to him."

"He may want a higher authority," April muttered.

"Oh, yeah? Whose?"

"I don't know. The Captain, an A.D.A. I get the feeling different parties here have different agendas."

"Fine. I'll take care of it." She sneezed again.

"*¡Válgame Dios!*" Mike grimaced.

"All right, already. I heard you the first time," Joyce barked at Mike. "I take it you'll be wanting to go, too?"

To Westchester to interview Dickey's wife? Mike lifted his palms. Of course he did.

"Great. Now we got an efficiency problem." Joyce's beeper bleated. She sighed. "Where's the nearest phone?"

Mike pointed to the one on the dead man's desk.

"Not that one." Idiot.

"There are some secretarial offices at the end of the hall. I used the phone there earlier," April said.

Sergeant Joyce went to find a phone. A few minutes later she returned and said, "You wait for the crime boys. I'm out of here."

She paused for a second, then told them the phone call was to tell her that half an hour ago one of their African-American decoys had been pulled off the street by a soft-spoken, well-dressed Caucasian twice her size who wanted extra help with directions to a certain part of a building. They had a suspect in the rape case.

forty-one

At three-thirty it was still an unseasonably warm afternoon as Mike and April headed up the Henry Hudson Parkway in Mike's red Camaro toward the town of Hastings to meet with Harold's widow, Sally Ann Dickey. April swallowed the last of her coffee and squashed the cup. It seemed a bit too coincidental that two unnatural deaths had occurred while, or very soon after, the victims had talked to Clara Treadwell. Okay, Cowles was a suicide, but what about Dickey?

April shook her head. Oh, sure, there were thousands of coincidences in police work. In fact, sometimes it seemed as if coincidence was the detective's only ally. Consider the carjacked Chinese jewel merchant hit on the head and locked in his own trunk as thieves sped away to keep his diamonds and dispose of his body. He happened not to be dead, however; he had his cellular phone in his pocket, came to, and called the police, who rescued him within the hour.

According to Sai Woo, this was a perfect example of Confucius alive and well in Chinatown, New York. Clear as day. No coincidence. Even a worm daughter should be able to see it. Heaven—which always did and always would rule the universe—made its own connections as the Earth and other planets traveled their course, providing every change necessary for the cycle of life and death.

"Heaven does not speak, but the four seasons proceed in their course and a hundred living things are produced, yet Heaven does not speak." This tidbit from the *Analects* was a scroll on the wall in the roach-ridden Chinatown tenement where April had grown up.

It meant four million things. One was that Heaven was the perfect being that determined what was coming down at all times. Two was that Heaven in its apparent silence actually never shut up. And three, one could hear what Heaven was not saying if one learned how to listen. Nothing, not one single thing, was random. Nothing happened by chance. April was taught she was put on this Earth to be quiet and listen while her mother interpreted Heaven's intentions for them both, according to Sai's own hopes and wishes.

Fortunately or otherwise, Heaven, like every member of the hospital staff and every member of the NYPD, had its own agenda. Always. April knew if she could only be still and quiet enough, others would reveal themselves to her. The deceitful Sergeant Sanchez always did.

On the surface April was thinking about what part Dr. Clara Treadwell really played in these two unnaturals. She was thinking of Sex Crimes expert Sergeant Joyce "interviewing" the hapless raper suspect. She was thinking of the possible reassignments of the Sergeant and herself and where the future would take them in the Department. But underneath her totally passive facade, she was fuming over the death of love.

For two and a half hours, they had hung around in the halls of the Centre organizing their case. April collected the names and fingerprint sources of people known to have been in Dickey's office for matches in the event others turned up. In addition, her list of people to interview had grown from twenty-five students, secretaries, colleagues, and patients to fifty—with the inclusion of the Centre's two security guards who had initially responded to the call and the paramedics, doctors, and nurses on call in the emergency room at the time.

The two Crime Scene Unit partners photographed and sketched the exact locations of all files and papers and furniture; took samples of the dried vomit and other material on the carpet; listed, labeled, and categorized every single feature in the room including the nearly empty glass on Dickey's desk. Among dozens of other items, they found traces of blood and some white hairs on the corner of the desk; two shirt buttons under the green vinyl couch; several shiny brunette hairs about four inches long; a soiled woman's handkerchief; as well as the imprint on the carpet by the door of some black substance from the front wheels of the gurney used to take the victim away. The CSU partners had a few witty things to say about working on a site without a corpse but were able to piece together where Dickey had been standing when he fell, how he had fallen, and some of what may have happened after that.

Still at issue was the hour and a half Mike had spent in the hall negotiating with Ben Hartley and a person to whom April had taken an immediate and violent dislike when first she careened into view teetering on black patent-leather spike heels with her boss striding ahead of her—Hartley's snotty, fat-assed associate, Maria Elena Carta Blanca.

"Like the beer," she'd said, letting the words "Carta Blanca" roll off her fat red lips, as if she personally owned the company and reaped its profits.

Maria Elena was at the other end of the spectrum from the tall, thin, gray-suited, white-shirted, blue-and-red-striped-tied, uptight, upper-class, white-bread Hospital General Counsel Benjamin Hartley. Whether she had been hired for her legal skills or her ability to communicate with the largest portion of the local community the hospital served was not immediately clear. What *was* clear was that Maria Elena was the generic rival of April's high school and police academy days, one of those cliquey, showy, flashy, cheesy girls whose walk was a male reveille—those girls who bounced their bodies around like Ping-Pong balls, talking dirty, acting dirty, eating men for breakfast. Getting all the attention. They were the kind of girls who made a Sergeant Margret Mary Joyce look like a debutante and April Woo like a flat-faced, flat-chested prude.

Maria Elena was a woman with lots of very curly black hair and an extremely pink suit several sizes too small for her that emphasized her large round butt. Under her suit jacket she wore a white crocheted blouselike thing with holes in it that allowed her flesh to bulge through, and a huge cross on the unavoidable bosom. And, unlike the self-effacing, modest, attentive, perfect person of Taoist teaching, she did not remain silent for a single second. She glommed onto Mike with an avidity that churned the acid in April's flat and empty belly.

"I'll be your contact," she told him, licking her plump, moist lips in anticipation. "I'm Mr. Hartley's associate."

April took that to mean Maria Elena was a lawyer and not his secretary. Then, before any discussions were even begun, Maria Elena whipped out two—count 'em, two—of her personal business cards and wrote her home number on the back in case Mike needed to reach her at night. Mike pocketed one of the cards and ceremoniously offered the other to April, who did not want to take it.

Then the negotiations began. Hartley told them as spokesman for the hospital, he would have to ask them to limit their investigation to personal interviews, as that would be the least disruptive to the organization and its staff, and to get these personal interviews over as soon as possible. Mike said that was not possible because of the nature of the material found in the deceased's office and the bearing such materials might have on the case.

The ensuing bickering centered around whether the police would box the files and the laptop and take them away or whether they would remain exactly where they were with the office sealed. Sergeant Joyce had indicated that impounding the files and laptop was her first choice. Hartley was insistent that Maria Elena be present to document and initial every single document. Further, Hartley's stance was that while the personnel charts could be reviewed by the police investigators, the patient files were privileged information and therefore could not be examined for any reason by any outsider, death or no death. Beyond that the lawyer was fundamentally and unconditionally opposed to having a single document leave the building. That meant the detectives would be forced to return there many times to examine them.

After two telephone consultations with some unidentified person at the Two-O and the D.A.'s office, Mike was finally able to strike a deal that made him look extremely reasonable and magnanimous. The files would be impounded where they were, completely confidential for the time being. April knew all it meant was that they were starting at the other end of the string. It was when Mike gave *his* card to the big-chested Spanish beer bottle with the cross on her chest that April became seriously annoyed.

She put the squashed coffee cup into the brown bag that had contained their lunch—two plain bagels with cream cheese and two cups of coffee they'd stopped for at H&H Bagels on Broadway. April had taken some time to sip the coffee, chew and swallow the warm, fragrant bagel. Throughout the drive she had remained silent, her window open and the fresh wind blowing on her face, ruffling her hair.

They passed the site of a terrible crack-up on the Henry Hudson Parkway two weeks before and crossed the bridge out of Manhattan. It wasn't until they were in the Riverdale section of the Bronx that Mike made a stab at conversation.

"I live around here," he said abruptly.

Just where they were on the Henry Hudson Parkway the apartment buildings looked like luxury towers and the private houses like mansions.

"No kidding." April knew next to nothing about the Bronx except that the Cross Bronx Expressway passed through a splashy, noisy, heavily populated street world of sights and sounds that were more like Puerto Rico than New York. She'd interviewed suspects in Coop City, Hunts Point, and knew the places where nobody would want to get a flat tire.

"Yeah, over that way, though, in Knightsbridge."

"Looks nice. Close to work."

"About fifteen, twenty minutes," Mike admitted.

"Better stay there," she said pointedly. "It takes me a lot longer."

"I have a reason for moving. I could show you on the way back." Without looking at her, he smiled his sexy smile.

"You mean you want me to go to your place?" April shook her head. No thanks. Last weekend she'd taken a big risk for him, spent half a day visiting three moldy, run-down, four-room ruins with exaggerated descriptions: "Delightful four-room townhouse"; "Charming, garden apartment"; "Sun-drenched and quiet"; "Townhouse with garden." All were way farther out in Queens than Astoria, where she lived, and none had even a low rent to recommend it. And she'd had hell to pay for it.

The truth was, she was still a little conflicted about his showing up at her house over the weekend, trying to make friends with her parents, showing off, tempting her with spending more and more time with him so she'd miss him when they were apart. She didn't enjoy having to take his side against Skinny Dragon Mother, worrying all the time about how long he was going to keep his hands off her and what she'd do when his hands started taking independent action.

The very last thing she needed was to go to his place.

"Not *my* place. My mother lives there." Mike laughed easily. "You should meet *Mami*."

Yeah, right. April leaned out the window and made a noise.

"What's that supposed to mean?"

"Nothing. A cough." April scrunched up his napkin and empty cup, stuffed them in the H&H bag.

They'd passed through Riverdale and were heading toward Yonkers up the Saw Mill River Parkway.

"You have a problem with meeting my mother?" Mike demanded.

"Jesus," April muttered softly. Where was he going with this?

"Now you're swearing. A nice girl like you." He slapped his Camaro's custom-leather steering wheel with one hand. "Very nice. Insulting my mother and my religion at the same time."

The man wasn't a cop for nothing. He knew exactly which buttons to push. April made another noise. Then, "What's your problem, Mike? What's with you? I'm not insulting anybody."

"The hell you aren't. I met your parents. I met your cousin Mei Mei—"

"Judy. Her name is *Judy*."

"Her name is Mei Mei. Only Judy for show." He mimicked Skinny Dragon Mother.

Oh, now he was into the race thing. An angry retort rose to her lips and stuck in her mouth like a fat trickster dumpling from a low-class dumpling house—two inches of thick, crusty, tasty-looking dough that turns to glue in the mouth and has only the tiniest hint of filling. Mike wanted to fight. April felt the possibility of saying some things no high-quality person would say. The appropriate thing would be to say nothing and show Mike that he was a fool. But the nasty four-letter words she was forbidden to say struggled around inside of her, eager to jump out and make her a true American.

"Slut" was the best she could do.

"Judy?" Mike said in surprise.

"No. The one you devoured with your eyes. Gave you her home number." April pursed her lips in disgust.

"Devoured with what— Who . . . ? I never even noticed her."

"Impossible not to notice."

"Ha!" Mike exclaimed, taking the exit. "You don't want to meet my *Mami* because you don't like Latinas."

"Come on, Mike. You know that's not true."

"You think you're high-class and we're low-class people."

"I don't want to hear this. Turn right here." They were almost there. April rolled up her window.

"You said Maria Elena was a slut."

"You saw her."

"Sounds politically incorrect to me."

"You saw her. How would you describe her dress and actions, Sergeant? Would you say the lady was altogether professional, or was she offering something more than hospital services?"

Mike sucked on his mustache. "I'd say most women go both ways on that. Liking guys is not a cultural thing."

It was a cultural thing, though. Where April came from, women were not supposed to go both ways on that. She was absolutely certain that if a person went the wrong way, only bad things—*no* good things—could happen. She could cite a hundred—no, a thousand—cases of disaster brought on by going the wrong way on this monkey-business issue.

"You know what I'd say?" Mike said.

No point in saying she didn't want to hear it. April was silent as they drove through a neighborhood of big houses with big front lawns that were free of dead leaves and still deep green in color. She hoped he wouldn't tell her and thought she might be spared when he pulled up fast and close to the curb in front of a white stucco place with a red-tiled roof, then cut the Camaro's engine.

He turned to her, his features serious as if he'd moved into another compartment in his mind, was about to be arrogant and advise her on how to do the interview with Dickey's wife. Unfortunately, there was no other compartment in his mind at the moment.

"I'd say you're prejudiced about Latinos because we're so sexy and you're pissed off about missing out. . . . Maybe you're afraid you can't compete."

Asshole. April smiled benignly, wishing him dead, and grabbed her bag. "That must be it."

She saw his chest puff out under the leather jacket with the certainty that he'd nailed her, so now she'd have to relent and meet his mother. This victory freed him up to move into a different compartment in his mind. He noticed his surroundings were not like Queens or the Bronx and got out of the car, shaking out his pant legs and breathing in the air of wealth.

"Nice," he murmured. "Be nice to live in a place like this. What do you say, *querida*?"

April shrugged and headed up the walk.

forty-two

Sally Ann Dickey looked like an aged Doris Day. Her eyes were cornflower blue, her cheeks pink, her hair a shade that used to be called strawberry. It was exactly the color of Doris Day's hair in the fifties. She wore a pearl-gray wool dress and served tea to the two detectives as if it were a social occasion. If they didn't exactly fit in in her fussy Westchester living room, Mrs. Dickey was the last person to let them know. She patted the pillow on the settee with its back to the window and cocked her head at them politely.

She had placed April and Mike in the delicate chairs that faced her and the very few cars that passed on the street. April cleared her throat. "Thank you for taking the time to see us," she murmured. "We know this must be difficult for you."

"Not at all." Sally Ann Dickey poured tea and turned to Mike. "Sugar?"

"Ah, yes, please."

"Milk?"

He glanced at April. She was too busy watching Mrs. Dickey's pouring technique to help him. He shrugged. "Sure."

Mrs. Dickey put the silver strainer in its silver holder, set down the teapot, picked up a silver creamer, clouded the tea, and handed Mike his porcelain cup.

"Thank you," he said.

Then Mrs. Dickey picked up the teapot again.

"It's a delicate situation . . ." April began.

"So I understand. Sugar?"

"No. Thank you. Plain is fine." April took the cup and set it on the table in front of her without tasting it.

The new widow had fine white skin meshed with a thousand tiny wrinkles. Her hard blue eyes held April in an unblinking stare until April understood she was expected to sample the tea. She took a sip. As she did so, she was distracted by the sight of a dark blue Ford that looked a lot like some agency's unit passing slowly in front of the house. Nah. Lots of people drove Fords.

"I'm sorry we're going to have to ask you some difficult questions," April said softly.

Mrs. Dickey bent her torso graciously toward Mike. "More tea, Sergeant?"

"Not yet, thank you."

April could feel some tension developing in Mike. She followed his gaze to the street, where the dark blue Ford cruised by in the opposite direction. Now his antennae were up.

"What would you like to know?" Mrs. Dickey inquired.

"Was your husband taking any kind of medication?"

"Oh, my, what kind of question is that?"

"It's a background question only someone who knew your husband very well could answer. We need to establish what kinds of medication he normally took."

The blue eyes regarded her. "Harold was a healthy man. I'm not aware of any."

Not aware of any. Interesting way to put it. April inhaled. "If it would make you more comfortable, why don't you tell us in your own words a little about your husband and his habits the last few weeks?"

"Harold was a great doctor, a great teacher, a wonderful man." Mrs. Dickey poured herself some more tea.

"What about his personality? His moods?"

"Oh. Well. Of course he was preoccupied. He was always preoccupied."

"Would you say he was depressed?" Mike threw in.

"Depressed? My husband? Never. He had too much to do. More tea?"

"No, thanks. I'm fine." Mike smiled at April. *Be direct and let's get the hell out of here.*

All right, all right. April nodded. "Mrs. Dickey, did your husband take antidepressants?"

"Of course not. Harold didn't take anything, wouldn't even touch an aspirin."

"What about alcohol?" Mike murmured.

The widow sniffed. "Occasionally he had a drop. To relax."

"How would you describe his mood lately?" April asked.

Mrs. Dickey looked from one to the other as if she'd suddenly thought of something. "Which one of you is the good one and which one the bad?"

"Excuse me?" April said.

"One of you is the good cop and one is the bad. He must be the bad one. Are you Mexican?" The cornflower-blue eyes were on Mike.

Mike was startled. "How can you tell?"

"I come from Texas, honey. Lubbock. My husband, too. We've been here a long time. So have you."

"Since I was four," Mike said.

"Still, some things don't change." Mrs. Dickey sighed. "We married when we were twenty-one. Harold was going to be a great doctor and help his fellowman. And he did." A ghost of a young smile passed over the frozen features. "What is it you really want to know?"

"Your husband was in his office most of Sunday."

"He left around nine in the morning and I knew he was going to the office."

"Did he tell you why?"

"He didn't tell me anything."

"Then how did you know where he was going?"

"He wasn't dressed for tennis and he took his briefcase and laptop computer with him. He'd gone to the office on Saturday, too. I assumed he was working on something."

"Do you know what?"

"I heard him talking on the phone. There had been a death, a patient, I believe."

"Raymond Cowles."

"Who?"

"Raymond Cowles was the patient who died."

Mrs. Dickey shook her strawberry-colored head. "No, I don't believe that's the one he was concerned about."

"Another patient died?"

"Well, I just guess so. Overdosed on Elavil." Mrs. Dickey touched her hair. It was as rigid as cotton candy, molded into a single piece.

"Do you know the patient's name?" April asked.

"It was very unpleasant, I seem to recall."

"The death was unpleasant?"

"Yes. It was very unsettling at the time."

"So it was not a recent death."

"Oh, no. It happened last year, I think."

So there had been another death a year ago. "What was unsettling about it?" April pressed on.

Mrs. Dickey looked confused. "I really couldn't say. Harold was a very private man. More tea?"

"Ah, no, thank you. Your husband had a phone call about a dead patient. When was that?"

"No, he had a phone call about something else. It reminded him of the dead patient."

"I see," April murmured.

"You're the good cop, I can tell. You have a sweet face. Do you have children?"

April moved her chin to the no position. She saw Mike tense as the blue Ford passed the house a third time. Inside, a man in a slate-gray suit was talking on a cellular. His face was hidden by the appliance. He didn't look their way as he slowed, then sped up at the next house. He wasn't a cop. Cops didn't have cellular phones.

April tried one more time. "Other than the phone call on Sunday morning, Mrs. Dickey, can you tell me if there was anything different in your husband's life in the last few months, anything at all? Did he seem worried, anxious? Was he more withdrawn than usual?"

Mrs. Dickey thought for a moment. "Harold was very worried about the snake. Is that what you mean?"

"The snake?"

"I call her the snake. She's like a rattlesnake except you can't hear her coming. She came back, you know, just to tease him after all those years. That's the kind of woman she is. Well, no more about that. I'm not a gossip."

"You can say whatever you like to us," Mike said softly.

"You're the bad cop. I'll tell *her*."

"Go ahead, I'm listening."

"Well, I wouldn't be at all surprised if *she* killed him. That's what you're here about, isn't it? You think Clara Treadwell killed Harold."

"Ah, Mrs. Dickey, at this time, we're just trying to establish how your husband might have ingested enough Elavil and scotch to kill him. Whether it was an accident . . . or he was depressed and did it—"

"*She* put it in the scotch."

"Dr. Treadwell?" April asked.

"Yes. She hated Harold. She was trying to get rid of him, and he didn't want to go." Mrs. Dickey crossed her arms over her chest. "And that's what happened. She took my husband. And then she killed him when she didn't want him anymore."

And then Clara came and took away the scotch bottle when she returned to lock Dickey's office after he was dead. April glanced at Mike. She could see he had a few problems with Sally Ann Dickey's theory. If the head of the Centre had poisoned her former lover's scotch, why risk being on the scene when he died? April shrugged. Well, maybe Clara hadn't known Harold would die. But there was another Elavil-related death. Maybe an investigation of that death would lead them in another direction.

April stood. "Thank you for your help, Mrs. Dickey. It's been very useful." She put her empty cup on the tray. "Oh, by the way, did your husband have an office in the house?"

"Of course. Would you like to see it?"

Now it was three offices. The man had three offices and a wife who may have watched too much television over the years.

"Yes, thank you, we would. But I'd like to use the bathroom first."

"That door on the right." Mrs. Dickey pointed to a door under the stairs. She put the rest of the tea things on the silver tray.

"I'd be happy to carry that tray for you." Sanchez winked at April and picked up the tray.

"Oh, my, are you sure?"

"Of course. I do this at home all the time."

"I don't believe that, Sergeant. But thank you anyway. That old thing is getting heavier every day."

"It happens." Mike was suddenly being very nice.

April figured he didn't like being identified as Mexican *and* the bad cop within minutes of an introduction. As soon as they passed into the kitchen, she ignored the door on the right and headed up the stairs.

forty-three

After April Woo's visit to her office on Wednesday, Clara Treadwell had swung her chair around and stared out at the Palisades across the river in New Jersey. She needed to calm down and get things straight in her mind. In less than an hour she'd be meeting with Daveys, the FBI agent Arch Candel had assigned to her case on Monday but who hadn't been able to schedule an appointment until today. Monday the situation had been complicated enough. Now with Hal's death under investigation, it was a lot worse. Clara was disturbed, annoyed at the wasted time and further possibility of scandal. Still, she didn't believe there was anything she couldn't handle.

She shook her head wearily at the rippling expanse of Hudson River. For four days she'd been on the phone talking endlessly about Hal's tragic, sudden, fatal heart attack. She'd spoken to the Dean of the medical school, the Vice President of Medical Affairs of the university, the Chancellor of the university, the trustees of the Psychiatric Centre, the chief psychiatrist of the state of New York, so vital to the Centre's funding, who reported to the Commissioner of Mental Health. The Vice President of Medical Affairs called the Dean of the medical school, who called the Commissioner of Mental Health, who called her while she was on the phone with the Chancellor. They all knew one another well, worked together on the committees that funded and regulated the academic and medical services the university and Centre provided, both to their students and the patients they served.

There was a great deal of interest in the case because Harold Dickey had been a well-known figure at the Centre for over thirty years. A lot of people had liked him. People's liking and respecting Harold had been one of the many problems Clara had had with him. People had been foolishly loyal to all of Harold's outdated views. Clara thought bitterly of Harold's influence on the Ray Cowles case. Dickey had killed Ray.

And not only had Harold been genuinely liked, he had been the head of the Quality Assurance Committee and had died under suspicious circumstances right here in the Centre. During her many talks with all of her colleagues, Clara hadn't exactly prepared for big trouble. Never, in her wildest dreams, would it have occurred to her that there would be any. She had talked to everyone and thought she had the Harold's-death piece of her nasty situation all nailed down. Arch had assured her that the FBI person would take care of the other piece. Boudreau.

All Clara had needed today was the Chinese policewoman, who had bungled the Cowles case, suddenly back in her life to cast suspicions on *Harold's* death. It was infuriating, outrageous. Clara could feel the tic jumping in her cheek as she tried to process the information April Woo had given her, make sense of what she'd heard and not have a seizure herself. For a moment she was possessed by the fear that, like Hal's, her heart might run amok, too.

Ray was a suicide. Did that make sense after what he told her that night? No, it didn't make sense. Now it seemed Hal was killed by a combination of Elavil and alcohol. But everyone knew Harold didn't like to take medicines. Clara made a steeple of her index fingers and tapped them together. Ray wasn't depressed and Hal wasn't depressed. Ray never talked about suicide in any real way, and Hal was much less interested in his mood than his mental processes. Hal would never have taken anything to jeopardize the way he thought. The chemical uplift was for other people, Hal's wife, maybe. His daughter. Not for him. He was a purist.

Clara stared through the triangle of her fingers, seeing Hal so clearly even after all these years, even after his ugly death. She saw him sitting in his underwear in the old easy chair in the bedroom of her apartment, the faded quilt thrown over the chair, always the jubilant peacock after sex, a glass of Johnnie Walker in his hand. For the sex he had no apology, but the scotch he had to analyze and explain.

"Every man has his weakness and his poison. Scotch is my poison," he'd say, holding the amber liquid to the light.

He didn't admit to his other weakness, which was women—most particularly her. Wouldn't acknowledge the appetite because he never had any intention of paying the bill. A little knot of bitterness still remained deep inside Clara because of that. It was like a painful lump of otherwise benign tissue that became sensitized only with strenuous exercise. Occasionally the feeling had resurfaced with Hal's pedantry in meetings when he pretended compliance and helpfulness to some innovation of hers, then stopped the progress cold with a few modest questions that generated endless debate. Now even his death had to raise questions.

Hal was a drinker, plain and simple, an old-fashioned lush. The steeple fell apart as Clara's fingers stopped tapping. One hand gripped the arm of the chair. The other rose to her mouth and began stroking her lips and her chin.

Someone you love is going to die. If Hal had written that note, he most certainly hadn't meant himself. For one thing, she didn't love him anymore, hadn't loved him for years and years, and he had known that. Not only that, for him the cold fact of the death of her love was old news. Hal had considered her loving someone else a challenge, a hurdle he could get over. He'd been arrogant. He would manipulate her, torment her any way he could. She could see him getting a little crazy and finding ways to scare her. But she didn't see him hurting *himself.* And no one else would, either. Hal's death would simply not be written off as a suicide.

Her agitated fingers moved back and forth across her lips, rubbing the soft skin as if it were a rough surface that needed abrasion. She hadn't loved Ray Cowles, either. And now he was dead, too. What did the story tell? Suicide and suicide? Ray because he couldn't face coming out of the closet and Hal not because she wouldn't love him but because he couldn't accept her accusation of harassment, the threat of being thrown off the Centre staff.

What about accident and accident? That sounded better in both cases. Neither had left a note. Maybe neither had meant to die. It didn't sound good enough, though. Hal had been very busy when he died. He had wanted to clear himself, keep his job. He wouldn't have taken Amitriptyline. If he hadn't taken the medication on purpose, could he have taken it by accident? Clara thought of Bobbie Boudreau leaning against a tree, smoking, as she returned to the Centre after Hal's death. Boudreau knew the building well. Boudreau was a mischief-maker, a poisoner. Boudreau had killed that way before. He'd been fired under extremely unpleasant circumstances. The pieces fit. Boudreau had killed Hal because Hal had found out Boudreau was the one who was harassing her.

Clara decided it was time to take the used condom out of her freezer, where she'd put it last Friday before leaving for her meeting in Washington. She was going to nail Boudreau with his own nasty little gift. Clara leaned back and checked her watch. She had ten minutes to relax before Special Agent Daveys arrived.

bobbie

forty-four

Bobbie's day off was on Wednesday. On the Wednesday after the death of Harold Dickey, he walked back and forth through the underground corridors in the Medical Center complex—from building to building and back—looking as if he had important business to do. As always, he seemed to belong there. As far as he was concerned, he did belong there.

He had become attached like a plant in a garden and didn't intend ever to leave. Before last year the wards in the Psychiatric Centre had been the garden where Bobbie thought he'd stay forever. Some years he'd worked the day shift, some years the night shift. Always he'd been available to fill in whenever needed, to help the damaged people in the wards. He didn't like regular people. He lived for his work.

Bobbie saw his patients as sacred victims of the vicious world that systematically destroyed them—made them sick, incarcerated them, made them sicker, then spewed the lost souls out onto the street again where they couldn't possibly survive. He believed it was the same kind of destruction done to him in the Army. He took comfort in the crazy. He felt God sent him there to the crazies, to be the one in control of them. He told the patients what to do. He gave them what was good for them. They got it when he said so and not before. If they had to go into restraints, he was the one to put them there. He was the one to release them. Every cigarette, every privilege they had and couldn't have was up to him. It was his job to protect the crazies from their doctors and from the world. Bobbie gave them their medicine with love. He mourned their loss when they were tossed back into the unspeakable life outside.

After that patient jumped off the terrace last year and Bobbie was blamed for it, he'd felt even worse than when he had been transferred out of his first MASH unit and over the next years was systematically demoted from one nursing job after another until he was no longer doing any procedures at all, was forbidden to touch the patients—even to bathe them or change their dressings. Demoted and demoted again *for no reason but pure mean spite* until all he could do was carry the bedpans and mop up the blood. Bag the corpses of all those medical fuck-ups. He'd bagged a lot of corpses before he left the Army.

But now he felt good again. One vicious bastard who didn't deserve to be a doctor, much less breathe the air of the living, was gone from this earth. Bobbie felt real good seeing Dickey as a dead man, rushed down the street on a gurney with all those asshole paramedics trying so hard to keep a dead man alive. God surely had a hand in putting Bobbie out on the street at that exact moment to serve as witness to the punishment of true evil.

God was surely good to give him a death he could see again and again. He played it over and over in his mind, particularly the part with the bitch Treadwell hurrying back to the Centre alone, probably going back for the bottle. Bobbie had been interested to see that Clara Treadwell's face had not been white with shock. Nor had it been gray with grief. Treadwell had completely forgotten the man who'd died just minutes before. She was preoccupied, busy with what she had to do next. Bobbie laughed at the panic the bitch Treadwell must have felt when she saw that Dickey's scotch bottle was missing from his office. Now the bitch would know she wasn't safe. Bobbie had been there: He knew what she had done.

Monday Bobbie felt good. Tuesday he felt good. Wednesday he felt good enough to travel up to the third floor and pay a visit to the old bag. He wanted to see Gunn's fat face get all red, wanted to hear her protest and complain, get all scared about what would happen, what would happen. *And what the hell happened since the good doctor was just fine when I saw him and gave him the files on Friday?* He wanted to hear her whine about all the trouble they'd get in. And ask again and again what had he done, what had he done, what had he done? Blah, blah, blah. Gunn didn't know he was in control of this. For once he knew what was going on and Gunn didn't. It made him feel good to think about it.

Bobbie arrived at Gunn's office soon after five. She was sitting at her desk, still as a stone. He was disappointed that her face didn't get red with embarrassment and fear when she saw him. She sat there staring straight ahead of her as if she'd been turned to stone. She looked beaten, looked old. He wondered how he'd gotten involved with such an old woman.

"Hi." He pulled on the brim of his baseball cap.

She shook her head.

Malika, her dim-witted associate, walked by and didn't even say hi. "I'm goin' now" was all she said. Then she left.

"What's up?" Bobbie asked Gunn. "You look funny."

"Something's wrong. Some guy from the FBI was here."

"Huh?" Bobbie was startled. "What'd he want?"

"Take a guess, Bobbie."

"Don't fuck with me, woman. What'd the asshole want?"

"He wanted to know why friends of Dr. Treadwell's were suddenly dying here."

Bobbie almost laughed. A bubble of air rose from his gut. He belched loudly, tasted the meatball from his meatball-hero lunch. "What friends?" he asked innocently. "I didn't know the bitch had any friends."

"Oh, come on, Bobbie. You know what I mean. Two people died. Not only poor Dr. Dickey—but a *patient,* too. Another patient died."

"*Another* one since last week?"

"No, the same one from last week. Isn't one enough?"

Bobbie shrugged. "Is the FBI here to nail the bitch for her crimes?"

Gunn shook her head. "Bobbie, you worry me to death. You really do."

"Why should I worry you to death?" He almost laughed in her fat face.

"Because you don't always think about the consequences of doing things . . . of people *dying.*"

"The shit I don't." Now he was getting angry. He didn't have anything to do with anybody's dying. Gunn had no idea what was going on. She was pissing in the wind again, going off on some crazy suspicions that were as far from the truth as falseness could get.

"I don't even work here," he protested. "I don't even know the guy. You told me it was a private patient. I don't even know the guy's name. How could I have anything to do with it?"

"Well, you know Dr. Dickey's name, Bobbie," she said haughtily. "And the police were here, too. The police *and* the FBI. What am I supposed to tell them?"

"Right, the fucking FBI. Let me tell you something—when the fucking FBI investigate things, they don't tell you they're fucking FBI. So you're imagining things. You're in cuckooland. You don't know what you're talking about."

She nodded. "Oh, yes, they do. I told this guy to go away if he didn't have proper authority to ask me questions, so he showed me this FBI *thing.*" So there.

"So what do you want me to do about it? I haven't done anything wrong. I don't even know what you're talking about. Dickey had a heart attack and croaked. I don't know about the other guy. I never even heard of him."

Now she got agitated. She started crying. "Poor Dr. Dickey. And now they won't release my files. I'm just so upset, Bobbie."

"Don't worry. I didn't have nothing to do with it. I didn't even know the guy."

Gunn blew her nose. "That's what you *say*. But you're not supposed to be here. What are you doing here? You knew the police were here, didn't you?"

She was crazy. He made a noise with his mouth. Who said he couldn't be there? No one said he couldn't be there. Only *she* said he couldn't be there. It pissed him off. He had to be smart about this, couldn't fly off the handle at her. He shook his head.

"No, I didn't know nothing. I just stopped by to see you. Don't try to make something of it."

"Let's go, Bobbie." Gunn's face was mad. "After everything I've done for you," she muttered. "I don't know why I put up with this. I don't want you ever coming over here again, you hear me?"

"What do you want me to do, leave town?"

"It wouldn't be a bad idea. Then you'd be safe." She waved her short, fat arms at him, shooing him away. "You go first. I don't want us seen together."

She was nuts. Bobbie made another noise and walked out.

forty-five

"How's it going with us, Jason?"

Emma leaned against the back of her green and black bistro wicker chair and tapped the end of her fork on the white tablecloth soundlessly. In the soft light, her smile was wistful. Wistful and sad always made Jason feel guilty. Guilty made him defensive. He didn't want to be defensive.

They were dining in a restaurant Emma thought was engaging enough to unite them against their private, ever-absorbing preoccupations. Emma was still waiting for word about her play and Jason had been sucked into the black hole of hospital politics and was never off the phone. The restaurant Emma had chosen to divert him to her own interests, however, was opposite the museum, around the corner from the Twentieth Precinct. From their table at the window, Jason was able to watch the street and wonder if April Woo was on duty. And if so, what she was doing.

"How's it going with us, Jason?" Emma repeated.

At the question, he hastily focused on Emma. In the old days Emma would never have asked such a thing. How was it going with them? What kind of question was that? How did he feel? Did he love her, miss her? Before six months ago she would never have demanded that he talk to her about these things. She used to know better than to try to swim in such tricky currents. But that was then. Now she felt she had the upper hand. The tables had turned. Suddenly she was a person of substance, an earner. She wore expensive clothes, had her hair colored, and dropped names of Hollywood people he was pretty sure he didn't ever want to know. So now Emma figured she had the right to ask any question she wanted.

Well, it just so happened one couldn't answer questions like that no matter how the tables were placed. Love was not an "ever-fixed mark that looks on tempests and is never shaken," as proclaimed by Shakespeare in a once favorite sonnet of Jason's. In fact, love was as chaotic, unpredictable, and dangerous as the weather.

How did he feel? How many times did the winds shift in a day, pick up and ease off? How many degrees did the temperature vary? Pressure built up and storm clouds gathered. Then, just as they accepted the inevitability of a real set-to with the elements, the winds died down without warning and the sun broke through.

Emma began twisting her wedding ring around on her finger, impatient for his answer. After a second Jason smiled and covered her hand with his own. "You already know the answer to that."

"Yeah, what is it?"

"We're catching up. We're just trying to catch up and work it out."

It must have been the right answer for once because she nodded. "Fair enough." Her fingers curled around his.

"I wouldn't have let you go, anyway," he added after a moment. "I need you."

That did it, got her where, all along, she had wanted to go.

"But what do you think about the play? Do you like the play?" she demanded.

He grimaced, stared out the window. "I'm sure everyone will like it."

"So what's the matter?"

The lifestyle, the jealousy. Everything. He couldn't go out and eat this late. He was too tired. If Emma did a play, there'd be no quiet dinners at home. No quiet at all. Or maybe too much quiet. At night when he was alone, undernourished and exhausted, she'd be out on the town working, eating late with a lot of groupies who were likely to flatter her and tell her she was wonderful. How could he stand that? In the daytime, when he was working like a fiend, she'd be lolling around in bed. It didn't sound like fun. On the other hand, if she didn't get the part, she might go back to California, and he wouldn't see her at all.

He picked at the spaghetti on his plate, irritated that even the tomato sauce on the spaghetti was compromised. When he'd ordered, the waiter had insisted it had no cream in it, but the sauce had arrived thick and creamy, hardly tinged with pink.

"It doesn't make any difference what I think. You'll do what you need to do," he murmured.

"Darling, you've always done what you needed to do. You never cared what I thought."

"Let's not get into parity. It's apples and oranges."

"It's apples and apples, Jason. Work is work. I don't love yours, but I guess I love you. So . . . ?" She shrugged. "It's the same thing."

Jason grunted and paid the bill. It never came to much: Emma needed a perfect body and wasn't eating entrées these days. That hurt, too. He couldn't even feed her. He put the receipt in his pocket, annoyed at himself for such pettiness.

"Come on, take your stodgy husband home. If you're really nice to me, maybe I'll give you a good time," he murmured, determined to bring the sunshine back.

"Promises, promises," Emma grumbled. Still, on the street she took his arm and hugged it to her.

They headed west toward the river. "Did that guy find you?" she asked.

"What guy?"

"Some man in a gray suit. White shirt. Short hair, blue eyes. Rang the apartment bell and asked for you."

"What did he want?"

"Well . . . since I'm not supposed to ask people looking for you who they are or what they want, I didn't ask. He wanted to know when you'd be free, and I said he'd have to ask you."

They walked across Seventy-ninth Street. "Hmmm. Cop? Insurance investigator?"

Emma shook her head. "Not a cop."

"How did he get upstairs?"

"I have no idea. I thought he was a patient."

Jason made a mental note to talk to the doorman in the morning. He tried to remember which one was on this morning, figured it must be Emilio, who was not always as attentive as he should be. As they went in their building, he stopped to ask the night doorman if anyone had asked for them. The former marine was the size of a bantam cock and still reeling from Emma's abduction down the block on his watch while it was still light at six P.M. last spring.

"No, sir, absolutely no one," the man said a touch defensively, looking away from Emma.

"Thanks, good night."

Upstairs in the apartment the phone was ringing. Jason unlocked the door and headed for it.

"I bet it's my call." Emma pushed past him into the kitchen and got there first. "Hello." Her voice was neutral.

"Ah . . . is Jason there?" It was a woman who sounded surprised.

"Who's calling?" Emma replied coldly.

"It's Dr. Treadwell. Clara Treadwell."

Jason was right behind her, standing there questioningly. Emma handed over the phone, rolling her eyes. She wasn't going to tell.

Thanks a lot. After a pause he said, "Hello?"

"Jason, it's Clara. I need to meet with you right away."

"Okay." Jason checked his watch. It was nearly eleven-thirty, and Emma was frowning at the intrusion. "Um, I'm all booked up tomorrow. How about tomorrow, early morning? At seven?"

"Come to my apartment."

"Ah . . ."

"Seven A.M.," Clara said impatiently. "It can't wait."

The line went dead before he could ask what was so urgent.

forty-six

In spite of his fatigue and the wine at dinner, Jason did not go to sleep when Emma did. There were a number of things he wanted to take up with Clara. He decided to finish the Cowles file before his meeting with her the next morning. He gathered up the papers and took them into the living room, where he sat in his favorite chair, reading, as Emma slept. At one he heard each of his clocks chime once. And then on the half-hour he heard them chime one again. He found it a little eerie to be sitting in the dark, with only one light shining on his page, married again with all the attendant complications of ambivalence and longing. Nothing about their relationship was the same as it had been before Emma left, least of all the old sense of security. Still, the need for love was a powerful motivating force. Jason had found he could endure life without it, but only just.

A sense of sadness touched him as he turned the pages to find his place in the file. Doctors don't like to lose patients at any time in their lives, but this patient of Clara's and Harold's was by no means silenced. Ray Cowles was still crying out to them, demanding their care and attention even now. Jason did not have to see his body, or the death report, or the confusion and sorrow of his widow to be touched by the tragedy of his death. Cowles had been a year younger than he. Jason thought of him as a very young man, hardly at the halfway point of his life.

What had changed his mind after all these years? What had made him leave his wife, then feel he could not endure the freedom to be himself? Jason searched through the ancient history of Ray's analysis, trying to find the seeds of his final self-destructive act. He was looking for a thread of depression and suicidal feelings that should have been noted and followed more closely at the time of his original treatment. And he was deeply aware as he read Ray's story that the only other witness to the dead man's treatment with Clara Treadwell was now also dead.

Six months into the analysis, Jason stopped at an entry and shook his head. It was clear to him that something more than the supervision of a therapy was going on between Dickey and Treadwell. There was no question that her supervisor's mind was on the seduction of his resident—

not the needs of the patient—and the supervisor was using the patient's remarks as a kind of direct foreplay with Clara.

Jason sighed and stopped again on a love issue that occurred over two years later. The patient RC was infatuated with a professor at the university. RC's description of his feelings included being overwhelmed by the way the man looked and by his smell. Dickey had told his student Clara that those were not true feelings of love. Dickey had insisted the patient was really in love with Clara. He remarked that RC never acted on his feelings for Professor S. and that proved he was not gay and not in love with him. In her following sessions Clara led the patient to believe Dickey's interpretation of his feelings was the correct one.

It was obvious to Jason that indeed the patient's description of his feelings for Professor S. had the clear ring of truth. And that by year two and a half of RC's therapy, his therapist and her supervisor were involved in a sexual relationship and were more interested in each other than they were in him. Jason didn't sleep very well that night. Neither did Emma. Both of them rolled around for hours, periodically coming together to hold and stroke each other in the dark.

It was unseasonably balmy at six-fifty-five when Jason walked up Riverside Drive to meet Clara Treadwell. He was a little hung over from too much white wine and not enough sleep. As he approached her building, the night doorman stood outside by the curb polishing the brass on the canopy supports.

"No one goes in there," the doorman said coldly when Jason tried to enter the building.

"Dr. Frank to see Dr. Treadwell. She's expecting me."

"I'll have to call up."

Jason nodded. So call up.

The guy jerked his head toward a man sitting in a car at the curb, then called up, spoke on the intercom, and said to Jason, "You're okay. Penthouse."

Clara opened the door even before Jason rang the bell, then, without greeting him, passed through the foyer to the kitchen. "Come in here. I'll make coffee" was the first thing she said.

She didn't look as if she'd slept much either. Jason followed her into a kitchen not unlike his and Emma's. It was large enough to sit in, modern but not trendy. She did have a microwave oven on the counter, which they did not. Jason wasn't sure what microwaves were good for, but only the night before Emma had said she wanted one.

He watched Clara grind some coffee beans from a Zabar's bag and dump them into a filter without measuring. Then she found milk in the refrigerator, poured some into a pitcher, put the pitcher in the microwave. Hit a button.

"Sit down," she said.

Mystified by the milk in the microwave, Jason sat in one of the two chairs at the kitchen table. After a few seconds the machine beeped. Clara took the pitcher of steaming milk out of the machine and set it on the table. "Café au lait," she said.

"I don't speak Italian," he murmured.

"It's French."

"Ah. I knew that."

She smiled. Sure he did. She set two mugs on the table with a sugar bowl. The microwave beeped when the milk was ready. The coffee machine beeped when the coffee was ready. It was a beeping kitchen. Clara poured the coffee and the milk in the proportions she felt were correct for the item she was making. Jason ladled in four heaping teaspoons of sugar, then put down the spoon.

"Ben Hartley called me here last night. Raymond's insurance company's lawyer called him yesterday. It looks like the insurance company has to pay the widow. I thought suicide wasn't covered, but apparently if the policy has been in place for more than a year the company has to pay no matter what the cause of death. They're going to sue us for the money."

"Who's us?" Jason asked.

"Oh, me, the hospital, and anybody else they can think of."

"What's the basis of their case?"

"Oh, I treated Ray eighteen years ago. I had an appointment with him two days before he died. They're going to allege we failed to treat him properly initially and then failed to identify him as a candidate for suicide two months ago when he called and asked to see me again. The insurance company is looking for a million dollars in damages. The widow wants twenty-five million. Ben said that that sum represents a combination of what the widow believes Cowles would have earned in a normal lifetime, plus some kind of compensation for her loss of love and companionship. You know of course he was gay. He'd left her months ago."

"Isn't that sort of beside the point?" Jason asked. "Where does Hartley see the liability?"

Clara ignored her coffee and started chewing the lipstick off her lips. "The hospital's insurance company may take the position that I was treating Cowles, at least this last time, as a private patient and therefore they have no liability. So it's complicated. Have you read the file?"

Jason nodded. He didn't ask why she had kept such detailed notes of such a botched job or why she had given them to him.

"The suit is nothing," she said. "I'm not worried about it. That's not why I asked you here."

"Oh?" Jason was worried about it. He sipped the coffee and burned his mouth.

"The police are investigating Dickey's death. Did you know that?"

"Oh? What are they looking for?"

Now Clara picked up her cup. The liquid on the surface must have been just cool enough. She drank some. "They don't think Dickey's death was natural."

"What do they think?"

"They don't know." Clara studied her cup.

"What do you think?" Jason asked.

"I think he was murdered." Clara let out a sigh and stirred her coffee thoughtfully. "You probably noticed the surveillance downstairs."

"Surveillance?"

"Yes, I've had to call in the FBI." She brushed her hair back with one hand, indicating her importance.

"Clara, how did the police get involved in the first place?"

She narrowed her eyes, looking back on Hal's last moments. "Something wasn't right. In ER, when they finally stopped working on him, I just said it seemed—medically odd. I thought it might be useful to run the toxes." She shrugged. "I was right. Poor Hal had a lethal mixture of alcohol and Elavil in his blood. If I hadn't asked, the murderer might have gotten away with it."

She looked at Jason and shuddered. "Who knows, I might have been next."

Jason frowned. "How do you know it wasn't an accident?"

"Jason, you saw me cut my hand. You saw that used condom at the meeting Friday morning. You yourself told me something had to be done about it. Well, I've done something. I'm having the FBI take over the case."

"I see." Surreptitiously, Jason added another teaspoon of sugar to his coffee. He wondered what the police had to say about that. "Well, that about does it," he said.

"Not quite."

"Oh?" What now?

"I'd like you to have the specimen tested for me privately, Jason."

"What specimen?"

"The sperm from the condom."

"You're kidding."

Clara shook her head. She wasn't kidding.

He was appalled. "Why?"

"Because I know who killed Dickey. I want to make sure he's caught."

"Then give the condom to the FBI agent. Or give it to the police."

Clara shook her head again. "I want to be sure there aren't two people involved."

"Two people?"

"Right."

Jason swallowed the last of his syrupy coffee. He couldn't get a fix on what game Clara was playing. He was beginning to think that Clara might be disturbed.

"Who are the two possibilities?"

Clara pressed her lips together. "A male nurse from the Centre overdosed a patient with Elavil about a year ago. The young inpatient had a psychotic incident and jumped off a terrace. The nurse's name was Robert Boudreau. Dickey was the one who investigated the case and had Boudreau fired."

"You think this man Boudreau was angry enough to murder Harold?"

Clara nodded. "I saw him outside the ER the day Hal died."

Jason was silent. "What about the condom?"

Clara answered the question by retrieving a package from her freezer. She put it down on the table between them, pushed it to his side with one finger. "I think Boudreau was behind the incidents with the scalpel and the condoms, too."

"Then why not let the FBI deal with it?" Jason suggested.

"There is a very slight possibility there won't be a match with his blood type."

"I see. Who else do you suspect?"

"I'm not entirely sure." Clara did not look at him.

If Jason hadn't spent so much time reading Ray Cowles's file the night before and seen such intimacy between Dickey and Clara, he would never have made the leap. But Clara had given him the file and Jason had studied it. He knew how deeply involved Clara had been with Dickey.

"Someone you don't want implicated," he said, "like the victim."

"Yes." Clara met his eyes. "You know Hal took advantage of me years ago. He manipulated Ray's case, and he manipulated me. He was my supervisor. I had no choice but to follow his instruction."

But Clara had not been acting under Hal's supervision when she met with Ray two days before his death or when she spoke to him only minutes before he put the plastic bag over his head. Jason could see the strings. Clara didn't want the FBI to know about her troubled relationship with Dickey. Jason had the Cowles file, which incriminated her in both cases. Now Clara wanted him to take the condom.

"Well," he said finally. "I'll have the condom tested if you want me to, but I'll have to give it to the police. I have no choice about that. This is a criminal investigation. I have to cooperate with them."

"The police are not competent to deal with this."

"I would disagree with that view. But it's up to you. I can't take evidence in a homicide unless I turn it over to the police."

Clara hesitated. He could see her weighing the pros and cons of different alliances. For some reason she wanted the protection of the FBI but did not intend to fully cooperate with them. She was playing a dangerous game. After a few minutes, however, she agreed and handed over the plastic package. Jason left with it almost immediately, pulling on the ragged growth of his new beard. He didn't have long to reach April Woo before both their days got complicated. He wanted the thing out of his possession within the hour.

forty-seven

"Let's get this straight." Sergeant Joyce stopped to sneeze all over the phone as she replaced the receiver. "Jason Frank gave you a used *condom* that came from Treadwell's appointment book a week ago?"

April stood in front of Sergeant Joyce's desk and nodded. She wondered if this was a good time to tell her about the FBI.

Joyce sneezed again and barked, "Sit down—you're giving me a headache."

April flinched and moved over to the windowsill, where the air was still leaking cold. She knew of some Chinese remedies that might help her supervisor's condition, but she didn't think the Sergeant would appreciate them.

"And you did *what* with it?" The Sergeant honked.

"Uh, I took it to the labs to be tested."

"Give me a hint, April. Tested for what?"

"Well, to get a blood type, to try for a match with—"

The door opened and Mike came in with a funny smile on his face. "You asked for me?"

"What's with you, Sanchez?" Joyce hacked into a paper napkin.

"What?"

"You know something I don't?"

Mike turned to April and winked, then shook his head, looking serious. "What's up?"

"Oh, nothing, just the Feebies want in, that's all. What the fuck is going on here?"

Mike's crooked eyebrows came together. "The feds? In what?"

"I just got a call from Special Agent"—she glanced down at the note she had scribbled, then sneezed on—"Stephen Daveys. He wants to work closely with us on the case. He'll be in to chat with us at four. That gives us about four hours to clear it." She barked out a short laugh.

April didn't share her enjoyment. They'd been talking for several minutes and the Sergeant had waited until Mike appeared to mention it.

Mike scratched his nose. "Excuse me, I must have missed something here. What case are we talking about?"

"It remains a little confused, a little hazy, Sanchez. What would the feds want with the case of an unnatural death of a shrink at the Psychiatric Centre? You tell me."

"Hmmm. Could be a number of things." He went silent, then glanced at April. "I heard you were at the labs this morning. We missed each other."

"Detective," Joyce said sarcastically, "why don't you tell the Sergeant what you were doing there."

April made a clicking noise with her tongue. It was the same noise Skinny Dragon Mother made when she was about to release her pent-up rage. April sniffed cautiously, wondering if Joyce's cold happened to be traveling her way, clicked her tongue again. Then she cleared her throat and smiled at Mike.

"I had some sperm I wanted tested."

"Oh, yeah?" he said. "Whose?"

"Dr. Treadwell thinks it came from the guy who offed Dickey."

"Oh, yeah?" Mike said again. "I don't remember any sperm at the death scene."

April kept her face straight. "It came up before the death. It appeared at some meeting Dr. Treadwell was having to discuss the Cowles case on Friday. Someone put it in her appointment book."

Mike chewed on his mustache. "Uh-huh," he said. "And how did you get it?"

She squirmed a little. "Jason Frank gave it to me."

"No kidding. How did *he* get it?" Frustrated, Sergeant Joyce grabbed a hank of hair to torture.

"Jason Frank is Dr. Treadwell's consultant on the Cowles suicide."

"And what does that have to do with this?" Joyce screamed.

"Dickey was Treadwell's supervisor on Cowles's treatment eighteen years ago. And Treadwell and the hospital are being sued for twenty-six million by the widow and the insurance company."

"Oh, shit." Joyce let go of the hair to blow her nose. "Oh, shit. I don't like this."

"And you think . . ."

April threw out a possible. "Dickey's the only witness to Cowles's treatment. If he's dead, he can't testify in a malpractice case."

"What are you suggesting here, April? You think the Director of the Psychiatric Centre—a woman who happens to be on the President's Commission on Mental Health—killed her former supervisor to prevent him from taking the stand against her in a case he supervised eighteen years ago? That sound plausible to you?" Joyce was still screaming.

"They getting much federal funding?" Sanchez drummed his fingers on the armrests of the chair he finally fell into.

"Who?"

"The hospital, hospital community programs—"

"Bingo, a nice fed connection. Fine—let them deal," Joyce muttered, wiping her hands of it.

"Yeah, but it might not be that. Hell, the Feebs can come in on anything. They've got a thousand excuses to step on any toes they want. Hey, maybe it's not homicide they're interested in. Maybe it's some kind of corruption." Sanchez turned to April. "So what's this about a used rubber in your possession this morning, April?"

"There's more to the Treadwell thing," April said. "Jason confirmed what Mrs. Dickey said about Treadwell and her husband. They did have an affair while Treadwell was in training there. After Treadwell qualified, she left for a dozen years, married, divorced, worked in California; married again, divorced again. She came back here as head of the psychiatric hospital three years ago.

"About six months ago she started dating a U.S. Senator and about the same time began getting threatening notes. Last week Jason was present when she reached in her desk drawer and was cut by a surgical scalpel someone had rigged up in there. The used condom turned up at a meeting when she opened her leather appointment book—"

"And Jason Frank told you all this?" Joyce interrupted skeptically.

"He told me about the events he witnessed. Her personal history I investigated on my own," April replied.

"Well, good work, Detective," Joyce said sarcastically.

April lifted a shoulder. *Thanks.*

"So what's his interest?" Mike demanded.

"Jason's? I'm not entirely sure."

"And what's the relationship, huh? What does he stand to gain here?" Mike again.

April shook her head. "I don't know."

"So, Dr. Treadwell is seeing a U.S. Senator. Whew." Joyce blew her nose loudly. "And what about the threatening letters?"

"Apparently, she didn't take them seriously." April spread out her hands, palms up. "She didn't want anyone to know."

"And now I guess she's changed her mind."

"Now she thinks Dickey was murdered by the guy who's been

harassing her." April didn't add that Clara was responsible for involving the FBI.

"Uh-huh. Does Treadwell have a name for this guy?"

"Yeah. Boudreau, Robert Boudreau. He was a former nurse, fired last year after the death of a patient—a young guy who jumped off a terrace. . . ."

Joyce's eyes were wide. She chewed on her lip with dismay. "I remember the case. This is real sketchy stuff, April."

April nodded. "It has a strong odor," she agreed.

"And why did Jason Frank tell you all this?"

"I guess Dr. Treadwell doesn't trust us. She told Jason she's having the FBI take over the case. Maybe he's afraid we can't handle them," April murmured. "But then again, maybe he likes me." She smiled.

"Likes you!" Sanchez exploded. "Likes you? I'll break his fucking head."

"Shut up!" Joyce screamed, then went into a coughing fit.

"You want some water?" April asked evenly.

"I'm fine. Ghhhh." Joyce cleared her throat and spit. "So Treadwell had a pretty strong motive for killing Dickey. And let's not forget that she was with him when he died."

"Let's not forget it," Mike said. "And maybe the Feebs are here to help her cover up."

Joyce started plucking at her hair again. "So this mischief may be a fairy tale. Anyone see the threatening letters?"

"Well, the condom sighting is legit—"

"That's a fucking fairy tale, too. What are we supposed to do with that? Why did Frank take the condom? Why did he give it to you? Give me a break."

"Look, Jason says all Treadwell wants is to have the thing tested to see if the blood type matches Boudreau's. Then we can nail him."

"Who the hell is this Boudreau?" Joyce screamed. "How does he tie in? What do we nail him with? Shit, the victim died. Either his death was a suicide, an accident, or somebody offed him. For all we know, Treadwell could have balled this guy Boudreau a week ago and held on to the happy results for just this purpose. The woman kept it for a *week.* Give me a break, April. This whole thing stinks."

"So, what do you want to do?"

"Check it out. Check it all out, every piece. Every scrap. I want to know the story here." She sniffed toward Sanchez. "What about you? You get anything?"

"Only one tiny thing." Sanchez shrugged. "The Amitriptyline was in syrup form. The in-patients get it in a little cup. They call it bug juice. It comes from the pharmacy on the third floor, but every floor has its own supply. Dickey apparently drank his with the scotch. There were traces of both scotch and Amitriptyline in his empty glass."

"Dickey was a doctor. He must have known that mixing the two would be dangerous. . . . Suicide?" Joyce said hopefully.

Mike shook his head. "Remember, there was no bottle of scotch, no container of the drug on the scene. No note."

Joyce tore at her hair again. Then suddenly she threw up her hands. "Get out of here. Fill in the dots by four—and get me some chicken soup for this damn cold."

forty-eight

The bean burrito and guacamole sat heavy in April's stomach as she headed out into the field after lunch. Lunch with Sanchez when it was his turn to choose—and he chose Mexican always—made her want to get into bed and sleep it off. Aside from the earthy spices and thickness of food in her mouth, she had to be on her guard with him all the time. He was as hot as the small red chilies on the plate you weren't supposed to eat, and there was always another meaning to everything he said. April had no background for this kind of banter.

Playfulness was against everything Chinese. Severe punishment as a spur to improvement was the hallmark of her culture. There was no such thing as positive reinforcement. Compassion was something she'd learned on the streets of New York. And sex—well, as her Italian supervisor in Chinatown used to say, "Get outta here. Forget about it."

Out of sight, out of mind was the Chinese philosophy on sex. Better if you didn't have it, but if you *had* to have it, you didn't talk about it. April had never heard her father refer to the physical aspect of married life. On the rare occasions Ja Fo Woo chose to say anything about anything, his remarks were limited to what children owed their parents, what wives owed their husbands, and what courses should be served for dinner. Occasionally, he had some things to say about his digestion. He had no sense of humor in two languages. Likewise her mother.

As for her former boyfriend, Jimmy Wong, forget about it. Jimmy used to tell April she didn't love him enough (and didn't do enough for him) to make her insecure about her ability to please him and motivate her, like Avis, to try harder.

At lunch Mike had reminded her of the Latinas in high school, with their pushed-up breasts and glued-on pants, the can of hairspray whipped out in the girls' room. Always talking, laughing, teasing, spraying their hair, getting ready to hit on boys.

"You see Carlos over there? He es sooo cool. The way he look in those tight jeans—so good. You see hes bike, so low. *Esta noche* I take heem. *Véalo usted mismo.*"

Mike kept telling her that kind of thing was normal, that she should lighten up and enjoy it. It seemed an impossible assignment. What if she lightened up about him and he decided he didn't like her after all? What if he opened the wrong door and some bad guy's Glock blew him away? It didn't seem worth the trouble.

"*Querida.* Hey—wait a minute." Mike hurried after her.

She ignored him. There wasn't an unmarked unit available, so she was debating taking her own car over to the Psychiatric Centre, where she had three interviews lined up. The trouble with taking her own car was the Centre's parking garage was nearly two blocks away from the Centre and the wind was fierce over by the river. But if she left her car on the street, someone might try to steal her radio.

Mike caught up with her and took her arm. "Hey, what's the matter?"

"You know."

"Oh, come on, can't you take a joke?"

"Don't play with me, Mike."

"Oy, *querida,* playing is life. What else is there? *Dios,* I pity the guy who gets you. Can't do this. Can't do that."

She punched him lightly on the arm. "Knock it off."

"Some life he'll have. With your sulks all the time, and never any play, I bet his *cojones* will shrivel up and die."

April laughed in spite of herself. "Eat your heart out, Mike."

"I am," he admitted, then, "What's the matter? I thought we had a good time at lunch."

"Maybe *you* were having a good time. I don't like the secrecy and games. If you know something, tell me."

"If you don't like secrecy and games, then you're in the wrong business, baby. Go into hairdressing."

"You know what I mean."

He shrugged, smiling. "The whole thing is a puzzle, *querida.* These cases are the least of it."

"So something's coming down."

He nodded solemnly. "You guessed it, something's coming down."

"Am I being reassigned?"

He shrugged again.

"Come on, what's coming down? Are you telling or not?"

"How about not." Mike looked over as more uniforms joined the first two on the sidewalk outside the fence. The uniforms were talking and laughing.

"Thanks, pal." April watched them, too.

"Oh, all right, if you really want to know, give me a kiss and I'll tell you."

She shook her head. Not a chance.

"Okay, so sue me for sexual harassment."

"Maybe later, when things slow down," she muttered.

"*Bueno,* I'll look forward to it. See you at four," Mike said, and walked away.

At three April was sitting in the academic office of Dr. Lionel Hambug gathering her thoughts. Sally Ann Dickey had given her permission to check out her husband's private office in the Medical Office Building, so she had gone there first. She found a room furnished with leather chairs and a leather couch. It had an artificial bamboo tree in the corner that needed dusting. Books and periodicals lined the bookshelves, and in the cupboards below, the deceased had kept files and reprints of his articles. April looked through the reprints quickly. Genetics seemed to have been Dickey's area of interest. His files were full of graphs and charts.

In his middle desk drawer she'd found an appointment book held shut with a rubber band. She opened it to check out the coming weeks. Dickey's time had been fully booked for the whole month of November. According to his book, he planned to speak at an association meeting in Miami in mid-December. He'd made a note to himself to inform (his letters were a scrawl) about the subject of his talk. He had blocked out the following week as a vacation and written "Aruba" across the days. His wife had not mentioned any trip to the Caribbean. Nor had Sally Ann known that in the last year Harold had added two modest life-insurance policies to those he already had and named psychoanalytic associations as beneficiaries of both of them. April had not yet been able to reach his lawyer to find out the contents of his will. No medications were kept in this office, but there was a bottle of Johnnie Walker in the bottom drawer. Johnnie Walker happened to be the favorite brand of the Chinese. It was expensive, but even her father drank it—showed what a big man he was. This particular bottle of Johnnie Walker was full and had not been opened. April closed the drawer, leaving it there.

"How can I help you?"

Dr. Hambug regarded her with expressionless eyes. He had granted her six minutes of his time and by the look of his face and surroundings, it seemed clear he would not allow a second more. He was a small, curly-haired man, clean-shaven, thin as a rice cracker, and clearly a tense and aggressive person even in repose. He wore a brown glen-plaid suit with a pale green shirt and brown tie and sat in a wooden rock-and-rolling chair similar to April's in the squad room. It was like the old railroad stationmaster's chair, hard and unforgiving to the back and bottom, not the shrink-industry-standard padded-leather job.

The chair creaked as he rocked back and forth waiting for her answer.

"I'm investigating the death of Dr. Dickey."

"Yes, you told me that on the phone. What exactly are you looking for?" Now there was a slight gleam of curiosity in the doctor's eyes.

"Dr. Dickey was working in his office the day he died and it's not entirely clear to us what happened. We're trying to establish his state of mind so we can—"

"You think Harold Dickey might have committed suicide?" Dr. Hambug seemed surprised. "Harold?"

"It's a possibility. That or an accident." Or a homicide.

"Gee." Hambug stared at the reproduction of some frenzied sunflowers on his wall.

April knew it was a famous painting but not why. She didn't know anything about art. "Does that sound plausible to you, Doctor?"

Hambug tore his eyes away from the sunflowers and smiled at her. "Plausible?"

"Your office is next door to his. You must have known him pretty well."

"We had lunch together two or three times a week for about twenty years. I guess you could say I knew him well." Hambug glanced at the corner of his desk, where a small clock presented its back to April.

She guessed she had about three minutes left. "What was his state of mind, Dr. Hambug? Would you say he was a happy, contented man, or a disappointed, angry man? Was he happy, was he depressed? Was he tidying up for suicide?"

Hambug swung about while the chair complained noisily for a few seconds. His narrow mouth considered the question while his brow furrowed. "I know what state of mind means," he said coldly.

April waited. She didn't like being patronized by people who had dozens more years of higher education than she did and thought she was stupid because of it. "So?"

He shrugged. "Dickey didn't like the way things were going. His position had eroded at the hospital. Things were changing. Hal found that distressing."

"He was in conflict with Dr. Treadwell."

Hambug ignored that. "Things were changing, but Hal had a devoted following, his students liked him, the staff liked him."

"What about Dr. Treadwell?"

"I don't know about that."

"They had a relationship at one time, apparently he wanted to renew it. What about that?"

"I don't know about that," Hambug repeated. "He certainly liked women, always had a woman friend. As far as I know, he hasn't had anyone special for several years. His relations with his wife, of course, were strained. His children are estranged, I gather. However, Hal was an optimist. He was enormously respected in his field. His time was filled, and he was a fighter. He didn't have the profile of a suicide. . . . I'll miss him."

Jason had said similar things. But Dr. Treadwell had hinted that Dickey had been depressed. "Was something bothering him lately?" April asked.

Hambug glanced at his little clock again. "Well, there was always *something* bothering him. Hal was something of a tilter at windmills, but I don't know of anything in *particular*. I can't even hypothesize."

April bet he could hypothesize pretty accurately if he wanted to. Now that the specified time was up, he could look her over appraisingly. He was doing that when she stood up suddenly. She wanted to leave before she was asked to, reached in her bag for a card. "Thank you for your cooperation, Doctor. You've been very helpful. If you think of anything else, you can reach me at this number."

Surprised, Hambug lurched out of the creaking chair to take the card and open the door for her. It occurred to April that he hadn't expected her to leave quite so easily. Well, sometimes you got a strike on the first try and sometimes it was necessary to work the fish a different way, come back two, three, even four times until you got all a person had to tell. The heels on her ankle-high boots pounded the uncarpeted floor of the hall as she headed to her next interview.

Gunn Tram was sobbing at her desk in the personnel office when April found her ten minutes later. The woman who had made such a fuss about getting her files back was not as large as her name implied. Gunn Tram was no Viking, just a small, plump hen of a woman with a number of chins, yellow hair, and neon-pink lipstick. She had to take her glasses off to blot her eyes. As she bent her head, the gray of her roots made her scalp look dirty. April figured she had to be somewhere between fifty and sixty.

"Well, what do you want to know?" Gunn Tram reached for a tissue, looking distinctly hostile, focused on the gun in the holster at April's waist that showed when she opened her jacket, then abruptly changed the subject. "Did you hand in the bullets for that gun to the head nurse?" she demanded in a way that made April think she could be difficult to work with.

April nodded.

"You're not allowed to have a gun in the hospital."

"I'm acquainted with the regulations," April assured her.

"If an unstable person got a hold of that"—Gunn rolled her eyes—"anybody could get killed. We don't have a police guard like they do at Bellevue." She started to cry again. "You don't know the things that can happen in a place like this."

April could smell the remains of coffee in the Styrofoam cup on her desk. It was one of those gourmet blends. The aroma was strongly perfumed vanilla or hazelnut. Next to the cup, near the computer, two doughnuts wrapped in plastic wrap waited to be consumed.

"Do you mind if I sit down?" April didn't wait for an answer. She sat in the chair by the desk and took out her notebook, wrote down the day, the date, the time, who was with her, and what Gunn Tram had said so far. Then she wrote: DISKS???

The woman's chins trembled. "How long will this take?"

April shrugged. "Depends."

Gunn took a deep breath and tore apart one of the doughnuts.

"How well did you know Dr. Dickey?" April tried some subtle backtracking. It wasn't easy now. She was tired and didn't like the people there. They were like Chinese puzzle boxes, complicated and deceptive.

"I've been working here as long as he has," Gunn said stiffly.

"How long is that?"

"More than thirty years." She studied the pieces of doughnut, then took a bite of the smallest, chewed daintily.

"So you knew him pretty well."

"Very well." Of that fact she was proud. "We have to be careful about the people who work here. Accidents are"—her eyes teared up again—"costly for everyone."

"What kind of accidents?"

"Oh, in a hospital anything can happen. If a patient who shouldn't be out gets a weekend pass, then goes home and hurts somebody or hurts himself. Or somebody gets the wrong medication and . . ." She left the rest hanging in the air. "Or someone elopes."

April sighed. Elopements, wrong medication. Wrongful death in a mental hospital. "What's the procedure when something goes wrong?"

Gunn rolled her eyes again. "Oh, God, there's an internal investigation for everything—reports, meetings, disciplinary actions. No accident goes unpunished," she said softly, "except maybe the ones that do."

"Did Dr. Dickey often work on Sundays?"

"He never did that I remember."

"What was he working on last Sunday?"

"I don't know."

"Are your personnel files on disks?"

"What?" Gunn brushed sugar from her fingers.

April pointed to the computer. "Have you got the personnel files in the computer?"

"Only the business data. The personal stuff—evaluations, promotion information, histories, disciplinary-action reports—are kept separately in the files. There's never been the manpower to enter it all in."

"What about Robert Boudreau's file?"

"Who?"

"Dr. Dickey asked you for files. Was Boudreau's file one of them?"

The hostile look was back. "I have no idea what you're talking about."

"Dr. Dickey took files of certain people. Did he tell you why he wanted them?"

Gunn took another bite of the doughnut. "I think he was doing some kind of survey."

Uh-huh. "And what about Boudreau?"

Gunn frowned, then shook her head. "Dr. Dickey never mentioned the name."

"Gunn, I heard that you know a great deal about what's going on here. Have you ever heard anything about Dr. Dickey being depressed or drinking in his office?"

Gunn looked horrified. "Dr. Dickey? Never. He was a wonderful man."

That was as far as April got with Gunn. She gave the woman her card.

Then she had to wait ten minutes to get her bullets back from the head nurse. She wasn't out of the hospital yet, so she put them in her pocket.

Her next interview was in the cafeteria. She was meeting with John Flower, a resident who had been in therapy with Dickey. The untidy young man came in several minutes after she did. He was wearing a maroon knit tie and a wrinkled blue work shirt under his baggy sports jacket. They got coffee from the carafes on the beverage table and took a table. Wistfully, Flower told April that Dickey was the most compulsive person he'd ever met.

"Two years ago he had surgery on his knees. He put his whole life in order in case something happened and he didn't survive. Got someone to cover his seminars and everything."

The young man played with his cup of coffee. It had come from the carafe marked GOURMET BLEND. The flavor of the week was titled vanilla-hazelnut. April had passed it up for the carafe labeled REGULAR. Hers was not a good choice. The murky liquid tasted like mold.

"He never missed a session, was never late. Why are you asking me these things?" John looked at her with undisguised curiosity.

"Dr. Dickey had taken some medication that contributed to his death. We're trying to establish how that happened, Dr. Flower."

"Oh, please, call me John." John cocked his head, staring at her in a boyish way. She noticed that he had green eyes. "May I ask you what?"

"What medication?"

"Yes, it might help."

"I really can't say."

Flower made a harrumphing noise. "Well, I suppose it doesn't matter, except there are things you can take by accident and things you can't, if you see what I mean."

April smiled. "It was, apparently, something he didn't take as a general rule."

"The rumors say he was drunk."

"Was he a drinker?" April asked evenly.

Flower raised an eyebrow, continuing to stare at her speculatively. "From time to time I have had the suspicion. Not enough to incapacitate him, though. He never looked or acted drunk."

April nodded. She wondered what was wrong with the young doctor that he had to be in therapy. He seemed attractive and not unintelligent. "Do you think he was suicidal?"

Flower shook his head. "Once he got hung up at an airport somewhere and didn't think he was going to be able to make my session. He called me from the airport and left a message on my machine."

He fell silent, breathing in the scented steam of his coffee. Then he said, "I had a nine-o'clock on Monday."

"Uh-huh," April said.

"We were going to terminate soon."

"Terminate? Does that mean the end of treatment?"

"Yes, and I knew him very well. He wouldn't have done this to himself without making sure I was okay. And that goes for everybody else he treated."

"I understand." April glanced at her watch. She was going to be late for the FBI. "Look, I have to go. Thanks for your help."

Flower seemed disappointed. "Listen, I'd like to help. Can we talk again? I could nose around, ask a few questions, and get back to you."

"Thanks," April said, holding in a smile. Everybody there was so helpful. "I'll let you know."

"He was a great guy. I wouldn't like to think . . ." John Flower got up and followed her to the door. "You'll find out, won't you? You'll find out what really happened to him, won't you?"

"Yeah," April murmured. "We usually do."

forty-nine

The three chairs in Sergeant Joyce's office were already occupied when April arrived six minutes after the hour, panting a little from her sprint up the stairs.

"Thanks for joining us, Detective," her supervisor said sourly. She nodded at the narrow-faced man in the gray suit sitting next to Sanchez. "This is Special Agent Daveys from the New York Branch. Detective Woo."

Sanchez still retained his smiling Buddha countenance from the morning. He winked at April. April bobbed her head at Daveys.

"Detective." Daveys held out his hand so that April had to advance and take it. "Nice to meet you." The guy was thin and didn't look particularly strong, but he had a muscular grip that didn't let go when April did. Her expression remained blank as her bones crunched. She cracked a few knuckles when her hand was returned to her.

Sergeant Joyce raised an eyebrow at her. *Problem?* April's shoulders moved about half an inch. The agent looked vaguely familiar. She had a feeling she'd seen him before.

"So, Daveys, you were about to tell us the reason we're joined together this lovely afternoon," Joyce said.

Daveys smiled beatifically. "Sergeant Sanchez, Sergeant Joyce, Detective—Woo? Looks like the U.N. around here."

Joyce's eyes narrowed. "Yep, we can help in any language. You have a problem, Daveys?" She looked ready for a juicy sneeze, pressed a finger to the base of her nose to contain it.

"From what I understand, Sergeant, you're the one with the problem. I'm here to assist with the solution."

"Well, that's just great. Why don't you fill us in on the case and your reasons for involvement?" Joyce was the supervisor, so she was the speaker. She looked feverish, though, germy and damp.

"Why don't I start with the questions?" Daveys replied.

"Well, this is just a little unusual. Generally, when our department thinks we need help, we get people from our own bureau," Joyce said.

"Uh-huh," Daveys replied. "So?"

"So, what's the story here? What interests you about a local unnatural?"

"We want to help you out with your case. On our end there may be some question of conspiracy."

"Oh, yeah, what kind?"

"Corruption," Daveys answered.

"That's very interesting," Joyce said, not appearing very interested. "Corruption covers a lot of territory, Agent Daveys. It could mean something. It could mean nothing. You want to share with us what your connection is?"

"Well, that remains to be seen. What we're looking for at this time is some cooperation. You let us see what you have, we'll work closely with you on the thing, help you with your case, give you the use of our people, our facilities, our labs. Whatever you need."

Sergeant Joyce sneezed suddenly. The sound resembled the explosive blowout of a tire. No one blessed her. When she recovered she murmured, "That's very decent, very generous of you, Daveys."

"We try to please."

"We try to please also, don't we, Sergeant?"

Sanchez stopped licking the ends of his mustache and said they did.

"So . . ." Daveys spread out his hands. "What've we got here?"

Joyce glanced at April. April had a finger in one of the ivy pots on the windowsill, testing the soil for wetness. The plant didn't look so good. Maybe it had caught the Sergeant's cold.

"You want to brief us on the investigation, April?"

Now April knew where she'd seen Daveys. The dark blue sedan. He'd been cruising the street in Westchester while they were interviewing Dickey's widow.

She said, "Dr. Harold Dickey died of a massive heart attack on Sunday afternoon, November 7, as the result of ingesting a large amount of alcohol mixed with Amitriptyline. He was with Dr. Clara Treadwell at the time of his seizure and death. Dr. Treadwell's story is that she returned from out of town and met Dickey at his office at the Centre. From his appearance she immediately deduced he'd been drinking for some time. Within minutes of her arrival, he collapsed. She tried to resuscitate him, called for the paramedics. They took him to the emergency room, where he was pronounced dead after all measures to save him had failed."

April glanced at Joyce. The Sergeant's head was buried in her hands. She looked bad. "Rotten kids," she muttered. "They're back at school, and I'm sick as a dog. I can't afford to be sick. Go on."

"As I said, the M.E.'s report showed that the victim was poisoned by the aforementioned substance. Our first line of questioning was to determine whether the victim might have ingested the drug by accident. We ruled that out this morning when the lab results showed drug residue in the glass he'd been drinking from. So far, there has been no indication that the victim was depressed at the time of his death and might have taken the substance voluntarily.

"Dickey was a drinker, but not a fan of medications of any kind. He has been described by his wife and colleagues as strictly conscientious. He had a full schedule for the coming weeks—classes, an academic conference, a vacation trip to Aruba in December. He had no family history of suicide. The six people I spoke to about him, including his wife, all said he was not the type to commit suicide. In addition, his behavior in the days before his death indicated that he was concerned about something and working on something. And although he left his office a mess, there was no sign of a liquor bottle or a container for the drug."

Daveys scratched his neck. "So you think someone poured him the lethal mixture. Like Socrates, the victim drank it, then the aforementioned murderer took away the evidence, hoping the death would look like a heart attack."

Joyce flashed him a dirty look.

Daveys didn't seem to mind. "Well, kids, that's pretty quick work. How many people had a reason to kill him?"

"At this moment the prime suspect seems to be Clara Treadwell, the person with him at the time of his death," Sergeant Joyce said flatly.

"And what's her motive?"

"She's named in a multimillion-dollar malpractice case involving the suicide of a patient about a week before. Apparently Dr. Dickey supervised her in the case years ago. He was also her lover."

"Anyone else?" Daveys asked.

Joyce turned to April. "Anyone else?"

"Dr. Treadwell suspects a former male nurse name of Boudreau. A year ago Boudreau gave an inpatient an overdose of Amitriptyline. The patient jumped off a terrace."

Daveys grimaced. "Messy. Have you talked with Boudreau?"

Joyce gave him another dirty look. "Not yet."

"Well, get him in here so we can talk."

"All in good time, Daveys."

"Well, you don't want grass growing under your feet, now, do you?"

Joyce turned to Sanchez. "Sergeant? Anything you'd like to add?"

"Not at this time."

"Well, thanks a lot, kids. Our people would like to see everything you have. Get the stuff together, will you."

"Stuff, what stuff?" Sanchez asked.

"Whatever you have—notes, lab results, death report." Daveys got up to leave. "Good working with you. I'll be in touch."

For a minute or so after Daveys's departure, no one said anything. Then Joyce checked her watch, shaking her head at how time had flown. The shift had ended half an hour before.

"Well, I'm out of here," she announced. "And so are you. April, go talk to Treadwell. Mike, go home."

April raised her eyebrow at Sanchez. He shrugged. Then, as they were filing out, Joyce added, "Good working with you," as if she'd just thought of it. She neglected to mention their gathering any stuff together to hand over to anybody.

fifty

It was hot and dry in Clara Treadwell's elegant living room. In fact, the whole apartment had that beginning-of-winter feeling prewar buildings got when the furnaces were turned on full force for the first time after a long humid summer. Clara paced anxiously in front of the windows facing the Hudson River, black as ink against the evening sky. Outside the windows the first snow flurries danced on the decorative black railings and were swept away without sticking. Around her, the room dimmed to deep gray without her noticing.

April Woo sat motionless in a Queen Anne armchair, her face completely empty. This detective was no friendly Connie Chung type, and the emptiness behind her eyes was a little unnerving to Clara, especially after the open approach of the FBI man, Daveys.

Clara considered how best to deal with the situation. Her area of expertise didn't have cultural sections like the humanities and sociology. Psychiatry still believed that all peoples developed pretty much along the same Freudian model. Lately, Asian psychiatrists had begun advising their colleagues about the Oriental character. Asian patients (even those born and raised in the West) were organized around a concept of the collective good and not around individualism, so patients urged toward a "healthy" Western standard of integration were threatened with becoming selfish, alienated criminals by their culture's standards. Asian shrinks warned that the incorrect integration of the two cultures could have devastating consequences.

Clara had never treated an Asian patient. She tended to snub Asian psychiatrists in the same way she snubbed the Canadians, the French, and the Italians—as hopelessly backwater and with nothing worthwhile to contribute to the field. The first time the two police detectives came into her office, she'd had them classified. Detective Woo was a definite petty-bureaucrat type, unimaginative, rigid, and unyielding. The Latino she figured was about on the level of the security guards at the door. Macho and clueless. Clara knew how to handle people like that.

Woo's notebook was open on her lap. Clara noticed that it was the same kind her assistant used, but that the detective's notes had a few Chinese characters in them. That bit of foreign secretiveness, too, fanned the deep hostility she had toward the police.

Clara believed April Woo had botched the investigation of the Cowles death and set her up for a malpractice suit that threatened the position she'd spent so many years creating for herself. She believed her whole life was on the line because of this young cop's fuck-up. And now—no doubt because she had allowed Jason Frank to overrule her own best judgment about the condom this morning—Woo was still hanging around, investigating Hal's death.

Clara suddenly realized it was dark and began to circle the room flipping light switches. Now she could see that the Asian detective's hands were not completely at rest on her notebook. The cop was getting nervous and impatient. Clara deliberately slowed her pace to let the other woman stew. She'd talk when she was ready.

Clara did not look at the policewoman, did not want to talk to her. It was Friday at five-thirty, now completely black outside. She had made the woman wait downstairs in the lobby for fifteen minutes. Then, up here in her living room, she had delayed several more minutes. Clara didn't like the police. She had been comforted by the emblems of her own class displayed by Special Agent Daveys, the familiar gray suit and white shirt, the briefcase, and the familiarity with the same English language she spoke. She seemed to recall from somewhere the fact that FBI agents had law degrees, and it was the FBI that set up the techniques of profiling serial killers. Daveys had assured her they would be able to obtain all the evidence in Hal's murder and do what was necessary to quickly apprehend the man who had killed him.

"What did you find out?" she asked suddenly.

"We don't believe at this time that Dr. Dickey's death was an accident," the detective said flatly.

Clara inhaled through clenched teeth. The sound she made was like the hiss of an angry cat. "The reason?"

"There were no containers of substances that killed Dr. Dickey in his office."

Clara frowned, raking her thoughts back to the day Hal died. There had been a bottle of Johnnie Walker on his desk. She remembered thinking it was almost empty and Hal was drunk. She had concluded that he must have been drinking all afternoon. She had assumed the bottle was still there.

"Why don't you tell me about that afternoon," the detective suggested.

Clara opened and closed her hand around the scab that had formed over the cut on her hand. A few more days and the scab would peel off. By then she was certain the man responsible for it would be behind bars. She tried to concentrate on that as she spoke.

"I returned to my apartment around four on Sunday—I had been in Florida for the weekend. There was a message from Hal on my answering machine." The tic that lived in Clara's cheek began to dance. She tightened up, resisting it. "He asked me to come to his office right away."

"Why?"

Clara fixed her gaze on the Chinese cop. "I'm being harassed. Hal was looking into it for me."

"And that was what Dr. Dickey called you about?"

"Yes. He told me who it was. He wanted to show me—I don't know—something that would prove it."

"And . . . ?"

"When I got to the office, I saw that Hal was drunk. Then, almost immediately, I realized he was having some kind of psychotic break. I didn't have any idea of the cause, of course. And then he collapsed. It was immediately clear to me something was wrong." Clara clicked her tongue. "Obviously he was poisoned by the man who was threatening me."

"Was it common knowledge that Dr. Dickey drank in his office?"

Clara traced the scab with two fingers, testing the skin around it as if for doneness. "I have no idea. I didn't know myself."

"Dr. Treadwell, the threats you were getting, the incidents with the scalpel and the condoms that Dr. Frank told us about"—the detective watched Clara play with her hands—"why didn't you report them to us?"

Clara stilled her fingers. "It was stupid. I realize that now."

"Dr. Treadwell, you're the director of a mental hospital. Surely you'd be the first person to understand how dangerous troubled people can be."

Clara smiled bitterly. "Sick people often get a bad rap, Detective. Sane people can be deadly, too."

"In any case, you didn't call the police."

"No."

"And a man died."

"Yes." Clara looked down at her hands. Now this stupid cop was accusing her of negligence. Her face blazed, but she kept her voice under control. "I said it was a mistake. I had no way of knowing this would happen."

"What about Raymond Cowles? Did you have no way of knowing that would happen?"

"Detective, the Cowles death has nothing to do with this. If you carry on in this vein, I'm going to have to ask you to leave. Nothing like this has ever happened to me before. I think you messed up. I don't believe Ray committed suicide."

"Nothing like this has ever happened before?" The detective looked surprised. "No patient connected with your hospital has ever committed suicide? I thought a certain percentage of mental patients commit suicide no matter what you do to help them. Even in the hospital it happens."

"Look, we work with very sick people. Of course it *happens*."

"In fact, it happens fairly frequently."

"It *happens*. I said it hasn't happened *to me*."

"But Dr. Dickey was familiar with such incidents. He dealt with them all the time. He was the chairman of the Quality Control Committee."

"Assurance. Quality Assurance Committee. Yes. And that was how we knew the man who jumped off the terrace last year was *not* a suicide. That man had been poisoned, just as Dr. Dickey was. They're not all suicides, Detective. Dickey was murdered by Robert Boudreau. We *know* that, so go arrest him before he kills someone else. That's what you're paid for."

The detective appeared undaunted. "How do we know that? Did Dr. Dickey show you what he called you to his office to see?"

"No." Clara took a breath and calmed down. "But there was a nearly empty bottle of Johnnie Walker on Dr. Dickey's desk when I got there."

"Where did it go?"

"I saw Boudreau outside of the emergency room when I left. Maybe he put the drug in the scotch bottle and then took the bottle after Hal was taken away. In the confusion, I didn't stop to lock the office. But even if it had been locked—well, obviously he can get in."

"Wasn't the bottle there when you came back?"

Clara shook her head. "I never looked. I didn't go in. I merely locked the door and left."

"You didn't go in for the materials Dr. Dickey wanted you to see?"

Clara's face flared again. "A friend had just died. I wasn't thinking of anything but that."

"A friend?" the detective said with a small smile. "Wasn't Dr. Dickey's involvement with you causing you some embarrassment, both in the Cowles lawsuit and personally as well?"

"That's enough." Clara stood up. "You're way out of line here. I live by the Hippocratic oath," she said coldly. "I would never harm another human being. It's against everything I believe." She pushed air through her nose, outraged at even the hint of suspicion against her.

"Think about what you're implying, Detective. I called for the paramedics. I was the one who thought the death was suspicious. *I* requested the autopsy. Why would I do that if I wanted to get rid of Hal?"

The detective closed her notebook. "I'm not a psychiatrist, Dr. Treadwell. You're the psychiatrist. It's not for me to explain why people do the things they do. I just know people do the most unreasonable things all the time." April stood and hitched her bag to her shoulder. "And who knows, maybe somebody put the stuff in the liquor bottle as a prank, to make Dr. Dickey act crazy, to make him sick so he wouldn't be competent in his job anymore. Maybe the person didn't know he'd down the whole bottle in one go . . ."

"Get *Boudreau,*" Clara snapped. "This isn't a hard one. This guy has killed before. He's threatened *me.*" Clara closed her eyes. She didn't want to scream at this clever cop.

"I'm trying to help you," she went on, her voice tight and angry. "I've given you the man's name. Your job is to *go and get him,* not stand here fishing in my stream."

"It's my job to fish in all the streams," April said softly. "Any old fish doesn't count. I'm paid to catch the right fish." She headed for the door, then suddenly turned back. "So you didn't put the drug in the bottle and then take the bottle away after Dickey was dead?"

"No," Clara said angrily. "I'm a doctor. I could never use a medication to hurt someone."

"Well, thanks. It may have been painful, but I needed to know that. I appreciate your help." The detective headed for the door with no further comment.

fifty-one

As Jason watched Special Agent Daveys chew on what was left of the ice in his third glass of water, nine clocks began to chime the half hour. Eight-thirty. Emma was not going to take this well. On his return from the office, just as she was regaling him with the happy story of her final call-back and offer of the role for which she'd come East, Special Agent Daveys of the FBI had shown up without warning for a home visit.

Standing in the hallway angular as a heron, Daveys said he was thirsty and politely requested a glass of water, preferably from a bottle that hadn't been opened. Emma brought him a fresh bottle of Evian and disappeared. Then, unembarrassed at the prospect of being a nuisance, he asked for lots of ice. Jason went into the kitchen for the ice bucket and found Emma in there sulking. He had promised her he wouldn't be long, and now the minutes were adding up.

For an hour and a half, Daveys had been chewing thoughtfully on cube after cube of ice as he asked about Jason's history at the Centre, his knowledge of Clara Treadwell, his involvement with the Cowles investigation, Harold Dickey, the inpatient wards, the staff at the Centre, the condom with the scalpel that had pierced Clara's hand, the used condom in the appointment book, and a dozen other things Jason didn't want to talk about.

"Do you get paid for being a supervisor?" Daveys asked abruptly.

"No," Jason said. He stared gloomily at the empty water bottle, dying for Daveys to go so he could have a real drink.

"You work for nothing?" the agent said as if he didn't believe it.

"It's considered an honor to be asked."

"How does it work?"

"Oh, supervisors follow residents through their first psychoanalytic cases—look over their shoulders, comment on what they've said and done with their patients in sessions, illuminate the process for them. It takes a lot of time, several hours a week."

"So you teach them how to do it."

"That's about it."

"You lead them, as it were." Daveys pinched his hawk nose.

"We're supposed to show them the way," Jason conceded.

"And you can lead them astray."

Jason coughed. "We try not to, of course."

"But when they're led astray, who would you say is responsible?"

Jason shook his head. "What case are we talking about, er, Special Agent?"

"Call me Steve. I'm just trying to get the lay of the land. How often do supervisors have affairs with their residents?"

"I can't answer that question. I don't know. It's unprofessional at best. It's a big no-no." Jason felt the clocks ticking like time bombs.

"What happened to the condoms Dr. Treadwell found?"

"I don't know what happened to the first one. The police have the second one."

Daveys's eyebrows shot up. "The police?"

"As far as I know."

"Dr. Frank, I hear you're very tight with the NYPD."

"I've worked on a few cases with them," Jason replied modestly.

Daveys regarded the empty Evian bottle thoughtfully.

"You having cross-agency problems?" Jason asked with a smile.

Daveys's thin lips came together. "I grew up in Boston, Doctor. My father was a cop. My little brother is a cop. I don't have agency problems, or any other kind. We all do our jobs and try not to get in each other's way."

"I thought homicides were supposed to be handled locally."

"We're always available to help out when we're asked." Finally Daveys put down his empty glass and rose. "You should have some of that water," he said in parting. "Flushes the kidneys, don't you know."

As Jason closed the front door on the kidney-flushing federal agent, Emma emerged from the kitchen with a bottle of champagne. She looked a little miffed as she moved a clock and some books on the coffee table to make a place for the glasses. "Well, how did it go?"

Jason brushed his hand over the face of a round clock, set in the top of a marble obelisk on a side table. He noticed it was fast and frowned.

"I guess you're not in a celebrating mood anymore." Emma put the bottle down and curled up in a corner of the sofa, nestling into her big white sweater, resigned to a change of plan.

"Yes. I'm in the mood. I'm thrilled and excited for you. Really."

"You don't look thrilled and excited."

Jason pasted on an enthusiastic smile. "Well, I am. I'm proud, I'm impressed. I know you'll be great. I have only one bit of advice to give you."

"Oh, yeah, what's that?" She eyed the bottle of champagne hopefully.

"Don't drool."

"Don't drool. That's it?"

"That's it." He saw that counsel wasn't enough. She wanted the toast, too. He lifted the bottle and unwrapped the foil, trying—at least for a few minutes—to push back the tidal wave of Clara Treadwell that was swallowing up his life.

"What kind of advice is that?" Emma demanded, disappointed that he didn't have room for her even now.

Trouble brewed in her eyes. She was angry about Daveys's visit. Jason could just imagine her sitting in the kitchen stewing about how she was always relegated to the background of his life. How she never had the support of a loving husband to cheer her on when she needed it. Which always seemed to be at the most inconvenient of times—like now, when an FBI agent happened to show up out of the blue to spoil her party.

On the other hand, maybe Emma hadn't been grumping around the kitchen counting her grievances. Maybe she was really scared because she got the part in her play and hadn't thought she would. What if she had only used the audition as an excuse to reconsider the rotten marriage that gave her stability and the rotten husband who loved her? An ironic smile played around Jason's mouth as he began grappling with the champagne cork. There was nothing in the world like the unforeseen consequences of answered prayers.

In a splash of foam, the cork jumped out of the bottle. Jason grabbed a glass to catch it.

"Congratulations, darling. To your great success. As long as you don't spit too much, they'll love you."

"You'd probably rather have a beer," Emma murmured, clinking glasses. "Maybe you'll get what you want, too, my love. I hope someday you'll know what it is."

"Touché." He sat on the sofa next to her, thinking he'd rather have a gin.

"So, what did the masked man want?" she asked, not exactly sipping like a lady.

"Take a guess."

"This is nice champagne. We may need another bottle." She paused to drink the last of the glass down and pour another. "Well, he was FBI, right?"

"Hmmm. What makes you say that?"

"I don't know. The slab face, lipless mouth, colorless hair. Gray suit . . . Evian, and lots of ice—give me a break." She poured Jason some more champagne, too. "Or maybe it was the cute little snub-nosed .38 strapped to his ankle. He sure wasn't a cop."

"You noticed."

"How could I miss it? He crossed his legs when he sat down. Has the FBI come to offer you a job, too?"

Jason laughed. "You're funny. Is that why you're a star?"

"No, I'm a star because I'm brilliant and utterly fearless. FBI. Snub-nosed .38. Am I right?"

"Probably right. I don't know about the gun. I have a brilliant and utterly fearless wife."

"How's it feel to be visited by the FBI?"

"Feels great, except for the sinking feeling right . . ." He pointed to his nether regions. "Feel this."

"Ha, ha."

"Really, it's bad. I need attention."

"Yeah, well, who doesn't? Now tell the truth, Doctor. Did Clara Treadwell kill her lover? Did the President of the United States send his private army to get the goods on the great Dr. Treadwell so he could quietly kick her off his commission before she becomes a major liability? Or are the feds here to cover up some secret plot to liberate the insane? That would be right up your alley."

"Now where would you get a fool idea like that, my dear Watson? Are you sure you wouldn't rather explore the implications of my . . . ?"

Emma slapped his hand playfully, nicely flushed from the champagne. "Maybe later. First the story, Sherlock. You know, this is more fun than being the wife of a shrink. Why don't you join the FBI? That's the kind of secret stuff that's *fun.* And if you worked for them, then I could have a private army looking after me."

She got up a little shakily, tottered off to the kitchen to look for another bottle. "Well, did she kill him or not? Wait a minute, wait a minute. Don't say anything until I get back."

Which victim? Jason squeezed his eyes shut, allowing himself to enjoy the slight buzz from the champagne. A number of points struck him about Clara Treadwell from his close reading of the last pages of the Cowles file. Two years into the therapy, Ray's girlfriend had begun pressing for marriage. From the descriptions of their discussions it was clear to Jason that Clara believed marriage was a heterosexual male creation designed to victimize and dominate women.

Clara had not yet been married at the time and did not want to succumb to the state of domination. But although she did not want to marry herself, her notes indicated that she interpreted Ray's anxiety about marriage as heterosexual avoidance. She told Ray he was afraid to take his natural place in the heterosexual world. Jason saw this as a constant manipulation of Ray's mental state as a counterpoint to Clara's own. It made her a subtle dominatrix. It also contradicted her claim that morning that she had acted solely as a parrot to her supervisor's ideas.

After nearly a year, according to Clara's notes, Ray had agreed to marry his fiancée. When Clara and Harold discussed this in their supervisory sessions, Dickey applauded the patient's decision. Nine months later, Ray Cowles was married and securely adjusted as a heterosexual. Since his marriage, he told Clara, he had not once engaged in any self-destructive activities. He and his wife had sex fairly regularly. The couple socialized in a predictable way. They had a staunch yuppie, upwardly mobile life. At this point Ray had raised the question of termination of his analysis.

Clara had told him she would think about it and then had a brief consultation with Dickey about it. Two things bothered Jason about this termination. It seemed clear to him that although apparently "cured" of his homosexuality, Ray was chronically depressed. His sessions with Clara were marked by long, arid silences. After he married, he produced no fantasies or free-associations about pleasure. He described his experiences at home and at work in gray, unemotional tones, expressing anhedonia and a low self-esteem. He said he was afraid he could never feel really loved or have any genuine satisfaction. He felt guilty and frequently had fantasies about dying. Cowles was an adjusted, stable, deeply unhappy homosexual, living the heterosexual life his analyst and her supervisor enjoyed together. Clara Treadwell and Harold Dickey had no intention of marrying each other but satisfied their own needs by getting Cowles married off.

Jason imagined that the consultation to terminate Ray's therapy probably lasted two minutes. Clara was clearly bored with him—he was no longer a lively and poetic patient. In the last months, unable to engage with him, she had made up crossword puzzles, thought of other things, drifted off during his treatment sessions. Her notes commented frequently that this was because Ray wasn't saying anything anymore. He was finished. He no longer had anything to say. On these grounds, Dickey, too, recommended termination. So, after four years with Harold and Clara, Ray Cowles was released to his own recognizance.

Jason found the notes regarding their last session particularly poignant. When Ray had asked if he was ever going to see his analyst again, Clara had responded by asking him what his fantasies on the subject were. Here Cowles finally produced a pleasurable fantasy. He said he imagined Clara as a kind of fairy godmother he could visit every Christmas. They could exchange Christmas cards, maybe even presents. Or they could have coffee on their birthdays and meet yearly like the couple in the play *Same Time Next Year*, only he and Clara would be friends, not lovers. Clara squelched this by remarking that termination was termination. She asked him to analyze his fantasy of reunions with her.

"Why do I have to do that?" he wanted to know. "It's so rejecting," he said.

"Termination is termination," Clara insisted, and refused to allow the fantasy to stand. She was treating him like a rejected lover and at the same time telling him that was not the case. Ultimately, to please her, Ray came to the conclusion that he "was proud" to be able to leave someone in his permanent past. And on that note, the treatment ended.

Would that Ray Cowles had left Clara behind in his permanent past. If he had, he might now be alive and well and living with the man he loved.

Clara wrote up the case as the unqualified success of the conversion of neurotic homosexual to well-integrated heterosexual. Ray Cowles's being nonimpulsive for a long period meant to Clara and Dickey that his superego had developed as a result of his Oedipal conflicts being resolved under their guidance.

Jason brooded about this as he prayed there was no more champagne to give him a headache later. Clearly Clara had organized her treatment of Ray Cowles around the firm beliefs of her mentor and supervisor, Harold Dickey. Jason knew at that time the concept of homosexual acts as impulses that were voluntary and governable was still widely held, in spite of the change in psychiatry in the definition of homosexuality as a perversion. The official change was written in stone in the Diagnostic and Statistical Manual of Mental Disorders Fourth Edition (DSM-IV), the textbook used by psychiatrists throughout the country; but old biases die hard, and clearly Dickey had clung to outdated convictions. Jason's diagnosis of the Cowles case was that it was a bad analysis. Clara had been supervised by a professor in the department with whom she was having an affair. The fact that the patient survived for more than fourteen years was offset by the fact that he died almost immediately after renewing contact with her. Clara had had a six-minute conversation with Ray just before he died. Could what Clara said to the man have triggered his last destructive act? And if she had said something, surely, Dickey could not have been responsible for that. Clara was claiming that a former nurse had murdered Dickey in revenge for being fired. She'd insisted that Dickey's death was not related to Ray's. Jason couldn't help wondering about that.

Emma returned with another frosty bottle. "Look what I found."

Jason groaned. There went his evening's work. Still, Emma's eyes were less stormy now. The neckline of her sweater had slipped down over a bare shoulder. She was smiling, and tipsy, happy to have Jason to herself. Clever girl. He resigned himself to marital bliss.

fifty-two

The sound of the radiator in Harold Dickey's office sounded like a hammer pounding on a lead pipe in an echo chamber. It felt about the same to April as Chinese water torture. She wondered how anyone could think in such a place. The radiator clanked relentlessly all through Saturday as she moved around the office sorting through the scattered personnel files while Mike sat at Dickey's desk retrieving and printing out what Dickey had labeled "special cases" from the dozens of documents in his laptop computer.

The laptop had been impounded to certify the chain of evidence. The D.A.'s office and the hospital lawyers had ruled that nothing in the computer could be tampered with or changed, nothing removed from it without being initialed by witnesses. That meant Maria Elena Carta Blanca was there with them all day, hanging on Mike's neck and peering over his shoulder at the screen, clicking her tongue at the sensitivity of the material that she had to initial as it spewed forth from the printer.

April glanced up from her perch on the ugly green couch from time to time to observe Maria Elena's large breasts grazing at Mike's shoulder like some hungry animal. By midafternoon April had a bad headache. Most parts of her job she enjoyed, but she was not enjoying today. The files she was searching represented disharmonies of monumental proportions. She was also sickened by Maria Elena's blatant play for Mike.

The sheets of papers from the files were a hopeless tangle of reports to and from and about social workers, nurses, nurse's aides, residents, supervisors, attendings, and private physicians. They involved case accidents with outcomes of varying degrees of seriousness and contained some hair-raising stories. Dickey's notes in the computer revealed his own thoughts about the more egregious cases of staff negligence—and a completely different set of cases involving young doctors.

"Listen to this, *querida,*" Mike said in a rare moment in the early afternoon when Carta Blanca was out of the room relieving herself and they were alone.

"'Second day of July.' That was last summer. 'Resident with one day of experience screens a suicidal person in ER. Suicidal person had a long history of drug and alcohol abuse and numerous visits to ER. Resident wrongly diagnoses situation, discharges patient who walks out of hospital and suicides an hour later.'"

Clank, clank, clank from the radiator and not the slightest hint of warmth. April shivered. "What was the outcome for the resident?" she asked.

"Not a thing. Dickey says, 'Why ruin a young doctor's whole career?' "

"What did they do, alter the chart?"

"Looks that way. Here Dickey says about the suicide, 'I hate these Goddamn coke addicts fucking up the system.' I guess they protected the resident."

"You see anything in there about a resident or a doctor being dismissed?"

Mike gazed at her contemplatively, stroking his mustache seductively. He shook his head. "Not so far. The disciplinary action seems limited to the staff. . . . And they say *we're* a blue wall."

"You find anything about Boudreau in there?" April was thoughtful, too. Dickey had collected these personnel files because he was concerned about another patient's death. So far, they hadn't found the details of the one they were looking for.

April sat cross-legged on the green couch used by patients telling about their dreams and desires—their sex lives. She had read about therapy in psychology courses she'd taken at John Jay. It sounded disgusting. The last file listed off her lap. She held the papers down with one hand.

"Oh, yeah, here it is. Dickey writes, 'That troublemaker Boudreau has really done it this time.' Yeah, this is it. Unipolar depressive, sixth floor north, checked in Monday A.M. At four P.M. guy goes manic, walks off the ward in his pajamas to the next floor. That's the manics-on-lithium floor. Door's locked, he can't get in, trots down another floor. It's an office floor, stairway door is not locked. The patient goes to the end of the hall, where there are French doors and a small terrace. It's a beautiful day and the doors are open. Apparently smokers go out to that terrace to smoke. Guy walks out on the terrace, jumps off before anyone can stop him, and hits the spikes on the fence around the garden. Guy's impaled on the spokes. According to Dickey's notes here, guy came down by the windows of the adolescent outpatient clinic, where a dozen kids saw the body. Boudreau was the one who gave him the overdose that made him manic. Dickey says, 'Bobbie Boudreau can't weasel out of this one. No one trusts him. It's just the last straw.' Well, there's more . . ." His voice trailed off, and he suddenly looked sad.

"What?" she asked.

"Oh, nothing. I may not be at the Two-O for long. I'll miss this."

"Oh." For a few seconds April's headache had eased. Now it started pounding again.

"But then, neither will you," he added with a smile.

The son of a bitch. April's head split in half. "We going somewhere, Sergeant?" she said, struggling for calm.

"Maybe, baby," he teased.

"You going to tell me where?"

"You want the short-term or the big picture?"

Who had Mike gone to? What had he asked for? How could he make requests on her behalf when *she* didn't even know what she wanted? She stared at him, furious. "How do you know these things?"

"After you've been around for a while, you get a few friends. Some of them move up." He shrugged again. "You have some friends, too. You just haven't discovered it yet."

April's cheeks burned. *Hijo de puta* jumped into her head. She didn't say it. *Mierda.* It occurred to her that she knew Spanish.

"Pendejo," she muttered.

Mike laughed uproariously, almost exploding with mirth.

"What's so funny?" April put the file down carefully.

"Pendejo, querida? You think I'm a *pendejo*?"

April lifted a shoulder. "What's it mean?"

"I'm a pubic hair? I'm a good-for-nothing, a coward, a *pubic hair*? Is that what you think?" Now the laughter was gone. Mike's voice rose with anger at his injured honor.

The door to the tiny office swung open. It wasn't the pushy Latina lawyer. It was the pushy FBI. Special Agent Daveys shoved himself into their space, his humorless face gray as stone. "Hi, kids. What's up?"

"Just wrapping for the day." Mike checked his watch.

"Did you find that file on the boy nurse?"

"I told you it wasn't here," April said.

"Bastard must have taken it."

"Yeah," April muttered. Or someone else had. Gunn had sworn Dickey never mentioned Boudreau. She tapped her fingers on the files. Time to go.

"There's a neat coffee bar over on Broadway. Let's go there and make a plan of action," Daveys said. It was not an invitation.

Mike glanced at April. "We're still investigating. We're not ready for action yet." He pushed a few buttons to shut down the computer.

"All the same, it's time to powwow."

"You going to tell us something we don't know, Daveys?"

"Many things, many things, children. This way to truth and justice." Turning around, Daveys bumped into Maria Elena, who was charging through the doorway.

"Oops, sorry." She backed her breasts out of Daveys's chest with a big smile.

"All yours, sweetheart. You can lock up now." Daveys swept by without even a peek at what he was missing.

fifty-three

Sunday, November 14, dawned clear and bright. Maria Sanchez awoke deeply worried about what the day would bring. For two Sundays in a row Diego Alambra had walked home from church with her, and she was disturbed because she didn't know what such a handsome man could want from an old woman like her. She also worried because Señor Diego Alambra was something of a mystery. He had a Spanish name but spoke Italian.

The mysterious Diego had started coming to her church some months before, and she could not help noticing him. He was a handsome man with hair still mostly black, like hers. Her hair was pulled straight back into a low roll at the base of her neck. His was swept up in a high curling wave above his forehead and cascaded gracefully down the back of his head to the top of his shirt collar. His mustache lay like a twig between his lips and sloping nose. He had full lips over slightly protruding teeth, a long face out of which deeply serious eyes watched her while she prayed. Sometimes his eyes were sad, sometimes thoughtful; always they seemed intelligent. He moved closer to where she sat in the very front so the priest would always be sure to see that she was there. He moved slowly, pew by pew, as the weeks passed, perhaps drawn to her by the intensity of her prayers.

Diego Alambra began by nodding at her, then bowing. And when he finally spoke, he called her *"la bella signora."*

Maria Sanchez was an old woman, nearly fifty-five, and for a long, long time she had been oppressed with a deep sadness that made her feel closer to a hundred. This sudden attention from a handsome man when she had not expected ever to be noticed again made it not seem proper to leave the apartment without a touch of powder on her nose, a touch of color on her round, dusky cheeks.

She was deeply disappointed when Diego finally spoke to her and his words came out Italian. Maria Sanchez did not think highly of the Italian men in the neighborhood, so she ignored him, caressed the plastic beads of her rosary, looking severe, as the organ music swelled and the Mass ended.

"Bella signora, sì, sì." He nodded vigorously and told her his name. *"Mi chiamo Diego Alambra, e Lei, cara signora?"*

What? The name made no sense.

Her lips curved up without her permission. A giggle as old as time rose from the deep well of memory and slipped out. "He, he." She laughed.

Then came Father Altavoce's command for the Kiss of Peace and suddenly, without her knowing how it happened, Diego Alambra had taken her hand and was holding it in both of his, gazing into her eyes so deeply it gave her a stomachache.

"Sì, sì. Molto bella." This Italian who called himself Diego had to be over fifty himself but certainly had a young man's enthusiasm for the single idea.

It was a small opening, but he bent so low over her hand, the gesture could not fail to be noticed elsewhere in the church. Maria Sanchez's faded flower of a mouth, unrenewed for many years by lipstick or the hope of ever tasting a man again, smiled in spite of itself.

"Español?" she ventured tremulously.

"E." He shrugged eloquently.

She had to turn the other way to move toward the exit. She felt a little stunned by the encounter and was glad she did not see him again on the street. Then later, when she was home, she worried that she had somehow done something wrong but wasn't sure what.

This fear of being wrong was not a new feeling for Maria. For a long time she had been worried about doing things without meaning to and being punished for it. She was deeply fearful that she might have grievously sinned in the past, that she was continuing to sin even now, and the constant accumulation of those unknown sins (for which she could never atone) was the reason for her past suffering, her present suffering, and quite possibly a future of suffering that would never end.

This was the deepest and most tightly held of her concerns. Maria did not know the nature of her sins but believed only sins committed by her could be responsible for her present condition, which was a sadness that went beyond reason. She was familiar with loss. She had lost her mother and father when she was very young, had lost two sons in infancy before she was twenty. Mysteriously, she could not have more children after Mike. She and Marco did not question that. They had their sorrows, but they had a long life together, nearly thirty-four years. She did not believe she deserved more.

It was the loss of life within life that defeated her. Her son who ran around all night, worked in places that worried her. Married a woman who was cursed with so many troubles she couldn't go out, couldn't shop or cook, just sat by the window and cried all day until finally one day her brother came and took her away. Inexplicably, Mike's wife, Maria, had gone back to the pitiful, broken-down house in the border town she had come from.

After that Mike fell even further away from his beliefs. He fell away from her and his father. He went back to his old ways, didn't call them and didn't come home. Maria would never forget the night her son came home—how surprised she was to see him, how he took her arm by the front door of the apartment and led her back into the room. "*Papi* is dead," he had told her. "He had a heart attack and died at the restaurant." He took Maria in his arms and held her so tight, she could feel the gun tearing at the armhole of his jacket.

Marco had died while making a crab quesadilla. He had not, as she had always feared, been assaulted on the subway coming home late at night from Manhattan. He had not been run over by a cab or a bus or a truck. All his life Marco had been a quiet man, so quiet Maria had often felt alone when she was with him. But when he was gone, it felt as if he'd taken her spirit with him. She did not understand how such a thing could happen. They had not talked together very much through all those years. But with Marco she had never felt constricted. Living with her son, she was tied in many knots.

This Sunday morning it had become cold again. Mike was still asleep in his room. The powder was on her nose. Rouge tinted her cheeks. Maria was ready to go to church. As she sipped her thick sweet coffee early in the morning, she studied the frosted dead grass on the playing fields in Van Cortlandt Park and worried about Diego Alambra. What if he walked with her a third time, would politeness require her to ask him in? What would she do about her son? What did she want?

She licked up the last and most syrupy drop, then washed the cup and looked around. The kitchen was perfectly neat. There was coffee in the pot for her son. As she closed the door of the apartment, her guilty wish was that Mike would wake up and go someplace far away. Her prayer was answered. As soon as he heard the door close, Mike threw the covers off, shivered, and headed for the shower.

fifty-four

At nine A.M. Mike Sanchez met Judy Chen in her family's deserted real estate offices in Astoria, Queens.

"Where's April?" she asked when he arrived alone.

"Oh, she had things to do."

Judy handed over the list of apartments she had to show him. She was a smaller woman than April, with a flat chest, wide hips, and curly hair. She looked him over appraisingly as he studied the listings at her desk in the window of Chen Realty, which never opened until noon on Sundays.

He looked at the last column first, frowning over what seemed to be very high rents.

"What's the story with you two?" Judy asked.

He didn't answer, had moved on to WBF, EIK, RIV VU, UTL INC, and thirty other abbreviations that weren't familiar to him.

"You wear that gun even off-duty?"

"Yeah." His eyes were focused on the information on the sheet. It didn't exactly tell him the things he wanted to know, like which one of these places April would like. He was a detective, but he didn't know what April liked, only knew she had class. Her Chrysler Le Baron was classy. Her clothes. So was the way she moved around, elegant, not flashy. He wanted a place where a classy woman would feel comfortable.

"You always wear it?"

"The gun? Yeah, I do."

"April doesn't wear hers." Judy leaned over, breathing in Mike's strong, sweet scent.

"Yeah, she does."

"You sure?"

Mike looked up, finally distracted. "Yeah, I'm sure."

"So what's the story with you two?"

He gathered some of the ends of his mustache into his mouth and sucked on them without being aware of it, then shook his head as if he weren't sure himself. It used to be that he just reached out for whatever female attracted him at the moment and didn't think about it too much. He might even have reached out to flat-chested Judy Chen if the mood hit him just right.

He never saw any reason to get personal. They wanted it. He wanted it. The idea was to satisfy the urges without getting attached or diseased. He'd always been careful about both those things. Then he got personal with Maria and they got married. Look what that led to.

After that eight-year disaster for which Mike felt deeply hurt and responsible, he developed into a first-rate detective and lost interest in the opposite sex. In his free time he hung out in bars, drinking and smoking and suppressing a profound rage. Then a year or so ago nature kicked in again. He got back to liking the easy-smiling, earthy ones with the big *chichis* who spread their legs without asking a lot of questions.

He got interested in April Woo only because she was sitting there beside him every day, not looking in his direction, not interested at all. It pissed him off and injured his healing ego. She just kept her head down and did her work, wouldn't let any man near her. He was intrigued, was impressed when she thought of things he hadn't thought of. When the other guys teased her, he started stepping in.

April Woo had sneaked up on him. He'd never met a female who said she didn't play around and meant it for more than a week—two weeks max. April had him *pendiente* for months. She meant what she said. She didn't fool around, wasn't going to sleep with someone she worked with. It was sad.

"What'd *she* say about the two of us?" Mike said finally.

Judy had a round eager face, a lot of powdered shadow around her eyes. Her curly bangs grazed the penciled-in eyebrows. She smiled slyly. "She said not to mess with you."

Mike sat back with a pleased laugh. "Oh, yeah? You likely to do that?"

"Of course not. I don't date my clients." Judy sulked a bit, pulling on her curly hair. The gesture made him think that's just what Judy did. Mike guessed she was older than April, over thirty and getting anxious.

He pointed to the listings. "What do you think I should look at?"

"Well, what are your priorities? What are you really looking for?" She gazed so deeply into his eyes, he had to look away or laugh in her face.

"I don't know. Something a woman would like. Sun, sky. Maybe a terrace or a little garden . . ." He stared out the window at the quiet Sunday street. "Bedroom," he murmured, and felt himself getting excited at the thought of April in his bedroom.

Judy Chen laughed. "They usually come with a bedroom. What's this for, getting married or getting laid?"

Two hours and five apartments later, Mike parked behind April's newly washed Le Baron on the street in front of the Woo house and waited as if it was a stakeout. It took five minutes before a window opened on the second floor.

"What's up?" April yelled across the frozen grass.

He got out of the car. "Want to come out for a while? I want you to meet someone."

"Yeah, who?" Without waiting for an answer, she shut the window.

A few minutes later she appeared at the front door. "What's the matter with you? You look sick." She was wearing her red turtleneck sweater and black slacks. The week before when he had turned up she'd demanded to know what he was doing there. This week she seemed to be expecting him. Probably Judy Chen had called and told her they were finished.

"You want something to drink?" she asked, stunning him with an invitation to come in.

"Sure." He followed her inside, looking around for her disapproving parents.

No one else seemed to be home, not even the dog. Still, April avoided the open door to the living room, where Mike could see a hard-looking sofa, two hard-looking Oriental chairs, some of the cheap red and gold things with tassels and paper coins that could be found in Chinatown, and not a lot else.

April entered the enclosed staircase to her place, gesturing for him to follow. At the top of the stairs he wiped his cowboy boots on a welcome mat that had lotus flowers and two Chinese characters on it. He didn't ask what they meant.

"It's kind of a dump. I never had time to finish it, and it's a real mess." Nervously April admitted him to the neatest place he'd ever seen.

"It's beautiful," Mike said, and meant it. "Really." He took in the plush deep pink sofa with two tapestry pillows of matching pavilions among the clouds and mountains with blooming cherry trees embroidered in pale pinks, blues, and gold. In front of the velvet sofa were two carved wooden tables. One had April's new nine-millimeter on it. It was still in its box because she had not yet taken the training to qualify for carrying it.

Mike's gaze traveled to the not-so-newly-painted walls decorated with several scrolls hung with braided rope of more mountain scenes April was never likely to see. The venetian blinds on the windows were up. He went to look at the view. The garden was shut down for the winter. A denuded hedge hid part of the house on the other side. He turned to the tiny kitchen. Two woks hung above a two-burner stove. The shelves were lined with colorful porcelain jars, bags of unidentifiable dried things. There was a wide rack that held many knives.

"Beautiful," he said with the solemnity of a person having a religious experience. "Can I see the rest of it?"

"It's really small," April muttered. "There's not much more to it. The bedroom is a mess. . . ." She indicated where it was.

"I'm sure it isn't." He passed her, moving to the front of the house, his heart hammering away in his chest with the violence of fifteen racehorses in the home stretch of the Kentucky Derby. Oh, God, she was going to do it. All the work, the pressure he'd put on people, the arrangements he'd made, were for nothing. She'd invited him in. She loved him. She was going to make love with him right here, right now, in her own house.

He was in ecstasy. He couldn't believe it. He'd thought of this moment, dreamed of how it would happen when they finally got together. For months he'd fantasized different April scenarios—April as a hungry tiger, fiercely passionate and aggressive. April ripping her clothes off and going straight for his zipper. April as a cherry blossom, tender and yielding. April touching him, embracing him with all her heart. He'd dreamed of their two naked bodies pressed together in *ardiente pasión.* April kissing him all over. April with her legs wrapped around him.

He was almost dizzy with anticipation as he went through the door to her bedroom. It had a single bed like his, only hers had a quilt with pink flowers on it. Not cherry blossoms, violets maybe. The bed was made. Two pillows were propped against the wall with the impression of her body on them as if she'd been lying there waiting for him. The chair beside the bed was piled with books.

The fragrance of the light scent she wore was everywhere. He wanted to put his face in the nightgown hanging over everything else on the closet door, sink to his knees, and die on the spot. His heartbeat was like thunder in his ears. He felt almost sick with desire as he waited for her.

But April didn't follow him into her room. He waited and waited, but she didn't come for his embrace. Why didn't she come in? He began to pace, unwilling to leave the bedroom but uneasy about forcing the issue. Finally he poked his head out the door. Steam was beginning to pulse out of the archway into the kitchen. The steam was not April's desire. The water in the kettle had begun to boil. In a second the kettle whistled, sending his heart into shocked awareness that she had not invited him in for love.

"Mike."

She summoned him. There was nothing he could do but leave the place of his dreams. As he emerged painfully from her room, she handed him the drink she'd been so busily preparing in the kitchen. He regarded the steaming cup of green liquid with deep distrust. It had a bitter smell.

"Maybe some other time," he muttered.

"Drink it," she commanded. "It'll make you feel better."

"There's nothing wrong with me. I feel fine," he lied.

"No, you don't." She clamped a hand on his forehead. "You're all clammy, you're sweating. You have a fever. Drink it, you'll get better."

That was how April allowed Mike Sanchez close enough to die for her but not close enough to touch. He had to drink the foul herbal tea to get out of there. And only after he drank the tea and told her he felt better would she agree to get in his car.

Then he told her where they were going. At one on Sunday, every Sunday without fail, his *Mami* always put dinner on the table. She invited some of her ladies from the building, or a cousin, sometimes a priest or a couple of nuns from the order. Always there was lots and lots of food.

April talked about the missing Boudreau file and how that bothered her, but she did not ask any questions. She glanced at him two, three times as they drove to the Bronx, as they parked on Broadway, then again as they waited for the elevator in the low brick building where he lived. He didn't want to talk about work. She could see how nervous he was.

"Don't worry, it's not a big deal," he kept saying. "I saw yours, you see mine. That's all. Not a big thing."

He kept saying it was no big thing, but his heart was going crazy again.

The aromas that greeted them as they stepped out of the elevator on his floor were almost unbearably delicious. Clearly his mother had outdone herself. He could smell onions and peppers, chicken mole, beans and melting cheese. He glanced surreptitiously at April. She didn't like cheese. He wanted her to like it.

"Smells good," she murmured as he turned the key in the lock.

"Yeah, my father taught her everything." Mike opened the door into a room warm with cooking and filled with heavy wooden furniture piled with bright pillows covered in coarsely woven fabrics with bold geometric patterns. He smiled encouragingly, then turned to the table by the window, where his mother sat bathed in the midday sun.

Maria Sanchez had her long hair down her back. She was wearing a purple taffeta dress, with a ruffle around the neckline low enough to reveal the tops of her plump, round breasts. When the door opened, one of her arms was outstretched and her hand was pressed to the lips of a dapper little man with a high pompadour and a bright green shirt.

Mike froze as if confronted by a couple of Uzis. Equally stunned, his mother gaped at him, then at the beautiful dark-haired woman in the red sweater and black jacket beside him, then back at him. Finally her surprised face relaxed into a wreath of smiles.

"*M'ijo,*" Maria breathed. "*Dichosos los ojos.* Come in."

fifty-five

Bobbie Boudreau did not need to send the Treadwell bitch any more messages. The old woman was right. Treadwell had called in the FBI. She knew he was out there now, and she was running scared. He liked that. A suit was guarding her building, an FBI agent, not a cop. He knew a cop would look like a homeless person or a delivery man from Pizza Hut. The suit you could pick out from two blocks away, right down to the device in his ear so somebody could talk to him from another planet. Just like they did for the President of the United States. Bobbie had to be pretty important if they had to call in the FBI to keep him out of Treadwell's office. He guessed by now there was another suit standing outside the executive suite on the twentieth floor. It made him want to laugh. Did they think he was stupid?

He could stand out in plain view and they wouldn't see him. They didn't know jackshit. Let the police come, let the FBI come, let the whole fucking army come. What would they find? Nothing. The whole thing made him want to laugh. How long did they think they could secure the area? A week, two weeks, a month?

They could hang around a whole year, for all he cared. This was his territory. He'd been here for fifteen years. He wasn't going anywhere. He stayed underground most of the time he wasn't working. Let them worry about where he was and what he was doing. Let them think whoever was bothering the bitch was gone now, far away. He wasn't showing up for any party with the feds. This wasn't Waco. This wasn't Oklahoma. This wasn't big-time stuff so they could hang out there for weeks just waiting for him to make a move. This was a fucking shrink who killed her patients with words. Whispered nasty little somethings in their ears and down they fell like bowling pins. Bobbie had heard the gossip about the patient who committed suicide because of her. Probably wasn't the first. These doctors could do anything. They were licensed to kill. Nobody could stop them. She was no better than the bastard back in 'Nam, practicing open-heart surgery on healthy hearts because he wanted to do bypass surgery when he got out. Nobody would say anything. Nobody tried to stop him.

So now it was proven. Words in the mouths of shrinks could kill. Same as guns. Same as explosives, same as poison. Shit—they were carrying concealed weapons that could maim and kill. And nobody had the power to stop them. Only God had the power, and He was taking care of them in His own sweet time.

It was no sin to be on God's side in this. It was necessary, like war. Sooner or later the FBI was going to be finished bugging and wiring the place. They'd get tired of watching and listening and waiting for him to do something they could nail him for. And then they'd go back to wherever they came from and he'd come out of the basement.

fifty-six

April didn't sleep well after the lunch with Mike's mother and the boyfriend he hadn't known anything about, and after she saw the place he wanted to rent in Queens. Her insomnia didn't have anything to do with the food, which had been impressive even to her. The apartment was all right, too. It had a terrace and was higher up than either April or Mike had ever lived. Judy was trying to get Mike a special deal on the rent because the landlord wanted a nice quiet cop in the building.

There were a lot of problems with change. April tossed around, worrying about why she was driven to push so hard for advancement when advancement would only take her away from the Two-O, where at least she knew who her enemies were. She had no idea where she was headed or what would happen to her and Mike if they messed up on the Dickey case. Nothing was exactly crystal-clear in this case except that there were a number of songs playing simultaneously and all they had picked up so far were the tunes of the dead men.

The easy homicides are the boyfriend/girlfriend cases. There's no mystery there. You can see them coming a mile away. Ten miles away. Was Dickey's death a boyfriend/girlfriend thing? Or was it a revenge thing by a guy who'd poisoned a patient with an antidepressant, harassed the head of the hospital—who conveniently neglected to tell anybody about it for a full six months—and then spiked a doctor's scotch bottle with the same drug that made the crazy patient a flier a year ago? It was pure speculation, right down to the spiking of the scotch bottle, because the bottle, if there had ever actually been one, had disappeared. April made a mental note to check the building's garbage even though it would be some job to find a bottle tossed out a week before.

And what was the story with this guy from the FBI? Daveys seemed pretty hot on Boudreau as the killer. But if Dickey's death was really connected with the Cowles suicide, then how did Boudreau fit into that scenario? Was he really the perfect suspect?

April rolled around in her single bed worrying about the case, trying not to think about sex with Mike in his apartment with its western exposure and view of the sunset. Clara Treadwell had had an affair with Dickey years ago when he was Clara's teacher. What if Dickey hadn't been able to handle Treadwell's being his boss? What if Dickey's wife was right and Dickey had wanted to renew the romance and his influence over Clara? Clara had a boyfriend in the Senate. Maybe she had been trying to get rid of Dickey and Dickey had been blackmailing her. That played. Clara could have mixed the alcohol and Elavil, not necessarily to kill Dickey, but to make him act crazy so she could discredit him and force him out.

April was also troubled by Daveys. She'd worked with the feds before, down in Chinatown, and she'd never seen a Feeb working on his own. Generally if you saw one Feeb out there in the open, there were dozens more holed up in a building down the street, watching and listening, waiting for a break while partying—eating and drinking on taxpayers' money.

Feebs and money was a sore issue with cops. Feebs made a lot more of it than cops, and they had an endless supply of federal money for their expenses. Feebs also had the kinds of labs and computers and technical equipment cops only dreamed of. So where were the rest of the Feebs on this case? What were they up to, and how were they about to ruin April Woo's chances for good luck and a long life?

"*Ni,*" Skinny Dragon Mother screamed up the stairs just as the sky was graying with dawn. "*Ni,* you not in hamony. That is the probrem. Not in hamony."

April did not love it when her mother called her "you," especially when she was miserable and trying to sleep. She dragged herself out of bed and found a note on her door. The note read, in Chinese:

In order to contract,
It is necessary first to expand.
In order to weaken,
It is necessary first to strengthen.
In order to destroy,
It is necessary first to promote.
In order to grasp,
It is necessary first to give.

It was a description of the transformation process—or what to do when things are out of harmony. A person had to be advised which one of the above things to do when something was out of whack. According to Chinese traditional thinking, the world and all its parts were in a delicate balance of Yin and Yang. Yin the dark—the passive, the brooding female—and Yang the bright—the positive, the active male.

When Yin and Yang were in balance, a person was in good health and good relationship with others, in an excellent position for long life and other good things like job security and status. When Yin and Yang were not in balance, the body became sick in ten thousand ways and relationships with others were bad. Work became impossible, and all kinds of things went wrong.

According to the same ancient Chinese philosophy, bad luck, illness, a rotten character (whatever was wrong) was never a person's actual fault. The fault was disharmony. If one was lucky and received the correct cure, harmony could be reestablished by one of the transformations described in the note on the door. Yin and Yang could be restored to their rightful balance and happiness achieved.

"*Ni,*" Skinny Dragon continued screaming up the stairs. It was clear from the piercing tone of her voice that she had not slept a wink the whole night, either. Her voice was so violent, not even the dog was visible when April opened her door, found the note, and peered down the stairs, yawning.

"Yeah, Ma, what?"

This morning Skinny Dragon Mother was wearing black pajama bottoms and a padded blue peasant jacket to fool the gods into thinking she was poor. Suddenly she started smacking her chest with an open palm and screaming in operatic Chinese that April's Protective *Qi* was weak, and this defect was the cause of all her troubles.

"What troubles?"

"You need treatment right away to get in hamony before your *jing* is so weak it's too late for anything."

"*Jing*? What's that?" April demanded.

"Neva mind what is. Clock ticking, losing more every day."

April yawned, bleary-eyed. If a clock was ticking, it had to be hormones. Jade Treatment was not for hormones. Any idiot knew that.

"Velly bad news. Come here," Sai screamed.

April padded down the stairs to her mother's kitchen, the official place of bad news. There Skinny Dragon told her that the Chinese newspaper had reported New York City was blanketed with a great fog of impure air so disease-ridden that no one outside or in a public place was safe from the dangerous colds and fevers all around. April was outside and in public places every day, Skinny Dragon said, scowling at her daughter. April breathed the impure air of rapists, thieves, and murderers. So April was in special danger.

April thought of Sergeant Joyce and knew this was true. The rest of yesterday's disaster she deduced from her mother's tirade about fat Foo Chang. Apparently the word had spread all the way to New Jersey (where Woo parents were visiting the Chang family) that April's monkey business with Spanish had spoiled her chances with George Dong and now no one worth marrying would ever have her. Foo Chang told Sai Woo that George Dong's mother, Mimi, had a cousin whose daughter's best friend was a Harvard docta. The girl was small size, only four foot ten, and not good-looking. She had curly hair, freckles, and a boxy figure. Also much older than April but . . . she was successful docta of women at Lenox Hill Hospital on Park Avenue, Manhattan. This small, old women's doctor, Lauren Cha, and George Dong had played tennis together twice in the big Queens bubble, and now there was rumor of a spring wedding.

Foo then mentioned April's Spanish boyfriend—everybody knew all about him—and this bitter news prompted Sai to tell the getting-very-fat Foo Chang that Spanish was highest-quality Sergeant, almost a Captain and a personal friend of the Police Commissioner himself. Foo countered by consoling Skinny Dragon with many kinds of food she did not want and by telling her she didn't *have* to have the same unhappy, unlucky life as all other parents whose children fell away from golden path never, ever to return.

The only way April could think of to appease her unhappy mother was to swallow the nasty steaming liquid Skinny gave her. It was a suspicious color. April sniffed it anxiously, almost fearful that her mother was angry enough to poison her. This Jade Treatment was unpleasant in the extreme, but Sai promised it would strengthen her Protective *Qi*.

Protective *Qi* was the energy of throat and lungs—not the energy of the whole body—only the upper respiratory system. To protect the whole immune system, you went for the Protective *Qi*, the energy of the throat and lungs. But who knew what it really was? It could be something to weaken her spirit and confound her purpose. It certainly didn't taste anything like the Jade Treatment she'd given Mike, and taken herself, yesterday to fortify them against Sergeant Joyce's cold. That Jade Treatment was like a eucalyptus tea, deeply green and spicy, an opener of the chest. Mike said he liked it—even though he hadn't known what it was for. April was eager to see if he was better today.

Leaving her mother lighting joss sticks for the gods of harmony, April left early for the Two-O.

fifty-seven

When April walked in at seven-forty-five, it was still dead in the squad room. The only person already busy at his desk was Mike, turning the pages of his notebook. Maybe he couldn't sleep, either.

"Yo, *querida*, how was your day off?" he asked without looking up.

"A real bummer. *Pasé el día en blanco,*" she grumbled.

"You didn't do a single thing? *¡Qué lástima!* You must be hanging with the wrong people."

"Must be. *¿Qué pasa, chico?*"

He smiled. Now he was *chico*. "What's happening is our new best friend wants a meet this afternoon. He says he wants to give us a present. All we have to do is pick it up and it's ours."

April dumped her shoulder bag on her desk. She sank into her chair. "The last time I heard a Feeb ask a cop to make a pick-up, it was an unauthorized search-and-seize they didn't want to take the heat for if we got caught."

"Oh, yeah? You do it?"

April looked him over for signs of fever. Today Mike was wearing a red shirt and a black tie, his first foray into color. Must want to attract a bull. She smiled. "You're looking better today, Mike. That Jade Treatment must have worked."

He made a face. "You mean that nasty green stuff you made me drink? What was it supposed to do, shrivel my balls?"

"A girl does what she can."

Mike leaned back in his chair, stroking his mustache and wearing his pirate's smile. "Well, it didn't work. You'll have to try again. . . ." He stared at her until she blinked. "So did you go in for the Feebs? Do the search-and-seize?"

She laughed. Laughing didn't feel too bad. "Not me. I don't take falls."

He changed the subject. "Well, we have to do a little homework here. Let's make a plan."

April nodded. They decided who would do what and where they'd meet to discuss their findings before meeting with Special Agent Daveys for lunch at the Lantern Coffee Shop. By nine-thirty April was back in the Psychiatric Centre. Gunn Tram hadn't told her the truth the last time they'd talked. April thought it was about time for another little chat.

Gunn Tram, however, wasn't in her office. She'd called in sick that Monday. The young African-American slumped at the desk in the outer office said Gunn had a bad cold and sounded terrible. April asked the woman if she knew an employee by the name of Boudreau.

"Uh-uh." The nameplate on her desk read Malika Satay. Malika had a spectacular head of braids that dusted off her shoulders as she shook her head emphatically with every statement. "Nobody by that name working here."

"How about a little over a year ago, in the summer?"

"Wouldn't know about that. I started last year at Christmastime." Malika clicked the gold beads at the ends of her extensions with her long gold-painted fingernails.

"Would you check for me?" April asked.

"Huh?"

"Would you look in your files and see if you can find a Boudreau in there—B-O-U-D-R-E-A-U."

"You with the cops? I seen you in here yesterday with that other guy."

April leaned against Malika's desk. April hadn't been there yesterday. Neither had Gunn; neither had Malika. "What other guy?"

"I don't know. Some other guy. Hung around all day bugging Gunn."

"You mean Friday."

"Whatever." Malika figured she'd done enough talking and shut her mouth.

"Whatever isn't good enough."

"I don't remember what day. One day last week."

"Okay, why don't we check the files?"

The woman got up sullenly. "Is that what he wanted?"

"The guy? What did he say he wanted?" April followed Malika's heavy steps to an interior space lined with banks of files.

"Uh-uh. He had a gun on his ankle. Made Gunn real upset."

"I can see how it would. What did this guy with the gun say he was looking for?"

"He just say Gunn knew what he wanted, and he'd stick with her till she tole him."

"Did you see this guy around here today?"

The secretary swung her heavy braids around, shooting April a look she couldn't read. "What's it to you?"

"You like Gunn? Is she a good person to work for?"

Malika turned back to the cabinet, pulled out one of the *B* drawers, shuffled through the files around B-O-O. "Yeah, she's all right."

"Then help her out, okay?"

"She in trouble? I knew she in trouble." The woman slammed the drawer shut. "I tole you, there's nobody with that name in here."

"It's B-O-*U*," April said patiently. "Try it again."

"Huh?"

"B-O-U-D-R-E-A-U."

"I done that."

"You've checked before?"

"Yeah, when that guy was here." Malika headed back to her desk.

"The file wasn't there then?"

"Uh-uh."

April turned back to the cabinet, wanted to see for herself. She shuffled through the *B*'s, found a file upside-down in the B-u section, and felt the hairs rise on the back of her neck. She pulled a pair of disposable rubber gloves from her bag and put them on before touching it. It was Robert Boudreau's disappeared, now magically reappeared, file. She looked around for a supply cabinet, opened a few drawers until she found a large manila envelope. The file disappeared again into the envelope. April went to see Malika.

She was slumped at her desk again. "Bye," she said without enthusiasm when April stood in front of her.

"I'm not finished. Did Gunn know which files were gone?"

"She real upset after Dr. Dickey died. Real upset. She say she the only one knew which files was missing. She had to get 'em back right away. All of 'em."

"Gunn told you she'd made a list of the files Dr. Dickey took?"

"Yeah."

"Did she tell you where she put it?"

"I tole you—that guy upset her real bad. He say she gonna go to prison. I heard him tell her."

"The guy with the gun?" April said.

"Uh-uh, the one with the ponytail."

Oh, now there was a guy with a ponytail as well as a guy with a gun. April's stomach churned. She could feel the burning acid attack a new clot of anxiety. There was another guy hanging around Gunn. Did Daveys know that? Neither April's voice nor her eyes betrayed the impatience her body was beginning to vibrate.

"Any of these guys have a name?"

"I didn't hear one." Malika didn't even bother to shrug. She didn't give a shit.

"Can you tell me what they looked like?"

"Uh, one guy looked like a cop."

Uh-huh. Cops came in all colors, shapes, and sizes. "The one with the gun on his ankle?"

Malika thought it over. It seemed to be a difficult question for her. "Yeah."

"What did he look like?"

Malika sighed at April's denseness. "Looked like a *cop,*" she insisted. "Like Tommy Lee Jones."

April didn't know any cops who looked like that. "Okay, and the other one?"

"Looked like a doctor." Malika nodded.

"The one with the ponytail?" April asked doubtfully.

"Yeah. He was wearing a white coat."

That didn't exactly make him a doctor. "Could you see what he was wearing under the white coat?"

Malika looked surprised at the question. "It was buttoned."

"Yeah, but could you see a dress shirt, a tie, a sports coat, the kind of pants he was wearing? Could he have been an orderly? A male nurse?"

Malika thought about it but stayed silent.

"What about his ID? Did you see that?"

"No."

"No ID or you didn't see it?"

"No ID. The cop had no ID, and neither do you."

Daveys would have a pass like hers. April pulled it out so Malika could see it. "One last question. Have you seen the guy with the ponytail before?"

"Yeah."

"Many times before?"

"A few times."

"When?"

"A while ago. Maybe a month, two months."

"Was he wearing a white coat the other times you saw him?"

"No."

"What was he wearing then?"

Malika pursed her lips with annoyance. "Street close."

"What kind of street clothes?"

"The kinda close you wear on the street. Jacket, sweatshirt, pants." Malika prolonged her skimpy description because April was jotting down what she said.

"Where did you see this guy with the ponytail, the jacket, the sweatshirt, and the pants?"

"Huh?"

"On the other occasions when you saw him. Where was he?"

"He and Gunn walking on the street. They drinking in a bar."

"Which one?"

"This is more than one question."

"You have more than one answer to give me, Malika. What bar?"

"French Quarter."

April nodded. She knew where it was. "This guy, was he white, black, Hispanic, tall, short? Fat, thin?"

"He beige, and he big."

Beige, now that was descriptive. "How big? Six foot? Hundred and seventy pounds, eighty pounds? Two hundred pounds?"

"Yeah."

That was all Malika was prepared to say at the moment. The guy had a ponytail. He was light-skinned with mixed blood of some kind and wore street clothes when he was not wearing a white coat. That did not put him in the doctor class. And he drank in a less-than-upscale bar way west on Ninety-ninth Street. April took Gunn's phone number and address, then headed to the lab to have the file dusted for prints.

fifty-eight

Gunn lived in a Gothic-style, highly decorated, four-story building with a heavy, curved stone staircase leading to a front door of leaded glass on the second floor. April shuddered when she saw it. The entrance to the apartments on the street level and below was hidden underneath the stairs, directly visible neither from the street nor the upstairs entrance. Arching over the sidewalk, the roof corner on each side restrained two attacking cement dogs with permanently gaping mouths and straining fangs. On the second and third stories three yawning bay windows with pointed vaults over dark stained-glass were faintly lighted from within. The house had a predatory look about it, almost as if it were alive and hungry. April parked her unmarked unit in a fire-hydrant space and hurried up the steps. She didn't have a lot of time to get this thing with the file sorted out.

Inside the front door, a tiny lobby had been created a long time ago with an inner door that was locked. The intercom system was very old. Gunn lived on the top floor. April pressed the button by her name and almost immediately heard static.

"Gunn," she said loudly into the intercom, "this is April Woo. Remember we talked on Friday?"

Crackle, crackle was the only response.

"Gunn, I need to talk to you. It's very important."

"Well, I'm sick. I can't talk."

"Listen, Gunn, this is urgent."

"Really, I can't—"

"Gunn, this is a homicide investigation. You don't have a choice."

There was a prolonged silence, then a click as the door lock was released. April let the door close behind her and trudged up a flight of creaking stairs that seemed to drag itself down as it turned the corner. Only one of the five bulbs glowed dimly in the ancient ceiling fixture high above. Gunn lived in the back apartment on the fourth floor. Her door cracked open as April rounded the corner at the top of the stairs.

"Hello, Gunn," April said.

Reluctantly, Gunn opened the door enough for a thin person to enter. April slid through. Gunn scanned the hall before shutting the door.

The apartment consisted of two small, very cluttered rooms with a galley kitchen tucked into one corner of the front room. The bedroom was in the very back of the building. The front and back rooms were separated by two huge, sliding wooden doors that were open most of the way.

"What do you want?" Gunn's eyes were red-rimmed and puffy, but she did not look sick. She was dressed in shiny black pull-on pants and several layers of tee shirts and sweaters. April could see the flickering light of the TV in the bedroom. She could tell that Gunn had not been lying on her bed watching it. The weepy-eyed little woman smelled as if she had spent the last few days on a diet that did not include any of the four food groups.

"Gunn, you lied to me about Bobbie Boudreau."

Gunn reeled back, bumping into a floral-upholstered rocking chair with a white lace napkin thing draped over the top, vibrating her head in tiny arcs of palsied denial. "No, I don't know anybody with that name."

"Oh, come on, Gunn, sure you know Bobbie. He's a drinking buddy of yours."

"Who said so?" Gunn looked surprised, moved away from the rocking chair, and collapsed onto a floral loveseat.

"Gunn, you've been seen with him in the neighborhood, in the French Quarter, right around the corner and other places. . . ." April paused to let her words sink in. "We know Bobbie lives right here in this building with you. We know everything."

"What? You can't."

"What we don't know this minute, we can find out by tomorrow."

"How? How can you find out?"

"By asking questions, Gunn. By asking a lot of people a lot of questions. One way or another we're going to find out, so you might as well tell me about you and Bobbie right now." April cautiously moved to the back of the apartment, her hand on the gun in her waistband. "Is he here now?"

"No, I haven't seen him since you people started hounding him," Gunn said sullenly.

"Fine, then we can talk."

"I didn't tell that other guy and I'm not telling you." Gunn shook her head. "Bobbie got a bum rap the last time. He has nothing to do with this. You can kill me if you want to."

"Nobody's going to kill you."

"Well . . . good. Now you can go."

"Gunn, you know I can't go."

"The other guy did."

"No, the other guy didn't go away. He told you he's with the FBI, didn't he? Well, the FBI doesn't ever go away, Gunn. You're going to have to tell one of us. Him or me."

"Well, Bobbie had nothing to do with it. You're just looking for someone to blame."

"Blame for what?" April asked.

"I know what you're trying to do. I'm not stupid. You think Bobbie killed Dr. Dickey the way they say he killed that patient last year, but he didn't have anything to do with either one."

"How do you know that?"

"How do you know the things you know? I *know*. Some things you just know, right?"

"Sure. Except it doesn't work that way in homicide investigations."

"I know how it works. Something bad happens and somebody has to take the blame. *Her* job was to blame Bobbie. *Your* job is to blame Bobbie." Gunn crossed her arms over her chest, mashing her bread-loaf breasts together. "I'm not going to help you do that."

"Who's her? Dr. Treadwell?"

"Yeah."

"She have it in for Bobbie?"

"How would I know? I'm only in Personnel."

April checked her watch. It was eleven-thirty. She was due to meet Mike and Daveys at one. This plump little lady was in trouble up to her pale blond eyebrows. April had a feeling Gunn knew every single answer, but she'd have to get all tangled up in lies before she'd start telling the truth. She said, "It's nice and cozy in here, Gunn. Do you mind if I take my jacket off?"

Gunn shrugged her square shoulders. "Do what you want, you will, anyway."

"Not necessarily." April unbuttoned her jacket and the navy blazer under it, revealing the scarf tied around her turtleneck. It was silk, one of the fake Chanels she'd bought on the street in Chinatown. The scarf had big gold chains and buckles on a blue background. Sometimes the chains looked like handcuffs to her. Tension pinched the muscles in her neck and shoulders. She took out her notebook and flipped over pages until she came to a clean one. Somebody had put Boudreau's file back in the personnel drawer—somebody who wanted it to be there but not readily visible. Now what kind of person would do that?

Gunn snuffled into a sodden wad of paper towels. "Bobbie is a great guy," she sobbed.

April watched her blow her nose and waited.

"He was a Lieutenant in Vietnam."

"Really," April murmured. "That must have been some time ago."

"Yes, he was, little Bobbie Boudreau, a Cajun from Louisiana. You know what a Cajun is?"

April inclined her chin.

"French-Indian. There are a lot of them in Louisiana. Some kind of mixture. They speak a funny French the real French can't understand at all. Have you heard of voodoo?"

"Voodoo?" April blinked. She'd heard of voodoo practiced in the big cemeteries in Queens. Kids dug up the graves because there was a market for the skulls.

"Yeah, black magic." Gunn's bleary eyes drifted across the room to a white mask on the wall. Ribbons dangled from it.

"Uh, does voodoo have something to do with this case, Gunn?" The mask didn't look as if it had come from Haiti to April. It looked more like the ones she'd seen in Italian restaurants.

"Bobbie thinks maybe he was tainted by voodoo back when his Daddy got the cancer." The old woman shook her head solemnly. "That visiting nurse he liked so much died, too."

April inhaled. What did this have to do with anything? "So what happened to him—Bobbie, I mean?"

"He went into combat *nursing,* of course. He said it was a sacred mission. He wanted to help America. He wanted to be white, you know."

April nodded solemnly. Who didn't?

"So I guess he was used to the blood or something because he was real good at it."

"Used to the blood?"

Gunn shook her head again. "I told you. He was very close to that visiting nurse. He went around with her sometimes, helped her. He saw a lot of sickness and blood."

A lot of sickness and blood.

"I guess it made him want to help people." Gunn was defensive now. "No good deed goes unpunished," she insisted.

April's watch told her she'd been there for seven minutes. A car horn sounded out on the street.

"Where is Bobbie?" she asked.

Gunn blew her nose again. "How should I know?"

"You know a lot about him. You must spend a fair amount of time together. He sounds like a close friend of yours."

"I know him. He's a good man." Gunn sucked in her lips, sullen.

April changed the subject. "What happened to Bobbie in Vietnam?"

"Oh, he was in an advanced MASH unit. He had a lot of bad experiences."

"People dying all around him? Missiles exploding? Drugs? What—?"

"Doctors practicing their specialties on soldiers who didn't *need* it, that's what." Gunn glanced at the mask again. "That comes from New Orleans. Pretty, isn't it?"

"How does all this fit in, Gunn?"

"You wanted to know about Bobbie. I'm telling you about Bobbie. The Captain of his unit was ordered to take a hill. They took the hill. The Captain lost an arm. His face was burned to a crisp. They lost thirty men. The next day they were ordered to give the hill back for reasons that were never explained."

"What about Bobbie?" Time was ticking away. April could feel him lurking out there somewhere. The story about the MASH unit didn't ring true, but April didn't want to challenge it.

"The new Captain had been in charge of body count—that's the number of enemy killed."

"Uh-huh."

"When he took charge of the unit, he started making up numbers." She snorted. "Some place for a moral kid. Everybody high on marijuana and opium, and drunk all the time. Bobbie was having nightmares, waking up screaming. They were making up numbers of enemy dead. And this Captain was a cardiovascular surgeon. He wanted to try new techniques out on his patients whether they needed the surgery or not.

"Marine came in, just a kid from Iowa. The Captain wanted to do some real dangerous surgery Bobbie knew the kid didn't need. He told the kid to refuse. The kid was scared but insisted the doc would never lie to him."

Gunn stared into the deep abyss that was Bobbie Boudreau's life in Vietnam. "It must have been terrible. The Marine died in surgery, and later that night there was a fight. One of the male nurses fragged the Captain."

"What's that?"

"I don't know, a dirty trick, I think. Threw a live hand grenade into his tent and blew him away."

There was a powerful old furnace in the brownstone. April felt the heat penetrating all around her. She removed her silk scarf. There was a dirty trick in Vietnam and the Captain died. A dirty trick on a ward a year ago and a patient died. A dirty trick last week and Harold Dickey died. What about Clara Treadwell?

"Gunn, did you know Ray Cowles?"

Gunn shook her head. She seemed bewildered by the question.

"Gunn, you're going to have to tell me where Bobbie is," April said softly.

"But Bobbie didn't do it. He wasn't the one. He got a bum rap. The MPs that investigated didn't like him. He was a Catholic, a Cajun. He talked funny. They were prejudiced against him, you understand?"

April didn't respond.

"They went to the real killer, who was crazy. They asked him what happened and he said he saw somebody French cursing the Captain after the Marine died." Gunn's eyes were wild now. "He killed himself, shot himself in the head."

"Who did?"

"The real killer. There was no murder trial because there were no witnesses, but Bobbie was finished for *no* reason. Just got transferred from unit to unit to unit and passed over for promotion. God, the system destroyed him. He ended up carrying bedpans and left the Army with a low-efficiency rating."

"Well, that was some time ago," April said. "And he's been in some trouble since."

"No, he had a perfect record until—"

"Until a patient died from an overdose of Elavil a year ago, just like Harold Dickey last week."

"It wasn't his fault," Gunn insisted. "He was a scapegoat. The pharmacist gave the wrong prescription. It's happened before. I should know. But did he lose *his* job? No. *Bobbie* lost his job. He lost his health insurance. His mother was sick. She couldn't get help. She died."

"Is that when you became friends?"

"What would you do with him if you found him?"

"Talk. Same as I'm doing with you. Is he likely to call or come see you?"

Gunn shook her head vigorously. "No."

"Are you worried about him?"

"Sure I am. I don't want him to get hurt."

"Gunn, did you help Bobbie get another job somewhere else in the hospital?"

Gunn sucked in her breath. "How did you know?"

Well, he had access to all the floors. "Did you know Bobbie was threatening Dr. Treadwell?"

"I don't believe it."

"Gunn, does Bobbie blame Dr. Treadwell for his troubles?"

"He says she's a hypocrite. None of the doctors ever get fired for their mistakes. And they make plenty, believe me."

"Does he hate her enough to hurt her?"

"He wouldn't hurt anybody," Gunn said flatly.

"Gunn, people around Bobbie get hurt. We don't want anybody else hurt. Now he's been seen in the hospital, so we know he has access. How did he get the keys?"

Gunn was silent for a minute, holding her breath. "He's in maintenance in the main hospital building," she said softly.

"Where's the office?"

"Below ER."

"Day or night?"

Gunn looked guilty now. "Day shift."

"Gunn, we're going to have to go into the station now. Get your coat."

"Why? I told you everything I know."

"Police work," April told her. "We need everybody's fingerprints."

The old woman started to cry. "Oh, my *God,* this is police brutality," she sobbed, "just like the movies."

fifty-nine

There was a message from Clara on Jason's machine on Monday morning when he came into the office at eight A.M. She said she needed to talk to him right away. He didn't return the call. At one P.M. he had a cancellation and let Emma persuade him to take a break and go out for lunch with her. As they left, he heard the phone stop ringing and Clara's voice talking to his answering machine. He didn't stop to find out what she wanted.

He was moody and distracted as he and Emma left the building. They turned east, away from the sharp wind off Riverside Drive, their breath making steam in the cold, wintry air. Emma bounced along, puffing the clouds happily, her hands plunged deep in her pockets, excited by her future.

Jason brooded quietly about his. He was losing time on all sides. He'd had to juggle patient appointments to carry out Dickey's teaching duties. He had spent many hours on the Cowles file. He now knew that Clara had given him the file because she wanted him to back up her story that she hadn't been responsible for the direction of Ray's treatment; her supervisor had betrayed both her trust and that of her patient. It was a nasty story that she was counting on him, the hospital, and its various committees not to reveal, for it would discredit them all. Unfortunately, the supervisor in question happened to die under suspicious circumstances in his office while Clara was with him.

Jason was shocked by Clara's arrogance. She seemed to believe that nothing could touch her. Never mind the suicide of her patient Ray Cowles and her six minutes of conversation with him before his death. Never mind her presence in Dickey's office when he died. Clara was going to rely on her position to stonewall her way through it all. She intended to come out of it unscathed, and Jason knew that she would sacrifice anyone and anything to accomplish her goal. There were some very good reasons not to get into a confrontation with her. Jason didn't want to discredit the Centre. On the other hand, he didn't want Clara to get away with murder by blackmailing the institution, either. He was torn, overworked, and overtired. And now he was taking the time to be with Emma and have lunch.

"Don't tell me you're not enjoying this," Emma said happily.

"What—winter, homicide, Clara Treadwell, or you?" Jason grumped.

"Thanks, that's lovely. I could have left you there and gone out to a fancy lunch, or gone shopping. Could have gone to the gym. Lot of things I could have done, you know."

"Sorry. Except for Clara, I'm having a ball, really."

"What's going on, Jason?" Emma asked, suddenly serious.

"I don't know, Em. I really don't."

"Oh, come on, you're a shrink. What's your theory?"

Jason inhaled on the question. His breath caught on the cold air, and he coughed.

"It's hard to imagine Clara a murderer," Emma mused when he didn't answer.

"There are other possibilities." Jason sighed, scratching his beard. "I really hate getting sucked into this."

"What are you going to do, baby?" Emma tucked a hand in his pocket, found some fingers. "You're rich. You don't have to put up with it."

They speeded up to cross West End Avenue before the yellow traffic light turned to red.

"Darling, *you're* rich. I'm not. I still have to put up with it."

"What does that mean? If you made lots of money, wouldn't you share it with me?"

"I didn't mean it like that." He fell silent, not wanting to seem churlish by pointing out that he couldn't exactly count on her good fortune since she'd only just returned from leaving him for six months. She might take off again at any time. And having a big earner for a wife would not be a complete joy to him in any case.

"Sexist," she muttered.

They got to their favorite place, the Lantern Coffee Shop, where they used to go years ago when they first met. At the door, Emma tugged at his arm.

"Look, there are those cops and that FBI guy." She turned away. "I can't go in there."

Jason peered through the dirty glass door. April Woo, Mike Sanchez, and Special Agent Daveys were sitting at a table in the back. As if she sensed Jason's presence, April suddenly glanced up. She saw Jason and smiled.

"What's going on?" Emma asked, her eyes troubled at seeing the two detectives who'd saved her life.

"We could go in and find out," Jason proposed.

Emma withdrew her hand from his pocket. "You're really into this crime thing, aren't you?"

"I thought you were interested."

She turned south on Broadway, forcing him to follow. "I was interested in the FBI. They need spook shrinks. You'd be perfect. Shave off your beard and let's go to Washington. But what's this thing with New York street cops? Why can't you stay away from them?"

"Emma, cops come in handy sometimes."

"Maybe. I don't know. I don't want to talk about it." She kept walking fast. Jason had to trot to catch up with her. He was dying to know what was going on. He wished he and Emma could sit down and join the law-enforcement party. But he knew from long experience that Emma did what she wanted and wouldn't be budged. She had to deal with things her own way. If she didn't want to be reminded of what it felt like to be a victim, fair enough.

Jason decided he'd put in a call to April and ask her if she'd drop by to update him on the case later. His breath frosted the air as he jogged to catch up with his wife.

sixty

Daveys chewed on an ice cube, staring at April's plate. "Something wrong with that?" He pointed at the uneaten last quarter of her tuna club.

"No." She watched his face twitch over the fries still piled up on her plate. He'd made a point of saying he never ate fried food. He'd said a lot of things. They knew the whole of his pedigree.

"You going to finish it?" Daveys asked.

"No."

"Can I have it?"

"Sure."

"You guys don't talk much, do you?" he said, pulling the plate toward him.

Smiling, Sanchez nodded at the waiter for some more coffee.

"Shouldn't drink all that caffeine, you know," Daveys told him.

Sanchez dumped two sugars in his fresh coffee. He didn't reply.

"Water's best, trust me on that one." Daveys took a bite of April's sandwich. "Not bad, want a bite?" He offered it to Mike.

April glanced up and saw Jason with Emma through the glass door of the restaurant. So the beautiful wife *was* back. April smiled at them. Emma caught sight of her and looked startled. She grabbed Jason's arm. Her lips moved. In a second they'd turned away. April's smile faded.

"So you're not going to trust me on this? What's with you kids? I'm offering you a present. You go over to Boudreau's place and you pick him up, take all the credit. Case closed. What's your problem?"

"Maybe you're our problem," Mike offered.

Daveys looked wounded. "I'm your solution. How could I be your problem?"

"Hey, Spiro," Mike called out to the owner, a fat man sitting at the counter under a No Smoking sign smoking a cigarette. "Ever heard of the saying 'Beware of Greeks bearing gifts'?"

"Want a baklava?" Spiro asked. "It's just out of the oven. I made it myself."

"I'm sure it's great, but then I'd end up looking like you."

"Ha, ha." The fat man laughed.

"So what's your point?" Daveys whined.

"Why offer us the gift? Why not make the bust yourself, split it with your team?" Mike said, winking at April.

This wasn't federal jurisdiction. That's why he couldn't do it himself. Daveys had another interest in this case they didn't know about yet. He was working with Treadwell, who was the girlfriend of a U.S. Senator.

"Oh, come on, guys," Daveys wheedled. "I gave you all you need. This guy was a misfit from the word *go*. The dirtbag fragged an officer in 'Nam. He's a pile of shit. We start digging into this, I bet we find out he's a mass murderer, like Dahmer or something. I'm doing you a big favor. Get him now before he does someone else. Trust me on this."

"So where's the rest of the team?" April asked abruptly.

"The team?"

"I've never seen a federal agent work a case alone. There must be more of you in the woodwork. Why don't you guys pull Boudreau in and get the credit?"

"Have I got a challenge here from a girl cop?" Daveys rolled his eyes. "You know why I can't do that. I'm handing it to you. What's your resistance here—are you kids nuts?"

Mike slammed his cup down. Coffee slopped over the edge. "Hey, Daveys, call us kids one more time—"

Daveys made a similar gesture with his glass. An ice cube jumped out and skidded across the table. "Look, I'm just being affectionate. My dad was a cop. My brother's a cop—"

"I thought your brother was a Green Beret," April interrupted.

"My other brother." Daveys caught the cube before it slid off the table, popped it into his mouth, and chewed.

Mike raised his hand for the bill. "Thanks for the family history."

"Look, if you pass up this opportunity, I can guarantee it'll be your ass. You can kiss your future good-bye."

Mike sighed. "Look, Daveys. We've got our own procedures here. We work with the D.A.'s office. We've got to get these things nailed down just right before we run in and arrest somebody, you know what I'm saying here? We don't like to fuck up, makes the Department look bad. But thanks for the tip about the scotch bottle in Boudreau's kitchen—funny how you know about it when you haven't even talked to the weasel yet. What does he do, leave his door unlocked?" Mike threw back his head and laughed.

"Yeah, it's a riot, all right."

Mike sobered. "But, hey, we'll check it out. Maybe we'll find out Johnnie Walker's his brand. Maybe we won't."

"I don't see gratitude here. What did you kids get on your own, huh?"

Mike glanced at April. On their own they'd gotten Boudreau's personnel file. He'd been a blood donor, so they knew his blood type, O negative. It matched the blood type of the semen in the condom. Bobbie had been arrested a number of times for drunk-and-disorderly, for assault—bar fights. No one had ever pressed charges. His prints were on file. They hadn't had time to find out if Boudreau's prints matched any of the prints that had been lifted from the file, but somehow they doubted he'd been the one to put it back in the drawer in Personnel. They knew about Boudreau's history in the Army and his dishonorable discharge. They knew where he lived and was currently working. Now they knew where he was hiding out.

"Thanks," Mike said. "You've been a big help. We'll go for it tomorrow."

"Good man." An apparent stickler for details, Daveys nevertheless forgot to pick up his tab when he left.

sixty-one

At a few minutes before seven P.M. on Monday night April adjusted her blue silk Chanel scarf nervously in the cage elevator that hauled her slowly up to the fifth floor of Jason's building. It occurred to her that Jason's wife had many real designer scarves and could spot a fake a mile away. She scraped through the lint at the bottom of her jacket pocket for a shred of tissue to blot her lipstick.

April had been upset that afternoon at the coffee shop when she saw Emma's face freeze at the sight of her and her lips move, *I . . . can't go in there,* as she turned away. But she wasn't really surprised. The two women hadn't met again after the perpetrator in Emma's case died. Not meeting again was usual. Unusual was April's working with a victim's husband on another case since. And yet another one after that.

If she was there to answer the door, the movie-star wife would look her over and April knew she looked a wreck. Her hair was absolutely flat on her head. Her clothes were wrinkled, smelled of mental hospital and the Victorian potpourri from Gunn's apartment. Her stomach was making terrible noises. She didn't feel up to Jason's wife tonight. She was in a state of panic, terrified about messing up the case.

Right now she knew that the Chinese god of messing up (whoever he was) was hanging over her as her Yin and Yang wrestled hopelessly out of harmony. She could feel him hanging around out there, just beyond her vision, waiting for the perfect moment to disgrace her and destroy her life. Maybe he'd come in the form of Special Agent Daveys. Maybe the NYPD was being set up somehow and she'd be the one to take the fall for this. She had a bad feeling about the situation with Boudreau. It didn't all fit together the way it should, and she had no idea how it would be resolved tomorrow.

Jason's elevator made a few little lurching hops before the two levels settled into one and the folding metal door clicked to let April know she could get out. Usually she and Jason talked in his office where the clocks didn't chime. Tonight he'd asked her to come next door to his apartment where the clocks did chime. April hadn't been there since the night Emma disappeared. Jason's wanting her to come there must have something to do with his wife.

April hastily retied the scarf one last time. Emma opened the door before April touched the doorbell. She was caught fiddling with the silk folds, felt she lost face. She was also stunned by Emma's loveliness. Emma had the kind of classic American features that were admired and coveted by the entire planet Earth. She was the standard of beauty by which all else was judged and found wanting. Emma's creamy pure skin, wide hazel eyes, slender (slender!), graceful, slightly upturned nose. Her hair, more golden than ash now, had just enough curl at the ends to give it body and bounce. Her mouth was larger than April's, which was on the rosebud scale, and she was taller. April felt small and ugly and utterly humbled.

"Ms. Chapman," she said. "I'm really sorry to bother you at home."

"Oh, please, call me Emma. Everyone else does."

Emma was wearing toast-colored suede trousers and a celadon silk blouse. Tied around her neck by the arms was a soft-looking sweater of the same color. That pale, almost translucent green was greatly prized in the Chinese pottery of the Sung dynasty for what was believed to be its magical power to detect poison in any food served in it.

"I'm glad to see you, Detective. You saved my life, after all. And who knows, maybe Jason's, too. Come in, he's waiting for you." Emma's slightly uncertain smile made April feel shabby, in addition to everything else.

"Ah, please call me April." April shrugged a little, returning the courtesy. The truth was, Emma shot the guy, too. And Emma shot him first. Who knew, maybe it was that first shot that saved both their lives.

The French doors were open. Jason was sitting in the living room that April thought was so eccentric. It was filled with books, ticking, bonging clocks, and aging upholstered furniture that was kind of threadbare and needed a face-lift. The curtains on the windows fronting the river also looked as if they had seen better days.

Jason put down the nearly full glass of clear liquid he'd been holding and got out of his chair to greet her. "April, thanks for coming. How are you?"

"Fine. Please, don't get up." No one else she knew got up for women. The gesture always startled her.

"Would you like something to drink?" Emma asked.

April eyed Jason's glass. "Club soda?"

"Nope, gin. Want some?"

April shook her head, glanced at Emma for guidance.

"I'm drinking white wine," Emma said quickly. "But we have everything. Pepsi, juice, beer . . ."

April realized that the movie star's offer of refreshment meant this must be some kind of ceremonial occasion. She struggled with the idea of white wine for a few seconds. George Dong was the only person she knew who drank white wine. She thought of it as a wimpy Yuppie drink. It didn't taste good or do much for her.

"Thanks, white wine would be fine," she said.

Emma went to get her a glass while sixty-three *ding*s, *dong*s, and *bong*s proclaimed the hour. April pulled off her jacket and took a chair, tried to arrange herself to fill it. She didn't succeed.

"So," Jason said. "Where are we?"

April smiled. "Still bearded, I see." And back with the splendid wife.

Jason raised his hand to stroke the stubble. "Yeah, I'm still polling opinions on it."

"What does Emma say?"

"I say it scratches." Emma gave April the glass of wine, chose the sofa, and sat gracefully.

Ah. Six months ago this was the wife who hadn't come to the station to discuss her own case. At two this afternoon she hadn't wanted to come into the restaurant where cops were eating. Now Emma was part of the team, willing to sit down in the same room with her. Clever girl. April smiled.

"So, fill us in," Jason said with a smile that confirmed her insight.

"The blood type of the semen in the condom matches Boudreau's, as I told you on the phone." April sipped at her wine, then put the glass down. "It looks like he's the one who's been harassing Dr. Treadwell. He's been in trouble before—"

Jason nodded. "The inpatient suicide a year ago."

"Even before that. Boudreau was a former Vietnam MASH unit surgical nurse. He may have killed his Captain after a young Marine the Captain was operating on died in surgery. Someone threw a live grenade into the doc's tent that night. Boudreau was not charged with the crime but did not do well in the Army after that." That was the part that had gotten Daveys all excited. Daveys's brother had been a Marine and had died in 'Nam, apparently from the negligence—or cowardice—of one of his men.

Emma shivered.

"Boudreau was fired after the patient's death. He may have blamed the Quality Assurance Committee for fingering him and the head of the Centre for firing him."

"How did he maintain his access?"

"He has a friend in the personnel office. She helped him get a job as a janitor in the Stone Pavilion."

"So he has all the keys," Jason murmured.

"It appears that he does," April agreed.

"Is he in custody?" Emma asked suddenly. "Did he kill other people?"

April's wine tasted light and fresh, hardly like alcohol at all. "Not yet is the answer to your first question, and it's possible is the answer to your second."

Emma poured herself some more wine. "What now?" she asked.

"We're bringing him in for questioning tomorrow."

"You mean you know where he is?"

April nodded.

Emma fell silent. April didn't want to imagine what she might be remembering.

"What about Dr. Treadwell?" Jason asked.

"Daveys has that end covered."

Jason glanced at the phone. "Maybe I should give her a call."

"Why is the FBI involved in this?" Emma asked. The FBI hadn't come for her when she was abducted. April saw the other question in her eyes. *Why not me?*

"Dr. Treadwell's boyfriend is a Senator. Treadwell was being harassed before Dr. Dickey died and she didn't do anything about it. When someone got killed, the Senator may have stepped in on her behalf and asked someone for a favor. It's just my hunch. That kind of thing happens."

Well, that was enough for one day. Reluctantly, April dragged herself out of the chair. "Well, thanks for everything. I've got to go. I've got a big day tomorrow."

"You're not staying for dinner?" Somehow Emma managed to sound disappointed.

"We're having dinner?" her husband asked.

sixty-two

Maria Sanchez desperately needed to talk with her son. On Tuesday morning she could no longer restrain herself from speaking. "*M'ijo*— " She knocked gingerly on Mike's door. "Will you have some coffee?"

A grunt came from inside the room.

"Are you awake?"

Another grunt.

"It's six-thirty. Won't you be late?"

No answer from inside.

"I made some coffee."

A few thuds and rustles, then Mike appeared at the door rubbing the sleep out of his eyes. "What's going on, *Mami*?"

Maria looked modestly away, as her *hijo* had nothing on but the gold medal of St. Sebastian nestled in the soft thicket of curling black hairs on his chest and one of the smaller towels stretched across his groin. She directed her eyes to the door frame, not wanting to see any telltale bulge of *le verga en ristre* in the baby she loved so much and could no longer hold and caress. No longer even talk to.

"It's six-thirty, *m'ijo*," she said softly. "Won't you be late?"

It was Tuesday and she was back in her usual black. He squinted at her dress, plainer than a nun's habit and a very far cry from the shiny, stiff purple number of Sunday. "I never get up before six-thirty," he pointed out. "What's going on?"

"Are you leaving me, *m'ijo*?" Maria whispered. "I don't want to bother you, but— "

Mike closed his eyes. "Give me a minute, *Mami*."

She nodded as he closed the door, her son the Sergeant with the loaded gun on the chair beside his pillow and a Chinese girlfriend with very small *chichis* and no sign of being a Catholic. Sighing, Maria padded through the living room to the table by the window, sat on the wooden chair next to the one Diego had taken when he came to lunch. She was thinking, as she had for two nights, about the things Diego had said after Mike and his pretty *novia china* had left. She smoothed her hand over the rich surface of the wood, darkened and glistening after many years of polishing and repolishing.

"Marry a man who will respect you, Maria," her father lectured to her long, long ago when she was just a little girl playing before dinner under the dusty canopy of the old tree split down the middle by a bolt of lightning. He talked, she played with a rag doll. *Mami* had fed and sweated over the old woodstove making her father's, and only her father's, favorite things to eat.

"Marry a man who can cook," *Mami* had liked to tell her. And following that, "Mexican men are defective. *Hiposexuado.* They cheat on you and they're lazy, *también.* Marry an Anglo or an Italian, Maria."

"Where will I find an Italian, *Mami*?" Maria had wondered, in that old town on the border of Mexico and Texas.

"Rosario Tebrones married an Italian. He went to Canada, then came here to visit a friend. Remember Rosario, Maria? She went to Canada and became very rich."

Maria could no longer remember Rosario. She could hardly remember her *Mami,* dead of fever at thirty when Maria was only twelve. But she remembered the soft whispers, the exhortations like prayers in her ears each night before she slept. "*En el nombre del Padre, del Hijo, y del Espiritu Santo* marry a good man, Maria, or your life will be *fuego del infierno* from the first day to the last."

Maria got up to pour a coffee thick as soup for her *hijo,* anticipating his arrival only seconds before it occurred. She inhaled his morning collection of fragrances: deodorant, toothpaste, Irish Spring soap, shaving cream, some kind of *crema hidratante* to soften his skin after shaving—and the strong perfume of many flavors that overshadowed everything, lingering in the apartment for hours after he was gone.

He sat down, his eyes, for a change, soft with concern. He did not begin with a thousand questions about Diego, and for that she was grateful. "What are you worried about, *Mami*?" he asked.

She sighed. "I saw the papers in your room. Are you getting married?"

"To April?" Mike swallowed some coffee down and choked, laughing at the same time. "You jump to the finish too fast, *Mami.* I've never even kissed her."

Maria was surprised.

"She's a—serious kind of woman. She doesn't play around." He shook his head, lifting a shoulder as if a little ashamed at how hard he had to work toward that end. "It's complicated."

"What about the apartment papers?" Maria asked, puzzled. "You're moving to Queens? You never said anything."

He looked guilty. "I'm getting reassigned, so I'm thinking about it."

What did that have to do with it? Maria gave her son a searching look. "You want a *compañera de cama* in Queens. That's far away, *m'ijo.*"

She traced the wormholes in the polished wood with a tentative finger. She didn't believe her son had never even kissed *la china.* He was leaving home for her, so she must have grabbed him in the important place.

"She's very nice, *muy bonita, muy simpática.* I liked her, *m'ijo.*" Maria didn't say, *Even though* la chica *had no womanly flesh and clearly wasn't a Catholic.* She loved her son. What can you do?

Mike smiled. "Thank you, *Mami.*"

"Is your promotion in Queens?" She licked the tip of her finger and rubbed at an imaginary spot on the glossy table.

"Ah, no." Mike changed the subject. "*Mami,* I'm surprised at you. You didn't tell me you had a—"

"*Amigo.* He's a friend, *m'ijo.* I met him in Church," she said pointedly.

"I'm sure you did, *Mami.* And you told me you were finished with men, an old woman ready to fly up to Heaven. Remember?"

Maria's round cheeks pinked at the lie. Sunday Diego had told her his philosophy of women. It was very interesting and not the philosophy of a Mexican man, that was for sure. Diego's theory was that there was more to a woman who had finished with her babies than one who hadn't started with them yet. And he didn't mean thickness around the belly, either. He meant more enjoyment, more time for eating and talking. *Ola,* Diego liked to talk. He wanted a woman of his stage in life who'd lived through the things he had and wouldn't think him a fool.

Maria thought Diego was a wise man, possibly even a saint. And she felt his appearance in her life at such a time must be a sign from the Almighty Father Himself. It was not impossible. Such things had happened before. Not lately, perhaps, and not to anyone she knew, but *Todopoderoso* could do anything He wanted. And if He wanted a good woman to care for a saint, He could certainly reach down to such a woman from Heaven above—as she prayed in His holy place, don't forget that—and breathe new life into the deepest part of her soul. The Holy Book, after all, was full of such miracles.

"Maybe not yet," she said of herself and Heaven.

"Well, what do you know about Diego?" Mike said suspiciously. "When did he turn up? What does he want?"

"*M'ijo,* remember that dog your father brought home? Big as this table and covered with flies?"

"Fleas. Yes, I remember. He said the dog was Jesus and we had to keep him."

"That dog followed him home."

"Uh-huh." Mike remembered that bit of insanity. "So?"

"Diego *también.*"

Mike pursed his lips. "Diego is a dog?"

"No, *m'ijo,* the other."

"Diego is Jesus."

Maria nodded soberly. "I met him in Church. God spoke to me." Her meek eyes flashed with sudden passion. "That is more than you can say about *la china.*"

Mike put down the coffee cup. He was not smiling anymore. Diego Alambra was the headwaiter in an Italian restaurant. So far that was all he'd had time to check out the day before. Diego's parentage and country of origin were still a little on the vague side, but Jesus he was not. "*Mami,* we will talk more about this later."

"Forgive me, *m'ijo.* I only want you to be happy. And no one can be happy without the Faith. *M'ijo,* wait a minute. What's the hurry?"

Mike struggled into his leather jacket, adjusting the gun harness under his arm with a jerk. His voice showed how angry he was. "Maria had the Faith. And she had *me.* Was she happy, *Mami*?"

A giant tear collected unexpectedly in Maria's eye. All her sorrows puddled into a lake and tipped over the dam of her lid, gathering momentum as it rolled down her cheek. He hadn't gotten over it. Mike was still in pain, still suffering over that poor crazy *chica.*

"I'm sorry, *m'ijo,*" she cried. "Is it my fault that God's plan is so mysterious we can't understand it?"

Mike kissed the wet cheek. "No, *Mami,* it's not your fault. But if you believe in God"—he opened his hands, shaking his head like a wise man—"then you have to trust He knows what He's doing with me, too."

Maria felt God's presence in those words, too. She believed her son was assuring her that either *china primavera* would become a Catholic if they married or he was not that serious about her after all.

sixty-three

Bobbie Boudreau closed the door to the fire room he now called home in B3 of the Stone Pavilion. He had spent the last four nights here. It was dark, and all that could be heard was the machinery—the electrical relays of the elevators clicking and throwing off sparks one after another all day and all night long, as the buttons were pushed upstairs and elevators in the bank right next to him moved from floor to floor; the thud and creaky whir of the mammoth belts and gears on the pumps that drove the water; the hiss of the steam escaping from dozens of safety valves. It was very hot, like Louisiana in the summer, but none of the sounds there were animal or human. He liked that. He was in a hurry to get upstairs, though. He needed a bathroom, a hot cup of coffee, and a doughnut.

He had just turned the corner into the main corridor near the elevators when he saw a guy in a gray sports jacket and a female slope coming toward him. Bobbie looked at them warily, kept going. His bladder was full. He had to take a leak.

The man spoke. "Robert Boudreau?"

Bobbie thought of turning the other way and bolting, but he decided he didn't give a shit. He kept moving toward them, his eyes fixed way ahead on a better future. The man was nothing, one of those little Hispanic clowns like the building workers, shorter than he and at least thirty pounds lighter. He could knock the guy over with one hand. He planned to brush past them on the slope's side and just keep going. It didn't work out that way, though. When Bobbie was ten feet from them, the man opened his jacket and casually reached for the gun in his waistband.

"Stop. Police."

Stunned, Bobbie stopped short and put his hands up. "Hey, man, you got some kind of problem?"

The man shook his head. Bobbie was the one with the problem. "Are you Robert Boudreau?"

"You gonna shoot if I am?"

"No. Just getting your attention. I was addressing you. Didn't you hear me?"

"No."

"Do you hear me now?"

Must be some kind of undercover cop. Bobbie glared at him. Asshole never took the gun out of his waistband, but he kept his hand near enough to it for the display of power to piss Bobbie off. What kind of shit was this? Bobbie felt like peeing all over the spic.

"Yeah," he said. "I hear you."

"Good. Put your hands against the wall and spread them."

An electrical engineer from the maintenance staff turned down the hall. He came to a stop when he saw them. The blood rushed to Bobbie's face. Now he was being humiliated in public. He looked at the cop's gun, then at the slope. Her jacket was open and she had a gun in her waist, too. What kind of shit was this? He hadn't done anything to deserve this. This was an outrage. This was beyond an outrage. He didn't want to put his hands on the wall and spread them. He didn't want that slope touching him. But he'd seen people killed by cops before. He was clean. He didn't have anything to hide, so he spread them. It was a good thing the male patted him down. He would have lost it if the slope touched him.

A few minutes later the two cops had him in a cop car headed for the station, and it was happening to him all over again.

sixty-four

April put the coffee and doughnut on the table in the interview room and waited for the uniform to return from the bathroom with the charming suspect. Sergeant Joyce had finally succumbed to her fever and called in sick. Mike was in her office talking to the D.A.'s office. He was in charge now.

She sniffed the coffee and was tempted, but it was precinct bilge, decided against it. The door opened. It was not the officer and the suspect. It was Lieutenant Marsh. Since the Department had done away with Desk Sergeant, some precincts had Lieutenants, even Captains, in the command area at the desk downstairs. The Two-O was one of them. She had no idea why Marsh had left his command post and come up to the squad room, waving an envelope in her face.

"What's up?" she asked.

Marsh held out the sealed letter with a smirk. "Congratulations."

April had been pranked before, more than once. She regarded the official-looking envelope with suspicion. She didn't have time to be the butt of a joke. She had a suspect in the john.

"What is it?"

"I don't know, Sergeant."

Sergeant, what was this sergeant? She was a detective. April squeezed her lips together, afraid to take the envelope and get bad news.

"What is your opinion? Is this something I have to respond to right away?" she asked, meek as a lamb.

"I would say so, yes. Go ahead, take it, it won't bite."

"I'm in the middle of an interview."

"Maybe the interview can wait."

"Okay." *I'm a sucker.* April took it.

"Go ahead, open it."

She didn't want to open it in front of Marsh. But she could see he wouldn't leave until she did. She opened it. Inside was the request to report for the promotion she'd been waiting for. She'd made Sergeant. That was good. Her heart thudded. She'd made it. Had she made it, or was this a joke?

Lieutenant Marsh held out his hand. "Like I said, I wanted to be the first to congratulate you."

April shook his hand. “Thank you.” Where was the joke?

“Yeah.” He smirked.

April glanced at the date for reporting. “Report November 16,” it said. What was this? Today was November 16. She frowned. That couldn’t be right. There was supposed to be notice for this kind of thing. It was a big deal. You had to report in uniform. There was a ceremony and everything. People brought their families. Everybody clapped.

She checked the date again and got the joke. The letter from downtown was dated November 1. That was the day the Cowles case started, the day of the flooding toilet. April stared at Marsh. “Lieutenant . . . ?”

He shrugged. “Yeah, well, it got kind of mislaid.”

“Mislaid?”

“Well, I just found it. I don’t know what happened. Some screwup.” Lieutenant Marsh was a big red-faced man, the kind of guy who couldn’t run a block without stroking out. He wasn’t known for screwups. He was grinning now, totally unapologetic.

April lowered her eyes so her rage wouldn’t jump out and hurt her career. “Yeah, well, thanks for finding it. I appreciate that.”

Just then the uniform brought Bobbie back into the room. Boudreau ignored the Lieutenant and reached for the doughnut before he was even seated at the table.

“Well, you better deal with it, Sergeant,” Marsh said as he left. “Better hurry up.”

April checked her watch. It was 8:15. She was supposed to report for promotion at 10:30. One Police Plaza. She’d been through this before. It was the kind of thing that made a person crazy. Just when you were at the turning point of a case, you had to be downtown taking a test or getting a promotion or some damn thing. *Mierda.* She was angry, really angry. She could kill Marsh. She wanted to go downtown; she couldn’t go downtown. Mike was here all alone with their suspect—not to mention every crisis of the whole squad—and she was supposed to walk out on him and report for promotion with the wrong clothes, totally unprepared? She felt sick. She hadn’t gotten the letter in time. She was working a case and couldn’t leave.

“You all right?” Mike came in, frowned with concern.

“Sure.”

“Problem?”

“No. I’ll tell you about it later.” She put the letter in her pocket. It was her job to finish what she’d started. All that work to get ahead and now she was going to miss the glory. She felt sick, wished she could puke right there on the floor. "You all set?"

Mike nodded. She punched the button on the tape recorder. She told it the day and the date, the location of the interview and the persons present.

"Would you tell us your name and address," she said to the suspect.

Boudreau turned his head away from her, gulped some coffee, and didn't reply.

April waited for a moment, then tried again. "We're beginning our interview now. Would you tell us your name and address for the record?"

Boudreau screwed up his face at Mike. "You call this an interview?"

"We're having a conversation. How about making a contribution?" In spite of taking over command, Mike seemed relaxed, ready for a long, complicated day.

Bobbie glared at him but said, "What do you want to know?"

Mike and April exchanged glances. The suspect had some kind of authority problem with women. So, this one would be Mike's. April thought about leaving, going downtown, having the Police Commissioner shake her hand. She thought about becoming a Sergeant. Her old boyfriend Jimmy Wong had told her he would never marry her if she made Sergeant. Sergeant Joyce's husband divorced her when she'd joined the force. Lots of people had trouble with women in authority. Mike didn't seem to. He must already have known she'd been promoted when he took her home to meet his mother.

Well, they had to be professional to work efficiently. Never mind the shit she'd gotten from downstairs, or this snub from a slime. She couldn't let these things bother her.

Mike led Robert Boudreau through the preliminary questions. The suspect pushed his chair back from the table and thrust out his pelvis defiantly as he described his job at the Stone Pavilion, how long he'd worked there and what he did. When asked what he had been doing down on B3, he didn't respond. Nor did he ask how the cops had located him there.

Bobbie did respond to the question about his previous job by giving a long, rambling account of his work as a nurse at the Centre—the faithful service he'd given for so many years all for nothing. He'd been unappreciated all along, and betrayed at the end, he told them. It happened to him over and over. Agitated, he tugged on his greasy ponytail.

An hour passed. Bobbie's position in his chair changed as he became more intense and involved in the story of his life. One injustice after another. Another forty-five minutes passed. At ten o'clock April thought some more about leaving. Then the hair on the back of her neck prickled. She could feel Mike getting tense. She turned her watch around so she couldn't see its face. Still, she felt each minute tick by.

Bobbie leaned forward in his seat, his sullen eyes locked on Sanchez. "We went halfway around the world for them. And you know what they did to us? They blew us to bits. You had to be there to understand. Those people were worthless trash. They didn't appreciate what we were doing for them. They had no honor. I'll tell you, those slope women are nothing like American women."

Sanchez chewed on his mustache, uncomfortable with the Asian stuff.

"Those people weren't even human. They stole our stuff. They had diseases. They killed people. One of my buddies tried to help some slope cunt's kid—"

"Hey, watch your language."

Boudreau kept his eyes locked on Mike. "You know what they did to him? They stole his money. They led him on a fucking goose chase, and they killed him. You know what? I didn't give a shit when our guys raped the women, killed them. They're worthless trash. They're nothing, not even human."

April's scalp prickled. Ten-twenty. It was over. It was too late. She'd missed it. And for what, to hear this slime call Asians trash? Her stomach ached. She was tense, worried about where this was heading. She could see that Mike was bristling all over.

"I don't know how you can stand to work with one. These slopes are shit. They used their own kids as decoys. They killed their own children. The women were prostitutes—"

"Okay, that's enough. We heard you got into some trouble in 'Nam. Why don't you tell us about that?"

Boudreau's strange, pale eyes locked on Mike. "A man should work with a *man.*"

"Yeah, well, that's not for you to say."

"It just makes you wonder what kind of guy works with a slope cunt—"

There was no advance warning. No rumble, no growl, no muscle contraction. Nothing. They were in one place and then they were in another with no intermediate steps. The electrical charge hit Mike like a bolt of lightning, sudden and deadly. First he was sitting at the table listening to the suspect, sweating a little, uncomfortable. Then he was on his feet in the place beyond rage. He dragged the bigger man out of his chair and hauled him to a standing position. Then he rammed his knee into Boudreau's groin so hard, the impact of the collision almost knocked them both over.

Gagging, Boudreau tried to double over, but Mike was out of control. He didn't let go. He didn't let the man buckle and vomit on the floor as nature decreed. He kept his hold on the larger man, shaking and shaking him in a frenzy.

"You sick bastard. *Hijo de puta.*" He held Boudreau upright by the throat so close their faces almost touched. *"Culo,"* he whispered. *"Cagado."*

Then he smashed Boudreau backward over the table and pinned him down with one arm. His other hand was clamped on Boudreau's Adam's apple, squeezing so hard the man couldn't vomit, couldn't make a sound, couldn't catch the breath he'd lost.

April was horrified at the pure animal rage of Mike totally lost to the world. He was crazed, didn't know what he was doing. She'd seen this happen with other cops. Seen plenty of kicking and beating violent suspects on the street, seen cops so mad they could kill with their bare hands. The thing you did was open the door. Call for help. Subdue the cop.

Stop it. Her job was to stop it.

The suspect was choking. He was losing consciousness, was turning blue. *Open the door, call for help. Subdue the cop.* She couldn't move, couldn't make a sound. The tape clicked off. Sergeant Joyce was at home, sick. The A.D.A. wasn't coming in until they had something. There was nobody watching behind the mirror. They were alone. Mike was covered with sweat. He was at the man's throat, out of control. And April was too shocked to move.

Then it stopped as abruptly as it had begun. Mike removed his hand from the suspect's throat and pushed him off the table onto the floor.

"Now apologize to the lady," he said.

sixty-five

In about fifteen minutes Mike had cooled off and returned to being the professional cop. He had Boudreau back in the chair at the table and appeared to accept the man's mumbled apology to April. It was clear he was not going to leave Boudreau alone to think about what he'd done. He was going to go on with the interview as if nothing had happened, calm and cool.

April did not calm down, however. It was not unusual for suspects who hadn't been touched at all to demand lawyers, then claim they'd been beaten and tortured. Mike had almost killed this guy. If Boudreau asked for a lawyer and complained soon enough, there might be bruises on his neck to prove Mike had lost it. She was nervous and unsure of what she should do.

Healy was down at the courts waiting for a warrant to search Boudreau's apartment. Aspirante was searching the basement of the Stone Pavilion. Their investigation was moving along. There was no way to change the configuration of who was doing what without Sergeant Joyce's intervention. April had no doubt Joyce would take them both off the case if she knew what had just happened.

Mike's sweat dried. He'd calmed down, but the threat of violence lingered. April did not consider the problem resolved when Bobbie did not immediately ask for a lawyer, or when both men pretended nothing had happened. Or even when Mike got a uniform to bring in more food at twelve-thirty and Bobbie ate it. This was bad news, an unstable and potentially dangerous situation. She debated calling in another detective. But there were problems with that. All the detectives were out in the field. And even if everyone were in, she was not in a position to take any independent action. Mike was in charge. He was the supervisor of the squad and he had not adequately supervised himself. All she could do was stay in the room as long as Mike was with the suspect.

April was deeply disturbed. She had worked with Sanchez over a year and had no idea he was capable of nearly killing an unarmed man in his custody with his bare hands. She could not take over the interview because the suspect hated Asians. But she could not leave, either. She was pinned to her chair for hours in the airless interview room as Mike tried to make the crucial bridge between Boudreau and the murder of Harold Dickey.

She would not leave him. The balance had shifted and things had changed between them. It wasn't simple anymore. When he'd shoved his own body between her and a raging fire months ago, Mike had viewed protection of her as his duty. He'd have done the same for a man, for anybody. Some cops saved the other fellow first no matter who the other fellow was. This defense of her *honor* today was mad and unreasoning, totally out of control. There was no excuse for it.

April sat uncharacteristically mute. Over the hours, as Mike questioned Bobbie, she remembered all the times she and Mike had been alone together in tight places, in dangerous places, in boredom—in the maelstrom of other people's violence. In extreme situations he would punch somebody once, jerk someone's arm behind his back. But his way was to subdue quickly and efficiently. He wouldn't use force unless he had to, and never extended it beyond what was necessary to get the job done. He had a reputation for being laid-back, almost too laid-back.

Now she knew Mike's self-control was new, learned relatively recently. The going-over-the-edge was an old thing. And now he wouldn't look at her. He was ashamed, like a reformed alcoholic who'd fallen off the wagon. That was how she guessed he'd been in the gangs when he was a kid, was no stranger to violence.

She was stunned. She had thought she knew him. She thought she knew herself. Right and wrong always seemed so black and white to her—what you were supposed to do and what you weren't. It was clear. It was written down. April always felt she would hold to the side of right no matter what happened or who was involved. She didn't like violent people. Didn't respect cops who went around bashing people who taunted them. But she still respected Mike, even after what he had just done. She knew that when she hadn't stopped him, she herself had gone over the edge. And now they were both out there.

But there was no time to talk about it. At three-thirty Daveys charged into the supervisor's office, where the four detectives were reviewing their day.

"Where is he?" he demanded.

"Ah, Daveys," Mike piped up from behind the supervisor's desk; "we were just talking about you. Where've you been all day?"

"Where's the suspect? This is the second fucking time you've done this to me."

"What? Done what?" Mike protested. Aspirante and Healy shifted around in their chairs. April sat on the windowsill, probably for the very last time. The ivy was dead.

"You're supposed to cooperate. You kids aren't cooperating."

"We worked according to plan today. You knew exactly what we were going to do. We did it. If you got a better offer today, that's not my problem."

"All right, all right. Let me see the video."

Healy scraped his chair on the floor. Aspirante coughed. Daveys glared at them. "What's your problem?"

"This isn't L.A., Daveys. We don't have a video."

"No video?" Daveys was impatient and aggrieved. "Well, you got a confession, right?"

Mike's face was impassive. He glanced at April. It was maybe the third time he'd looked at her all day. He didn't get a reading, so he turned back to Daveys. "We can link him with the Treadwell incidents. There were newspaper articles about Treadwell and her condom campaign taped to the wall in the basement room at the hospital, where he hung out. Also packages of condoms, scissors, paste, several fake IDs, different uniforms. Metal toolbox. Guy didn't have any trouble getting around."

"What about Dickey?"

Mike shook his head.

Daveys made a face. "What's the matter with you kids? Don't you know how to do an interview?"

"He said he didn't do Dickey."

"Oh, yeah, then what was he doing there when Dickey was brought in to ER? What about the fucking scotch bottle?"

"It's at the lab, being tested." Healy had found the Johnnie Walker bottle in Boudreau's apartment, right in plain sight, just where Daveys had said it would be.

"It's a smoking gun," Daveys said with satisfaction.

Mike glanced at April.

"What?" Daveys demanded.

"Nothing."

"What, for Christ's sake? Don't hold back on me."

"Boudreau says he took the bottle out of Dickey's office because Treadwell was setting him up with it."

"Treadwell was setting Boudreau up," Daveys said with heavy sarcasm. "They were that close?"

"Boudreau says Treadwell knew he was harassing her, so she decided to get rid of him."

"By murdering one of her oldest friends?"

"Well, it's complicated, Daveys. Dickey was Treadwell's lover years ago. They were being named in a lawsuit over a patient who'd suicided." Mike chewed his mustache thoughtfully.

Daveys closed his eyes, then opened them. "You're fucking up here. The guy had the *evidence* in his *home.* If it turns out the Elavil was in the scotch bottle, you have a smoking gun. What else do you fucking need here?"

"Treadwell was with Dickey when he died." April spoke up for the first time.

Daveys rolled his eyes at her. "Ah, another country heard from. So, little girl, Treadwell was in the office. Boudreau was down on the street. So what?"

"So there are two threads leading to the truth here," Mike said. His eyes blazed at the FBI agent's insult to April. "Aren't you guys supposed to be interested in the truth? I thought I heard somewhere that the FBI was dedicated to uncovering the truth."

Healy guffawed.

"What a bunch of fuckups. Where is he? You still got him here, don't you?" Daveys demanded. His stony face was getting red.

"Yeah, we got him," Mike said.

"Okay, give me a few minutes with him." Daveys shook his head. "Do I have to do everything for you kids? Bring him out, I'll show you how to get a confession."

"Fine." Mike glanced at April again. This time her eyes flickered. She pushed off the sill and went to the bathroom.

sixty-six

Bobbie was slumped in his chair in the interview room when Daveys walked in with his FBI credentials held in front of him as if he were warding off Satan with a cross.

"Hi, Bob, ma man. I'm Special Agent Daveys, FBI," he said.

Well, look who joined the party. Bobbie felt like laughing. The other asshole. The Fed. This morning he'd been humiliated at work by spic-and-slope cops. The spic had tried to kill him, and it got him nowhere. Now they had to get this FBI crud he'd seen hanging around the bitch Treadwell to take a crack at him.

"FBI, you hear that, Bob?"

"So what am I supposed to do: shit in my pants?"

"Most people do."

Bobbie snorted.

"I see you're a man with a sense of humor. How're you doing with the police—they treating you all right? You want some coffee, a cigarette?" Bobbie didn't reply, so Daveys shrugged and lowered himself into a chair.

Bobbie watched the asshole with cold, pale eyes. He'd seen guys like this before. In the service they were the ones who used clubs to do their questioning and made up the answers after their victims were dead. He flinched when Daveys suddenly reached down to his ankle where a gun was strapped. He glanced over at Bobbie with raised eyebrows as he scratched an imaginary itch on his calf.

"I want to make this easy for you, Bob. We know all about you. Everybody here knows everything there is to know about you."

Bobbie glanced uneasily at the tape recorder. The asshole hadn't turned it on. Bobbie had a feeling it hadn't been an oversight. He made some faces at the mirrored wall opposite him, wondered if anyone was watching on the other side of it.

Daveys rubbed the side of his calf just above the butt of the gun. "Make it easy on yourself, Bob, tell me about Dr. Dickey and his drinking problem, how you put the Elavil in the old man's scotch." Daveys's hand moved to the butt of his gun. "Let's get this over with, save ourselves a lot of time and aggravation."

Bobbie licked his lips and glanced at the mirror again. Anybody out there, or was this asshole going to finish what the other asshole had started?

"I didn't off the bastard," he said finally.

"You didn't—then who did?"

Bobbie pulled on his ponytail. "You know who did."

"Oh, Bobbie boy, this is no way to treat the FBI. We're not stupid, you know. We've got the goods here. We're going to put you away for a long time for what you did to Dr. Dickey."

"Don't give me this FBI shit. It means nothing to me." Bobbie shook his head. They had nothing to charge him with. They had nothing on him that could put him behind bars for a single day, and this asshole knew it. He hadn't killed Dickey. He wasn't going down for it.

"Sure it means something to you, Bob. The FBI is everybody's nightmare. We don't let go."

"I'm not going down for it. The bitch was in the room with him. Ever think about that, FBI?" Bobbie waved at the mirror. "Anybody out there? The—fucking—bitch—killed—her—old—man. You gonna let her get away with it?"

"You know, Bob, you're not being cooperative. Is that smart?" Daveys looked pained. "You want to be smart, Bob, don't you? You don't want me to think you're stupid, do you?"

"You're trying to fuck me. Why should I give a shit what you think?"

"Because I'm important to you. I can save your life—"

"Can you?" Bobbie sneered.

"—or I can end your life. What do you want it to be?"

Bobbie was silent. He did not see a choice here.

"You know, you're never going to get another job, Bob. You're done, finished. Your wiping Dickey is not just a suspicion of ours. We *know* you did it. Your girlfriend told us you killed him. She told us all about it."

Bobbie shook his head. Gunn wouldn't have done that.

"Yes, man, she did. She told us what a bad boy you are."

Bobbie squirmed in his chair, uneasy. "That's a load. She doesn't know shit about it."

Daveys laughed. "Believe me. I don't lie."

Bobbie snorted. "Well, neither do I. I didn't like him, but I didn't off the guy. Why should I? His girlfriend did it."

"Uh-uh-uh-uh-*uh*." Daveys got up and slouched over to the chair where Bobbie was sitting. "I don't want to hear this cowardly shit about Dr. Treadwell. This is a life-or-death matter, understand? Life or death,

Bobbie. So make it easy for all of us." Daveys leaned into Bobbie's space, crowding him. "I said, speak up."

Bobbie didn't speak, didn't move. He stared at Daveys.

"Are you telling me you're not a *man,* Bob? You know what I think you are? I think you're an un-American sack of *shit.*" Daveys leaned closer. He whispered, "You *smell* like a sack of shit, too."

Bobbie looked down at the gun on Daveys's ankle. He kept his silence.

"You're a chicken-shit coward. You kill like a girl, Bob. You're a disgrace to your country. You fragged an officer in 'Nam. That's as low as they go. How many innocent people have you killed since, you mulatto sack of shit?"

The blood rushed to Bobbie's head so fast he was almost blinded by his rage. Then Daveys backed away. For a second Bobbie thought he was going to take out his gun and shoot him right there in the interview room.

"I want a lawyer," Bobbie managed to croak out. Now he was scared, really scared. "I know my rights," he cried. "You either let me out of here or you arrest me."

It was over, and Daveys knew it. He banged his hand on the table. "I want you to know something, asshole. It's my job to rid society of vermin like you, and I do my job whether I like it or not." He spun around and smacked the table again.

"You're a blight on this country, on the whole world, you hear me, you little shit? And I'm going to bring you down not because it's my job—my job just makes it legal—I'm going to get you because *I* want to. And I may break you, and you may be dead first." When Daveys finished talking and hitting the table, he walked out of the room and slammed the door.

An hour later Bobbie was back on the street.

sixty-seven

Gunn kept trying the phone in the basement apartment all Tuesday. It rang and rang and nobody answered. Where was Bobbie? She knew he hadn't shown up at work because she called and asked for him. The person who answered the phone in the maintenance office said he didn't know where Bobbie was.

Gunn was worried. When Bobbie got upset, he went out drinking. When he drank, he got in fights. She was glad she'd told the Chinese cop she had no picture of him, and there hadn't been one out on display to prove her a liar. She was glad he'd never put a card with his name on the intercom board. Bobbie didn't want to be found. Maybe they wouldn't be able to find him. She felt so guilty for what she'd done.

As the evening hours crawled by, Gunn became more and more concerned. She'd never liked the game of hide-and-seek when she was a kid. Concealment scared her. It always upset her to be in a game where she couldn't see what was going on. Days had gone by, over a week had passed since Dr. Dickey drank from his scotch bottle and died. And every second she was more afraid. Last time Bobbie got in trouble, she was right there in the middle of it all, knew every detail of the incident, but was never in any danger herself. Now she was the one in trouble and didn't know which way to turn. She had nobody but Bobbie, and he was out there somewhere, wasn't coming home to her now that she'd been to the police station, had her fingerprints taken and talked to the cops. Bobbie would forgive her for everything else, but he wouldn't forgive her for talking about him.

The Chinese detective had given Gunn her business card last Friday, just in case she thought of something else. Gunn had put the card in her purse to be polite. This morning she took it out. She still felt guilty about letting the detective into her apartment and then not telling her the truth about what she'd done. Maybe Bobbie had seen the cop come in last night and was too unnerved by it to come home. Gunn was pretty sure Bobbie hadn't slept in the building. Maybe the cop had gone to find Bobbie at work this morning and that was the reason he hadn't shown up. Gunn hadn't shown up at work, either. She hadn't slept and was terrified because she was out of her depth and didn't know what to do. She wished Bobbie would come back so she could explain everything to him.

From time to time she played with the Chinese cop's business card. It wasn't a real business card. It was a police department card that said on it *20 Detective Squad* and below that *Det.* ———. April Woo had written her name in the blank by hand. The blank below that was for a case number, but no number was written there. Maybe Bobbie's case didn't have a number yet. Gunn thought about calling the cop and asking what was going on about Case number-nothing-yet. She thought about calling all day, about giving herself up. Then it got too late.

At eight o'clock she went downstairs and peeked out the glass front door to see if someone was watching the building. She didn't think Bobbie would come home if there were cops around. She prowled around the back windows of her bedroom, but it was dark out there in the garden and she couldn't see anything but the shapes of old heaps of garbage. She went down the stairs a second time at nine, then a third time at ten-thirty. There was no light under Bobbie's door. Each time she returned to her own apartment she had a few drinks. At eleven, she went down the stairs one last time. This time something didn't feel right. The last of the three dim lightbulbs in the hall ceiling fixture had gone out. It was dark in the hall, and dark under Bobbie's door. It didn't feel right. Gunn leaned close to the door. She heard the toilet flush.

"Bobbie?" Gunn whispered. "Bobbie? Are you there?"

Nobody answered.

sixty-eight

Tuesday was a quiet night in the squad room of the Two-O. Except for the Boudreau case, nothing much was going on. One detective was at his desk on the phone; everybody else was out. Mike and April sat at the table in the locker room, the tension between them unrelieved. It had been a long day. Their shift had been over many hours before, but neither wanted to go home. April knew that she would be out of there tomorrow, headed toward another life, but she wasn't ready to detach from this one yet. Mike had sent Detective Andy Mason to watch Boudreau, whose only response to his interview with Daveys had been to ask for a lawyer. The D.A.'s office felt there was only circumstantial evidence, no direct evidence, that the suspect had tampered with Dickey's scotch bottle. In addition, Boudreau's prior history, though persuasive to Agent Daveys, was also based on circumstantial evidence. In any case, nothing he'd done in the past would be admissible in court in the present instance. They needed a stronger case before they could make an arrest. Behind the mirror, April and Mike had watched Daveys put on a show for nothing. They didn't feel good about him.

Boudreau had been released for the moment, and a completely unapologetic Daveys took off after him. A bad day was turning out to be an even worse night. After Daveys had gone without leaving a forwarding address or beeper number, they'd received some disturbing information from the lab. Lab techs confirmed the presence of Elavil in the Johnnie Walker bottle found in Boudreau's apartment. Boudreau's fingerprints had been found on the bottle along with those of the deceased.

But the print experts also found smudges and partials of a third person on the bottle. Those partials turned out to match the only other set of prints found on the folder containing Boudreau's file: Gunn Tram's. Dickey's fingerprints on almost all of the pages of Boudreau's file suggested that the file had been in his office and he had read it. Gunn's prints were mingled with the dead man's in such a way as to suggest that she had handled it after he had, and she had probably been the one to return it to her office. If Boudreau had taken the file from Dickey's office, April and Mike reasoned, he would never have returned it to the personnel office. He would have destroyed it.

Gunn's prints showing up in two places where they weren't supposed to be bothered the two detectives enough to keep them sitting at the table with their notes, and Boudreau's file, for many hours. April dialed Gunn's number a few times to make sure the little lady hadn't gone anywhere. Her line was always busy.

At ten P.M., they'd been on the job for fourteen hours, and they were still debating what they should do next. A lot of people would have gone home hours ago, waited for another day, another supervisor to deal with it. Tomorrow was their day off; whatever came down would be off their watch. But Mike and April didn't see it that way. They had one suspect they considered dangerous out on the street who was being tailed by one or more FBI agents, as well as by one of their detectives. And now they had a brand-new suspect, the first suspect's girlfriend, who happened to be a little old lady. Suddenly the case was beginning to sound like a boyfriend/girlfriend thing after all. April sighed gustily. They had to bring Gunn in and talk to her. Should it be now or tomorrow?

At ten-thirty Andy phoned in to say Boudreau had gone into his building and looked as if he might have settled in for the night. April suppressed a yawn. If all was quiet, maybe she could go home now. She picked up the phone and dialed Gunn's number again just to make sure the old woman was all right. She let the phone ring ten times, then hung up, shaking her head.

"It's been busy for hours and now suddenly she's not there."

Mike tapped a pen on the arm of his chair. "Maybe she's in the bathroom."

April made a skeptical face. "Maybe she's not."

"You're worried?"

"Yes, aren't you? Boudreau was harassing the one doc; and he, or Gunn, or both of them, killed the other doc. The whole thing stinks." April actually looked at him for the first time in hours. "You know we have to make a move."

"Hey, I don't have anything scheduled right now. I'll go over and bring the lady in for a chat. Would that make you feel better?"

"Yes."

"Fine. You go home and get some sleep. I'll go get her." Mike tapped the pencil, shrugged again. "Will I see you in the morning?" he asked.

April shook her head. "They've probably got somebody new coming in here tomorrow."

"Look, April, I've been thinking about what happened this morning and I know you're wrong about me being a loose cannon. I'm not a wild man. I just—" He took a breath and let it out. "I just didn't know it was there, that's all. Sometimes you just go along with certain assumptions and then something happens to knock them out."

Uh-huh.

He gave her a helpless look. "You *know* I'm a gentle person."

She frowned and looked at her hands. "No, I don't know that anymore."

"Yes, you do. You know me. That wasn't me. That was . . ." He searched for a word.

April didn't help him find one.

He dropped the pencil and started tapping his finger against his lip, glanced through the open door at the other detective out in the squad room. He was a young black man, new to the squad, talking heatedly on the phone. From the tone of his voice it sounded like an argument he didn't want to lose. "You're making it hard," Mike murmured to April.

She didn't say anything.

"Okay, you're right. I did play with some rough people in my time. I did get into some trouble, but it was a long time ago. I never hurt anybody who didn't deserve it, and I got out of it, didn't I? You know I'd never hurt *you*. You know that, don't you?"

That was the excuse they all gave: every thief, every abuser, every batterer, every killer. Now April looked out at the other detective on the phone. He was winding down now. It was time to go.

"I didn't know it was there. I know now, so it's a factor," Mike said.

"What's the factor?"

He glanced around, caught—guilty, lifted a shoulder. "I guess I love you. . . . It took me by surprise. I didn't know I would get . . . violent about it."

April glanced down at her hands as the heat rose to her face. There hadn't been a lot of people in her life who'd said that to her. Certainly not any of the people who should have. Somehow that made it worse.

"*¿Y qué más?*" he said softly.

She shook her head. Somehow it hurt not to feel the way she'd always thought she would when a man she admired finally said he loved her. Safe and secure and happy like in the movies. A lot of things were in the way. A cop couldn't be unpredictable, couldn't fly off like that—should never, never fall in love with a partner and go crazy over her honor. Love made Mike dangerous, not safe. He was always going to be dangerous. She wondered if real love was like this.

"*¿Y qué más?*"

"*Nada más.* Let's go."

"You're coming with me?" He was surprised.

"Yeah." Wearily, she reached for her bag.

sixty-nine

Bobbie left the police station on Eighty-second Street and headed west toward Broadway. He had a lot of things to be angry about—the humiliation of cops coming to get him at work was the least of it. Then, as he thought about it, he got angrier and angrier. The cops had evicted him from his home, from life itself. He wanted to go to work, back to his patients and his old life at the Centre, even headed in that direction. But even as he walked west, he knew he couldn't risk going back there right now. Maybe later.

He told himself he didn't give a shit about the tail. He didn't see a tail, but he knew there had to be one. The cops and the FBI asshole thought he'd killed Dickey. That had to be the biggest laugh of all time when they were the ones who almost killed him. Where was the justice? There was no justice. Had to be cops and FBI behind him. They wouldn't let him go without a tail.

Whoever it was, Bobbie wasn't about to give the bastard the satisfaction of turning around. He didn't care. He didn't give a shit, craved a drink, wanted to think things over. The temperature was dropping. It felt as if there'd be another freeze that night. Bobbie was wearing his nylon zip jacket. He needed something warmer, couldn't decide where to go.

If he went to the French Quarter, the Mick might bother him. It wasn't safe to hang out at the hospital now. Someone might hassle him. He picked up a bottle in a liquor store he never bought from and walked around with it for a while, trying to figure out where to go. He didn't like not having a place to go. It upset him. He drank from the bottle as he wandered the area. When he was tired of looking at people, he headed over to Riverside Park and watched the Hudson turn into a choppy black oil slick.

He was angry that the only thing the assholes did all day was bug him about old stuff from his life, real old stuff nobody in the world could possibly care about anymore. Who gave a shit what happened thirty years ago? It didn't matter anymore. No one cared. Bobbie sat on the cold ground and watched the lights in New Jersey, knowing that the old bitch was responsible for all this. She'd given his file to Dickey. She'd talked to the cops. She'd told them things about him that were private, that he'd never told anybody else. He didn't know why he'd ever bothered to talk to her. He felt hurt and wounded. After all those things she said about loving him, she turned out disloyal, just like everybody else. She talked to a douche bag of a cop who didn't know anything—anything about life at all—and who tried to kill him. A piece of shit who worked with a slope almost killed him. She'd told the FBI guy that he'd killed Dickey. That really made him mad.

As he sat in the park, he was aware of the dog walkers and joggers running on the paths after work. He knew the old bitch was out there somewhere anxiously trotting around like someone hunting for a lost dog. He was pretty sure if he went one block up Riverside Drive, he'd run into her. He hoped a car ran her over.

As he took some time to think about that, Bobbie was aware of some black guys hanging around thirty yards up the hill from him. The hoods of their sweatshirts covered their heads, and they were smoking dope. The sweet smell of grass drifted out toward the Hudson in the frosty air. The whole thing disgusted him. He'd never smoked dope himself. He thought it was dangerous, made a person stupid. He muttered to himself, really annoyed about these coons menacing people and polluting the environment. For a while he thought they were going to come over and try to mug him. If they did, he knew they'd be stupid, and he'd bash their coon brains in.

They left him alone, and after a while he was mad enough to go home.

seventy

Bobbie liked the basement apartment even though the heat from the hot-water pipes was so intense, no one else could stand it. He said it reminded him of Louisiana. Sometimes in winter the pipes were so hot a splash of water could turn the place into a steam bath. Bobbie said where he came from there had always been a lot of steam rising off the bayous, where his father and brothers went out fishing almost every day before the war in 'Nam changed everything.

Bobbie said he never did have the patience for fishing himself, and even now the smell of fish made him sick. He told Gunn how his father used to tease him about his chickens. The men in his family fished and never did anything else since time in Louisiana began. Gunn imagined Bobbie as a good boy. He always gave his mother the money he made from those eggs.

Bobbie, Bobbie, Bobbie. Gunn's head was full of him, his stories of the oyster pies and tickling the crayfish holes in the hard ground with a stick to tease them out, and the heat, and the father who wasted away for years before he finally died coughing up streams of bloody phlegm. And his brother who went to prison for killing a man Bobbie knew for sure his brother never even got close enough to touch. And Bobbie's humiliation in Vietnam, where everybody saw things through the haze of drugs and Bobbie was the only one sane enough to see what was going on. He was too good. Gunn reviewed the events of the last year in the light of the questions the Chinese cop had asked.

Gunn remembered Bobbie's gentle way with the patients on his ward, how soft and kind he had been no matter how crazy and vicious and off the wall the patients had been. He had picked them up and put them down, wrapped them and unwrapped them like precious dolls, never, never hurt anyone. She knew he'd been hurt over and over, but he had never hurt anyone else.

For hours Gunn lay rigid on her bed in her pull-on pants and several layers of tee shirts. She had not wanted to go to bed in case Bobbie called, even though she knew Bobbie would not call. He was mad at her for not destroying his file a long time ago, for keeping it there in the wall of files for somebody to find someday and use to put him out of the Centre. He'd been afraid of dying, homeless, on the street. No matter what she said to assure him such a thing would never happen, he had refused to believe her. He didn't understand that the files were sacred. Gunn knew other people tampered with them, lost them, destroyed them, but she never would. That's why she'd had to get Bobbie's file from Dickey's office and put it back. The whole point was to keep Bobbie out of it.

In the flickering light of the TV, Gunn shivered, even though the woman cop had pointed out it was warm in the building. Very warm. She turned off the TV and lay back on her bed, shivering in the dark. She worried about the toilet flushing in an apartment where no one was home and wondered if she was just a crazy old fool.

Her eyelids began to feel heavy, and she drifted off into a familiar nightmare. She dreamed her cozy little apartment—with all its overstuffed furniture, floral fabrics, pillows, and lace—burst into a wild, raging fire that forced her up against the leaded window, which she could not open. With the fire at her back, Gunn tried and tried, but the window would not budge. It was rusted shut.

She could hear the crackling flames eat up her couch, her rocking chair and the lace shawl hanging over the back, feel the heat press her against the frozen, leaded glass. Then a burst of cold air hit her face as the window opened. She whimpered with terror as the dream changed shape and she tried to wake up.

As she struggled in her dream, she heard a voice in her ear. "Gunn, wake up." Two powerful hands took her shoulders and shook her roughly.

She opened her eyes. "Bobbie?"

"Get up," he ordered.

Gunn started crying. "Bobbie, please don't be mad at me. I've been so worried."

"I said, get up."

"All right, all right." She got up, pulled her tee shirts down over her hips, and scrubbed at the tears on her face.

"Go in there." He marched her into the living room and sat her on her pretty couch. "What did you tell them?" he demanded.

Gunn's mouth opened. "I didn't tell them anything."

"That's not what they said."

"Bobbie, I—did something bad."

"You stupid bitch." He kicked the couch.

She cringed at his anger. "Don't be mad at me. I was afraid. I'm . . . still afraid."

Bobbie's eyes were cold. "That FBI guy you were so friendly with said you fingered me."

Gunn's eyes widened with shock. "I told them how good you were with the patients, how much they all liked you. That's all I told them. Bobbie, that's not how I was bad."

"Oh, yeah, Gunn, how were you bad?"

Bobbie looked so mad. Gunn wrung her little hands, unsure how to say it. "I only wanted to help you. I didn't mean to hurt anybody. I just did it—to help."

She had no time to scream. He grabbed her and squeezed her neck until the roar of asphyxiation filled her ears. Her lungs screamed for air. She reached for Bobbie with both hands, couldn't reach him, ended up clawing at the pillows and peeing in her pants. The next thing she knew, Bobbie was sprinkling her all over with water from the antique brass watering can that she never used for anything but decoration.

Gunn gasped, coughed, couldn't catch her breath. She was aware of being wet all over and stinking, tried to vomit. Nothing came up. Bobbie stood over her, his broad, freckled face and huge, bulky body a mountain. He held the watering can above her so that it continued to dribble all over her. His face was bloated, swollen with rage. She'd never seen anything like it. She looked around wildly for the cops. The cops had to be watching him, watching the building. She probed the throbbing bruises on her neck. She was terrified. Bobbie had described killing chickens like that, then cutting their heads off after they were dead. It occurred to her for the first time that he was crazy.

"Bobbie, don't hurt me. . . ." Her voice was a croak.

"I don't *hurt* people." His strange blue eyes pulsed with the death-rays of the voodoo people. He once told her people with eyes like that could kill.

"You don't hurt people?" she whimpered.

He banged the watering can against the sofa arm.

"I'm a good person, loyal to a fault. I don't *hurt* people." He stuck his fingers in her face. "Do you hear me? I don't hurt people."

She wanted to throw up.

"I told you I don't *hurt* people," he insisted.

"You hurt me," Gunn said softly. "You almost killed me, Bobbie." Gunn hung her head.

"You hurt me, Gunn. Say you're sorry."

"You know I'm sorry."

"*Nobody* says they're sorry. They fuck you over. And then when they're wrong they don't say they're sorry— You bitch! You set me up."

"No, Bobbie, I was trying to save you." Gunn started to cough and cry again.

"You set me up."

"No." He was wrong about that. She shook her head. She'd helped him. Tried so hard to help him. Her eyes jumped around, looking for something to save her from this.

"Loyal to a fault," he spat at her. "I took care of you."

The wrongness of this made Gunn shake her head. Bobbie was all mixed up. The truth was she, Gunn, had taken care of him, got him a job, brought his old mother up north, found her a place to stay, took care of her while she was sick. She'd given Bobbie money and seen that the old lady got buried right. It had been expensive, but she had done it for him. "Bobbie—" He was all wrong. She wanted this to stop now.

"Admit you set me up," he said, his wrath erupting again.

"I'm sorry, Bobbie. . . . I feel real bad. I didn't mean to kill Dr. Dickey. I just wanted him to get a little confused and forget about you. Please believe me, I didn't know it would kill him."

"You killed him?" Bobbie screamed. "*You?*"

"I was trying to help you, Bobbie—"

"You . . . *bitch.* You didn't help me. You finished me!" He shook the watering can in her face. The water was all gone. Furiously, he slammed it down on the side of her face, splintering her nose and cheekbone. He hit her with it again, bashing her skull in with almost no effort. Then he dropped the watering can and without a backward glance returned to the bedroom, where Gunn never locked the leaded window because she was afraid of fire. He went down the fire escape and out through the garden.

seventy-one

April drove her own car up to Ninety-ninth Street. Mike sat in the passenger seat, unusually quiet until they hit the block. She had a feeling he was upset because she hadn't said she loved him, too. But who knew, maybe he had other things on his mind.

"I'll go up and get her," he said.

"It's my call," she protested. "I'll go up. You wait in the car."

"I'm not waiting in the car."

Good sign, they were fighting again.

"Fine. How do you want to do it?" April asked.

"I go up. You sit in the car."

"She'll respond better if it's me," April argued.

"You want to both go up?"

"If I have no choice." April parked the car at a hydrant. She switched the lights off and killed the motor. The night sky was overcast. Not many people out on the street. She got out of the car and spotted Andy running toward them from the alley by the building. He had the hood of his parka up and a scarf wrapped around his neck.

"He got away—" he panted. "Daveys went after him."

"Fine, let Daveys deal," Mike said.

Then they went up to Gunn's apartment. Another old lady was standing in the hall, banging on Gunn's door. "I heard him screaming at her. I called the police," the old woman cried. "Gunn, it's all right now. Open the door."

seventy-two

A light powder of snow filled the sky as Bobbie went over the wall into the garden of the house next door and disappeared. He didn't think anybody had seen him come out onto the street six houses down, almost at the end of the block, and saw no shadow behind him. Somewhere behind him an asshole or two were huddled in the cold, watching the building he'd left. So he thought.

But he didn't really care who was behind him. Like an animal seeking his lair, Bobbie was driven by a great urgency to get to the Centre, without any clear idea of what he would do when he got there. If only he got there, he knew he'd be all right. He was a survivor. He'd been trained in combat years ago and still knew how to fight and hide. If he got there he'd have some time to work things out. It would be many hours before anyone called Gunn. Maybe a whole day before anyone found her.

Bobbie hugged the side of the buildings on Riverside, keeping as far out of the lights as he could. He was still furious at Gunn for killing Dickey and then telling the Fed bastard *he* had done it. He was stunned by the magnitude of the betrayal. It was the worst betrayal ever, and now it seemed clear to him that Gunn had been at the bottom of all his troubles. Dickey hadn't set him up a year ago. Dickey hadn't gotten him fired from the job he liked. It was Gunn, all Gunn. She was the one they questioned about every case. She was the one who kept the files. She knew what was added and subtracted to every file and why. She had control of everyone through the things written in their files. She helped people get raises and get fired. She got him fired because it was a way to make him dependent on her, to need her. She even killed his helpless, innocent mother.

The wind picked up, whipping the fine, stinging snow into Bobbie's eyes. The storm whirled inside him, too, as he tried to make sense of all the bad things that had happened to him. The dumb old bitch had ruined his life, but God had raised His hand against her and now she was punished. With this analysis made, Bobbie tried to calm down and focus on survival. He told himself that if he could just go back to where he used to be safe, he'd be safe again.

Habit propelled him to the Centre, where he'd gone year after year, day and night—where the patients liked him and he'd been in control. At night no doctors were anywhere near the north dorm on the sixth floor where he used to work. Behind the glass wall in the nurses' station sat just one nurse. There were maybe two or three aides for the whole floor. From midnight to seven-thirty or eight all the patients would be heavily medicated and asleep. Nobody would go in there; there he'd be safe.

As Bobbie moved quickly through the snow, he began to feel better. He had some time. Hours and hours to collect himself, to think. He didn't have far to go and kept his thoughts on the sixth floor, the community-service area, where he'd worked for so many years. He needed to sit on a chair in the fourteen-bed ward in the north dorm and feel the patients sleeping all around him. They had always liked and responded to him, even the really crazy ones. He'd taken care of them. Now he'd see them again, and they would protect him for a little while, give him the space he had to have to think things over and get himself together. He knew he couldn't go home again, and couldn't go back to the basement room where the two cops had found him this morning. He kept thinking of that chair in the middle of the unit, where his silent, crazy family would be sleeping, and no cop or FBI asshole would ever find him.

Bobbie entered the hospital complex through the loading dock at the morgue. The guard in the tiny office with the windowed door had seen him before and didn't even bother to wave him through. He traveled the musty corridors two stories under the ground that twisted and turned and sloped downhill into the basement of the Psychiatric Centre.

No one ever challenged anyone at night. There was no security on the graveyard shifts. Still, Bobbie played it safe and dropped into a supply closet to change into hospital whites. As he took his jacket and pants off, he noticed spots of blood on them. He changed, then buried the tainted clothes deep in a garbage can that was still full from the previous day's waste. He checked his watch and came out of the closet. He felt fully in command of the situation. The halls were empty and silent; so was the elevator that took him up to the sixth floor.

The sixth floor was the community-service catchment area, the place where anyone could be admitted. People on welfare, homeless, beggars—all those who couldn't pay for treatment or their stay in the hospital. They were admitted, stabilized with medication over a period of days or weeks. Then they were released. Out on the streets again, they stopped taking their medications and soon spun out of orbit again. Many of them had to be admitted over and over.

In Community Service they sometimes had people who couldn't

speak English, couldn't speak a language anybody knew. Once they had some kind of illegal alien. No one knew where he came from or what language he spoke. No one could talk to him, and he didn't even have a name.

Bobbie had chosen the last elevator on the bank, the one that wasn't visible from the nurses' station. He got off and saw a bent, graying head. He checked his watch. It was just after eleven. The nurse was probably going over the M.D.s' order book. Eleven-thirty was the latest they gave medication. Most everybody was already juiced by then, but sometimes the doctors left special orders for problem patients. Before the nurse lifted her head, Bobbie ducked and turned left. He streaked past the small elevator hall. Then he straightened up, took another left, and strolled down the long, dim hallway, jubilant at being back where he belonged, safe and sound.

Bobbie had always liked the unearthly quiet of night on the wards. There were rules here. No TV, no radio after ten P.M. On either side of him, doors were closed on silent double and triple rooms. Everyone had to follow the rules. Bobbie felt ever more confident as he headed down the hall.

The north dorm was a large circle with no doors at the very end of the long hall. There, too, the lights were low but not off. Bobbie could see everything clearly. He checked his watch again and assessed the situation. Several patients were up, but only one was on his feet. An angry-looking guy paced a five-foot area. He was wearing only pajama bottoms, and even in the dim light, Bobbie could see this one was trouble. The patient had a web of scars on his chest. His eyes burned in what looked like a death's head; half of one ear was missing.

That was the only bad one, though. Most of the other patients were in their beds, staring at the ceiling or snoring. Two were playing a silent game of checkers. One guy was reading a nudie magazine, fondling himself under the covers. Bobbie pulled up a chair and sat down facing the pacer. He wanted to keep an eye on him.

As soon as Bobbie sat down, the guy stopped pacing and bunched up his fists. As if hit by an electrical force, the man in the next bed sat up. Then the one next to him rolled over onto his back and sat up. Bobbie ignored them. The man with the scars started punching at the air in his direction. Bobbie sat in the center of the dorm and watched him. He checked his watch. As he expected, at 11:20 a nurse came in.

At first she didn't see Bobbie. She walked over to the patient punching the air. "Seamus, how are you feeling?"

The man stood still, his eyes on Bobbie. "I'm feeling . . . tense."

"Really? What's bothering . . . ?" Slowly the nurse turned around. She saw Bobbie and looked confused. "Seamus, excuse me for a minute. I have to find out something."

The nurse headed across the ward toward Bobbie, her brows knit in puzzlement. Bobbie ignored her. The two checkers players started chattering in Spanish.

"I need to pee—" A short bald man got out of bed and started crying.

"Get back in bed, Alberto. . . . Excuse me." The nurse stood in front of Bobbie, a puzzled expression on her broad face.

Bobbie ignored her.

"Who are you?" she asked softly.

Bobbie couldn't think of a good answer, so he looked the other way as if she wasn't there.

"Excuse me, I don't remember having a need for anybody here tonight." The puzzlement turned into a frown. "Do you speak English? I need some clarification here."

Bobbie didn't move. He wanted to stay frozen in time until the nosy bitch left. She didn't seem to get it. He didn't want to talk to her. He didn't have anything to say.

She persisted. "Are you specialing somebody?"

Without meaning to, Bobbie snorted and spoke. "Yeah, I'm specialing. That's it."

"I got to pee!" Alberto cried.

"No, you don't. Get back in bed." The nurse spoke automatically, her eyes narrowing on Bobbie. "I'm sorry. I don't know you. Who are you?"

"I said I'm specialing, so you can beat it." Bobbie was getting really upset. He'd worked on this floor for almost fifteen years. And this nosy nurse had to humiliate him by demanding to know who he was.

The nurse flushed at his tone. "Who do you think you're talking to?"

"I don't need this, okay? I don't want trouble, so just go away." Bobbie bit off the words.

"I'm in charge here. I have to know."

Bobbie tried to keep the pressure down, tried to think of something to say to make the bitch go away. Seconds passed and then she spoke again.

"Look, where do you work? Who do you report to?"

Bobbie made an angry noise. He'd warned her. He didn't want to have to warn her again. He didn't answer. Alberto shuffled over to where she was standing and raised his hand to her arm.

"Alberto, please get back into bed." The nurse had her hands on her hips now. She didn't want to be bothered by the senile man. Her face was red and angry. "What's your schedule?" she demanded of Bobbie. "Show me your identification."

For the first time in his life, Bobbie didn't have one. He didn't have any ID at all, not for any department. The nurse's insensitive treatment of the senile patient and her humiliation of him joined forces. He lost his concentration.

"Fuck you." Bobbie half rose, then slammed his butt down on the chair. None of them needed this shit. Finally he made up his mind and stood up. He was a good eight inches taller than the nurse. "Get out of my face, you hear me, bitch? Get lost."

The nurse gasped. "I'm in charge here. You're in the wrong place. *You* get lost. *Now!*"

That was it. There was no negotiating with this bitch—no way was he leaving. Bobbie raised his arm. In one quick motion, he backhanded the nurse, knocking her down. Alberto just missed getting knocked down with her. The old man backed away from her still form, whimpering. Then he dropped his pajama bottoms and peed on the floor beside her.

Seamus stopped punching the air. In two catlike leaps he was across the floor, pummeling Bobbie, kicking him, biting whatever he could reach with his teeth, and tearing at his ears.

seventy-three

April and Mike stayed in Gunn's apartment until there was a response to their call for help. It took less than six minutes to secure the area and explain the situation to the uniforms who arrived on the scene.

Mike phoned the squad room three times to see if Daveys had called in with his location, but there was no message from him. At eleven-ten, there was a call from Andy Mason. Daveys left a message at the station that Bobbie had gone into the Stone Pavilion and disappeared in the basement. So had Daveys.

Four blue-and-whites were on the street with their lights flashing when Mike and April left Gunn's building at eleven-twenty-five. The snow had stopped, but the temperature was still dropping.

Mike checked his watch and sighed. "How many Feebs you figure Daveys has in the hospital by now?"

April shook her head and tossed him the keys to her car. He took the driver's seat, turned on the engine and the lights without comment.

"I don't think any," she said to Mike after the heat started to come up.

"No other Feebs. How do you figure that?"

April shivered, thinking of Daveys's interview with Boudreau. "Some of what he said was the usual bullshit. But some of it was personal." April studied Mike's profile. "Like what you did was personal with you, know what I mean?"

Mike pulled away from the curb. "No," he said curtly.

"Daveys kept talking about his family with us, remember? His big brother died in 'Nam. His little brother is a cop. He's a big family man, an all-American racist."

"So?"

"So he hates guys like Boudreau, really hates them. It wasn't just a line to get the guy to squawk when he said he'd get him. It was personal."

April studied the side of Mike's face. She'd seen his profile a thousand times. His right ear was scarred from the burns he'd received in the fire. She, too, had some scars that would never go away. They were connected by those scars, by the ghosts of the victims whose deaths they'd investigated, by the cases they'd cleared together.

"It was personal when you lost it, Mike. But afterward it was over.

You didn't want to kill the guy. Daveys wants to kill him, and he can't have a bunch of buddies with him. I'd guess there won't be any team. He'll be alone."

Mike sneaked a look at her. "Is this your way of telling me you love me, *querida*?"

April stared out the window. "I'm telling you Daveys went alone. We have the advantage here."

"Oh, yeah, what's that?" Mike ran the red light at Riverside, headed south to the hospital.

"We know where Boudreau went."

"No, he wouldn't go back to that room in the basement. He knows we know about it."

"That's right. So where would he go?"

"The Medical Center is a big place. He could go anywhere. If he really wanted to get lost in there, we'd need an army to find him."

"Uh-uh. Think about it. Guy worked in the Psychiatric Centre for a lot of years. He'd go there."

"Thanks, *querida*, that's a big help." Mike passed the Stone Pavilion. The Centre was on the next block.

"Oh, come on, *amigo*, you've been staring at his file all day. What did it tell you?"

"It said they tried to move him to another unit several times because of his hostility to the community-service patients . . . but he—— refused to——leave——the——sixth——floor."

Mike braked in the white lines outside the door of the twenty-story building. The car skidded sideways on a patch of ice, then stopped. They jumped out into the freezing night and headed for the revolving front door. It was locked. They went in through the wheelchair-access side door, their shields already out for the guard. But no one was around to challenge them, so they traded glances and headed for the elevators. It was eleven-forty-five.

seventy-four

At eleven-forty-five, Ellen McCoo, the beefy middle-aged nurse who had discovered Bobbie on her floor and been knocked unconscious after confronting him, groaned and tried to open her eyes. Ellen had crumpled in the middle of the ward, oblivious to the chaos made by all fourteen patients of Six North, out of their beds and deeply into their own crazy behaviors.

Joe Penuch, a thirty-year-old delusional-aristocrat street beggar, gestured wildly, muttering curses as he approached and retreated from the melee. Roberto, a forty-five-year-old Puerto Rican who had been lobotomized because he had the compulsive habit of ripping and tearing gaping wounds in his body, and Cesar Garcia, a young man who had tried to commit suicide many times, most recently by cutting his wrists and injecting air into his liver, chased each other around a bed, arguing violently in Spanish.

Peter Austin, a friendly twenty-five-year-old disordered artist who drew happy landscapes in oils but couldn't make sense when he spoke, wept as he saw Seamus tear some of Bobbie's hair out, then copied Seamus by ripping out some of his own.

Terry, a short, fat man of indeterminate age and origin, who had recently amputated three of his fingers, was beating on the back of the Haitian known as Herbert, an HIV-positive patient who had raped his wife and then tried to hang himself after she became HIV-positive, too.

And Seamus had started it all. He'd seen Bobbie backhand the nurse who took care of him, saw her fall, and let loose with everything he had. And Seamus had a lot to let go. He was born with the XYY chromosomal abnormality associated with the most violent of criminals, was a hyper-aggressive alcoholic and heroin addict. He'd become the object of extremely detailed Psychiatric Centre and police negotiations after his last release, when he'd slashed his boss's throat with a knife while working in a vocational-rehab halfway house. Readmitted to the hospital instead of going to jail, he was presently contained with massive doses of Thorazine and Haldol.

When the throbbing began to ease a little and Ellen registered what was going on, she feebly tried to call for help. No one came. She struggled to a sitting position and was horrified to see Seamus try to bite off one of Bobbie's ears.

"Stop that!" she screamed. But she might as well have asked a tornado to calm down and stop twisting.

The interloper in Seamus's territory had attacked someone he knew. Seamus was going after the intruder with the force of a natural disaster—punching, kicking, tearing at Bobbie's nose and hair and ears, growling, spattering blood.

He had sent the other patients into a frenzy. They had become a troubled school of fish, vicious and hungry. Seamus himself seemed unaffected by the one milligram of Haldol he was on orders to take every hour in the evening until he was out cold. His opponent was bigger and heavier, but Seamus had the advantage of a chemical imbalance in his makeup that—in spite of all efforts—was not adequately tranquilized. He was all violence and no restraint. Bobbie fought just as hard and began to gain momentum as his own anger mounted. With the little finger of his right hand sticking straight out of his hand sideways and blood all over his face, Seamus abruptly backed off.

Bobbie shook himself like a wet dog, thinking it was all over. A cut on his forehead had filled his eyes with blood. He'd been fighting blind. Blood also spurted from his already-swollen broken nose. He wiped the blood out of his eyes with the back of his hand. For a second he saw his opponent's eyes burn as Seamus retreated. Bobbie turned away, figuring he'd won.

Then suddenly Seamus circled and leaped on him from behind. He wrapped his legs around Bobbie's waist and his arms around Bobbie's neck. Bobbie made a choking noise as the crazy man crooked his arm, trying to bend Bobbie's head back and snap his thick neck. Not a chance of that. Bobbie swung around, then bent forward, throwing Seamus to the floor with a loud crack. Then he picked up the chair he'd been sitting on.

Ellen dragged herself to her feet. "Hey, stop that. . . . That's enough. . . ." She pulled at the chair in Bobbie's hands. "Stop . . . it."

Bobbie swung at her. Ellen McCoo was a heavy woman, but tough, and now very angry. She ducked, screaming for help. This time her voice carried and two nurse's aides rushed in. A third went to the phone to call for help. Doors started opening up and down the hall.

The whole ward was fighting when Special Agent Daveys ran into the brawl with his snub-nosed pistol held out in both hands.

"FBI," he croaked, then found his voice. "FBI! Freeze!"

No one froze. At the sight of the gun, the screaming in Spanish and

English, the curses and imprecations, the wild gesticulations only got louder and wilder. The school of fish had been frenzied; now it was terrified. Daveys pointed his gun at Bobbie, who still held the chair over his head in his hands. From the hall came sounds of people screaming and wailing.

"Get back!" Daveys screamed at the throng behind him. "Get out of here!"

"You get out of here!" Bobbie shouted back. "Don't even think about coming in here."

"Freeze, Bob. I've got a gun," Daveys said. But he didn't look too confident about it, hadn't seen too many psycho wards.

"I don't give a shit about the gun. Shoot the place up. Go ahead, you might get a gold star." Bobbie laughed at the thought.

"That's it, it's over, Bob. Put the chair down." Davey gaped at the spectacle. "Let's calm it down in here," he said reasonably.

"Fuck you."

Ellen saw her chance and started wrestling Bobbie for the chair. Seamus pulled himself to his knees and grabbed Bobbie's ankles. Bobbie wrenched the chair out of the nurse's grasp and slammed it down on Seamus's head. He collapsed and didn't move again.

Daveys moved the gun from side to side, trying to get a clear sight. "Stop it! I said, *stop it now*. This has gone far enough." Daveys lost his reasonable tone. "I mean it. I'll shoot."

"Oh, sure you will." Bobbie grabbed Alberto, the closest patient, who still stood close to his nurse, weeping and holding onto his penis for dear life. Effortlessly, Bobbie picked up the half-naked old man and held him like a shield. He was laughing when he said, "Go ahead, asshole, shoot."

At 11:56, Mike and April charged down the hall, past a dozen frantic aides and nurses, who had arrived from other floors to reestablish order on Six North. They raced into the opening at the end of the hall just in time to see Daveys's arms tremble, skewing his aim from Bobbie's foot to his head. Alberto screamed and wept for help. Daveys missed whatever he'd been trying for when his gun went off. The discharged bullet hit Bobbie and Alberto. Locked in a fatal embrace, they went down together.

seventy-five

Wednesday morning brought a white sky, punctuated with dark pockets of brewing storm. The temperature had sunk ten degrees below freezing during the night. The snow was gone, but crusty patches of ice had formed in the puddles on the streets and sidewalks.

Clara Treadwell saw the ice on her terraces and some lacy frost crusting the corners of her windows. She decided to take the cold storage tags off her mink coat. She was no longer troubled by winter or anything else. At two A.M. she had been awakened from her medicated sleep by Special Agent Daveys. He told her that Robert Boudreau had killed Gunn Tram in her home, then fled to the Centre, where he caused a disturbance among the patients on Six North and killed one of them. When Clara asked about the outcome, Daveys told her Boudreau and another patient had been fatally shot when Boudreau took the patient hostage in an effort to escape. Clara counted the victims of the Centre's former employee, Robert Boudreau. Because of him, five people associated with her institution were dead.

Clara spent the rest of the night on the phone, telling different versions of the truth to different important people. At six-forty-five she called Jason Frank and told him to meet her at her apartment with the Cowles file at seven-thirty. Jason seemed distracted by other things when she called, but after she told him what had happened, she managed to persuade him to leave the arms of his wife and get over there.

Then Clara took a long, hot shower to warm her bones and thought not of the day ahead but of Florida. Abruptly, she had decided that Florida was not such a bad place if you owned two or three big houses and thousands of acres of orange groves. It was not as bad, say, as her life with husbands one and two had been in California. Those husbands had been difficult and jealous. Arch Candel was powerful and protective. He'd brought the FBI in to solve all her problems. Arch would see that she came out of this clean. Maybe after a few years, when her contract at the Centre was up and all this was forgotten, he'd arrange a presidential appointment for her. Surgeon General or Secretary of Health Education and Welfare would be nice.

Full of her bright future, Clara Treadwell dressed in a neat black suit, as was appropriate for a day of gravity and mourning. She was composed and serious as she opened the door of her apartment for Jason Frank at seven twenty-nine.

"Come in, Jason. It's good to see you. I've already made the coffee. You must be freezing." She went through the door to the kitchen without stopping to take his coat.

"It's cold," Jason admitted. "How are you doing?"

"I'm shocked and saddened, of course. Deeply saddened," she added.

Jason unbuttoned his coat, then opened his briefcase and pulled out the thick Cowles file. He put it down on the table. It was clear he was troubled and not as sanguine about the whole thing as she.

Clara didn't give a shit. "Milk?"

"No, thanks."

"Is that the complete file, everything I gave you?" she asked as she carefully opened a fresh carton of orange juice.

Jason nodded at the file. "Yes. It's all here."

"You didn't make a copy?"

"No, Clara, I didn't make a copy."

Clara's briefcase was open on the kitchen table. Her tape recorder lay on top of a pile of papers. Realizing the button for voice-activation was off, she put the juice container down and rearranged the papers in the briefcase as a camouflage to pressing the button on the recorder.

"This has been a terrible ordeal. I want to thank you for your counsel, Jason, and for your time. I'm glad it's over. You'll be free of the unpleasantness of all this soon."

Jason considered his mug of inky coffee. "I didn't realize the case was closed. I thought lawsuits took forever. Did the hospital settle so quickly?"

"No, no. It's all still up in the air. But I know it will all go smoothly now." Clara poured herself a half-glass of orange juice and drank it, savoring the freshness of the taste. Then she poured some more. "Doesn't the FBI renew your faith in the system?"

"The FBI?"

"Yes, they came in after the police failed to solve Harold's murder. Can you imagine what a disaster this could have been for me without the FBI? Those stupid cops actually suspected me of some involvement with Ray's death, Hal's death. . . . It was the FBI agent who followed Boudreau to Six North. Boudreau had started a riot among the patients." Clara poured herself some coffee before going on.

"The police incompetence in all this is absolutely shocking. If I were you, Jason, I'd cut back my involvement with them before you get in serious trouble." The nerve in Clara's cheek jumped.

Jason studied her, frowning. "You think the police were incompetent? In what way?"

"Jason, they thought I was responsible for a patient's suicide. They came to my office and harassed me, practically accused me of murder. And then when poor Hal died— Well, they were sure I killed *him,* too. Me, a murderer. Can you imagine people going around saying that? It was slanderous, damaging to the Centre and all of us—absolutely intolerable."

Jason glanced at the briefcase, then studied Clara's face. "Clara, may I be absolutely frank with you?"

"Of course. More coffee?"

He shook his head. "Did you know, Clara, that the police don't feel that truth is a relative thing? They think if you lie about one tiny thing, you're likely to be lying about everything. It makes them really suspicious."

Clara laughed. "What are you talking about? I never lie."

"You spoke to Raymond Cowles the night he died. You talked to him for six minutes, a very short time before he killed himself. The police have the phone records to prove it."

"So what?" Clara demanded, suddenly angry. "It's none of your business and none of their business."

"Clara, this is a very compelling piece of evidence that was important to the police and believe me, it will certainly be used against you in a civil suit."

"I don't *ever* want to hear you say any such thing, Jason. That conversation was sacred, inviolable. It's confidential. The police are absolute bunglers; they don't know anything about it."

"Well, they're paid to find out all the confidential things people don't want them to know, and in this case they did."

"They didn't find out anything. Don't make me angry."

"Then don't say the police are incompetent when they make a connection between you and a suicide, and you and a homicide. You were involved in both."

"They weren't connected."

"Maybe not to each other, but they were both connected with *you.* And you talked to Cowles before he suicided. You can't hide your head in the sand, Clara. You were practically there in the room with him."

"I don't want to hear this," Clara said coldly.

"You can't hide your head in the sand," Jason repeated.

"Nothing Ray and I talked about had anything to do with his suicide."

Jason didn't comment.

"All right, if you really have to know, Jason, I'll tell you. Ray wanted to go into treatment again so he could get my blessing for choosing to be a faggot, after all." She took a sip of coffee and swallowed it with a sneer. "Can you imagine what that meant to me, after all I'd been through with him?"

"What did you tell him?"

"What did I tell him?" Clara's face hardened with the memory of Ray's plaintive voice. Even now it made her shudder with revulsion.

"Dr. Treadwell," Ray had whined at her, "I don't want it to end this way. I need to see you again. Haven't you ever been in love? Don't you know what it feels like to be happy, to be free to be yourself?"

"If you're happy in your choice to be a homosexual, Ray, you don't need me," she had replied, hardening against him.

"This is not a choice. I am a homosexual. I've always been a homosexual."

"Then what do you want from me? Do you want to punish me by telling me all our work together was for nothing? Do you want to punish me for trying to help you achieve a normal healthy life with a woman who loved you, probably loves you still? You're regressing, Ray. You're returning to your self-destructive ways. And if you do that, you're at risk of dying of AIDS at the very least. But you're wrong about being able to punish me. You can't punish me; I'm not your mother."

"I don't want to punish you." Ray's voice was as soft as he was. "I would never hurt you. All I want is to have you accept that for me, this is not a choice."

"You're regressing," she'd told him flatly.

"Look, I just want closure, what's so wrong about that? I just want to be able to go on with my life feeling I've gotten over the hurdle."

"You want my blessing for being a faggot?" Clara remembered her angry indignant voice. "Well, absolution is not my department. You need a gay shrink. I'll refer you to someone who can help you."

Remembering every word, Clara gritted her teeth at the perfidious way Ray had ended the call by accepting what she said as final and irrevocable, by politely taking down the telephone number she gave him when he didn't intend to use it. She would never never forget the quiet docile manner with which he had thanked her and said good-bye. Ray Cowles had even wished her good luck in her own life. After all the years of their relationship, she could not imagine why he had done such a terrible, terrible thing to her. He'd defied her before. How could she have known that he cared so much about what she thought he'd stupidly kill himself over it? Son of a bitch. She would never never get over it.

She ran her fingers through her hair to clear her head. "Jason, the truth is I told him going back into therapy with me was out of the question. You know I don't take private patients anymore, and I most certainly don't give my blessing for self-destructive actions. Frankly, I told him absolution is not my department. I said if he wanted a blessing for being gay, he could always go to a gay shrink—I told him the most competent doctor I knew was Harold Dickey and gave him Hal's name and number."

Jason looked shocked. "Clara, Hal wasn't gay."

Clara tossed her head defiantly. "So what?"

"There are many highly competent gay psychiatrists. Why didn't you refer Cowles to one of them?"

"Oh for heaven's sake. Hal knew the case. He seemed the best man at the time, so I gave him Hal's name. What's the difference?"

"Hal bore some responsibility for the outcome of the first treatment, so a renewed involvement wouldn't have been the best thing for the patient." Jason spoke with a passion that annoyed Clara.

Her eyes became shrewd. "Don't get moral on me, Jason, there's no percentage in it."

"Percentage is not my department. What did Cowles say then?"

"He said he'd do that, he'd call Hal. He sounded fine. And that was it." Clara stood up, poured herself some more coffee, then sipped it standing up. "It was extremely inappropriate for him to call me in the first place. We'd talked about boundaries, we'd talked about termination. There was nothing new here." Except that he'd tried to ruin her life, and she was not going to let him.

She glanced at the clock on the wall. Seven-forty-five. She had to go. She put her cup in the sink and cleared the table of the orange juice carton and the file. She didn't bother to look at Jason. She didn't care what he thought. She could destroy him if he didn't do what she wanted. He had to know that. She released the chain on the back door and went out into the back hall.

She opened the garbage chute and stuffed the file in. It took a minute to position the bundle to fit the slide, but finally she heard the satisfying *thunk* as it dropped twenty stories to the basement. When she returned to the kitchen, Jason had buttoned his coat and was ready to leave.

"Let's get one thing straight about the Cowles case," Clara said. "It was a blip in the screen. Ray couldn't accept his sexual preference. He chose to end his life. These are the facts that have significance for us. The other incidents, the harassment of me that you were witness to, Hal's death—they brought a kind of hysteria to us all, led us in another direction. Now we're centered on this unfortunate case of a disturbed young man again. If we stick together with a clean story, we'll all benefit. If we waver on it, we all stand to lose. Do you understand me, Jason?"

"Gotcha." Jason patted his pocket and turned to go.

Clara nodded grimly, satisfied with the outcome of the interview. She was glad Jason had the sense not to annoy her by asking about the staff appointment she'd promised him. It made it easier because she'd never intended to give it to him.

Only much later in the day did Clara realize Jason had stolen her tape recorder with their conversation on it. It wasn't where she'd left it, and she looked for it everywhere. For a while she waited for him to blackmail her. When the shit hit the fan and she was fired, she tried to reach him on the phone. She suspected him of using the tape to discredit her. Stealing was a flaw Clara would never have suspected in Jason's character. The whole thing baffled her until she moved out several months later. Then she found the recorder. It had been in the bottom cupboard near where Jason had been sitting. Hiding it there, letting her think he had stolen it to blackmail her, must have been his own little joke.

But it was not the tape about the suicide of her patient that cost Clara Treadwell her job. What cost her her job was the scandal of FBI intervention on her behalf in the homicide investigation of Harold Dickey. That intervention had caused a riot on Six North and the shooting deaths of a patient and a former employee in a hospital that strictly prohibited guns on its premises. It also cost Clara her future in Washington. The good Senator from Florida changed his mind about being in such a great rush to remarry so soon after the death of his beloved first wife.

epilogue

Wednesday, November 17, was Mike Sanchez's day off. After hanging around the Psychiatric Centre with April for several hours to house-clean three deaths in a psycho ward, they both went home to sleep it off. At four P.M. he was awakened out of a deep sleep to get the unofficial word that he had been transferred to the Homicide Task Force of the NYPD.

"You know where Sergeant Woo has been assigned?" were Mike's first words.

"Nope, I haven't heard anything on that," said his contact in Personal Orders.

"Well, let me know, will you?"

"Yeah, yeah. Congratulations, Mike."

"Thanks."

Mike hung up. His mother wasn't at home to hear the good news. He wanted to tell someone. He took a long, hot shower and thought of April Woo.

An hour later he pulled up in front of April's house in Astoria and honked the horn. About five minutes later she came outside. He was leaning against his car waiting for her.

"What's up, another triple homicide?" She ambled down the walk toward him. Her purse was hitched to her shoulder. She was wearing a new camel-hair winter coat and new boots. Her hair looked different. Suddenly it seemed a lot longer. The lipstick on her rosebud mouth was now a deep red-brown.

And something else was different, too. For a second Mike couldn't figure out why April looked so spectacularly different. Then he saw a knee appear as her coat flapped open. With a shock, he realized April was wearing a skirt. He'd never seen her in a skirt, never seen her legs. April had always worn trousers to work, didn't want anyone to look at her.

He chewed on his mustache, smitten.

"Cat got your tongue?" She grinned.

"You look great, *querida.* I never knew you had such great legs."

"Well, now you know."

"Now I know."

"What's the news? Anybody going to get arrested in this case?"

Mike shook his head. He thought of Ray Cowles, Harold Dickey, Gunn Tram, Bobbie Boudreau. Then his thoughts wandered to Clara Treadwell and Special Agent Daveys. Rumor had it Daveys would take a vacation for a while and probably not resurface in the New York area.

"I guess there are crimes people die for, crimes people lose their jobs for . . ." Mike stopped as he caught sight of Sai Woo's head in a downstairs window.

"Yeah?"

"And crimes people get away with."

April turned around and waved at her mother.

"April, you think I should take that place in the Garden Tower?"

April leaned against the car. "It has a nice terrace . . . and a view of Manhattan—"

"If you crane your neck." Mike shrugged. "And a dishwasher. You ever had a dishwasher, *querida*?"

"Do you have to wash the dishes before you put them in?"

"I don't know, but you don't have to dry them when you take them out." Mike opened the door for her. "They're standard everywhere now, look good. What do you say—want to take another look?"

"At a dishwasher? Is this a proposal, Sergeant?" April laughed and got into the car.